TRUST FALL

Also by Lynn Painter

Better Than the Movies

The Do-Over

Betting on You

Nothing Like the Movies

Fake Skating

TRUST FALL

LYNN PAINTER

SIMON & SCHUSTER

London New York Amsterdam/Antwerp Sydney/Melbourne Toronto New Delhi

First published in Great Britain in 2026 by Simon & Schuster UK Ltd
This edition was first published in Great Britain in 2026 by Simon & Schuster UK Ltd

First published in the USA in 2026 by Simon & Schuster Books for Young Readers,
an imprint of Simon & Schuster Children's Publishing Division,
1230 Avenue of the Americas, New York, New York 10020

Cover designed by Sarah Creech
Interior Design by Jacquelynne Hudson

1 3 5 7 9 10 8 6 4 2

Simon & Schuster UK Ltd
7th Floor, 199 Bishopsgate,
London EC2M 3TY

www.simonandschuster.co.uk
www.simonandschuster.com.au
www.simonandschuster.co.in

The authorised representative in the EEA is Simon & Schuster Netherlands BV,
Herculesplein 96, 3584 AA Utrecht, Netherlands. info@simonandschuster.nl

Simon & Schuster Australia, Sydney
Simon & Schuster India, New Delhi

A CIP catalogue record for this book is available from the British Library.

PB ISBN 978-1-3985-6550-0
eBook ISBN 978-1-3985-6551-7
eAudio ISBN 978-1-3985-6552-4

Printed and Bound in the UK using 100% Renewable Electricity at CPI Group (UK) Ltd

FSC
www.fsc.org
MIX
Paper | Supporting responsible forestry
FSC® C013604

This book is dedicated to

Emily Grage Kirkle

(7/1/98–3/24/26)

The ULTIMATE MAIN CHARACTER

I mean, think about it . . .

When writing a new book, an author brainstorms who they want their main character to be.

First, they give the character a name. *How about Emily?*

YEAH, GREAT NAME—ADORABLE.

Then they give some thought to the details of her appearance. *Is Emily pretty? BEAUTIFUL, ACTUALLY.* Stunning green eyes with the longest lashes, perfect eyebrows, lovely teeth, great skin, and a smile that lights up a room. Oh, and her sense of style? *Perfection.* The girl *really* knows how to dress.

OKAY—READERS WILL LOVE HER.

After that, they might assign some distinct character traits, those little details that make a character SO VERY unique to themselves. Okay, well, for starters, Emily is a JoBro stan (first notes of "Paranoid" begin playing).

OOH, THAT'S GREAT.

She's the quintessential autumn girl, a pumpkin-patch-loving, hard-cider-swilling Kindle reader with two fluffy cats (one is crazy, of course, because CATS). Em is super into Marvel movies, and—get this—she's also a Cubs fan.

Of course she is. LOVE THAT FOR HER.

And even though she's the sweetest, *kindest* human, she's also got fire underneath it all. Hilariously sarcastic, wildly competitive, has been known to cheat at Uno—that sort of thing . . .

SO, LIKE, THE NICEST GIRL BUT ALSO KIND OF A BADASS UNDERNEATH IT ALL?

Exactly.

Is this character too perfect to be realistic, though?

IT ALMOST FEELS THAT WAY, DOESN'T IT?

But Emily was one thousand percent the real deal, the perfectly unforgettable main character we were somehow blessed enough to know in real life.

Dedication #2

To YOU, Reader.

You might think you're alone, but you're not.

Your people just haven't found you yet.

They're coming, and they're going to LOVE you, so don't give up.

They're on their way . . .

Julia's Prologue

"If I die in Nebraska, I'm leaving everything to the hot dog people."

—Remington

Sometimes life is ridiculous.

For example, on the eve of what would come to be known as one of the most monumental days of my life, I was hauling around an old ice cream bucket just in case I wasn't done feeling sick. I'd had an unfortunate run-in with some surprise cashews after school, which led to an ER visit, and now someone was at the door.

Wonderful.

And the rest of my family was in the backyard with the new kittens.

Perfect.

I hit the porch light and pulled open the door, unsteady on my feet, expecting to see one of the neighbors.

Instead there was a man standing there.

A silver-haired man in a *very* nice suit, looking like a mob boss or an FBI agent. His gaze was alert—intense—as he watched me.

"Hi," I said, pushing open the screen door, wondering where this well-dressed stranger might've come from. "Can I help you?"

"Good evening, miss. Are *Clint* or *Shawna* available?"

It was almost as if his voice had applied air quotes around my parents' names, like his lips had never uttered such unsophisticated Midwestern labelry before.

His appearance on our porch felt . . . worrisome.

Ominous.

My stomach clenched.

Damn you, cashews. I knew I should've blown off the "free cookies" table in front of the counselor's office, but I'd been so depressed after hearing about Will and Hannah that I'd completely eaten my feelings instead.

I kept my hand on the door handle as I felt tiny beads of sweat forming on my forehead. "Um, may I ask—"

"Hey." Liam, my twin brother, popped up behind me. "What's up?"

I rolled my eyes. Leave it to Liam to just casually *what's up* a stranger from God-knows-where who was standing on our stoop with the intention of doing God-knows-what.

"My name is Bernard Elizando, and I'm looking for your parents, young man," the guy said in an accent that could only be called cultured. It wasn't technically British, I didn't think, but it was so locked-in on formality that it felt . . . noble. "Might they be available?"

"They're feeding the cats out back," my brother volunteered, ignoring my handle-grasping hand to push the door all the way open in a gesture that begged the potentially murderous stranger to enter our house. "Come on in."

"We don't even know him," I whispered under my breath as the man stepped over the threshold. "What are you doing?"

"He rang the doorbell and said 'might they be available,'" Liam said in a surprisingly good imitation of a British accent. "Bernard's obviously not the Golden State Killer."

"I can assure you I'm not here on violent business, Miss Lowell," the man said, meeting my eyes. He wasn't smiling, but there *was* some sort of reassurance in his calm expression, amusement in his ice-blue eyes. "I simply need a moment with your parents."

"I got you, Elizando," Liam said, leading the guy through the living room and toward the back door. "Do you want anything to drink? Busch Light? Water?"

Stop offering refreshments to foreboding strangers, you idiot!

"No, thank you," Bernard replied. I trailed behind them as Liam slid open the patio door and they both stepped outside.

And as the ick of nausea returned to my body, my world went off the rails.

Because after introductions were made and an entire conversation transpired about the adorable feral kittens living underneath our hydrangea bushes, Bernard Elizando started saying the craziest things I'd ever heard.

He calmly informed my parents they'd been named the primary beneficiaries in the will of some guy named Remington. Apparently there was money *and* a house, which now belonged to them.

Us.

My mom's mouth dropped wide open as Bernard shared the news, and my dad laughed like this was the funniest thing he'd ever heard.

"I'm so sorry, Bernard, but that name doesn't even sound familiar to me," my dad said, shaking his head. He smiled a confused grin and asked, "Are you sure you have the correct Clint and Shawna Lowell?"

"Of course," Bernard said, and that response felt right. I somehow just *knew* this steely-haired man never made mistakes. He quickly listed off our address, the address of my parents' market, and a brief bio of my parents' life.

"That *does* sound like us," my dad quipped, still looking amused as hell.

"And this stranger seriously left us money and a house in his will . . . ?" My mother squinted and her eyebrows scrunched together. "That doesn't make sense. And we don't have to *do* anything to accept this inheritance . . . ?"

"There actually *are* some stipulations, Ms. Lowell," he said with a nod.

"Okay, here it is," she replied lightly, pursing her lips.

"Entirely aboveboard, I promise," Bernard assured her.

But then he spewed utter madness.

He looked my parents in the face and told them (in his very dignified voice) that the house they were to inherit was in New York City. It was a five-story single-family home on the Upper West Side, and the fact that my parents didn't just die on the spot when he said that told me they had no idea what this meant.

But I did.

And I gasped so loudly when he said it was in the Gardenwood neighborhood by Riverside Park, not that anyone in the backyard (aside from me and Bernard) knew what that clarification meant either, because holy, holy *shit*.

I'd binge-watched *The Woods* (prep-school drama series) multiple times, so *of course* I knew, but my parents and brother—clueless as to what this implied.

Gardenwood, also known as the *beau monde blocks* (a pretty nickname for the neighborhood), was an area where Manhattan felt quieter and more residential, where uptown old money lived in buildings that looked like rows of ornate mansions, all glued together.

I listened in shock as Bernard gave my parents a brief description of the "house"—*two kitchens, wine cellar, elevator, five wood-burning fireplaces, two-thousand-square-foot roof deck with Hudson River views*—and then he informed them we would need to *live in it* for no less than six months if we wanted to inherit.

Those were the two stipulations: We had to live in the house for at least six months, and Liam and I had to attend the very exclusive Gardenwood Academy during that time.

I took in a deep breath of fresh air and clutched the ice cream pail a little harder, fairly certain I was going to have to vomit in the next five minutes but unwilling to walk away from the conversation because *what the hell??* Every sentence he uttered was more unbelievable than the last, though the sudden notion of moving far away from the place where Will had moved on from *me* and was probably actively planning his homecoming proposal for Hannah *as we spoke* kind of sounded like sweet escape.

God, how can he be dating her already?

"Wait a minute," my dad said, screwing his thick eyebrows together and looking at Bernard like the man had just suggested he glue feathers to his chest and start clucking like a chicken. "Are you telling me that in order to 'inherit' whatever this stranger left behind, we're supposed to up and move to New York for six months?"

"Precisely," Bernard said, as if he wasn't aware my dad was mocking the idea. "In the next thirty days."

"Oh, well, we can't do that," my mom said, looking worried. "I'm a teacher and can't leave my classes—school just started. Liam's got baseball, Clint's got the store—"

"She's right, Bernard," my dad said, nodding. "There's just no way we can move our entire family across the country, especially when we know nothing about this stranger who apparently left us something."

I swallowed and closed my eyes, dizziness washing over me. I could feel sweat on my back, on my forehead—*God, I need to go in*—but I just couldn't walk away from this bizarro situation without some sort of answer or resolution to the great WHAT THE HELL.

"I understand, Mr. Lowell," he replied. "But perhaps you'd like to give this a little more consideration. I can return in the morning for further discussion, if you'd like."

"That won't be necessary," my mom said. "Springfield is our home—"

"What are we talking here, inheritance-wise?" Liam interrupted, unconcerned with the two kittens that appeared to be scaling the front of his T-shirt as he asked the million-dollar question. "Obviously we're not gonna pull up stakes for two grand and a shanty; I mean, come on, Bern. You gotta give us a little more info before we can agree to move to the 212."

I expected my parents to call him out for being rude and mentioning money, but all eyes turned to Bernard as we collectively wondered.

How much?

I put a hand over my stomach as the queasiness got even worse.

Bernard flipped his gaze to my dad and asked, "You'd like an estimate on the inheritance amount?"

"If possible," my dad said, looking embarrassed. "I mean, just a ballpark would be nice, uh, in the decision-making process."

I swallowed.

"A ballpark." Bernard gave a nod, tilted his head just a fraction of a degree, and said, "I believe that ballpark would sit somewhere in the range of . . ."

And then he said a massively huge number.

A number with a *lot* of zeroes.

Multiple, multiple millions.

"Million?" my dad wheezed.

My mother gasped. "Did you say *million*? Dollars?"

"Holy *shitballs*!" Liam yelled.

At the exact second I threw up into my bucket.

Damion's Prologue

"Sometimes people do inexplicably weird shit."

—Remington

"Damion?"

I glanced up from the risotto I'd been zoned out on, only to see my parents watching me from their spots at the far end of the dining room table. My dad was still sporting the suit he'd worn to the office, which meant he was definitely going out after dinner, and my mom was wearing her "hot barre" workout clothes, which meant she wasn't going with him.

"Yeah?" I said, irritated they'd interrupted thoughts of Remi.

Every time I had risotto, I thought of him because he'd *hated* it.

Remi was my mom's uncle, an eccentric old guy who was like . . . well, *shit,* like no one else I'd ever met. I swallowed hard, that marble-in-my-throat feeling back again as I pictured his face.

How can Remi be dead?

It seemed impossible that he was gone.

"What do you mean, yeah?" My dad raised his eyebrows, and I could tell by the expression that I'd tuned out something he deemed important. He had the kind of face that should've belonged to a king or a world leader on the wrong side of good, the kind of face that wielded powerful expressions with little effort.

You could tell if he wanted you praised or executed simply by the speed of his blink. "Your mom asked if you stopped by the office after school."

"Quinn," my mom snapped, letting out a long-suffering sigh as she glanced at her annoyingly intense husband. "Not tonight—I'm too tired for this."

The "this" she was referring to was any conversation with my father whatsoever.

God, adults are wonderful.

"I was simply trying to get our son to answer a basic question," he snapped back as he set his knife on the edge of his plate. "My apologies."

"I *did* stop by the office," I said, doing my best not to sound like a judgmental dick. It was hard when they were once again discussing *the season*, which was an exorbitant waste of time and money, in my humble opinion.

A formal ball for high school seniors that felt like something out of Regency England, with multiple parties leading up to said ball?

Fucking asinine.

But I pointed my fork at my mother and added (with the congenial smile of an affable son), "And I dropped off the donation cards, so we're all good."

"Wonderful, thank you," she said, reaching for her wineglass. "I swear to God the planning is already killing me, and it's only getting started."

"Oh, you love the PTA," my dad muttered as he lifted the lowball glass in his hand and tossed back the last of whatever brown liquor was lining the bottom. "What would you do without festivals and balls to plan?"

"Million-dollar question right there, honey," she quipped, raising her glass to her mouth, pausing to say, "Talk about your swoony thoughts. What *would* I do if there were no festivals or balls for me to plan?"

"Shop more, perhaps," my dad suggested.

"Oh, good one," she replied with an eye roll.

Your parents are shitty to each other and you need to know that's not how you talk to someone you love.

I could hear Remi's voice as if he were actually there. He'd spent half my life trying to undo what he saw as the damage my parents were doing to me with their "adolescent thoughtlessness."

How can he be gone?

It was impossible that he wouldn't be there anymore.

My parents already seemed to be *over* his death. Since the moment we'd heard, they'd been on this whole *he was probably ready to go* kick, mostly because good ol' Remi had been in his eighties, living far away and off the grid.

But they'd had no clue.

Uncle Rem's last letter to me—sent at the beginning of May—had been all about how I needed to come to Nebraska and fish with him. He'd mentioned the good steaks, the woman at the bait shop he said he "might've had the hots for," and the possibility of me bringing him another cat because Mr. Dipshit was lonely.

Why didn't I drop everything and bring him another damn cat?

And who's taking care of Mr. D now??

The guilt was going to kill me, I swear to God.

And a thousand question marks about my future surrounded me now, a future I'd secretly plotted with Remi.

Could it still happen? Could I make it happen without him?

My gut said yes, that he'd somehow drafted a plan in case of his death because that was just the kind of guy he was, but I wasn't sure how to find out. I alternated between wanting to send a letter to the Nebraska address in hopes of a response from Bernard, and worrying that someone else—someone on my dad's payroll—might intercept the note and all hell would break loose.

So for now I was just waiting. Longer than I realized I had been, because Remi had died months ago. *Months* ago, but we weren't notified until a few weeks ago.

My parents were pissed at Bernard for being so grief-stricken that he hadn't thought to let them know immediately, but I wasn't buying into that shit. There was no one on the planet more focused and intentional than Bernard fucking Elizando, Remi's right hand. If he didn't let us know, that meant Uncle Rem had made arrangements *in advance* for Bernard to keep it on the quiet.

But why?

He did whatever the hell he wanted, all the time, sure. But it felt . . . I don't know . . . *shitty* that he hadn't let *me* in on the ending.

Whether he was surfing in Rio, exploring ancient ruins, or just hanging out in some random highway town, he always sent letters to the PO box he'd opened *for me* when I was in third grade.

The PO box I'd checked on a daily basis *since* he opened it.

The PO box that I probably needed to close now.

The sound of the doorbell cut through the quiet awkwardness of our family dinner.

"Um, hi . . . ?" Jeffrey Callahan, one of my father's trusted attorneys, walked into the dining room a minute later. Every item of clothing on his body was expensive and perfectly pressed, but the way his glasses slid down his nose and the ever-present sheen of sweat on his forehead made it clear to all that he was an outsider.

What are you doing here right now, Jeffrey? Go. Away.

There was something about my father's lack of work-life balance, the fact that he never stopped working at all, that grated on my nerves. He was like a mob boss, the way his colleagues were constantly popping over to the house at all hours. Only instead of addressing urgent things like family feuds and murder contracts, they were discussing mind-numbingly boring financials that could definitely wait until the next morning.

But Quinn Rutledge never let anything wait, not when money was attached.

"Listen—Quinn, Whitney," Jeffrey said, his voice an urgent whisper. "I'm so sorry to interrupt your dinner, but I thought you'd want to know that I just found out the will is already out of probate and disbursed."

He looked agitated and slightly terrified, like the human embodiment of nervousness, as he spit that statement directly at my parents.

"What are you talking about, Jeffrey?" my dad said with a calm smile, though I could hear the irritation in his voice.

"Remington," he replied, scratching his neck. "I'm talking about Remington's will."

"Would you like to have a seat, Jeffrey?" my mother asked with a bright smile. "Are you hungry?"

"No, thanks," Jeffrey said to my mom, then to my dad, "Can I speak to you in the other room, perhaps?"

NO.

My gut clenched, and I wondered what this was about as my dad and Jeffrey went into the study and closed the doors.

Had Remi mentioned me—and our plans—in his will?

I was ninety-nine percent sure he wouldn't—he was way more off-the-books than that, especially when it came to me—but I still felt dread as silence settled over the dining room. Dread that quickly turned to confusion and fear when my dad's voice erupted from behind closed doors a few minutes later.

Shit.

My dad returned to the room, his relaxed smile a thing of the past as he ushered a now-mortified Jeffrey quickly out the door.

Shit, shit, shit.

He was in full-on freak-out mode, fast-pacing around the dining room as my mother scrambled to keep up with him. He was ranting in a low voice that only allowed me to hear every few sentences.

But they were *big*-ass sentences (and not about me, thank *God).*

Apparently, Remi had left a big chunk of his estate to some randos in Nebraska.

As in *millions* of dollars, left to strangers in the Midwest who no one had ever heard of.

"Can he do that?" my mom asked my dad in a hushed tone, her hands wrapping around his bicep. My eyes got stuck on that—diamond-ringed fingers clutching at him in a gesture of support—because whenever drama ensued, my parents always came together.

It was somehow sweet and toxic, all at once, the way they bonded over crisis.

Although, what was the crisis here?

Since Rem had never married or had kids, I think my parents sort of assumed his assets might be left to our family. But Dad was good at his job and great at investments—we had more than enough money, so if Remi wanted to give everything away, why shouldn't he?

"Well, of course he *can*," he said, rapidly typing something to someone in his phone as he spoke. "But the bigger issue here is that he *wouldn't*. This screams of coercion. Of fraud. Of someone taking advantage of a little old man."

I snorted.

Because the idea of someone taking advantage of Remi was ridiculous. Even in his eighties, he was balls-to-the-wall and get-out-of-my-way, one hundred percent of the time. I mean, his letters had never changed. Their tone—and even the handwriting—remained the same from the time he first started sending them when I was in elementary school, until the very last one arrived a few months ago.

"He'd obviously slipped into some form of dementia, if this is truly what his will and testament looked like," my dad said, shaking his head. "And the fact that he had it disbursed before we even knew about his death is *beyond* problematic. Talk about your red flags."

I kept my mouth shut (not easy), but part of me wondered why he cared. Yes, it was a lot of money, but we *had* a lot of money.

So did it *really* matter if the old guy threw his money at some nobodies in Nebraska?

It was funny, actually, and the more I thought about it, the harder it was not to smile.

So on-brand for my badass weirdo Uncle Remington to say *fuck it all* and just give it away to strangers.

"Is it too late to contest the will, since it's post-probate?" my mother whispered.

"Oh, we're contesting," my dad said with so much ferocity I almost felt bad for the Nebraska randos. "Jeffrey will get to the bottom of this bullshit and jerk every penny from their grasping fingertips."

I said, "I don't want to be the voice of dissent—"

"Yes, you do," my mom interrupted.

"Not now, Damion," my dad warned.

"But what if this was what Remi wanted?" I said, needing to finish my sentence. "Shouldn't he be allowed to leave his things to whoever he wants?"

That made my dad send every bit of his attention my way. He glared for a long moment, icy blue eyes pinned on me like my question had greatly disappointed him, before saying, "Did you know that the house is included in his estate, Damion? That these strangers from the middle of nowhere will be moving into his *house*?"

"I'm sorry, did you just say—"

"It includes the house."

In an instant it felt like the oxygen had been sucked from the dining room, from the world, from my lungs.

NO.

I stared back at him, not believing what I was hearing.

It couldn't be true.

Remi would *never* do that.

"Not only did he leave it to these people, but he included a stipulation that they must live there for six months; I *did* discover that much. They're going to *move into* the home that Remi said, and I quote, would be *Damion's to play in forever*. So these . . . *grifters* are going to be living in your house, and they can do whatever they want to the space. They can sell off every belonging, paint the walls pink, and then auction it to the highest bidder after the six-month requirement is met."

I could feel that he was still watching me, but I wasn't there anymore.

No, I was at Uncle Remi's.

Because that house . . . that house was so much more than a house to me.

One of the original "seven beauties" of the Upper West Side, it had hidden rooms, library walls that moved, a bar that F. Scott Fitzgerald himself had carved the initial *Z* into with a pocketknife; the place was legendary.

Rich with history.

But more importantly, my entire childhood with Remi was centered there, hanging out with my favorite person in the world while he taught me countless lessons and told me a thousand cool stories. It was like I was *built* in that place, raised by the echo of Rem's booming voice as he let me be . . . *me*.

So yes, that house was technically just real estate, but *fuck*, it was also the only piece of *him* left in the world.

And if he'd left them the house, did that mean he *hadn't* set anything aside for my "alternate" college plans, the ones my parents knew nothing about?

"Dementia seems like a stretch, though," my mom said to my dad. "He was always so sharp. And fraud . . . ?"

"The only way Remi would give up that house was if someone forced him to. Think about it." My dad gave my mom a serious look and said, "He's all alone, in his eighties, and some small-town nobodies in Springfield-Nowhere, Nebraska, discovered he had money. They could've befriended him, listened to his stories, and slowly convinced him they cared."

I wanted to puke as I listened, because the idea of anyone manipulating Rem felt nauseating.

"All we know about these people so far is that they own a tiny grocery store—a store that was hemorrhaging money—and a house that's mortgaged to the hilt. They were *this* close to losing everything when suddenly Remi leaves them his fortune? They *had* to have played him, Whitney."

Could my dad be right about this? Could some small-town hucksters have wormed their way into Remi's life to steal his everything?

"Maybe," my mom said, her eyes wide on my dad like she was looking to him for next steps.

"At the very least, I'm going to do some digging," my dad said, taking off his suit jacket. My mother swooped in with the assist, helping with the blazer removal before rushing away with something close to a smile on her mouth, presumably to fetch him caffeine and tea cakes.

"Brace yourself, Nebraska," my dad muttered under his breath as he read something on his phone screen. "Because we're onto your bullshit."

My dad acted like he *was* a mob boss whenever he faced conflict. It never entered his mind that he couldn't fix something once he drew up battle plans, and I wasn't sure I'd ever seen him lose.

Usually it was all in business, but this time it was personal.

And for the first time in my life, I found that to be really reassuring.

CHAPTER ONE

Thirty days later

"Never half-ass New York. Snag a bagel, walk with purpose, draw into your lungs that intoxicating mix of exhaust fumes, garbage, and the best food you'll ever fucking taste. Let the city mark you."

—Remington

Julia

"So maybe you two should just go . . . um . . . walk around the neighborhood for a bit."

"Are you serious right now?" I asked, leaning into the front seat of the minivan from my spot in the back, just so I could peer into my parents' eyes and figure out if they were, in fact, being serious. "You want us to just randomly wander the streets of New York City when it's going to be dark soon and we have no idea where we are?"

According to the internet, once it got dark in the city, the criminals came out.

"Dead serious," my mom said, glancing over at me with a sardonic smile. "We've got an hour to kill, and I've had more than enough time in the car with you guys over the past few days. You and Liam can go find some food, and it won't be dark for another hour. You're going to have to get to know the neighborhood since we live here now, anyway."

For the thousandth time in the past month, I couldn't believe this was actually happening.

We were seriously about to *live* in New York City and be in possession of a massive fortune.

Howwwwwwwwwwwww . . . ??

We'd lived a relatively "comfortable" lifestyle before the inheritance, financially speaking. Our house was nice enough and we had plenty of food, but our *comfortability* was in a super Midwestern sort of way. My parents' tiny supermarket paid the bills (or so I'd thought), any labeled clothing came from nationally branded mall stores and places like Kohl's, and our family cars came from Jim's Dodge Country down the road (where Jimmy Bob had been dealing vehicles since before I was born).

We weren't uncivilized and we knew how to fit into a normal city, but I had no idea how we were going to learn to fit into a place like Gardenwood.

Thank God we had Bernard; we at least stood a chance with his expertise at our disposal.

For starters, he'd sat us down and thoroughly schooled my family on the details of the inheritance, once we'd decided to accept.

"I don't want to scare you, but there *will* be interested parties who won't want you to inherit," he said, pacing as he spoke to us like no information had ever been this important. "Those parties could benefit from knowing the details of the will and manipulate the outcome, so it is imperative that you tell no one the stipulations, do you understand?"

He gave us a cover story and answers, in case anyone had questions, but under no circumstances were we to let on that we'd recently come into money via an inheritance.

The Lowells had always had a fortune, but they didn't flaunt it—that was the vibe.

Clint and Shawna have always wanted to live in New York, and after a lifetime of hard work and skilled investments, they're finally doing it.

Key phrases: diverse investment portfolio, robust interest earnings, investors.

As if that weren't enough, Bernard had been instrumental in getting us ready for the move, showing up at our house every day with itemized lists of things we needed to accomplish in order to get planted in the new house. He arranged everything, waving around a black credit card that magically made everything he wanted to happen . . . *happen*.

People showed up to pack our things. Other people showed up to move boxes.

A team appeared at our doorstep to clean and stage our house to get it ready to put on the market. Although, my dad pumped the brakes on that, changing his mind the day a broker showed up and stuck the For Sale sign in the yard. He couldn't say goodbye to the farmhouse he loved, and we still hadn't decided what to do with the dogs (and cats and chickens), anyway, so instead of selling the house before the move, we called my cousin Lauren instead.

She was already working two jobs and putting herself through college, so she jumped at the chance to live rent-free in exchange for taking care of the house and animals—and working at the store—while we determined if we were staying in NYC past the six months or not.

"Anything to get out of this car," my brother said, reaching for the handle of the sliding door and pulling it open.

Cool air rushed at us as we stepped out of the Honda, and I stared at the "house" in disbelief yet again. My parents might've forgotten their key *and* the paper with the backup security code in case they misplaced their key (which was why we were just sitting in the car in front of the building, waiting for Bernard to save us), but we were, in fact, the owners of the building in front of us.

Impossible.

Im-freaking-possible.

It had ornately carved columns beside the gold-trimmed black double doors, and the words "Riverside Manor" were etched into stone above it.

It'd been designed by a famous architect in 1899 and had ten *thousand* square feet of living space inside that, according to the photos and videos we'd seen, was unbelievably luxurious.

It was stunning.

It was picturesque.

It was *ours*, what the hell.

Liam and I started walking up the block, which seemed very quiet for a New York City street. It was building-connected-to-building-connected-to-building, like a street of mansions all smooshed together (just like I'd seen on Google), and it had *You've Got Mail* vibes in the very best way.

"You know someone's probably watching us right now," Liam said as he zipped up the front of his jacket. "Some socialite is peering out her window this very minute wondering why the fuck a *minivan* has dared to set its ugly little wheels in the fancy neighborhood."

"I definitely think Dad missed the mark when he turned Bernard down on the car thing," I agreed as I walked beside him. "The Odyssey's going to get us the wrong kind of attention."

Bernard had also been trying to help my parents by preparing them for what was going to be our fancy new life. Like finding us a "more comfortable" luxury vehicle that was in line with the norms of our new neighborhood, but my parents were far too practical to take his advice and insisted on keeping their minivan.

Why would we buy a Maserati SUV when the Honda is almost new?

As we walked down our street, Liam and I freaked out about the grandiose buildings that were part of our neighborhood.

Our neighborhood?!

Impossible.

"Check out that one." Liam pointed to a residence with two enormous lions—one on each side of the entrance—that looked exactly like the ones that sat outside the New York Public Library. It should've looked absurd, having huge animal statues in a quiet residential area (wearing wreaths of autumn leaves, no less), but in Gardenwood it somehow worked.

"Maybe we should have lions," I said, my stomach getting a little nervous as I remembered we'd be going to school with people who lived in these very buildings.

Dear *God*, what would we ever have in common with people who had lion statues?

"We definitely should," Liam agreed, his eyes on the stone cats.

We'd had a family meeting—multiple family meetings, actually—after Bernard dropped the inheritance bomb on us, because my parents wanted to make sure we did the right thing. *Money is important,* they'd said, *but family is everything.* We talked through all the scenarios and all the endings, we talked through what we'd be losing and what we'd be gaining if we moved, and then the four of us had voted—with actual secret ballots—on whether each of us wanted to make the move or not.

And it'd been unanimous—the Lowells all wanted to move. Although, "want" was a confusing word in this instance.

"Need" was probably more appropriate.

Because, as it turned out, the grocery store had been upside down for a long time. Like, to the point that my parents had literally been about to lose the store and maybe even the house, which they'd second-mortgaged in an attempt to keep the store afloat.

I'd had no idea that right about the time Bernard showed up on our doorstep with his massive news, my parents had been out of options.

So *of course* I voted to move—how could I not? What were the other choices? And who walked away from millions of dollars, regardless?

On top of all that, Liam insisted it was a good time for me to get out of Springfield because my "obsession" with my ex wasn't healthy.

And he was both right and wrong, by the way.

It *wasn't* good for me and escape *was* probably healthy, but I was *not* obsessed with Will and that comment really pissed me off.

Mostly because, before we left, Hannah told half the school that I was a "stalker who wouldn't let go of Will" because she saw me drive by his house one time.

One time.

I'd spent half my life hanging out at Will's, yet she moved to Springfield and a month later had my former boyfriend's devotion and the ears of half the school listening to her filth.

Don't think about it, I reminded myself. *Forget all about everything back home and focus on this fancy new life sponsored by Lou.*

Another thing about the move decision was that it became far less terrifying once we realized who our benefactor was.

Remington was actually the guy we knew as "Lou."

Lou had been a little old man who lived in a fishing cabin just outside town. None of us knew how long exactly he'd lived there before he'd started placing grocery orders a few years ago.

Ironically, we didn't do online orders. But we did for him.

And we didn't do delivery, either, but we did for him.

Because how could we not? Lou was . . . *Lou.*

He *emailed* his order every Sunday night, complete with SKU numbers and prices, and Lou became, in a weird way, like family to us, even though we knew nothing about him.

Every week one of us delivered his grocery order, and whichever of us was lucky enough to do it usually ended up staying for at least an hour, conversing about anything and everything. Lou was no-nonsense and cursed like a sailor, but that didn't make him any less endearing.

And then a couple of years ago my dad casually invited him to come over on Thanksgiving, which turned out to be our favorite Thanksgiving ever.

Because Lou entertained us with stories about what it'd been like to live in New York on parade days, he helped my mom by whipping up a batch of homemade cranberry stuffing (from memory), and he even stuck around to decorate the Christmas tree with us at the end of the day. It was almost like we had an unofficial don't-ask-don't-tell policy with Lou, where we ate up every bit of information he chose to feed us from his life, but we also never pried or asked questions because *something* had led to him living all alone in a tiny fishing cabin near the Platte River.

So when we had our family meeting about moving, my family agreed that as weird as it might sound, we trusted Lou. We couldn't believe he'd had a fortune or that he'd left it to us, and we had no idea what to make of the stipulations, but we had faith in his motives and his noble character.

My parents were adamant about the fact that if any of us hated Manhattan and wanted to move back, once the time requirement was met, we could. Lou had the inheritance set up where as long as we met the stipulations for six months, we kept the fortune.

We'd lose the house if we decided not to live in it, but we'd have more than enough money to buy whatever home we wanted, after the fact.

Including *our* house, back in Nebraska.

"Holy shit, look at this," my brother said, pointing when we reached the corner.

"Wow," I said, shaking my brain out of Springfield because I was in New York, dammit, about to embark upon a life far more fabulous than Hannah Holbrook's. She could have Will and his classic Ford F-250 that didn't have air-conditioning, because I was about to lose myself in a cool new world.

Markets, coffee shops, restaurants, nail salons—the streets were alive, thrumming with businesses as far as the eye could see. Cars honking, people walking, delivery bikes, taxis—it was exactly like I'd pictured Manhattan, though to be fair, the only knowledge I'd had before now was what I'd seen on-screen.

"This street is definitely less fancy than ours," Liam said as we turned left at the corner and started up the block.

"Thank God," I said, because as little as I knew of life in the big city, seeing things like Panda Express, Raising Cane's, and Five Guys made me feel far more comfortable than a quiet block of mansions.

Because what in God's name do I know about that life?

"We should get Italian," I said definitively as we passed a place called Upside Pizza.

"You always want Italian," Liam countered, going around a slow walker in front of him.

"I know, but what's better than noodles and meatballs?" I said, hurrying to keep up with his long stride.

"Sushi," he said, pointing to a shop with blue neon in the window. "It's what all the fancy Manhattan kids are eating."

"Ugh." I could feel my chest tighten. "Don't start."

"I can tell you're already worrying way too much about school, but don't sweat it, Jules—who gives a shit if the richies don't appreciate us?"

"Maybe," I sighed, trying to release the tension running through my body, "but I'd also like to blend in at school. I don't want to be an outcast."

"We might not even stay, so I wouldn't worry too much," he said.

"First of all, we're staying for at least six months," I said, "And it's easy for you to say *who cares* because you're super social. You fit in everywhere."

"By fitting in 'everywhere,' you mean at the only school we've ever gone to?" he said sarcastically.

"Yeah, whatever," I said, because we both knew I was right. Liam was like my dad: He always knew the right things to say to make everyone love him. He was legitimately the most charming person in the room at any given moment, and I wished I could borrow just a fraction of his charisma.

Because, conversely, I was the most awkward person in the room at any given moment. Give me a new and uncomfortable situation, and I was always down to trip over my own feet and ramble incoherently with an awkward laugh.

While likely spilling something on myself.

"Oh my God, look at the baguettes in the window," I said, my stomach growling as I stared at a window display filled with crusty breads and delicate pastries.

Loaves was the name stenciled on the glass.

"I'll never understand how one person can like bread so much, but come on," my brother said, entertaining my unhealthy love of crusty carbohydrates. "Let's get a couple sticks for later, when we're moving shit into the house and have no food."

The bakery felt like something from a faraway corner of Paris. It had shelves of beautiful pastries behind glass, each row more detailed and gorgeous than the next. Macarons. Chocolate croissants. Brownies. Cake pops. You name it, it was here and looking delicious.

Afterward, we grabbed burritos at Chipotle and found a bench in this, like, mini park called Straus Park that was in the middle of an intersection, where we ate in silence while looking at our phones.

And I was hit with a pang of homesickness as life appeared to go on back home without me. I'd contemplated deleting all my socials because I didn't want to see anything from Hannah and Will, but that felt a little too final.

Now I had regrets, though, as everything back in Springfield seemed to be moving on like I'd never been there.

I closed my apps—*what's the point*—but when I went to put my phone back in my purse, I saw it was unzipped.

And my wallet was gone.

"Oh my God," I said as I opened the tiny bag and shifted things around, as if that'd make any difference. It was my super-small crossbody bag, and my wallet usually took up all the space inside.

It was clearly missing.

"What's wrong?" Liam asked through a mouth full of burrito, still scrolling on his phone.

"My wallet's gone," I said, panic rising inside me.

No, no, no—it can't be gone, I thought, my stomach clenching at the thought of never seeing it again.

"You sure?" he asked, looking over at me.

"Yes, I'm sure," I said, rolling my eyes.

"Maybe it's in the van."

"No, I used it to pay for the bread and burritos," I said, panic swirling through me. "I must've dropped—"

"Dad told you about the pickpockets, Jules," Liam said, looking unconcerned. "You're in a big city now and have to lock that shit down."

"Oh, this is helpful," I snapped.

"Relax," he said, setting down his burrito and dusting off his hands. "You're not going to be driving here, so the license is no loss, and good ol' Bernard will have a replacement debit card in hand within the hour. Nothing to get keyed up about."

Keyed up. That was how my family referred to my anxiety. I got *keyed up* about little things, and they just needed to say "calm down" and that would instantly relax me.

Not.

And what he said might've been correct, but he had no idea what that wallet meant.

"It might've fallen out of my bag after we got the burritos," I said. "I probably forgot to zip it and it fell out. I'll be right back."

He made a noise that told me he thought I was delusional as I got off the bench, but I didn't care. I needed to find that wallet, dammit. I started retracing my steps, staring down at the pavement and weaving in and out of clumps of pedestrians as I walked back toward where we'd been, freaking out.

Because it wasn't just a wallet.

Don't cry, I told myself as my throat got tight. *This is not a big deal,* I thought as I dodged everyone else walking down the sidewalk while keeping my eyes glued to the ground.

You needed to get rid of that wallet anyway, you dumbass.

Ever since the breakup, whenever I pulled it out of my purse, I knew I needed to hide it away. I needed to bury it in my box of Will memorabilia—which was a pretty big box, by the way.

But for some reason, I hadn't been able to bring myself to do that yet.

And it was ridiculous. Silly, stupid, and sentimental.

Last summer, Will lost his wallet and had to get everything replaced. New license, new debit card, new student ID; he had to get all of it redone. He bought a new wallet and filled it with the replacements, including the replacement copy of his favorite photo of me that he always kept in there.

The photo I'd teased him about.

Who keeps a photo of their girlfriend in their wallet anymore, boomer?

And God, I'd melted at the way he smiled at me when he said:

I do, because I like seeing your face every time I open it.

So when his dad finally found his lost wallet in one of the fields when he was cutting corn in August (it'd fallen out when they were spring planting, apparently), I kept it. Will had everything he needed in his new one, so I ditched my pastel wristlet and claimed his brown leather bifold instead.

But now it was gone.

It was gone, just like Will.

Lost somewhere in New York City.

God, just like me.

Stop overthinking this, I scolded myself as I approached Chipotle.

It's fine, I told myself as the guy at the counter dismissively reported that no one had turned in any wallets while also looking at me like I was an idiotic tourist.

But it didn't feel fine as I walked out of the building.

It felt like a bad omen, like the *this is fine* meme with the dog in the burning building.

And I wanted to rage.

I wanted to shout and maybe kick something over, because that wallet being taken from me today felt like the icing on the Will and Hannah cake, like the universe was doing a ball-spike on my face as if to remind me things were never going to be the same again.

And as I clenched my fists and stood there on the sidewalk, seething at the injustice, I saw it.

I saw *him.*

There was a guy in glasses and a hoodie, standing in front of the bakery on the other side of the street, and he was holding the wallet.

Oh my God.

Not only was he holding it, but it was open—*he was going through its contents, that asshole*—and he had a picture in his hand.

It was the stupid picture of me, laughing and surrounded by dogs, and it was in this stranger's hand.

And the guy was smirking underneath his backward Mets baseball cap like he found the picture hilarious. A shitty little know-it-all half smile was on his face as he looked down at it, probably the grin he grinned every time he picked an unsuspecting pocket, and that was the final straw.

I was taking back the wallet, dammit.

Even if it meant killing that guy with my bare hands.

CHAPTER TWO

"Oh, holy shitballs, here she comes."

—Remington

Damion

I couldn't stop looking at the photo.

At the stupid, cheesy wallet photo in my hand.

For starters, who actually kept pictures in their wallets anymore? This thing had to belong to someone at least seventy years old, right?

But there was something about the picture that I couldn't look away from.

I just wasn't sure what it was.

It was a photo of a girl wearing a winter hat and gloves, her body swallowed by an oversized barn jacket, and she was laughing.

Laughing while surrounded by *one-two-three-four-five-six*—six dogs.

Six golden retriever puppies.

She was on the ground in the snow, with her head thrown back and her mouth open wide, her eyes squinted as she laughed at the dogs, who'd obviously knocked her down in their bid for her attention.

I knew nothing about the girl, but it felt like I could *hear* her laughter.

Yeah, she was cute, but it was the *aliveness* of the photo that had me kind of wanting to keep it.

I mean, of course I wouldn't. Some idiot tourist (because no one in Gardenwood would have a wallet like *that*) had dropped his wallet on the sidewalk and was probably looking for it that very moment. I'd turn it in with contents intact because I wasn't an asshole, but—

"Hey!"

I glanced up at the shout, then did a double take when my brain registered what I was seeing.

Holy shit, it's her.

It was the girl from the photo, only she wasn't smiling in real life.

No, she was pissed.

Pissed and headed straight for me.

"That's my wallet!" she yelled, stepping into the street and crossing without even looking. A black Mercedes honked and slammed on its brakes, but this chick didn't even slow or look in its direction.

No, she actually started jogging, her eyes narrowed into an angry squint as she came at me like she fully expected me to start running in the other direction.

She had long curly hair the color of a pin oak tree in the fall, that cross between brown and bronze and the deepest of reds. *God, I'm even thinking like Remi now,* I thought offhandedly, but how else could I explain that specific thought? Uncle Rem was obsessed with trees, mostly because that was where his true obsession—birds—tended to live, so I'd spent a lifetime listening to the man wax poetic about tree types and foliage colors.

But he was clearly taking over my brain when *that* was what I was thinking as a clearly enraged girl with wild-ass *Pretty Woman* hair was now sprinting toward me.

I'm not sure why, but when she got close enough to grab for the wallet, I yanked it up and out of her reach.

Which wasn't hard because she was kind of short.

And I was not.

Short, that is.

"Give me the wallet," she said loudly, out of breath as she did a little jump and tried to grab it, "and I won't call the police."

I knew it was unwise, but I couldn't *not* laugh when she said that.

First of all, it was hilarious that she thought *I* would want to steal an ugly wallet that clearly belonged to someone who wouldn't have more than a Costco membership card and a ten-spot at their disposal.

But I loved the take-no-shit attitude.

"Wow, you're such a badass tourist, obviously knowing exactly how to deal with big-city wallet-stealing thieves like myself," I said. "'Speak firmly and tell them you won't call the police if they give it back'—I bet you read that on the internet."

"Just give me my wallet," she demanded.

"How do I know it's *your* wallet?" I asked, holding my arm straight up so she had zero chance of even getting close to it.

"Because you're holding a picture of *me* in your other hand," she said in outrage, her face scrunching into a scowl so overexaggerated that I had to laugh again. "A picture that came from said wallet."

"*Is* that you?" I looked down at the photo without lowering the wallet by a single millimeter. "I don't know. This girl looks happy and *nice*, whereas you look . . . well, I don't want to be rude, but *not*—"

"Come on," she snapped, lowering her arm to her side. "You know it's me, knock it off."

I could tell by the expression on her face that she was about to jump for it again.

"I'm just not sure," I said, for some reason wanting to mess with her. "And who carries a photo of themselves in their wallet? That doesn't make sense, unless you're a narcissist, so I'm not buying it."

"It's mine and you know it!"

"Do I?"

"I think you do," she said through gritted teeth.

And then she jumped again but only managed to smack my elbow.

Which made me laugh. Again.

Which made her make this little growling noise in the back of her throat.

"I mean, it appears to be a man's wallet," I said, wondering if the long lashes that framed those angry eyes were natural or extensions. "And you do not appear to be a man, so . . ."

"*Of course* you're a gender-stereotyping kind of guy who—"

"So I'm going to have to check the ID," I finished loudly, talking over her. "But you need to take a step back so I can do so."

She rolled her eyes and crossed her arms over her chest.

It wasn't a step back, but the arm cross felt like a concession. So I lowered the wallet just enough to pull out the driver's license, then I raised my arm back up again, still holding the wallet out of her reach.

Which made her give me another sigh and eye roll.

"Better be careful or they'll get stuck like that," I muttered.

"What?"

"Your eyes." She knew exactly what I'd meant. "It's obscene how hard they're rolling."

"Can we get on with this?"

I looked down at the driver's license in my hand, which actually belonged to a guy who looked like he would own a lot of unironic camo. "I'm sorry, kiddo, but the wallet appears to belong to someone named William Malone. This dude has blond hair, blue eyes, and a tragically awful mullet, so the judges are giving you a big, fat nope. Not yours."

"He's my boyfr—*was* my boyfriend," she said with a sigh. "Not that it's any of your business. But if you check behind where *his* license was in the wallet, you'll find mine."

"Will I?" I said, going back to the wallet.

"Yeah, you will, wiseass," she replied, so quietly that I almost didn't hear it.

"Wiseass," I repeated, shaking my head as I saw the top of what appeared to be another driver's license. "First you accuse me of theft and now you're calling me names. I am grossly offended."

"Sure you are."

I pulled out the license that clearly belonged to her.

The photo confirmed both the brown eyes glaring at me and the mass of auburn curls.

Julia.

The name suits her, I thought as the song by Mt. Joy started playing in my head.

Julia
Fix me a blue sky in the warm sun . . .

"This license belongs to Julia Lowell," I said, obnoxiously looking back and forth between the identification in my hand and her in-person annoyed face.

"That's me."

"How do I *know* this is you?" I quipped, unable to stop myself from antagonizing her. Something about the stubborn jut of her chin and the way she looked at me through narrowed eyes made it impossible to let her off the hook.

I was having way too much fun messing with her, this ridiculous person who thought I wanted her ridiculous *boyfriend wallet*.

"Just. Look. At. The. Photo," she said in frustration, her voice coming out as a groan through clenched teeth.

I looked down at the identification and then everything came at me, all at once.

Cold water, slap to the face, punch in the gut.

Holy, holy shit.

She was Julia Lowell.

Lowell.

With a Nebraska driver's license.

Nebraska.

And a Springfield, Nebraska, mailing address.

Springfield. Nebraska.

No way.

As my mind was wrapping around the insane reality that I was face-to-face with one of the Nebraska Lowells who'd come to town to steal Uncle Remi's house, she jumped up and reached for the wallet.

And this time she successfully knocked it out of my hand.

It fell to the pavement, and as I quickly bent down to retrieve it, because now I definitely couldn't let her win—at *anything*—she did the same thing.

Only she tried boxing me out, turning her body to push mine out of the way.

And as she did that, she somehow managed to throw back her head and ram it directly into my nose, the back of her skull slamming into my face with the full force of a major leaguer's baseball bat.

"Shit!" I managed, straightening my glasses as I saw stars and involuntary tears filled my eyes. My hands came up to cover my nose as I stepped away from her with a stumble—*dear God, it feels like she shattered my fucking face.*

"Shit," she said as she grimaced and raised a hand to the back of her head, rubbing the spot where I assumed she'd have a hell of a bump because my nose had to have dealt a blow to that hard-as-a-rock cranium.

She must've determined me to no longer be a threat now that she'd headbutted me, because instead of running off with the wallet, I heard, "God, are you okay?"

"Are you serious right now?" I asked, wondering if my nose was broken. I half expected it to be gushing blood for how much it hurt, but she didn't look horrified, so I was probably okay.

Although, she very well might be someone who *wasn't* horrified by the sight of blood.

She *was* one of them, after all.

Springfield. Nebraska.

Holy *shit*.

She looked worried, those long lashes blinking fast as she gnawed on her bottom lip and watched me cup my busted nose. "Can I, uh, I mean, is there anything I can—"

"I think you've done enough, *Julia*," I snapped as my nose started throbbing. "And let's not even pretend you feel bad that you broke my nose, okay? Just *run along* and go do whatever you were doing before you discovered me trying to find the wallet's owner like a decent human being."

"I'm *sorry*," she said defensively, tucking a long curl behind her ear. "But you were the one who—"

"Who dared to touch your ex-boyfriend's ugly old abandoned wallet, yes, I know," I interrupted, done with this and done with her. "Run along, honey, and this time maybe look before you cross the street. People in the big city get killed that way."

Her mouth dropped open in outrage, and she just stared at me for a second, like my words had rendered her frozen.

But the girl recovered quickly.

"Y'know, you're kind of a jerk," she said, the remorse instantly gone from her face as she shoved the wallet into the front pocket of her jeans.

"Y'know, I kind of am," I agreed. "A jerk with a broken fucking nose. Thanks again for that."

For another half second we just glared at each other, her brown eyes moving all over my face while I wondered if she'd moved into Remi's house yet.

Are you sleeping in my favorite bedroom, Nebraska, the one I used to make blanket forts in?

The thought of it made my stomach *literally* clench as the grief came at me harder than a headbutt.

"No problem," she said, her teeth once again gritted. "Nice meeting you, um . . ."

"Damion." I let go of my nose and slid my hands into my pockets. "And I only wish I could say the same, *Julia*."

She made another snarling noise before turning and marching away, once again *not* looking before running out into the street.

This time there weren't any cars about to mow her down.

Talk about a lucky break.

CHAPTER THREE

"New York hypnotizes you with its autumn. Each falling leaf coaxes your consciousness into a long, sleepy sigh as you succumb to the dreamlike dance of the tumbling yellows, the falling reds, and those crinkling, crunchy browns."

—Remington

Julia

"You cannot be serious," I said, looking out the window.

"It's a tradition, every first day of school since kindergarten," my dad said, sliding his feet into his Vans. "You seriously think you're going to have a first day of school without me capturing a photo?"

"But we have new neighbors that we don't even know yet," I said, the stress of the morning making me feel absolutely nauseous. The combination of a new school and my utter confidence that we wouldn't fit in were *killing* me.

In the five days we'd been New Yorkers, I hadn't really seen a single neighbor out *doing* anything. Actually, I hadn't really been able to peg who were neighbors at all, because it was Manhattan: There were just people walking on the sidewalk all the time, people who might've been neighbors or might've been tourists.

Who could tell the difference, other than the fact that the ones with dogs were probably locals, right? Or maybe they were the dog walkers? Because, yes, my neighbors seemed to hire dog walkers who somehow managed to wrangle eight dogs at a time. Dogs that had better accessories and style than I ever did.

But it looked like there was a girl around our age—terrifyingly fashionable and overconfidently cool—who maybe lived in the white stone house across the street. She had long blond hair that only came from good genes and a lot of money, like she'd been visiting the very best salons since the day she was born.

No Supercuts for that girl.

"Don't you think it would be bad luck not to get the photo we've always gotten?" my dad asked. "It seems like it'd be tempting fate to mess with a lifetime of memories."

"Just let them take the damn picture so we can get out of here," Liam said, pushing his glasses up the bridge of his nose and making me think of *that guy*.

The jerk with the glasses and probable broken nose.

I still couldn't believe that'd happened. Like, who *did* that? Who messed with strangers for fun? Hopefully, he was just a random terrible New Yorker and not what the typical locals were like.

"Can we at least take it inside?" I asked. "Why have a gorgeous staircase if we're not going to use it for photographs?"

"We've always done it outside, come on," my dad said, brushing off the suggestion.

"Miss Julia," Bernard said with a twinkle in his eye, "I suggest you acquiesce before your stubbornness makes you tardy."

I rolled my eyes as I followed Liam and my dad to the front door, with my mom trailing behind us as we headed outside, because *of course* she'd want to be a part of this.

"Oh my gosh, you guys look so cute," she said, smiling and clasping her hands in front of her chest. "You're like something out of a show on Disney. I'm in love with this whole look."

She was referring to our uniforms, which I was on the fence about.

For someone who was already pretty sure she wasn't going to fit in among wealthy New Yorkers, at least the uniform would level the playing field a little bit. I liked the pleated skirt, the blazer, and the tie.

It felt very Chilton-esque.

My brother just looked . . . *strange* wearing nice pants and a sweater with a big crest on his breastbone, mostly because his usual wardrobe made him look like he was ready for a flash-mob impromptu basketball practice at any given moment.

This . . . this ensemble made him look like he was ready to study for his SATs at any given moment.

We quickly smiled for the camera, my dad trying to center us perfectly between the columns, but movement caught my attention as my mom said, "Awwwwww!" way too loudly.

Oh, geez—the cool girl.

The girl across the street was walking out her front door—talk about your crappy timing—going straight for the black SUV that was waiting. Seeing her in the same uniform that I was wearing added to my nervousness, the confirmation that people who looked like her would be attending my school.

As my mom *awwww*ed over our adorability, Cool Girl tossed her perfectly coiffed head and looked in our direction.

Shit, I thought, mortified that she was witnessing our geekery.

Her eyes narrowed and she looked at us like we were out of our minds, which was probably what inspired my smart-ass brother to raise his hand and yell, "Good morning, neighbor!"

Her eyes narrowed even more before she slid a pair of dark sunglasses over her eyes and got into the waiting car.

"Oh, we're going to be best friends, I just know it," Liam said.

"Why did you have to do that?" I said through gritted teeth as we went inside.

"You saw her and the stick up her ass," he replied with a shrug. "How could I not?"

"Okay, go get your stuff together," my mom said, oblivious to it all. "We should leave now so you aren't late."

I ran up to my room, still in shock that this was actually happening.

I was starting a fancy private school in New York.

Me.

Life didn't make sense anymore.

Especially as I walked up the grand staircase, passing by all the luxurious decorations that adorned the walls of the place that was apparently our house.

I wasn't one to be impressed by something just because it cost a lot, but Lou's house—our house—was unbelievable.

Not only was it gorgeous and huge, but it had all this incredible history locked up inside it. If you pushed down on the first-edition copy of *The Great Gatsby* that sat on a shelf in the library, the shelf actually slid over, and there was a secret library with *better* books that you could access via the coolest little ladder.

And every bit of the house was like that, I swear to God.

Liam and I were constantly finding what felt like little treasures.

My mom had zero plans to change any of the décor, because she said it felt like this was how the house was *meant* to be dressed. She wasn't wrong—it was somehow very Lou-coded.

It'd never make sense that Lou had had something so amazing and then wanted to leave it to us. *Us?* Had he not had someone else in his life to leave it to? I mean, the lower level of the house he'd left to Bernard—it had its own private entrance from the outside—but shouldn't he have left the rest of it to . . . *someone*?

My parents thought it was because we felt like family to him, but that seemed too good to be true, in my opinion.

I went into my room and slid my feet into my new shoes. Over the weekend, my mom had taken us to Fifth Avenue and shuffled us in and out of designer stores, stores with names on them that we'd never even heard of (even though I considered myself to be relatively fashionable). I read *Vogue* and watched celebrity styles, but a lot of these designers I still didn't know.

I tied my Louis Vuitton sneakers, grabbed my Fendi backpack, double-checked that my diamond studs were fully backed and not going to fall off. I took one last look in the mirror. Ugh. Could I really do this? Did I have a choice?

It's now or never.

And how I wished it were never. Gardenwood Academy was *beyond* imposing.

Very efficient, very uniform.

A string of black vehicles—all luxury—lined the curb in front of us, and when each car reached the front, back doors opened and students emerged like celebrities getting out on the red carpet. I watched as they exited vehicles and found each other, coming together and walking into the building in groups that made me want to vomit in nervousness.

Because NYC private school cliques were far more intimidating than the cliques back home, and even *those* had given me endless anxiety. As long as I'd been in school, I'd been ridiculously in my own head when it came to socialization. Logically, I knew that no one cared what I was doing, but my brain was constantly convincing me that everyone was talking about me behind my back.

Which was probably why I'd only had two *true* friends—Teanna and Lauren—back home (not counting Will and Liam). I never wanted to put myself out there and talk to new people, because what if they hated me?

I pulled out my lip balm and ran it over my lips while we rounded the block where my mom had conveniently dropped us off in the minivan—away from prying, judgmental eyes—and took a deep breath.

The crisp of the autumn morning sent a chill over my face, and I froze when I looked at the school because it felt too big for me. Not in size but in stature. It was all brick, with just enough ivy crawling over the facade to make it look overpriced and like somewhere I shouldn't be.

I adjusted my very expensive backpack as I got out, but as someone walked past me, a random girl with long black hair and a beret that managed to *not* look stupid, I noticed her bag. I didn't recognize any discernible logos, but it reeked of money. Quality leather, soft and without flaws . . . *exclusive*.

Somehow you could just tell.

That drew my eyes down to her shoes, because shoes and bags were kind of the only creativity you had when the uniforms were in play, and her shoes had the same vibe as her bag. They were some cool variety of loafer, with frilly socks underneath, but they were understated, obviously luxe, and expensive without screaming a brand name.

I looked down at my own shoes, covered in logos, and wondered if I'd made a bad choice.

"Come on, we're going to be late," Liam said, going around me.

My whole life people had asked what it was like having a twin, but times like this solidified the very best thing about it.

You always had someone with you. My brother could be a smart-ass, but he was always there.

"Coming," I said, scrambling to keep up with his long legs.

It was impossible not to notice people glancing our way, which wasn't a surprise.

It's just because we're new, I told myself.

But, ugh—people were definitely watching us, especially girls looking at Liam.

So shocking, the sarcastic voice in my head quipped. He was tall and funny and girls *always* liked him. Liam was naturally comfortable in his own skin and good at everything—the cool twin—whereas I was in my own head and rambled too much, aka the uncool twin.

The first thing I noticed when we walked through the main doors was that it smelled so *good.* It didn't smell like industrial cleaner or school lunches, which was public school's scent potpourri, but instead smelled like . . . *lilies*?

It smelled like freaking lilies and maybe old books (?) but in a good way.

I followed Liam toward the office, walking atop dark, shiny wood floors, but as I glanced around, I was distracted by the lighting.

The *lighting.*

Chandeliers, sconces, lamps—the place was lit like an exclusive hotel, not a school. I half expected to see a lounge somewhere off in a corner where students were sipping on martinis. Instead my eyes landed on three uniformed girls (who looked like models) sitting on a sofa, talking quietly while holding delicate china mugs, and two blazered guys (who also looked like models) on wingback chairs, laughing as they listened.

And holy *shit*—it smelled like lilies because of the *actual* lilies sitting on the table between the wingback chairs.

How was this a high school?

I followed Liam into the office—more floral arrangements, dear *Lord*—where the woman behind the desk smiled, *thrilled* to see us.

"The Lowells—of course," she said, grinning and nodding. "So nice to meet you. Headmaster Green has been waiting for you, so go ahead back to his office."

She gestured toward a thick wood door on the other side of her desk. Liam shot me a glance and we walked in the direction where she'd pointed, pausing to knock at the headmaster's door.

Headmaster. So, so strange.

"Enter," we heard someone say, so Liam grabbed the doorknob and pushed open the door.

"Miss Lowell, Mr. Lowell," the man behind the desk said, standing and coming around to greet us. "How lovely to meet you. I'm Headmaster Green."

Headmaster Green was not at all what I would've expected. Instead of a scowling white-haired man with demerits to distribute and maybe flowing robes, this guy looked nice. He was probably in his fifties, his smile warm, and he was wearing a thick wool sweater with perfectly tailored pants.

"Nice to meet you," I mumbled nervously as my brother reached out and shook the guy's hand.

"Welcome to Gardenwood Academy."

"Thanks," Liam said in that comfortable way he had with everyone he met, like he knew exactly how they'd want him to respond. "Great to be here."

"Is your family all moved in?" the man asked, his eyes dipping down to Liam's loosely tied tie.

"Not at all," Liam said, and I just smiled and nodded beside him as he added, "But we were able to find our notebooks and pencils, so we're all good for school."

"Wonderful," Headmaster Green said, and then he reached out a hand and started fixing Liam's tie. "Speaking of school, why don't you two have a seat? Since we have a few minutes, I just thought we'd go over a couple things before I send you on your way."

"Thanks," Liam said with a grin as Green stepped back, and Liam looked down at his now perfectly tied tie. "Nice work."

"Always here to help," the man said as he went around the desk and sat in his chair.

Of course they'd already bonded.

Liam plopped down in one of the two guest chairs, so I lowered myself to the other, wondering how I was going to make it through the day when my stomach was so full of nervous butterflies.

"Miss Lowell," the headmaster said, his wise, owl-like gaze on me behind his thick black glasses. "You're quiet. Are you nervous about your first day?"

"Yeah," I said, then quickly corrected myself with "Yes, sir."

"First of all, call me Mr. Green, or even Seth if that makes you more comfortable. Second of all, try not to be too anxious. We have a wonderful student body who I think will make you feel quite at home."

"Oh. Good. Okay," I said, picturing Mr. Mets Hat scowling at me like I was a raccoon in a dumpster after I broke his nose. Pretty much any human would make me feel more welcome than that guy, the only person I'd met since we moved.

"After speaking with your parents and the administrators at your previous school, we have carefully curated your schedules for this semester."

"Excellent," my brother said, as if this were something he had been concerned about.

I wanted to roll my eyes.

"Yeah, great," I said, the mention of my schedule making my stomach ache even more.

"We do need to have a quick touch-base about your math scores," he said, eyeballing me with a seriousness that hadn't been there when he was talking to my brother.

"We do?" I said, my stomach dropping even lower.

"You see, Miss Lowell," he said, crossing his legs and leaning back a little in his high-backed chair, "Gardenwood Academy has a reputation for excellence that we take quite seriously. We hold our students to the highest of standards. Each year there are hundreds of applicants we would love to admit, but simply cannot because they don't meet those standards."

"Okay," I said, not sure where this was headed, but I knew it wasn't good.

"We're always happy to work with alumni families and those of generous donors, and we pride ourselves on our ability to foster student improvement. But ultimately, the scores *do* matter and must reach a certain level in order for a student to remain enrolled at the academy."

"Okay, spell it out for us, Seth," my brother said, glancing over at me like he knew I was never going to work up the courage to actually ask what the headmaster was getting at. "What does she need to do, or how off are her scores? I feel like you're trying to lay something down for us that we're missing."

I wondered if my mom knew about this score issue, because she'd had a meeting with administration the day after we'd moved in. And were we the family of "generous donors"? Had my parents donated money to the school in order to get us in?

"Do I have your permission to discuss this with you and your brother collectively," the headmaster asked me, "or would you prefer I dismiss him and we can talk privately?"

It was so bizarre, the way he was talking to us like we were adults. In the world we'd come from, teachers and administrators talked to students like they were kids. This man, however, was talking to us like we were business associates.

Something about it was kind of cool, but it also felt . . . *weird*.

"No, it's fine," I said, knowing it'd be better to hear it with Liam in the room.

"Your test scores in mathematics fall rather significantly below our standards," he said.

He quickly held up a hand as if to say *don't talk*. "Which is okay. We have some of the world's best educators here at Gardenwood, as well as a host of tutors who will absolutely work with you to get those scores raised."

"Okay, well—"

"That being said," he continued, "I think the best course of action is to schedule a tutor *immediately*, because we need to get these scores turned around and rectified as soon as possible. We have no time to waste, unfortunately."

My cheeks got hot and I felt embarrassed in the way I always did when it came to math. I considered myself to be a relatively intelligent person, and I did fine in all my other classes, but when it came to math, especially algebra, it was like trying to translate another language.

"Our standardized testing season begins in six weeks, and as willing as I am to make allowances for special families and students, your results on those tests are irrefutable. It boils down to simple data, and my hands are tied once the numbers come in. The scores alone will determine your ability to stay here or not."

Suddenly it felt like my blood was quickly draining from my face. If I wasn't able to stay at this school, that meant we wouldn't meet the stipulation and wouldn't inherit the money, right? And even though my family had agreed that wasn't everything, I didn't want my non-math brain to complicate things.

Especially now that I knew we'd been about to lose *everything* before the inheritance bomb.

"So," Liam began, shooting me a glance that was telling me to calm my ass down, "we can set her up right away with your best tutor and get cranking on this?"

I could tell he didn't get it. He understood that I needed to do better as a student at Gardenwood Academy, but he hadn't caught on to the fact that our millions could possibly be in jeopardy if I didn't score high enough on the tests.

And I wasn't going to enlighten him.

I felt dizzy from the stress of this news and definitely didn't need more pressure from him or my parents.

"Absolutely we can," Mr. Green said. "I will speak to the teacher in charge of the tutoring staff and we can determine who might be the best person to work with her."

"That would be great, thanks," I said, feeling the need to speak up because suddenly it felt like Liam was my dad or something. "And is there a way to, like, keep this kind of quiet so I'm not—"

"We employ complete discretion," he said, making relief settle over me as he added, "I absolutely understand that as a new student you might worry about the optics of needing extra help. I know with one hundred percent certainty that you would not be judged for taking your grades seriously, but we can definitely arrange after-hours, off-site help if it eases your mind."

"Yes, thank you," I said, glad he understood. "That would be great."

"Why don't you two take these," he said, grabbing two folders from his desk and handing one to each of us. "Your schedules and student handbooks. Let's get you on your way to starting your first day, and Julia—just stop in and see me before you go home and we can get the tutoring scheduled."

"Okay. Sounds good," I said, even though it didn't sound good at all.

Liam and I opened our fancy schedules, printed on thick card stock, as Mr. Green—*Seth?*—continued. "I have two volunteers waiting for you in the office, student guides who will help you get assimilated. They will accompany you to your classes, facilitate introductions with staff members, lead a tour of the facility, and foster peer-to-peer new engagements."

Peer-to-peer new engagements? Dear Lord, this truly felt like a different world.

"You can feel comfortable leaning on your volunteers and assigning them any requests and inquiries. They will eat lunch with you and are at your disposal. *Use* them."

We stood and followed him out of his office, and as we headed into the lobby area, I wished Liam and I had the same classes, like when we were little. It'd always been nice to let him go into a nerve-racking situation and be his social self while I enjoyed the protection of hanging in his shadow, comfortably invisible.

"This is Jasmine," the headmaster said, gesturing toward a girl with a long black braid, wire-rimmed glasses, and dark red lipstick who was clearly waiting for us. "She will show you around, Miss Lowell, and provide all the assistance you'll need in getting comfortable at Gardenwood."

"Hi," I said awkwardly, because what was I supposed to say to this stranger? "Um, nice to meet you."

"Nice to meet you, too," she said with a really warm smile, making me feel marginally better. I glanced down at her shoes, and she *also* had subtle shoes that looked expensive but understated.

"This is *Mr.* Lowell—"

"Liam," my brother interrupted, extending his hand to shake hers.

What the hell is he doing shaking her hand?

Her eyes narrowed as she looked directly at his hand like she was confused by the gesture, but she smiled, shaking his hand and saying, "Jasmine."

"And this is Beckett," the headmaster said, pointing toward a tall blond guy in a blazer who looked like a Hollister model. "He will be your right hand as long as you need him, Liam."

"Nice to meet you," he said to my brother, then smiled at me.

"Classes start in fifteen minutes, so you should probably make your way along now," Mr. Green said.

"Thanks, Seth," my brother said.

Seth. So, so weird.

"Yeah, um, thank you," I agreed, always Liam's backup hype man.

"Miss Lowell, your first class is down the hall to the right. Mr. Lowell, you are on the third floor to start your day. Good luck, you two."

Liam tossed me an enthusiastic wave and followed Beckett up the grand staircase. Leaving me alone (with Jasmine) and a firestorm of nerves.

Here we go.

CHAPTER FOUR

"Manhattan isn't a place where you fit in. Millions of people, all crammed together, and not a one of 'em fits in. Just find your spot and start chiseling."

—Remington

Julia

"Everyone starts their day in their transition class, which is basically just homeroom," Jasmine said, leading me away from the office and down a busy hallway. I could still feel eyes on me and I tried to ignore them, I really did.

But every time I glanced away from Jasmine, I just saw a very intimidating army of beautiful, uniformed robots. Girls with long hair in blazers and skirts, guys with short hair in sweaters with ties, dudes in jackets who looked like they were ready to take over their fathers' businesses—they moved in groups of three and four, appearing as if they'd all been cast for a *Vogue* private-school photo shoot.

"You and I are in the same transition, so that's good," Jasmine said. "Also—ask me any questions about anything while we walk."

"Okay," I said, wishing I could just say, *Tell me who to avoid and who to watch out for*.

"So what made you guys move here?" she asked, shifting the bag on her shoulder. "Business?"

I thought back to what Bernard told us to say.

"Yes. My dad has a lot of business here, so my parents decided it was finally time to put down roots in New York," I said.

She nodded. "Have you been here before?"

"I haven't, but they have," I said, which wasn't a lie. When I was little, my parents took the Amtrak to New York a few times for their own little vacation, but I didn't need to pitch it as a tourist situation.

No, I was going to pretend they'd been business travelers who'd enjoyed the Big Apple for businessy reasons, multiple times.

"Have you always lived here?" I asked, immediately regretting how unsophisticated the question sounded.

"Yeah," she said. "My dad grew up on the Upper West Side and never wanted to live anywhere else. I'm a lifelong New Yorker."

My face was on fire as we continued through the halls, because *everyone* was looking at us when we walked by. And even though my uniform should've made me look like every other girl in the building, I somehow knew I wasn't doing it right.

Of course, my unmanageable hair played a huge part in that.

Because this looked like a school full of girls who knew how to wield a flatiron. My unruly hair, however, was another thing entirely. There were people who had curly hair, sure, but I had curly with volume that was almost impossible to tame. I'd gone to the salon a few times and paid a small fortune for relaxer treatment, but it never lasted long enough to make up for the cost.

Today I'd pulled the front up in a clip and kept the back down, unloading half a bottle of gel and hair spray in an attempt to keep it under control.

"Hey, Jaz," a blond girl said as she ran up to us.

Come on, I thought in disgust. *What is with the hair here?*

This girl had a blond bob with *perfect* blunt edges, and she looked like everybody's all-American. Like, her style aesthetic was *how every grandparent wants their granddaughter to look in a photo*.

"Did you already get the tickets for later?"

"Yeah, they're in my wallet," Jasmine said. "I'll give them to you at lunch."

“Hi, I’m Donovan,” she said to me.

“Julia,” I replied, happy that Donovan *also* seemed decent.

“Donovan’s in our transition and she’s also kind of always with me, so you’re either going to have to get used to her or hate her for the rest of the week,” Jasmine said with a smile.

“Yeah, I’m sure you’ll hate me,” Donovan said. “I’m a real pain in the ass.”

That made me let out a little of my breath. Maybe the private-school students would all be this normal—wouldn’t that be great? I’d imagined Gardenwood Academy to be very much a mean-girl situation, but maybe that was unfair?

“Also there’s already a rumor going around that your brother is crazy hot. Is he single?”

“God, calm down, Donovan! She just got here and also probably doesn’t want to discuss the heat status of her twin brother.”

“I just like to get business out of the way quickly. Single or not—it’s an easy question.”

“He *is* single,” I said, “but a little on the obnoxious side, so you might want to reserve your opinion until after you meet him.”

“Obnoxious I can do,” she said with a smile.

We kept walking, and as we did, Donovan started giving me information on the people we passed, quiet little drops of intel.

“That’s Colin Streeter,” she said under her breath as we passed a massive guy who looked kind of like a linebacker in a suit coat. “Great football player, nice guy, terrible boyfriend. Steer clear unless you like bossy.”

“Noted,” I said quietly, though I was pretty sure I wasn’t going to have to worry about being chased by football players.

“And the girls by the auditorium doors—see them?” she murmured, gesturing with her head to our left.

I glanced over, and five girls were standing there, five girls who were all staring down at the papers in their hands. The tallest one, who looked exactly like Sadie Sink, appeared to be reading aloud from the pages.

Jasmine said, "Donovan, you're not going to—"

"They're the Oscars," Donovan interrupted as we passed, her voice loud enough for me to hear but not for anyone else to register. "Theater kids with enough talent and connections to blow up any day now. Dasha—the one with all the eyeliner—was in a film with Leo DiCaprio last spring, and the short girl beside her is Anthony Hopkins's stepsister's granddaughter."

"But no one calls them 'the Oscars' anymore," Jasmine interjected as I wondered how girls who looked that sophisticated could be *my* age, students at *my* school.

"Don't you still think of the labels, though?" Donovan asked her, then explained to me, "In seventh grade, there was this whole thing where everyone created social labels for all little cliques at the academy. The Oscars, the Skins, the Toms, the Judges, the Dead Poets, and . . . well, I can't remember the rest. It was basically just middle-school nonsense, but my brain *still* catalogs people by those little tags."

"Yeah, same," Jasmine said. "But it became a whole huge thing where parents got involved, *such* middle-school drama, so pretend you never heard of it because people still have feelings."

"Got it," I said, watching as Dasha put a hand over her chest and took over for the tall Sadie Sink, speaking and gesturing wildly.

The Oscars.

We kept moving through the crowded hallways, and Donovan kept giving me info that I appreciated knowing, yet also terrified me because it was confirmation that the entire student body of Gardenwood Academy possessed a stronger sense of self than I'd ever dreamed of having.

The Toms were five guys—Corbin, Chuck, Hunter, Harrison, Jack—who pretty much ruled the school. Lacrosse superstars from the most powerful families. As we passed, I found them all to be intimidatingly handsome but in a red-flaggy kind of way.

"The trouble with the labels started when Corbin found out which Tom they were named after," Donovan said quietly as we passed the group. "He assumed it was like Tom Brady or some jock superstar, but it was actually Tom Buchanan."

"From *Gatsby*?" I asked, feeling nervous when I made eye contact with the red-haired guy in the group.

"Bingo," Jasmine said. "Corbin didn't like that, but his father—Edward Archington of the Chase Bank Archingtons—*really* didn't like it."

"Understatement of the century," Donovan said, nodding, and I was dying to hear how Edward Archington of the Chase Bank Archingtons had reacted.

But I was too afraid to ask, so I just said, "Oof."

"Oof for sure."

By the time we reached the classroom at the end of the hallway, I'd learned about the others. The Judges were three mean girls who harshly judged everyone and everything—and also their fathers were *actual* circuit court judges. The Dead Poets were a group of writerly students (the only ones who didn't sound scary) who constantly discussed literature and were also "wicked hot."

But the Skins? They sounded the scariest of all.

"They're like the female version of the Toms, in terms of power and popularity," Donovan explained. "'Skins' refers to the fact that they're so flawless, the only explanation is that they must be aliens wearing lab-created, perfect-human skins. Coco is their leader, they're each more disgustingly stunning than the next, they wear all the best clothes, and they're at every good party."

"Is this a big party school?" I asked, remembering the cornfield parties I'd been to back home.

"For sure during the season," Donovan said.

"The season?" I inquired, thinking of the debutantes in the Regency-era historicals I loved to read.

"That's a whole other thing. Come on, we don't want to be late," Jasmine said dismissively, pointing in the direction of the classroom doorway.

I swallowed down my nervousness as we went into the room.

"Hey, Mr. Sparks—this is Julia Lowell, a new student."

Jasmine walked right up to his desk and I followed. The man, who looked to be in his thirties with thick, dark hair, gave me a smile.

"Well, good morning, Julia Lowell. Where are you from?"

"Nebraska," I said, immediately aware of how quiet the room became when I said that.

"Wow, I expected a New York address, not a Midwesterner," he said, tilting his head. "We don't get a lot of those around here. This has got to be quite a change."

"It definitely is," I said, nodding and wishing I could go hide behind a desk.

"Less cows?" the girl in the front row muttered without looking up from her phone.

I didn't know if I was supposed to answer or if she was just being rude, but I said, "I haven't seen one yet, so probably yes."

That made her look up from her phone, her long-lashed eyes narrowed. "Probably?"

I shrugged. "Probably."

"Well, welcome to Gardenwood," Mr. Sparks said. "Hopefully, you'll find that my class is not too daunting—"

"Or boring," Donovan added.

"Or boring," he agreed. "Although, you can't listen to anything Donovan says because she finds everything boring."

"Not true," she said.

"Totally true," someone said from the back.

"There's an open desk over there, and I will get you a textbook as soon as the bell rings."

"Thank you," I said, nodding.

I turned and headed for the empty spot, and I was almost there when I heard someone say *his* name.

"You're so wrong, Damion."

My head whipped around. There was no way there could be more than one person in New York City named Damion, right?

Okay, *not* right, but still. What were the odds I was going to meet two Damions in the short time I'd been in Manhattan when I'd never met one in my entire life?

Please let those odds be high.

No such luck (what did I expect?), I thought, because there he was, walking through the doorway with another guy.

He was tall—*whoa*, even taller than I remembered—wearing a gray crested V-neck sweater with a shirt and perfectly tied tie underneath it.

Nice black pants, brown leather messenger bag slung across his body, big-faced silver watch that looked a lot like a Rolex, and a signet ring.

Not the same aesthetic as the man I'd assumed to be a pickpocket, but oh my God—it was definitely him.

No, no, no, no, nooooooooo!

"I'm so right and you know it," he said, smiling at his friend, until he saw me.

He saw me.

Our eyes met, and I swear to God everything froze. Everything froze for a solid ten seconds before his mouth flatlined.

His throat moved as he swallowed. His smile disappeared in an instant, like it'd never been there. His jaw flexed.

And then he said, in the *most* sarcastic tone, "Holy shit, as I live and breathe, it's Julia Nebraska."

What the fu . . .

I watched him swagger toward me, my brain unable to process this unexpected turn of events.

Is this what it feels like to go into shock?

The guy whose nose I thought I'd accidentally broken, the dude I accused of stealing my wallet, the person I called a THIEF, was a student at my school.

A Rolex-wearing student at my fancy private school.

Which meant he was rich.

Oh God.

His shoulder bumped mine slightly as he walked past—*oh my God, was that an accident or is he intentionally bumping into me?!*—which made me stumble into the desk behind me.

It was nothing, my little trip, but enough of a *something* that I heard a few chuckles float around me.

Embarrassed, I sat down and pulled a notebook out of my backpack as dread settled in the pit of my stomach.

Ugh. What have I done?

No wonder he'd seemed so annoyingly amused as he'd held Will's wallet just out of my reach that day. He was a snooty prep-school guy. I bet it was just *so* entertaining to mess with the chick who'd naively assumed he was a petty criminal.

There was no way he wasn't going to tell everyone that hilarious story, right?

I shot a glance in his direction, relieved to see he was looking down at a book as I studied him and his dark hair, thick and a little curly on top. The tortoiseshell glasses he wore looked . . . well, really *good* on him. He had brown eyes, no—*hazel*—a sharp jaw, and a somehow . . . muscular neck. He was, annoyingly, a very attractive guy.

Hot, even.

But I'd engaged with him enough to know it didn't matter. He was a jerk.

And probably a hyper-entitled trust-fund baby.

Yep.

It only took a few hours for him to prove me right.

I was walking down the hall at the end of the day, leaving my mind-bogglingly disappointing after-school meeting with Mr. Green, the meeting where I learned some extremely unfortunate news about my math tutoring situation. I was juggling an armful of freshly assigned text-books when I lost my grip and dropped them all. I sighed and kind of wanted to cry—it'd been that sort of day—as I knelt down in the busy hallway and scrambled to pick them up before being trampled to death by the young coastal elites who all seemed to hate me.

I was reaching for the English book when I glanced up to find Damion walking in my direction. He was with two other guys, laughing and talking, and they were oblivious to my existence.

But *he* definitely saw me.

He gave me a sly smile as his dark—*wicked*—eyes took in the details of my situation. But instead of slowing or swerving to go around me or, God forbid, bending down to help me retrieve my books, he completely walked over them.

He walked. Over. Them.

Walked over them!

The tip of his fancy loafer made contact with my lit book as he passed, sending it spinning farther out of my reach as he continued on like I hadn't even been there. Like I didn't even exist. I cursed him under my breath as I watched him walk away.

What a dick.

An *asshole.*

And, as Mr. Green had just informed me, my potential new math tutor.

CHAPTER FIVE

"Beware of freckle-faced girls."

—Remington

Damion

"Just grab them and go," I said, in a hurry to blow out of school and get to the courts.

"Yeah, no shit," Beckett said. "What do you think I'm going to do? Stick around for happy hour with administration?"

"I have no idea *what* you're doing," I said, glancing at my watch. "Hurry up."

I'd been irritated ever since transition, when I had to sit and stare at Julia Lowell for the entire thirty-minute period. I mean, I didn't *have* to stare at her, but I couldn't seem to bring myself to look away from the back of her head.

Because the sight of her just pissed me off.

Even her curls pissed me off, to be honest. Too long, too curly, too . . . *auburn-y*. Shit.

Her *existence* just pissed me off.

And how dare she look like a lost puppy in the halls of Gardenwood, like a wounded animal?

I'd felt like a giant asshole for a half second when I saw her in the hall earlier, but then I remembered that she'd be going home to Remi's house after school, the house I hadn't seen the inside of in way too long, where she'd probably put her feet up on his furniture and laugh with her parents about how easy their grift had been.

Boom—any urge to help her disappeared.

I'd walked on by as if she *hadn't* looked utterly helpless.

"Hey, Mr. Green, I just need to grab those council forms," Beckett said, half yelling into the headmaster's inner sanctum as we pushed into the office. "I forgot to grab them this morning."

"Oh. Yes," Headmaster Green said, getting out of his chair and crossing his office. "They're over here."

Mr. Green went over to one of the office cubbies, grabbed a stack of papers, and handed them to Beckett.

"Thanks," Beckett said.

"How's everything, Damion?" Mr. Green asked, tilting his head and looking at me like he was surprised to remember I existed.

I used to tutor for him and the office all the time my freshman year, but once my sophomore year hit, I found better things to do with my time. But I kind of missed it. There'd been something oddly satisfying about helping somebody else get better at something.

"Good," I said, wondering what he knew.

Green was shockingly aware of every tiny thing going on with the student body, right down to who was dating who, whose parents were cheating, and which student was secretly not getting into the college they'd told everyone they'd gotten into.

No one really knew how he knew what he knew, but the man knew *all*.

"Listen, your timing is impeccable, because I'm in need of help and I cannot think of a better person to provide the assist. Do you have a quick second?"

I wanted to say no so badly because I was beyond ready to bail, but no one said no to Green. "Sure," I said, shrugging at Beckett when he looked at me like *what the fuck*.

Green wasted no time as we sat down in the chairs on the other side of his desk.

"So I know you don't really tutor anymore, Damion—"

"Sorry, Mr. Green," I interrupted, cutting him off because I *couldn't*. "But I'm going to have to stop you right there. My course load this year is crazy heavy, and I cannot—"

"*I* can," Beckett interrupted, looking annoyed that he hadn't been asked.

Beckett actually *was* an active tutor, so it made sense that he was confused by the request.

"You're fairly booked, Mr. Schwab," Green said, his eyes narrowing as he looked at Beck's shirt. "And I need someone brilliant who can help me out immediately. We're on a tight deadline, you could say."

What the hell does that mean?

"An emergency case of tutorial necessity?" I leaned back a little in the guest chair. "Someone's going to die if they don't get smarter in a hurry? What's going on?"

"If you're too busy, that's fine," Green said. "Sometimes there are just situations that require a little—"

"Who's it for?" Beckett asked. "Whose grades are in this much trouble?"

"No one's grades are in trouble," Mr. Green said quietly, glancing toward the door. "There actually are no grades set at all yet—"

"Oh, wait, wait—is this the new kids? One of the twins?" Beckett looked at me and said, "Is it Julia Nebraska?"

Beckett found that to be a hilarious nickname for the new girl "with all the hair."

"I really need your discretion on this, guys," the headmaster said. "This particular student, as a new arrival, wishes to avoid any negative first impressions that could potentially accompany a need for educational assistance."

He came around his desk, walked past us, then went so far as to close his office door.

This was serious.

"I cannot get into the details, but Miss Lowell needs a math tutor," he said.

"So it *is* Julia Nebraska," Beckett said, giving me a smirk.

"Your tie needs attention, Mr. Schwab," Green said. "Perhaps focus on that instead of buzzing over salacious gossip."

"Come on, Seth," Beckett said, looking down at his tie and straightening it. "I buzz because knowing the gossip is fun, but you know I'm a vault."

It was true. Beckett enjoyed hoarding secrets and intel, but he didn't really run around spreading information.

No, that was what everyone *else* in Gardenwood did.

But as I watched Beckett retie his tie, my brain slammed the door on this Nebraska situation. Not only was I too busy to take on a student at the moment, but I was a thousand percent unwilling to help that particular girl out.

I *wanted* her to fail.

And my nose was still sore, for the love of God.

"Regardless of who I tap for this assignment, confidentiality is key. Our new classmate needs to focus on her studies, and she cannot do that fully if she's anxious about appearances. I'd like to set up a tutor who's willing to go to her house or meet her off-site, to be honest, just to ease her mind."

It's not her house, it's Remi's house.

"I'm telling you," Beckett said, "I can squeeze her in."

There must've been a question in my look because Beck shrugged like he was helpless and said, "You have to admit she's interesting, Damion, come on."

Interesting. Everyone was chirping about the new girl, but "interesting" was probably the most complimentary thing I'd heard about her.

New money (the biggest insult one could receive) and *Louis Vuitton* (I had no idea what that one was referring to, but it wasn't good) were the nicknames she'd already secured, and the day was barely over.

"This is not what I'm looking for here," Green said, rolling his eyes but looking amused because, well, who wasn't amused by Beckett? My best friend was fucking endearing in his utter Beckettness, God help us all.

He was *that* guy, the guy who was honest all the time, for better or worse.

"The Lowell residence is over on Riverside, Damion," Mr. Green said, raising his glasses to the top of his head and rubbing his eyes. "So if you *did* have any availability, it's conveniently located between the academy and your house. You could arrange the sessions to occur on your way home, so it really wouldn't be schedule-intensive."

As if I didn't know where the "Lowell residence" was located.

God, hearing it called that really pissed me off.

"Maybe," I finally replied to Mr. Green after I was able to unclench my fucking jaw. "If I have the time."

Mr. Green sighed, obviously disappointed in me.

Not the answer he wanted.

Yeah, well, I didn't want the house I love to be occupied by thieves, so call us even, Seth.

"Very good" was all I heard him say as I blew out of his office, ready to move on to the part of the day where I *wasn't* pissed off about every-fucking-thing.

I closed the door as Beckett took off for the basketball courts.

"Damion!"

Jesus! I almost had a heart attack as the loud voice and assault of curls appeared out of nowhere in front of me. She was clutching her textbooks nervously to her chest, but those eyes were trained on me like she was ready to rumble.

Julia Nebraska.

Fan-fucking-tastic.

"Jumping out at people in abandoned hallways," I said, wishing for the power to make someone disappear with a finger point. "Is that what they do for fun on the farm?"

"First of all, I have no idea because I've never lived on a farm," she said, looking grossly offended. "Second of all, did you agree to do it?"

I looked down at her upturned face and damn, I liked the expression she was wearing.

It reeked of desperation.

Of panic.

For some reason, that fast-blinking anxious gaze gave me a wicked sort of satisfaction.

You should *be nervous, Nebraska.*

I played dumb just to make her beg for it.

"Agree to do what, exactly?" I asked, injecting obnoxious innuendo into my tone to mess with her. I leaned in a little closer and said, "Because I'm game for almost anything, Nebraska—just tell me the plan."

She blew an unruly curl out of her face as a wrinkle formed between her brows. "Agree to be my tutor. Look, I'm not thrilled about it either. And I know we didn't start out on the right foot."

"Understatement from the nose crusher," I scoffed, straightening.

"But Mr. Green said *you* are the best tutor there is."

"Is that a question?" I asked, working for a look that said *insulted*. I narrowed my eyes and said, "Because you sound surprised."

"No! I mean, I'm not. Surprised, that is." She sighed, and I suspected she wanted to stamp her foot in frustration.

I, on the other hand, wanted to laugh at how hard she was trying to keep it together.

She lifted her chin and said, "I'm hoping you'll accept my apology for the whole wallet misunderstanding and consider helping me."

I leaned against the wall and crossed my arms over my chest.

Said nothing, just waited.

Beg, I thought. *You're gonna have to beg me, honey.*

"Please," she said, blinking fast and gnawing on the corner of her bottom lip.

So, so desperate.

I fucking loved it.

"I mean, if I were to do this," I said slowly, drawing it out because it felt so damn good to torment her, like I was somehow doling out micro-justice for Remi, "that would mean you'd owe me a favor."

Her eyebrows bunched together even harder. "What kind of favor?"

I could tell she was uncomfortable with my word choice.

Good.

"I'm not going to tell you now, come *on,*" I said, letting my eyes slowly travel over her face. "Where's the fun in that?"

She took in a deep breath through her nose, her wide-eyed gaze locked on mine. I could see a thousand thoughts screaming through her Midwestern mind, and for a split second I thought she was going to back down.

But then she raised that stubborn chin and said, "Fine."

"Fine, what?"

"Fine, I'll owe you a favor for helping me," she said, looking over her shoulder as if checking for spies before she nodded. "So you'll do it, then? You'll tutor me?"

"Um," I said, straightening and looking down at my watch. "I don't know, I'm not sure." Honestly, I was surprised she'd agreed to it.

And part of me got a thrill from the challenge in front of me.

Still, I couldn't help but make her sweat for it a bit. I leaned down toward her, closer than before, those curls tickling my bruised nose as I whispered, "We'll see."

I could hear the catch of her breath as her eyes turned so close to mine.

"We'll see?" she repeated in disbelief, her forehead creased with confusion wrinkles.

"Yup." I backed up, getting a clear view of the nerves lining her face.

That and the freckles on her nose.

So many freckles.

"We'll see," I shouted, walking away. But I could feel her eyes on my back. Feel her frustration bubbling.

And it felt oh so good as I sensed her watching my exit.

Take that, Nebraska.

CHAPTER SIX

"There is nothing quite as terrifying as the sound of the doorbell. *Ding-dong*, asshole, someone's on the porch and wants inside."

—Remington

Julia

I didn't actually know what to do when I heard the doorbell.

Who could it possibly be?

I glanced down at my Dozer Day crewneck and ratty sweatpants, briefly considered running upstairs to change, but since we didn't know anyone yet, what were the odds the person on the other side of that door was here to see me?

It was probably someone selling security systems or vacuums door-to-door.

Honestly, though, was it even safe to answer the bell when you lived in Manhattan, a place where random strangers were always walking past your house?

I got off the kitchen stool, where I'd been trying to get a handle on the massive amount of homework I already had, and I dragged myself to the door, not wanting to speak to any other living human who was remotely related to or familiar with Gardenwood.

Perhaps ever again.

Because it'd been a brutal first day.

Donovan and Jasmine had been nice, but they were the only ones (not counting adults).

To be fair, technically no one had been *mean* to me, at least not to my face, other than the girl who'd mentioned cows during my transition and of course . . . *him*.

No, it was more about the icy stares, the quiet comments I couldn't hear but knew were directed my way, the loud laugh around the words "new money" when I'd had to cross paths with the Toms. In other words, it'd been a socially anxious girl's worst nightmare.

At lunch, Jasmine sat with me for five whole minutes before she was called away to the office, leaving me to sit all alone at a table with the eyes of the entire student body upon me. It would've been bad enough in a regular cafeteria, but the *dining hall* at the academy was ten times worse. The shiny floors, stone walls, and high ceilings made it super echoey, so simple lunchtime conversation made the place feel like a thousand people were all shouting at each other.

And I just knew, without a doubt, that I was the main topic of said lunchtime conversation.

It had been a nightmare.

Add to that my hallway run-ins with Damion the Evil, and the day could be safely filed away as one of the worst ever.

I saw my brother briefly after school, but he was with two other guys, laughing too hard with his apparent new friends to say anything other than "Hey, Jules" as he walked by.

Typical.

I sighed before I opened the front door, but when I pulled it back, my sigh turned into a gasp.

Because Damion the Evil was on my front porch.

This day is CURSED.

"Hey . . . ?" I leaned forward a little, looking to see if anyone was with him, because it didn't make sense that he was standing on our stoop between the mums and pumpkins that Mom and Bernard had strategically placed on our front porch.

I blinked hard. This had to be some autumn-fueled nightmare.

"What are you doing here?" I heard myself ask.

"Oh, now that's a polite way to answer the door," he said, his mouth turning up in the mocking grin that set my teeth on edge.

His eyes dipped down to my sweatshirt and threadbare pants, and I regretted my decision not to change.

"Sorry," I said, not at all sorry, "But I just didn't expect to see *you* at my door."

"Why do you stress the word 'you' like I'm the last person you would ever want to see on your porch?"

"Because we aren't friends and I don't even know you," I said, irritated by the cockiness in his smile.

What the hell is he doing here, what the hell is he doing here?

And how does he know where I live?

"I thought you wanted me." His smile grew even bigger. "To be your tutor."

Oh. My. God.

I didn't know what I'd expected him to say, but it wasn't *that*.

I still couldn't get over the fact that Damion was the brainiac Headmaster Green had raved about when I stopped by his office at the end of the day. He'd said he had a "brilliant" student with a "genius IQ" and a "real talent for teaching."

His favorite tutor he was *confident* could turn around my scores.

And then he uttered the name.

DAMION.

I'd had a slight mental crashout when he said that, because though the universe could be cruel, it couldn't be cruel enough to make the biggest jerk in Manhattan my best tutorial option, could it?

Why him?!

After realizing he hadn't agreed to tutor me, desperation had forced me to swallow my pride and beg, yet this oversized tool on my stoop had looked at me like I'd bored him before he dismissed me with his little "we'll see."

We'll see.

Yeah, no.

I shook my head and crossed my arms. "Um, I think I've changed my mind."

"You think you've *changed your mind*?" he said, his grin creeping even higher. The late afternoon sun was giving him a killer glow as he smiled down at me from his high height. "How come?"

"Because you, like . . . ," I said, trying to come up with something. I didn't want to bring up the wallet thing or the hallway thing or the homeroom thing because discussing his awfulness would make it seem like I cared, so I said, "I don't know, it's just not a fit—"

"Whatever," he interrupted, still smiling like my rambling was hilarious, amused by my discomfort.

I wanted to slam the door in his face so badly.

But then I heard the headmaster's voice like it was on a loudspeaker in my brain.

The scores alone will determine your ability to stay here or not.

The last thing on earth I wanted was to be in Damion's debt, to owe him a favor—*whatever that even fricking looked like*—but if I didn't nail those tests, my family might not inherit Remi's money, which would send us back to Nebraska, where we would lose the store and probably the house.

And I couldn't let that happen.

So if the demon in front of me was the best person for the job, I needed to suck it up and make a deal with this devil, right?

Damion shrugged and said, "I was just being a nice guy, stopping by, but if you think you've changed your mind, I'm out—"

"Wait," I said, reaching out and grabbing his blazer, needing to stop him.

"Yes?" he replied, his eyebrows going up as he looked down at my gripping hand.

I quickly let go.

The cool autumn wind sent his scent—*something expensive*—right in my direction as he said, "What exactly am I waiting for here?"

I cleared my throat and said, "I actually *do* want you—"

"I knew it," he said with smirk.

"—to be my tutor—"

"Ah—"

"—please." It was hard to say with my teeth gritted, but necessary.

I needed Damion's help, and I was going to do whatever it took to get it.

Even if it kills me.

I took a deep breath and tried to negotiate. "As long as I have your word that you'll keep this confidential, I will grant you a favor in return for your services."

"My . . . *services*," he said in a low voice, those hazel eyes—very green at the moment, strolling all over me like he was considering multiple scenarios in his wicked imagination. I knew he was messing with me, but there was something about his expression that made my stomach get a little . . . flittery.

God, what is with this guy??

"I like the sound of that, Jules," he said, "Although, your negotiation tactics are a tad bit moot because I already know your secret, so I could blab it to the world if I wanted to, regardless."

"My *secret*?" *Oh God, oh God—does he know about the inheritance?* "What 'secret' do you think you know?"

That erased all teasing from his face, which went seriously intense. His eyes narrowed slightly as he gave me hardcore eye contact. His eyebrows screwed together, and he watched me for one second, two seconds, time and space hovering before he quietly stated, "That you need a tutor."

"Oh," I said, a little unsure what was happening between us. I felt *accused* of something, though I wasn't sure what. "That."

"Oh, *that*." His voice lowered even more. "Tell me, Nebraska—is there another secret that you're keeping?"

I rolled my eyes and pushed back the hairs that'd fallen out of my bun, disliking how off-balance this guy with the sharp jaw and muscular neck made me feel. "Dozens of them, in fact."

And as he stood there on the stoop, watching me like he was waiting for some kind of confession, I wanted to curl up in a ball on the floor and whine at that realization that I needed him.

I had no margin for testing error. He *did* already know my secret, which left him as my best and only option.

God help me.

CHAPTER SEVEN

"Home is where the leftover Patsy's pizza is."

—Remington

Damion

"Does that make sense?" I asked, watching her as she looked down at the equation.

There was something about the way her long lashes fluttered when her eyes dipped down to the paper that I found distracting, but the motion had nothing on the utter mindfuck that was her teeth nibbling on her lower lip and the way her hair was messily twisted into a knot on top of her head.

Those random traits were bugging the shit out of me. They were inexplicably annoying, and when you paired them with her ridiculous shirt—which had a picture of a Caterpillar bulldozer on it with the words "Dozer Day" on the front—the girl was too ridiculous for words.

"It actually does," she said with a crease between her brows, like she couldn't believe that it *did* make sense.

That I had been the one to make it make sense.

Yeah, I'm as shocked as you are, Nebraska.

Not shocked that I was getting through to her—I was a good tutor—but shocked that I was helping her at all. I'd swung by just to mess with her, to torture her a little more, yet suddenly I was her teacher.

But I hadn't been able to stop myself.

Because of the house.

Being that close, seeing the walls behind her as she stood in the foyer; it hadn't been enough.

I'd needed to get inside.

And *shit*, I'd been in serious jeopardy of crying like a little baby boy when I followed her in, because they hadn't changed anything yet. The furniture, the artwork, the over-the-top dining room wallpaper—aside from random boxes sitting around, the house looked the same as it had the last time I'd been there.

And it *smelled* the same, which was making it hard to focus on anything other than how much I missed Remi. When she'd led me into the kitchen, I was grateful for the math all laid out on the island because it provided a distraction from how emo being in the house was making me.

"That's because I'm the best tutor," I said.

"Okay, you actually *do* seem really good at the tutoring," she agreed, still sounding shocked.

"I *am* good, but maybe they're just shit at teaching math in Nebraska, did you ever think of that?"

"No," she said, her left hand grabbing her right arm and giving it a stretch. "I'm sure this is impossible for someone like you to believe, but Nebraska is actually not that different from New York in some ways."

"The hell you say," I said, watching as she switched to stretch the other arm.

"Seriously," she argued. "We've got good schools, running water, EV charging stations, and great cell service."

She sounded like a billboard for *shop local*.

"Wow," I said, looking down at my watch. "Progressive farmers—how fascinating."

"Not everyone's a farmer, for the record, but just forget it," she said as she reached up and tugged the hair tie out of her hair with one hand, holding the mass of curls in place with the other. She quickly wound her hair into another massive knot while looking at me with judgment in her eyes. "You wouldn't understand."

"No, enlighten me. You said you didn't live on a farm, but I find that hard to believe, because what else is there to do out there? I mean, whatever it is, your parents obviously do it well enough," I said, gesturing to the interior of the house. "Is your dad the dude who owns every gas station in the state or something?"

I was curious to see what she had to say about her family's new money.

"Technically, my parents ran the grocery store in our town, not the gas station, but probably like *your* dad, he's got, uh, a *lot* of different business things going on. He doesn't talk to me about his investment portfolio, y'know?"

His investment portfolio.

You mean the money he took from my uncle, honey?

I could tell she was uncomfortable with my question, which made sense. People who weren't wealthy, *truly* wealthy, were awkward as shit about discussing finances, like they weren't sure how to bridge the gap between humility and simple facts.

The truly affluent, which included every household in Gardenwood, didn't give a rat's ass. It might be gauche to ask about money, but if someone dared to ask the question, Old Money would always lift their chin and drop the numbers, because it was good to be king.

"And we *didn't* live on a farm," she said defensively, offended by the stereotype. "No combines, no tractors, just a normal house with indoor plumbing and Wi-Fi."

"Any animals?" I asked, imagining her feeding cows and horses while remembering the photo of her with all those dogs.

Were they *her* puppies?

"No," she said, making a face like I was ridiculous. "I mean, we had chickens, dogs, and cats, but those aren't *farm* animals."

"Chickens don't count as farm animals?"

"I mean, people in the city have chickens," she said with a shrug. "I read that you can have chickens in Manhattan, so . . ."

"No shit?" I knew that, but I also didn't know anyone with chickens. "You can have chickens here?"

I had no idea why I was pretending I was unaware.

"Only hens, but yes."

"Are you sure?" I said, looking at her like she was nuts.

Why does this girl make me want to mess with her twenty-four seven?

"Yes," she snapped.

"So tell me about the grocery store."

"I don't want to," she said with a shrug. "No, thanks."

"Why not?" I said with a laugh, surprised by her answer.

"Because I just don't feel like you genuinely want to know," she said, her suspicious gaze taking a trip over my face.

"I do, though," I said. "I genuinely want to know what it's like to run a little bitty grocery store in the middle of nowhere. How big is your Nebraskahoma hometown? Are there any businesses there at all, aside from your general store?"

"First of all, about fifteen hundred people, and second of all, it's not a 'general store' because the year isn't 1892," she said with an eye roll. "And yes—downtown Springfield has some great shops. There's a bridal boutique, a Thai restaurant, Black Sheep Coffee House, a very cool retro store called ReMain, and, if you must know, the Blind Pig has the very best bar food."

"I'm sorry, the town bar is called the Blind Pig?"

"Mock it if you like, but I'd kill for one of the Pig's steak Phillies right now. I doubt anywhere in New York has bar food quite as good."

"You sound ridiculous," I said. "The East Coast is where cheesesteak sandwiches were invented."

"Doesn't change my stance one bit," she quipped, tilting her head in challenge. "Do you want a pop, by the way? We've got Diet Pepsi and Dr Pepper."

She got up and went over to the refrigerator, the refrigerator that used to be stocked with all my favorite things. It felt like my breath was stuck in my lungs as she pulled open the door, as my brain desperately wanted to see a row of tiny chocolate milks and a door shelf full of Mountain Dew Baja Blast. Shelves of mismatched takeout containers, because Remi liked eating "other people's creations."

Disappointment shot through me as I saw a half-empty fridge full of things foreign to that appliance: gallons of milk and cartons of eggs and a random pizza box that *wasn't* from Patsy's.

Four baguettes.

Who in God's name would put a baguette in the refrigerator?

"No, thanks," I said, clearing my throat as she grabbed a can of soda and came back to the island. "So tell me about the *non-general, not-1892* store. What's that like?"

It was bizarre, the way I felt about her little slice of Nebraska.

On the one hand, I couldn't care less about some Midwestern nothing town. A landlocked farm town with a population of fifteen hundred?

Falling asleep just thinking about it.

But on the other hand, something about the place had drawn in Remi. My nomadic, world-traveling uncle had chosen to settle down there—when he could've gone anywhere—so my curiosity about Springfield was hella piqued in that regard.

"I mean, the market's pretty small," she said, settling back onto her stool. "Seven aisles, not counting produce and frozen."

"Did you work there? Are you like Laura Ingalls?"

"The Ingalls family didn't have a store," she corrected in a tone that seriously questioned my intelligence. "The Olesons were the ones with the mercantile."

"That's right," I said. "Nellie and Willie and the folks—I remember now."

"I can't believe a city kid like you watched that show," she said, surprise on her face. "*Little House on the Prairie* seems far too . . . out-of-date for someone who's been wearing a different pair of designer glasses every time I've seen him."

"Obsessed with my eyewear, are we?" I said, surprised she'd noticed such a tiny detail when she'd been so busy with things like bashing my nose and dropping her books.

"Hardly. It's more of a 'what a high-maintenance dude' observation," she said with an eyebrow raise.

"And I didn't watch the show; I read the books," I clarified, ignoring her comment.

"Probably when you were a baby, because you're the smartest tutor in all of Gardenwood Academy, right?"

"You're quite the smart-ass, aren't you?" I said, a little amused by the punchy wit that reared its head when you pushed her. Someone with a bit more edge hovered underneath all those curls.

I kind of liked poking until that chick showed up.

She just shrugged and gave me a look that was half challenging and half nervous, like she was worried she was going to piss me off and lose her tutor.

"So are you ever going to tell me about the market? Maybe this is your way of distracting me because your tiny grocery store was actually a mob front and you don't want me to know."

"The Springfield Mafia would never let the Lowell family in—are you kidding me with that? It's as if you've never been anywhere outside the city."

"I've been everywhere," I clarified. "Just not the Midwest."

"Paris?" she asked.

"Yep," I said.

"Italy?"

"Multiple times."

"Poland?"

"Krakow's a stunner in the fall."

"Brazil?"

"Rio *and* São Paulo. Almost surfed at Copacabana once."

"Almost?"

"It's a long story, but—oh my God, there's a cat in the kitchen," I said, interrupting myself because, holy *shit*, there was a cat in the kitchen.

A fluffy white Scottish Fold walked through the doorway and meowed. I couldn't believe my eyes. "You have a cat. In your kitchen."

Dear God, that is the cutest fucking cat I've ever seen.

"Oh. Yeah," Julia said, looking at me like I'd just insulted her. "We allow her to move freely about the building. We're wild that way."

Ah. She thought I was judging her for allowing her cat to be in the kitchen. But the truth was that I'd just never seen a cat *in* this kitchen. I'd seen a multitude of cats downstairs, because Rem had fucking *loved* cats, but he'd been weird about cats and food.

"What's her name?" I asked.

She still looked annoyed, but she said, "Clank."

"Seriously?"

"Seriously. And for the record, her manners are perfect, so she's better in the kitchen than my dad. Probably better than you, even."

"Her manners," I repeated, staring at the cat.

"She doesn't jump on counters, has never had an accident, and that girl doesn't know the meaning of a hairball." Julia's gaze was challenging when she looked at me and said, "Perfect."

As if she understood, Clank—what a fucking name—gave me a tiny meow before gracefully exiting the kitchen.

I was disappointed by the quick exit.

Come back, honey.

"Speaking of perfect—"

I was interrupted by the doorbell, which made her smile disappear and her eyebrows scrunch together.

"What is *with* this day?" she said under her breath as she set down her soda.

"Lots of visitors?" I asked.

"So far you're the only one," she said, "But since we don't know anybody yet and everyone at school hated me on sight, a second doorbell ringer seems excessive."

"Don't you have a brother, by the way?"

"He left in search of a basketball court," she said, standing and pushing at the hair that'd fallen out of her bun. "He said he was in dire need of a pickup game, and I am definitely not about that, so he's on his own. I'll be right back."

She walked out of the kitchen, and I felt like I could finally let out my breath when she disappeared. It'd been killing me, being in Remi's house and pretending I didn't belong there, that it wasn't somewhere that'd felt more like home than my actual home.

Because this was my safe place, the place where I could be myself.

Because Remi *let* me be myself in this place.

I could still hear the words he said to me that changed everything, the words he'd said in this very room.

He'd looked me in the eyes and said, *Figure out who YOU want to be, Gardenwood be damned. No one's opinion of you—except for yours—matters.*

Heavy words to say to a thirteen-year-old.

But it'd been right after a rugby match, when I got hurt from a cheap shot by a guy twice my size. I'd hated rugby, but my dad had forced me into it. *He'd* played and his father had played. It was "a Rutledge tradition."

Reputation and appearance were everything to him.

Which was probably why instead of asking me if I was okay afterward, my dad looked at me with disappointment and said, "Christ, Dame, you need to nut up and get dirty. You do whatever it takes to get the best of your opponent—to get the win. The win is all that matters."

I remember sitting on top of this very island, Remi bandaging me up, his words echoing.

You don't have to please your dad—you know that, right? You have to respect him and you have to follow his rules, but you don't have to please anyone but yourself.

And that was that.

No more following the herd for me.

Which . . . made me a rebel in my dad's eyes.

Something I leaned into, proudly.

So yeah, this place was important to me. Remi's presence felt heavy in these walls. I'd walked past the house every day since I'd learned it wasn't Remi's anymore, needing to know what was going on with it.

Are they moved in? What are they doing in there?

Does it look different?

It'd driven me crazy.

I started pacing while I waited for her to come back, and when I paced by the desk in the library, I couldn't believe my eyes. I leaned closer, my heartbeat picking up speed as I looked at the legal pad sitting out for all the world to see.

Holy shit.

I didn't know what it meant, but the masculine scrawl on the top page obviously had to do with Remi.

Holy, holy *shit*.

REMINGTON
BERNARD ELIZANDO
REMINGTON??
3-15
SCHOOL HOUSE

What the hell did it all mean, though? I pulled out my phone and took a quick picture, every cell in my body buzzing as I realized I'd actually found something. Underneath the legal pad were some random documents—moving company contracts—but I could hear Julia talking in the foyer, so my pulse pounded as I kept my ears open for any other sounds.

God, what am I doing? It seemed insane, creeping around like a spy, but at the same time, maybe that legal pad could provide the information necessary to get the house back.

After another minute of espionage, I put my phone away.

But I felt like laughing or jumping up and down because holy *balls*.

This was too easy.

I suddenly realized that tutoring her was going to be a golden opportunity. Not only did I get to visit *my* fucking house, but I already had something. My dad might employ a team of investigators on his payroll, but I'd found something already, praise *Jesus*.

I had to figure out what it meant, but at least it was *something*.

"We live close," I heard. "So it just makes sense."

I recognized Donovan's voice, so I walked out of the kitchen and into the foyer.

"Oh hey, Donovan."

"Damion?" she said, her eyes narrowing. "What are *you* doing here?"

Her eyes went back and forth between Julia and me, and you could almost *see* her brain churning out the story. *Damion was at the new girl's house—I'm serious!*

"He just showed up at my door," Julia said quickly, glancing at me in a way that let me know she wanted me to keep my mouth shut about the tutoring.

"I thought we could hang out," I said with a shrug.

Julia's eyebrows crinkled together, and I could tell she didn't like that answer.

Which I fucking loved.

"You guys are hanging out?" Donovan asked, her eyes huge. "Already?"

"You know me," I said. "I have a hard time stopping myself from diving in headfirst."

Julia's eyes narrowed, and I kind of wanted to laugh because of how uncomfortable—and irritated—I was obviously making her.

"Classic Damion," Donovan said with a grin, and I knew that was only going to confuse Julia even more.

I had a reputation at school for . . . hell, I wasn't even sure what. For daring to do and say the things that I wanted to do and say, as opposed to following the rest of the privileged sheep as they did whatever our insulated bubble of the UWS dictated they should do . . . ?

Yeah, that was kind of it.

"I just wanted to get to know our new neighbor a little bit better," I said, stepping closer to Julia.

"Is that right?" Donovan's eyes clocked the motion, and she asked, "So you just ran over here right after school, huh?"

"Sure did," I said with an intentional smirk.

"I didn't invite him," Julia clarified defensively, looking even more nervous as she took a tiny step away from me.

"It's true—she had no idea I was coming," I said, letting my face slide into the smile that I couldn't have kept away if I wanted to. "I took it upon myself to be a one-man welcome wagon."

"I just bet you did," Donovan said with a laugh, putting her hands in her jacket pockets. "Well, I'll let you guys get back to hanging out. I just wanted to drop by and invite you to help tomorrow morning if you want to."

"Yeah, um, thank you," Julia said, looking anxious and confused as she smiled at Donovan. "I'll text you."

"Cool," Donovan said, and then she headed for the exit.

And the literal *second* Donovan left, Julia whipped around and gaped at me, her eyes huge as she leaned her back against the door. "What the hell was *that*?"

"I thought you didn't want anyone to know I'm tutoring you," I said slowly, like she was the ridiculous one for not catching on. "So I said we were hanging out."

Her brown eyes watched me, like she was waiting for more.

"I was just trying to keep your secret," I added. "But I think I have Donovan's number if you want me to text her and tell her the truth. My priority was hiding the tutor thing, but if I overstepped—"

"No," she interrupted, looking more frazzled than she had when I'd showed up at her door. "The last thing I want is for everyone to think the new girl's stupid, so I'm glad you said it. I just—"

"You're not stupid," I heard myself interject, not really sure why I cared but . . . I mean, I *didn't* care, but also she wasn't stupid and it seemed wrong that she'd even suggest that.

"I know I'm not," she said quietly. "But I don't want anyone at school to think that before they even know me."

Oh honey, they're never going to know you. They're going to chew you up and spit you out without ever going deeper than your tragic fashion mistakes.

"By the way," I said, needing to kick her out of this moment of vulnerability, because it'd actually made me empathetic for a split second. Empathic to *her*, holy shit, what was wrong with me? I'd just found information that could help to eventually evict her squatting family, so I definitely didn't need to be concerned with her insecurities. "Donovan is pretty gossipy, so I'd get ready to field some questions about us tomorrow."

She sighed as if I'd just said the worst thing possible. "Why why why whyyyyyy did this have to happen?"

"This isn't a big deal, Nebraska. Just act like I'm a guy you met who came over and wanted your number. I'm sure it happens all the time."

She made a snort noise, like it *didn't* happen all the time. "You'd go along with that?" she asked, her eyes all over my face.

I shrugged. "I don't give a shit what people think."

"Hmm," she said, still watching me carefully as her teeth toyed with her bottom lip. "Maybe we'll just wait and see what happens. Maybe she won't mention it to anyone."

"Sure she won't," I said, smiling triumphantly as I turned to go back to the kitchen. "Because no one gossips about anything at Gardenwood."

I left not long after that, but when she closed the door behind me, something about her hand shutting me out of Remi's house, leaving me standing on the stoop like I didn't have any right to be inside, sparked my irritation.

Irritation that only grew at dinner, because all my mom wanted to talk about was the Lowells and the season.

My two *least* favorite subjects.

"You'll never guess who came to the planning meeting today," my mom said as she speared a beet in her salad with a fork.

"Who?" my dad asked, moving his fish knife through the salmon like a skilled surgeon.

"Shawna Lowell," she said, shaking her head like it was unbelievable. "Not only are the Lowells here and all moved in at Remi's, but she wants to be *involved* in the PTA. She actually volunteered to help with the planning of the season."

"You're kidding," my dad replied, setting his utensils on his plate with a clink before reaching for his brandy. "You met her?"

"Oh yeah," my mom said, lifting her fork to her mouth. "Shawna is just as permed and eyelinered as you would've expected from a woman with that name, and she seems utterly *enchanted* by the idea of the season."

You could tell by the mockery in her tone that my mother was quoting Shawna Lowell.

"God help us," I said under my breath.

"And get this," she said to my father, sounding outraged. "Claire had barely touched on potential themes for this year when Shawna jumped right in and said, 'What about New York literature?' I was ready for everyone to shoot her down because we were all leaning toward a color-themed masquerade with a midnight reveal—I mean, what a brilliant idea—but then she starts going off about books and how a specific book would be a great theme. Apparently she taught English back in Nebraska, so she started listing off all these famous novels and authors from the city."

I reached for a roll and thought it actually sounded like an interesting idea. I mean, I still wouldn't attend the overblown ball, but at least it wasn't something inane like a color-coded masquerade.

"Nobody looked interested until she said *The Great Gatsby*, and then—"

"Dear God, Mimi lost her mind, didn't she?" my dad supplied.

"Oh, you have no idea," my mom said with a dramatic sigh. "The woman was very nearly cackling with glee."

"I can imagine."

Mimi Carter was *allegedly* a descendant—through marriage—of F. Scott Fitzgerald himself, which for some reason drove her friends crazy.

"Then someone suggested *Breakfast at Tiffany's*, which made *everyone* lose their collective minds because of all the jewelry ramifications and the fashion possibilities, so now it's a done deal. The season's general theme is New York literature, the ball will be book-specific, and there's nothing I can do about it."

My mom sounded so disappointed, it was almost funny.

"What's the third book option for the ball?" I asked, and took a bite of the heavy hearth bun in my hand.

God, I love bread.

"What?" my dad said, not looking up from the phone, which had just beeped with a notification.

"Aren't there usually three choices the committee votes on?" I asked.

My mother talked about the season way too much if *I* knew how it worked.

"No one could agree on the third title, so we're reconvening tomorrow to brainstorm," she said, reaching for her wineglass. "But I'm really mourning the masquerade idea because it was so deliciously otherworldly. Mysterious, like something from *Bridgerton*. I'm terrified we're going to get stuck with something depressing like *A Tree Grows in Brooklyn*."

Yeah, not exactly a banging ball idea, I thought. *Have to agree with Mom on this one.*

"What about Edith Wharton?" I said, thinking through New York authors.

My mom said, "Honey, I can't remember who wrote wha—"

"*The House of Mirth*? *The Age of Innocence*?" As soon as I said the titles, though, I knew they wouldn't work. Both novels were basically just scathing critiques of New York's upper class, so it definitely wasn't a fit because Gardenwood did *not* engage in self-deprecation or irony.

We were far too elite to have a sense of humor about ourselves.

Also, why am I offering ideas for the thing I LOATHE?

"Wait—Edith Wharton wrote *The Age of Innocence*?" My mother set down her glass, her eyes going all big in her face. "Oh my God, I think that movie won the Oscar for best costume design!"

"The movie—"

She grinned and clasped her hands together. "I *loved* that movie. The bustles, the corsets, the fabrics—what an idea!"

"I thought it was supposed to be about the *literature*," I said. "You know, the book itself?"

"Oh, come on, Damion, artistic license," she squealed, beaming. "This is amazing; I can just see it now. *The Age of Innocence* ball. The hats, the parasols, the gloves . . . oh my God, I cannot wait to show up tomorrow and blow everyone's mind with this idea!"

"You know it's kind of a depressing book, right?" I said, wondering if *anyone* on that planning committee, aside from my mom, would see this as a good idea.

"You can't stop her now, Dame," my dad said, his eyes still on his phone. "Just let her go."

"But—"

"Eat another roll, dear," my mom said, grinning from ear to ear. "You've earned it."

CHAPTER EIGHT

"Eating on a park bench is far superior to dining anywhere else in the city. Give me birds at my feet, a sandwich in my hand, and the sun on my face. The only five-star spot I need."

—Remington

Julia

The new school sucked, but I didn't hate *everything* about our new life.

For starters, we had money.

A ridiculous gift, that, and something we were still getting used to.

My parents remained on-brand Shawna and Clint, making Liam and me ask before we could buy anything and then lecturing us about the importance of fiscal responsibility, but it didn't suck having a debit card that was connected to an account with guaranteed flow.

And our neighborhood was a dream.

Like, I was *obsessed* with it.

There was just something about the Upper West Side that I adored, the way you could get lost in the crowd and somehow be seen and not seen, all at the same time. I felt strong and independent as I walked the streets like a character in a Nora Ephron movie, popping in here and there with my tote bag over my shoulder as if my own personal theme music were playing in the background.

Side note: My theme music would obviously be "Julia" by Mt. Joy.

Duh.

And my love of our new city was accentuated by the season, because

New York in the fall was as lovely as every song and movie had ever purported it to be.

The air was cool, the trees tipped with gold and ruby hues, and the crunching noise of the leaves under my shoes sounded like heaven as I sampled bodega foods, loitered at coffee shops, and wasted far too much time in the bookstores.

I loved everything about it.

Especially my two parks.

Central Park was as magical as I'd always known it would be, with the bonus of it being a quick golden-leaf-strewn walk from our house. Huge and beautiful, with the reservoir and the castle and the tiered Bethesda Fountain that I wished upon every time I visited.

Please, no school drama.

But Riverside Park was my favorite. It felt smaller and like a secret (compared to Central Park), like it was *my* neighborhood park.

I liked walking Clank (yes, I walked my cat) in the mornings before school because I felt like I could breathe when I was there. No uniformed classmates were judging me; there was only Mother Nature doing her thing, along with the other early risers.

And this morning was no different.

It was the kind of morning that still had summer warmth in the rise of the sun, even though the temperature had cooled. The leaves were early-peak in the park, where every single color was mixed into the fray. Some trees were still green, some yellow, but others were blooming with brown and red and orange.

Every color was on display and it was stunning.

I was strolling leisurely, letting Clank lead me, and we were almost to the row of benches that faced the Hudson River when I saw a guy my age sitting on one of them.

Actually, he was on the *best* bench, my favorite bench.

The bench I most enjoyed reading upon, the bench where I liked to sit and watch the barges float up and down the river.

But the guy . . . wow, the guy was . . . curious. And familiar.

I kept out of his sight line as I walked slightly behind him, ready to pounce on the bench the moment the dude left. I was about to claim it when he finally hopped up, but instead of leaving, he lifted a pair of binoculars to his eyes and turned his head to the left.

I couldn't tell if he was looking up in a tree, or at one of the people walking around.

Hmm. *Is this guy a bird-watcher or a pervert?*

Almost as if hearing my thoughts, he lowered the binoculars and—

Holy shit! Holy shit! Holy SHIT!

Damion?

It couldn't be, right? For starters, no rich prep-school guy would be out and about this early in the morning. Surely boys like him had Scotch-fueled hangovers to sleep off from the night before that kept them in their luxurious beds until the very last minute.

And guys like him *definitely* didn't write in leather-bound journals. I didn't know Damion at all, but he didn't strike me as someone who'd be into jotting down his innermost thoughts while communing at the park.

No, he seemed like someone who'd be into *kicking* a journaler's journal *around* the park.

My heart leapt as I quickly started heading in the other direction, accidentally jerking Clank a little too hard and causing her to *meow* at me.

"Sorry," I murmured—quietly, because for some reason, I felt like I would be murdered if he knew I'd seen him.

Doing what, exactly?

What in the hell was he up to?

I swear to God it looked like he was bird-watching, but no. Impossible. Bird-watching? Damion the Evil?

It just couldn't be.

Was he some sort of *Harriet the Spy* member of the neighborhood watch? Did New York City even have a neighborhood watch? I wondered as I speed-walked through the park.

And why did I care?

And why was I still thinking about it later, when Liam and I were walking into school?

I was just as confused as I'd been in the park, because no way would someone like Damion the Evil watch *birds*.

No freaking way.

My phone buzzed, and when I pulled it out of my pocket, it was my cousin texting our three-way group chat.

Lauren: I just got a weird call at the store.

Liam: Heavy breathing?

Lauren: Yeah because I'd for sure text YOU if I got that call.

Me: BTW did you order pumpkins for the window display?

I squinted as we walked up to the entrance, dreading another day of school at Gardenwood.

Lauren: Your dad already asked me that and YES

Me: But he never orders enough. Get another case.

"Focus, Jules," Liam said, then texted: The weird call??

Lauren: Yeah, It was a guy with a LOT of questions about the owners of Lowell's Market.

I glanced over at my brother, who ignored me to text: What kinds of questions? Who was it?

So far things had gone smoothly with the inheritance, with no one—aside from my tutor—questioning our arrival or my dad's "business."

Lauren: He didn't say, but he wanted to know where you guys went, are you coming back, did you sell your house . . .

"Oh shit," I said to Liam, my stomach clenching as he looked back at me with a worried expression that probably matched my own. "Do you think this is what Bernard warned us about?"

"Probably," he said, "But relax. Asking isn't getting."

I texted: What'd you tell him?

Lauren: I put him on hold for an hour and he was gone when I came back.

Liam: NICE. Thank you.

Liam was good at not worrying, but I was stressed all morning because someone was actually asking about us.

Who was it?

Bernard had been very vague with his warnings before the move, saying something about how *vast fortunes bring all creatures scuttling to the surface*, but it was killing me, wondering who *specifically* was scuttling to get at Lou's estate.

I wished Bernard were there with me, at school, because I needed his calm demeanor to reassure me that everything was going to be okay.

Maybe Liam and I needed to create a group chat with him.

Although, I'm not sure he'd give me his number.

Bernard was funny that way. Close enough to know all our secrets, but formal enough to discourage oversharing.

I was still thinking about the mysterious call when I stopped by my locker after fourth period, and I nearly jumped out of my skin when someone yelled my name.

"Julia!"

I turned around, and the cool blonde who lived across the street from me was standing there with a few friends behind her. *One, two, three, four . . . four of them.* They were all four watching me, none of them smiling, and I just *knew* I was staring directly at the Skins.

There was no one else they could be.

Unease rippled through me, and I felt like I was under attack.

By an impossibly gorgeous girl band or something.

The tallest of the group, a size-zero redhead with a *lot* of cleavage exposed since her collar-popped button-down was *way* buttoned-down, eyeballed me like I'd just said something insane (even though I hadn't spoken at all). Her tie was tied in a loopy bow instead of like an actual tie, her legs were covered in over-the-knee brown boots, a demure pearl headband held back her long bangs from her shoulder-length hair, and she was wearing a backpack that was bright red patent leather.

If I'd been wearing any of those things, I would look ridiculous. But she was wearing all of them, together, and on her, it was money.

"What exactly is the deal with you and Damion Rutledge?" she asked, her tone and expression telling me she had zero interest in becoming my friend.

"I'm sorry—what?" I said, feeling attacked even though they were just standing there, looking at me.

"There's a rumor that you and Damion are seeing each other, which simply cannot be true," the blonde said, her tone accenting the utter impossibility of the notion. Her eyes were almost aqua, they were so light, and it was jarring how beautiful she was. Almost *disturbing*, really, like she was a robot or an alien.

Are you AI? Because your perfect face doesn't make sense to my imperfect brain.

And as she waited for me to answer, I just knew this was Coco. Something about her energy just screamed that she was the leader of this group.

"Oh. Um, no," I said, hating how my voice sounded. It came out breathy and high-pitched, like I was lying or scared of my own shadow. I cleared my throat and used my best *not a wimp* voice when I clarified, "I barely know him."

Which, coincidentally, made "I Wish I Knew How to Quit You," my favorite Sombr song, pop into my head, since it was from the *I Barely Know Her* album.

I felt like a liar as they stared at me, my heart rate skyrocketing while my cheeks got hot enough for me to know that anyone could see I *was* lying just by the bright red pops on my face. But I wasn't about to cop to the tutoring, not to these specimens of human perfection. I somehow just knew that these four girls were accomplished speakers of multiple languages and probably all had Ivy League possibilities; no *way* could I tell them about my . . . *problem.*

"If you barely know him," the girl beside Coco asked, the girl who had curly black hair that went down all the way down to her waist, a waist that I might be able to wrap my hands around, it was so tiny, dear *God*, "then why was he at your house?"

"Why was he . . . ," I murmured like an idiot, blinking and trying to formulate thoughts when I knew I was screwed. That was, in fact, a really good question. Why *would* he stop by if I barely knew him?

It didn't make logical sense, dammit.

For a split second I wondered if Donovan had said something, but as Coco's pale blue eyes bore into me, I remembered where she lived.

She could've *seen* him at my house.

I stared at the girls with my mouth open, probably looking like a fish as I tried recalling how to speak. My phone was in my hand because I'd been staring down at it before they approached, so when the notification sound rang out, I nearly jumped out of my skin.

All five of us glanced down at the display, and in the midst of my panic I saw a text from a number I didn't know.

I brought you a baguette, Nebraska.

I gasped, because I knew who the message was from, but Damion didn't have my number and this was impossible so what the hell, what the hell?? I stared at the display and didn't know what to think or do or say as four sets of long-lashed eyes settled upon me in judgment.

But then it got worse because I saw him coming.

Damion was walking toward us, coming from behind the Skins, grinning, with a loaf of French bread in his hand. He was so tall, impossible to miss with that wide chest and those long legs, somehow managing to look reckless and wild while wearing a blazer and tie.

"How do you know my number?" I blurted without thinking, holding up my phone.

Which made the entire group turn around and look at him—look at him as he gave me a very dirty grin and said, "I know lots of things."

I know lots of things.

I pushed at my hair, unsure how to even talk to a guy who said things like that.

The girl with the waist-long hair giggled, but I wasn't amused. "Seriously, though," I said, working hard at making sure these girls knew I *hadn't* given it to this guy I didn't know. "How did you get my number?"

"It's Rutledge," said the Skin who was wearing what appeared to be a choker made out of a hundred strands of pearls. Her neck wasn't even visible underneath the cover of so many pearls, yet they somehow accentuated the caramel highlights in her hair and made her green eyes pop. "He can do anything."

"I'm sure he can't do *anything*," I snapped, my gaze still on the towering boy with the dark hair.

"Anything," Damion repeated, giving me an eyebrow raise that dared me to argue as he held up *his* phone.

"I—I don't, um—" I stammered.

"Your bread, Julia," he interrupted with a grin, presenting the baguette like a lifeline for me to cling on to.

"Um, thank you, I guess . . . ?" *What is with the bread?* I grabbed the paper-wrapped loaf from Orwashers and said, "What was your name again?"

That made Coco snort—I wasn't sure if it was in disbelief or in mockery of Damion—but it didn't matter.

Because my feigned unawareness of him was received like some sort of a challenge.

He stepped closer, not releasing the baguette, pulling me slightly closer still by the loaf between us. His eyes were very nearly twinkling behind those *stupid-hot* glasses as he looked down at me and said, "It's Damion, honey, and it looks like I'm going to have to make some serious moves to ensure you never forget it again."

CHAPTER NINE

"Mean people suck. Mean people with money suck more."

—Remington

Damion

"What the hell was that?" Coco asked, looking at me like I was out of my mind.

I watched as wild curls disappeared down the hallway, feeling pleased that I'd left her unsettled and confused, even as I rebuked myself for giving away my damned baguette.

That was supposed to be my lunch.

It was like I was incapable of stopping myself whenever she lifted that stubborn chin in challenge. The chick made me want to leave her squirming while simultaneously messing up her hair . . . maybe pulling it a little.

"What do you mean?" I asked casually, even though I knew exactly what Coco meant.

"You know exactly what I mean," she said. "Why are you acting all flirty toward that . . . girl?"

She said "girl" as if it wasn't possible to come up with another word to describe how distasteful she found Julia. She said, "Not that I care, but I know you're not out here trolling for hicktown girls in ridiculous shoes. So what are you up to?"

"I'm not up to anything, but it seems to me that you care very much," I said, knowing exactly how to push her buttons. "Are you into me, Coke?"

"First of all, you never know. Maybe the gods are smiling on you today," she said with a smile, sending a frisson of unease zipping down my spine because I didn't like the way she looked at me when she said that.

She looked *interested*, and the last thing I needed was Coco Chattingham's interest.

She leaned a little closer and said, "But I just happen to find it bizarre that you're wasting time with . . . *that*. Is there some sort of a bet in play here or something?"

"There doesn't have to be a bet for me to find a new friend interesting," I said. "Don't be jealous."

She didn't even dignify that with a response, but simply turned and started walking in the other direction.

Naomi, on the other hand, gave me a smile with an eyebrow raise. "Seriously, Rutledge, what are you doing here?"

"You know me," I said, sliding my hands into my pockets. "Always looking for something to entertain me."

"Okay, this is true," she said, and I was slightly insulted by her easy agreement. "But *her*?"

I just shrugged. "Who knows?"

"What do we even know about her?" Bella said. "I heard she has a hot brother and that they're from Wyoming, but do we know anything else?"

"Nebraska, not Wyoming," I corrected, "And she has a *twin* brother."

"Does he *also* have awful hair and terrible fashion sense?"

"I will leave that judgment to you," I said, happy to walk away, because I was done with the conversation. I accepted my reputation because it was convenient, but that didn't mean I wasn't annoyed by its inaccuracies.

But as I headed for my next class, I was torn between feeling slightly bad for Julia because she was fitting in worse than I would've even imagined, and feeling hopeful that the absolute rejection she was experiencing across the board was going to somehow make her family disappear.

Not likely, but it was fun to dream.

I waited an hour before succumbing to my need to mess with her. I had study hall, so it was an entire free period to wreak havoc upon her flustered sensibilities.

Me: Did you enjoy my bread?

I was surprised by her immediate response.

Julia: Why with the bread? What's the bread about?

I replied: Bread is only ever about bread, Nebraska, come on.

Julia: Wow. So deep. NOW I believe you about the whole "smartest guy at Gardenwood" thing.

I smiled in spite of myself.

Texted: By the way, your legs are very long.

Julia: Um . . .

I knew that wherever she was in the building, she was staring at her phone while doing that fast-blinking thing, looking like she couldn't believe what I'd just said.

I loved the thought of it.

So I added: Are you taller than your mullet-inflicted, bad-wallet-carrying ex-boyfriend?

That was going to bug the shit out of her.

I saw conversation bubbles, so I typed fast because she'd *hate* it if I cut off her defensive response.

I sent: Btw I'm a busy guy, so if you want me to pencil you in for tutoring or . . . anything else that crosses your mind, we should probably set aside the time.

More conversation bubbles.

She's losing her shit right about now.

Julia: Not that it's any of your business, but he's taller.

Me: Who?

Julia: My ex

Me: Your ex what?

Man, I wish I could see her frustrated face, I thought. I bet those cheeks were going hardcore red while she tried coming up with a response.

Julia: You asked if I was taller than my ex-boyfriend

Me: The short king with the mullet?

Julia: He isn't short!

Me: Stop lying. William had pocket-sized energy.

Julia: You saw his license for five seconds, you couldn't know that

Me: So are we hooking up or what?

I heard myself laugh out loud when the conversation bubbles stretched on forever.

I couldn't wait to see what she came up with.

Julia: Are you drunk right now?

Okay, fair, I thought.

I texted: Sadly sober. Why would you say that?

Me: WAIT. HOLD ON, NEBRASKA. Did you actually think when I said "hooking up," that I meant . . .

God, this is fun.

So many conversation bubbles.

Then finally—

Julia: NO!

I snickered, looked up to see Mr. Kenseth peering at me from behind his tiny glasses like I was a criminal, then sent: . . . tutoring??

This is going to kill her.

A solid two minutes elapsed where no words were sent, just those little dots that let me know she was still there.

Finally she replied: If you have tutoring availability on Thursday, I can do it anytime after school. If not, that's fine.

I didn't know Julia Nebraska, not really, but I knew her head was exploding that very moment.

Me: Oh honey, I can do it anytime.

CHAPTER TEN

"I don't trust anyone who eats while wearing white. That kind of arrogance is annoying as fuck."

—Remington

Julia

"Is that text from Damion?"

Damion the Evil, who's making my head want to explode?

Yes!

I looked up from my phone to see Jasmine and Donovan standing in front of my locker, watching me with matching smirks on their faces.

"Um . . ."

I didn't really know what to say. They *seemed* nice, but could I trust them?

With no other choice, I responded, "It *is*, but I have no idea how he got my number; I swear I didn't give it to him."

"It's Damion Rutledge," Jasmine said. "If he wants something, he gets it."

Is that his motto or something?

"Really?" I hated that I wanted to know more about what he was like. I was positive the truth would make me trust him even less than I already did, but everyone's attitude about him made me curious. "What does that mean, exactly?"

"Just that he's one of those guys who, like, lives by his own rules," she said, as if that explained it.

"Yeah," Donovan agreed with a nod. "We've all gone to school with him since kindergarten, so we *know* him, but he's still got this mysterious thing about him. You can't ever be sure what he's going to do or say."

"So does he get into a lot of trouble?" I asked, not wanting to seem too interested but feeling like I needed to know whether or not he came with a warning.

"I mean, he's *gotten* into trouble, sure, but he's not really *considered* trouble, if you know what I mean," she said. "He used to get in the occasional fight, and most people think of him as a rebel, but he also comes from a good family and gets good grades. It's more of an attitude thing."

I had no idea what any of that meant.

How bad is he—how bad??

"Are you interested?" Jasmine asked, crossing her arms and tilting her head. "In Damion? Because he usually doesn't date girls from Gardenwood, so the fact that he's talking to you and showed up at your house on your first day has everyone *fascinated*."

Nooooo.

The last thing I needed was attention like this.

Talk about a nightmare.

The only thing worse would be people knowing I desperately needed their rebellious boy to help me with my abysmal math skills.

"I mean, I don't even know the guy—"

"Oh my God, what if he asks you to the season?" Donovan said in a squeal.

"Damion would *never* do the season," Jasmine said, shaking her head. "That is *so* something he would mock."

I said, "What exactly is the—"

"But his mom's in charge of planning this year, and he's a senior," Donovan said to Jasmine. "So you never know. His parents might make him."

"Ooh, true," Jasmine said, looking excited by the thought. "I'd do anything Quinn Rutledge said—he's got that stern-daddy thing about him."

Donovan made a face and said, "Gross."

"Is the season like homecoming?" I asked. "Like a prom kind of thing?"

"Oh, you sweet summer child from a foreign land, this is absolutely *not* like homecoming," Jasmine said with a laugh. "It's more like prom on crack."

"Times a thousand," Donovan added. "Think of the Met Gala and a slew of pre-parties leading up to it, and you're closer to the truth."

"Are you serious?"

That sounds insane.

"The ball is on Halloween night, and it's the most formal of all balls," Jasmine said. "It's magical."

"Imagine being whisked away to the gala by someone wild and unpredictable like Damion Rutledge," Donovan said with a smile. "I've got butterflies just thinking about it."

"Dear *God*," Jasmine said with a giggle. "That *is* a dizzying thought."

"Dizzying" and "unpredictable" were far better words than "magical."

Because the idea of a magically romantic event with a guy—any guy whatsoever—sounded completely nauseating to me.

Seriously.

The one thing Will had taught me was that no matter how solid or trustworthy a dude might seem, the simple truth was that that he wasn't.

Trustworthy.

No one was worthy of romantic trust.

NO ONE.

Because if Will Malone, the boy I'd known and loved since the fifth grade, my first kiss and first dance and the guy who'd cried actual tears when I had appendicitis sophomore year, was capable of waking up one day and deciding he wanted to rip out my heart, every single human male was also capable of the same violence.

And I wanted no part of that ever again.

So these girls might see Damion as someone hot and mysterious, but I only saw him as a guy.

And I had zero interest in those anymore.

Add to that fact that Damion was an enormous *jerk*, and all he became was a very attractive means to an end.

My evil tutor.

"Well, I barely know him," I said dismissively, wanting to shut down any ideas they might have about me and Damion and the season. It was one thing to let them assume he might be interested in me, but it was another thing altogether to let them think the season was a possibility for us. "So I'm not dizzy at all."

I was still reeling from the bizarre day at school when my brother and I walked into the kitchen and things got even *more* strange.

"What exactly is going on here?" Liam said as he stopped short to stare at the scene in front of us.

I nearly ran into his back when he froze, but I totally understood his inability to move forward as I stared in disbelief.

My parents looked ridiculous.

My father was wearing white shorts with a white polo neatly tucked into them, he had the cleanest white sneakers I'd ever seen on his huge feet, and there was a white baseball cap on top of his head as he stood in front of the sink, doing a dance move that might've been the Charleston.

As if this weren't strange enough on its own, my mother stood on the other side of the room, also fully clad in white from head to toe. A white sweater, white pleated skort, white sneakers—she was all in on the whites, and Bernard appeared to be tying a white ribbon around her low ponytail while she hummed whatever song my dad was dancing to.

"Did aliens abduct my parents and they're trying to fool us with replacements?" Liam asked as he went straight for the fridge. "Because no one who has ever met Clint and Shawna will believe that this is them."

"Right?" my dad said with a laugh, pointing to his waist as he stopped jamming. "I'm wearing a belt with shorts, so life doesn't make sense anymore. I told you I look ridiculous, Bernard."

"You look exactly the way you are supposed to look, Mr. Lowell," Bernard said with a calm smile, unfazed. "Distinguished."

"Like a cotton ball," Liam added. "Or a very distinguished Q-tip."

"What is happening here with the whites?" I asked, scooping up Clank.

"We are now officially members of the Gardenwood Athletic Club," my mom said, sounding in awe of that fact. "I actually had a tennis lesson today, and your dad worked on his putts with the golf pro."

"Grab me a pop," I said to my brother, then asked my mom, "Did you like it? The indoor golf and tennis?"

Golf and tennis weren't things my parents had ever really been involved in. Like, my dad golfed occasionally in outings with friends, but he didn't do it with any athletic intentionality.

He was a Busch Light kind of golfer, in it for the beer, not the birdies.

"I actually did," my mom said, sounding downright perky. "And I met a couple of ladies from the PTA who were surprisingly nice *and* are going to be working on the ball planning with me."

"Ball planning?" Now my mind was good and truly blown. My incredibly practical mother was involved in this ball nonsense? "Are you talking about the season, Ma?"

She nodded and looked excited. "It's so over-the-top I can't even believe I get to help organize it."

What is happening to my life?

"These ladies' faces were pulled really tight, so I don't trust them further than I can throw 'em," my dad added.

Which made my mom giggle. "Just because they don't age doesn't mean they aren't good people."

"I didn't say they aren't good people. I said I don't trust them," he said. "The guys I met on the putting greens were the same way. Nice enough, but smelling too much of cologne and hair product to be trustable."

I wanted to mock him, but somehow that seemed like maybe a decent way to filter trustability.

"How was school today?" my mom asked.

Awful, terrible, the stuff of nightmares.

The whole *everyone thinks I'm talking to Damion* thing had me feeling *very* unsettled. Coco and the Skins—*good band name*—definitely hadn't seem pleased.

"Good," Liam said, tossing a can of Diet Coke to me before grabbing the box of leftover pizza slices and carrying it over to the table. "Classes are good, people are good, everyone thinks Jules is being chased by some guy named Damion—all good."

LIAM!

"What?" my mom said on a gasp, as if the idea of a boy being interested in me was downright impossible to believe. Her eyes were huge when she asked, "Is this true, honey? Who is Damion?"

My parents had been concerned about my unwillingness to move on after the whole Will thing, so needless to say, she looked *thrilled* by the news.

Also, she said the name "Damion" with a breathlessness, as if it held magical possibilities or something.

"Yeah, who is this besotted student," my dad said, looking down at his belt and adjusting the tiny buckle, "and do I need to show him my gun collection?"

I rolled my eyes. "I doubt he's going to be scared off by your collection of Revolutionary War–era weaponry, so definitely no, and also they're wrong. He's not chasing me; he's my tutor."

“Oh, that’s the *tutor’s* name—Damion,” my mom said, her breezy words belying her eyes as they narrowed thoughtfully on my face. “It’s still going well?”

“Yep.” I nodded. “It’s fine so far, but no one knows he’s my tutor because of the confidentiality thing, so that’s why people are assuming he’s into me.”

“Well, that’s nice,” she said. “That it’s discreet. Not that there’s anything wrong with having a tutor.”

“No, I know,” I said with an eye roll. “It’s fine.”

But I felt the eyes of the kitchen upon me all of a sudden, and I wondered if everyone in the room was thinking about the tutor and wondering if there was any shot of him succeeding.

After the first meeting with Mr. Green, my parents and Bernard reassured me my test scores weren’t going to jeopardize our fortune.

But I didn’t believe them.

Because something in my dad’s expression when I mentioned it, the way he hadn’t *quite* met my eyes, made me think it worried him, too.

Did I actually have the power to ruin the dream for all of us?

CHAPTER ELEVEN

"Cats are funny little assholes who love you on their own terms. I respect them more than I respect most humans."

—Remington

Damion

Dad: Call me NOW.

"You're seriously going to just keep ignoring him?" Beckett asked as my phone chirped for the sixth time in the past two minutes.

"Yep," I said as I went down the park steps, glancing over at the yellow trees to my right, where I'd seen a Cape May warbler before school. "I'm going to be home in a couple hours and I can argue with him then."

"God, I could *not* blow off your dad," he said, dribbling as soon as we reached the path. "Quinn is fucking scary."

"He's all talk," I said, ignoring the knot of dread in my gut that was the direct result *of* his talk.

But what was the point of calling him now? He was at work, and I was on my way to shoot hoops. Arguing about the upcoming weekend served neither of us and would only result in a fight with zero resolution.

This weekend was a special event at his fraternity, so my dad wanted me and my mom to accompany him to Dartmouth. To my father, the idea of the three of us engaging in a weekend of alumni schmoozing was, like, the ultimate.

To me, the idea was fucking suffocating.

Mostly because it felt like a trap, like the walls were closing in on me.

All my dad wanted was for me to follow in his footsteps, to go to

Dartmouth next year like he'd done, like his father had done before him, like his grandfather had done before him.

Actually, it wasn't a want at all.

He expected it to happen, just like he expected the sun to rise in the morning.

His son was—*of course*—going to follow in his footsteps.

It was what the Rutledge men did.

They were born, they played manly games, they graduated from Gardenwood, and then they attended Dartmouth. After that they could take their rightful spot within Rutledge Investments, wherein they would spend the rest of their days poring over financial statements and hoarding wealth the way wild people on TLC hoarded animals.

As the heir apparent to take over the family business, it was just assumed that I was going to fall in line.

Nope, though—it wasn't for me.

I had other plans, better plans.

But the fact that my dad was on my ass to confirm I was coming along on the family trip meant he was pressing the gas on getting my future going.

He wanted a weekend to get a good visual on what the future would look like.

I wanted to avoid that weekend entirely.

So I wasn't going to attend.

Because if I went, I'd either have to lie the entire trip or tell the truth.

Each sounded equally awful.

"Just tell him," Beckett said. "Tell him you're not going. Tell him you have to help me with . . . something."

"First of all, you just said you're scared of him, so 'just tell him' falls a little flat, you wuss," I said. "And second of all, even if I had to help you give CPR to nuns, he'd still say Dartmouth is more important."

"I hate to break this to you, but your freshman year is coming fast whether you like it or not. You can't keep putting off the inevitable." Beckett shot me a look and said, "If you're actually going to do the damn thing, the conversation needs to be had sooner rather than later."

Beckett was my best friend, probably the only person who really *got* me, even though we were total opposites. He understood what I wanted and respected my goals, but he was all about following in *his* dad's footsteps and doing exactly what was expected of him.

He looked *forward* to meeting his parents' expectations, couldn't *wait* to go to Harvard and join his father's fraternity, and he was genuinely honored to follow in his dad's vocational footsteps.

He *was* the golden child.

So yeah—he thought I was out of my mind with my alternative plan.

But still, he supported me.

He was the only person in the world—now that Remi was gone—who knew what I *actually* wanted to do next year, what I was trying to make happen.

Everyone else on the planet just assumed I was doing what I was supposed to be doing.

"I know," I said, but I just didn't know *how* to do it.

When Remi was here, we'd had a plan.

Now it was just me, trying to find the words to disappoint my dad and the way to make it happen.

"Maybe do something terrible at alumni weekend," he said with a smirk. "Make him relieved you don't want to attend his alma mater."

"Vomit on one of his fraternity brothers?" I said, gesturing for him to give me the ball.

"Get arrested for taking a piss in the campus fountain," he suggested, sending me a bounce pass. "An indecent exposure charge will distract him."

"Great suggestion," I said.

His phone buzzed and he glanced down at it. "Oh, good, Liam's meeting us."

"Liam? Lowell?" I asked. "At the courts?"

"Yeah," he said, putting his phone back in his pocket. "Is that okay?"

"Sure," I said, dribbling the basketball. And yet the last thing I wanted to deal with at the moment was one of *them*.

A Lowell.

Beckett seemed to really like Liam—everyone did, actually, but they also didn't know what I knew about his family. The people of Gardenwood might suspect they were new money, but no one had confirmation of that rumor.

Or the fact that the money had come via questionable methods.

I'd briefly considered telling Beckett everything, but then I thought better of it. What was the point in mentioning it when I had no proof? It seemed smarter to wait and see if my dad was going to be able to reverse the will.

Please, God, let him be successful.

It felt urgent and imperative that we do it, like we'd all be failing Remi if we didn't right that wrong and get his house back.

But with each passing day, it felt less possible.

The longer they were in that house, the more it felt like it might actually be theirs.

God help me, Riverside Manor felt like it was slipping out of our hands.

CHAPTER TWELVE

"Red flag? I'll tell you what's a red flag. Abs. A dude with abs has chosen hotness over pasta, and that doesn't sit right with me. Fuck off with that."

—Remington

Julia

"Just come with me."

My brother, dressed in a faded Busch Light T-shirt and baggy basketball shorts, stood in front of my locker and looked at me like *I* was the unreasonable one.

"I don't want to 'hoop,' Liam," I said, wanting to go home and lose myself in a book.

The day had been relatively unremarkable, as in I hadn't been accosted by any mean girls or tall boys wielding bread loaves, but it'd still been a day filled with quiet murmurs and judgy side-eye.

"You don't have to hoop, you just have to hang out," he said. "You love the park."

"*You* can," I said. "And I love being by *myself* at the park. I definitely don't want to have a playdate with your new jocko friends."

"Jules," he said, sighing and running a hand over the top of his head. "Just listen to me."

We had the same hair color, but his curls looked perfectly tousled, as opposed to my mane of twirly corkscrews.

"The guys I'm meeting at the park seem pretty decent, so you should come and actually *talk*," he said. "You're never going to make friends if you don't say any words other than 'sorry' and 'my bad.'"

I shook my head. "I don't think Gardenwood *dudes* are where I should start, friend-wise."

"Because the girls have been so welcoming?" he said, raising an eyebrow.

"Ouch," I replied, grabbing my backpack and slamming my locker shut.

"How about this? Just walk with me to the courts and then make the call. It's so close to home that if you decide to bounce, it's right there."

"Fine," I said, giving in because at least he'd be there.

Liam might have his faults, but he'd kill someone before he let them be mean to me.

It was a quick walk to the Seventy-Sixth Street courts, windy in that autumnal way where you didn't really mind because the scattering leaves put on a show, but my stomach got straight-up jumpy when we got close and I saw a bunch of guys dribbling and shooting around.

"It's going to be fine," Liam said, reading my mind as we approached. "Don't get all keyed up."

I rolled my eyes. "I hate when you say that. Being stressed about something doesn't make me 'all keyed up.'"

"I'm just messing."

"Well, I don't like it."

"Why do you think I do it?" he said.

Infuriating.

I slowly took a seat on the bench outside the basketball courts, on the other side of the fence.

"It's about time," I heard someone say, and Beckett—the guy who'd showed my brother around on the first day of class—sent a chest pass Liam's way.

Which Liam caught, then immediately made a shot from deep court.

Show-off.

Ugh. It was truly unfair that everything came easy to him.

He was privileged that way, the ass.

Speaking of . . .

I felt every muscle in my body tense when I saw him.

God.

Of course Damion was there.

I mean, why wouldn't he be? It seemed anytime I was stressed or anxious, *he* magically appeared.

Before he had a chance to see me, I immediately pulled out my phone to commence Operation Look Distracted in the hopes he would ignore me, because I couldn't deal with him and his stupid glasses and his cocky grin and any more surprise loaves of bread.

Also, like, how did he already know my food weakness?

I'm leaving, I thought.

As soon as they started playing, I was going to go home. I'd use the distraction of bouncing balls to make a clean getaway.

But then the world shifted when they decided to play *shirts and skins*.

Because Damion's shirt came off and I very nearly fainted.

Not only was he tall, but he was broad-chested and ab-smacked and basically carrying around the chestal region of a god, dear *Lord*. I had to look away because holy *crap*, the way he had muscles on muscles was a bit too much for me to handle.

"Let's go," I heard Beckett say, and then they basketballed.

Liam seemed completely comfortable, not at all fazed by the fact that he didn't really know any of the other guys yet, and I found myself staying a little longer than I'd planned.

Not because I was making friends; no one even noticed I was there.

But watching the game was far more entertaining than I'd expected.

Mostly because Damion never shut up.

Like, *ever*.

He was almost obnoxious in the way he called *everyone* out, giving each and every person shit, but nobody was bothered by it. Rather, they seemed to enjoy it.

Damion was actually funny.

And unbelievably *good*.

Great. Mr. Perfect just got perfecter.

He was obviously the best one on the court, even better than Liam.

Which was saying a lot.

I hated it.

It wasn't right that someone could be rich, smart, athletic, funny—and also the world's biggest jerk.

"What the hell was that shot?" Liam yelled at Beckett after a ridiculous air ball.

"It's called a good look," Beckett yelled back.

"Bullshit it is," Damion commented as he dribbled between his legs.

I honestly forgot about my escape plan—that's how into watching them I was—until I saw Coco and Naomi.

They were walking toward the courts, coming from the other side of the park, wearing cool sunglasses and eating frozen yogurt as fall's brightest foliage stretched out as their backdrop. Coco had a scarf tied around her hair and was wearing a dress that would've made Jackie Kennedy proud, and Naomi appeared to be wearing leather shorts with a wool sweater and knee-high boots.

They looked ludicrous.

If they walked down the street in Springfield looking like that, people would be talking about them on the town's Facebook page.

But here, in the city, they looked *perfect* and I wanted to *be* them.

But I never would be.

I grabbed my backpack and was off that bench so fast, speed-walking in the other direction as quickly as my legs would take me, desperate to get away before they noticed me.

I couldn't handle the thought of dealing with them outside of school.

It was bad enough in the halls of the academy, where their behavior was probably in check because of the threat of teachers happening upon their dickery.

But having a run-in with them out in the wild, where they had free rein to dig in as hard as they wanted?

No, thanks.

I hauled ass through the park and didn't relax until I saw the general.

My general, in a way.

It was the statue that sat at the top of the park stairs, memorializing General Franz Sigel (of Civil War fame, *thank you, Google*). I could see Franz from our living room window, so the general had become my lighthouse, the beacon that led me home whenever I was in the park.

It was like ol' Franz was always there, waiting for me to come home.

"I've never been happier to see you, Franz," I muttered as I passed the statue and ran toward my house, the wind whipping my hair into my eyes.

My phone buzzed just as I was going through the front door.

Damion: I saw you watching, Nebraska.

I gasped and froze in place, feeling busted.

Oh my God, did he see me drooling over his stupid muscles?

"Is everything all right, Miss Julia?" Bernard asked, looking up from where he was sitting at the big desk, working on his laptop.

"Oh. Um. Yeah," I said, closing the door behind me. "I just, uh, forgot something."

I looked down at my phone and texted: Could you see how bored I was?

Good answer, Jules.

Damion: You actually looked very . . . engaged for someone who says she doesn't like basketball.

"Oh my God!" I said under my breath.

So arrogant.

Bernard asked, "Anything I can help with?"

"No, thank you," I said through gritted teeth, rolling my eyes. "Just dumb boy stuff."

"Ah, that," he said, going back to his work.

I sighed, toed off my shoes, and sent: I was playing Wordle on my phone, if you must know.

I made it up to my room before he made me literally scream with his cocky response.

Sure you were, Julia.

CHAPTER THIRTEEN

"New York coffee shops mirror the city itself in the way they're both welcoming and exclusionary at once. Their existence calls out to the passerby on the street, tempting him with everything he thinks he's looking for, but once inside, he wonders if he's come to the wrong place entirely."

—Remington

Damion

When Julia suggested meeting at Irving Farm Coffee for our next tutoring session, I was so damn disappointed, I almost refused.

Because I was dying to get back into those walls.

Julia: Running late but almost there.

Of course she was running late.

I set my phone on the table and sat back in my chair, sighing because what the hell was I even doing? I'd agreed to help her because I missed the house, yet here I was, waiting for Julia Nebraska in a coffee shop.

Coffee shop = not a house.

I was homesick for another visit to that place, but there wasn't a good way to explain away my clawing need to hang out at Riverside Manor.

I love your kitchen so much it brings tears to my eyes.

I want to take a nap on the thick rug in your game room.

God help me, I need to smell your parents' closet and see if I can still pick up hints of cigar smoke.

No, not weird at all.

But for real, it felt like Remi was disappearing more every day, and I was desperate to feel him, any little piece.

Just as I thought that, I saw Julia through the window, scurrying toward the entrance like she was running late for work—head down, curls flying.

God, even the way she moves screams that she isn't one of us.

She stood out like a sore thumb at school, with her wild hair and whatever was going on with her ridiculous Louis Vuitton shoes. Even though her uniform matched everyone else's, her accessories made her stand way the hell out.

Of course, at the moment she appeared to be wearing jeans, a plaid flannel shirt, and Chuck Taylors, dressed to traverse either a cornfield or a baseball diamond, so she was outdoing herself on the whole I-don't-belong-here front.

Which gave me joy because she *didn't*.

She didn't belong here, and I needed her gone. She had a key to Remi's house and I didn't anymore, and that was messed up.

The bell over the door rang as she entered, and I leaned back in my chair and cued up my best charming smile, so ready to mess with her.

Because I had realized something lately.

Keeping her off-balance was therapeutic for me.

Something I could control in my uncontrollable life.

Between my father's expectations and the gaping hole left behind by Remi's absence, I constantly felt pulled under, like everything was floating past me, coming *at* me, and all I could do was helplessly hang on.

And I *hated* being helpless.

Enter Julia.

Daughter of my enemy, inheriting my inheritance, residing in my residence.

The brown-eyed recipient of my future.

Her constant side glances, wrinkled forehead, and quick blinks when I messed with her told me she was in over her head.

Which was nice, because that was right where I wanted her.

Confused and at my mercy.

I gestured toward the seat across from me, where a baguette was waiting for her. "Hey, Jules."

Her eyebrows slammed together as she sat down. "It's *Julia*."

Oh, sunshine.

"So sorry, *Julia*," I corrected. "But I bet your friends back home call you Jules, don't they?"

"Some do," she admitted, eyeballing the bread like it was poisoned while at the same time failing to disguise the fact that she wanted to eat that bread more than anything in the world, which kind of made me want to laugh. "But we aren't friends."

"And don't you think we should be?" I replied, tilting my head and wondering if everyone dressed like that back in Nebraska or if it was just her.

She looked at me for a long minute, her mouth a little open like she was in shock and not sure what was going on. "You want to be friends."

It wasn't a question. Her gaze was all suspicion.

"Friends, or . . . *something*," I said, dragging my eyes down her body.

Dammit, I thought, abruptly returning my gaze to her face.

The goal was to make her uncomfortable, to irritate her, but that'd felt way too Corbin-coded for my comfort, leering at her like a fucking creep.

I crossed my arms over my chest and nodded my chin toward the bread instead. "You know I got that for *you*—you can eat it."

"Stop buying me bread," she said with an irritated laugh. "I *like* bread, but it's not going to work."

"What's not going to work?" I asked.

"I don't know," she said with a shrug. "Whatever this is. Why is this the second bread you've given me? What's with the bread, like, what are you doing?"

"So suspicious, Nebraska," I said, giving my head a shake. "I saw the stash at your house and assumed you're a junkie, and since I'd really like you to focus all that Midwestern energy on *me* for the next hour, I thought an investment in delicious carbohydrates might provide the assist."

"Why would I focus on *you*?" she asked, her eyebrows all crinkled together.

Right in the trap, sweet girl.

"Because I'm your tutor and want you to concentrate on math . . . ?" I said, narrowing my eyes like I didn't understand her. "Whoa. Unless you're suggesting something else, something less educational and more—"

"No," she said, rolling her eyes in exasperation. "Oh my God, *no*!"

CHAPTER FOURTEEN

"Gardenwood is a neighborhood I love with all my heart. The architecture, the history, the restaurants, the markets—I could wax poetic over the place all day long. The people, however, scare the living shit out of me."

—Remington

Julia

Whyyyyy does he make me so nuts?

Damion was staring at me in that unnerving way of his, like there were no less than a thousand wicked thoughts going through his mind. He seemed like an actual character from *The Woods* (the TV show), or perhaps a guy from a vampirical dark romance novel.

Basically, he seemed like he knew everything I didn't.

Something about his heavy-lidded eyes, or maybe it was his sharp jawline or those dark, slashing eyebrows—made it seem like he'd done *everything* and surely had a frame of reference for all of it. Sex, drugs, booze, fashion, sports—he was just *that* guy, the guy who oozed a dark knowledge of any and all things.

Donovan's words added to my intimidation when I felt like I knew absolutely nothing about any of it.

Most people think of him as a rebel.

Like, if *those* people thought of him as a rebel, then I was definitely out of my element.

I hadn't been sheltered in Springfield—I'd been to a few parties there, and knew a lot of people who drank on the weekends—but it felt different here.

The students at Gardenwood Academy all seemed *experienced*.

There was a confidence in the way they moved through the world, an arrogance that suggested they'd done about a million things I'd never even thought to try. This was true about Damion.

Especially true.

Just being *around* him, even sitting across from Damion in a quiet coffee shop, held an air of danger.

Quit being a stupid baby, Jules.

"I don't need bread," I said, clearing my throat, trying my hardest to sound unfazed when he always seemed to have me fazed, "to concentrate on the math—the *math*, thank you very much."

"Glad to hear it," he said with a slow-sliding grin, maybe the first genuine grin I'd ever seen on his face. Then he lowered his voice and mockingly repeated, as if it was hilarious to him, "The math, thank you very much."

Oh my God, could he be more arrogant?

I looked at his smile and wanted to slug him, but also—*wow*.

That smile.

Thank *God* I knew he was a jerk and I was immune, because the full-throttle power of his smile definitely gave the "dizzying" vibes that Donovan and Jasmine had been talking about.

Dear *Lord*.

And what is he wearing??

I hadn't noticed when I sat down, mostly because I was late and also slightly distracted by the baguette, but he was wearing a *Knives Out* fisherman sweater that looked absurdly, ridiculously, *monstrously* good with the glasses on his face and the waves in his thick hair.

It was offensive how handsome he was.

"I need a coffee before we start," I said, nearly knocking over my chair as I stood. "Do you want one?"

His smile simmered into more of a smirk, like he could read my thoughts.

Jackass.

Which made me look down at my Apple Watch to avoid his eye contact entirely.

I *heard* him say, "An Americano would be great."

"No problem."

I went to the counter and ordered our drinks, trying to get my brain and my emotions to agree on calming the hell down.

Who cares if he's attractive? I thought as the barista prepared our order. *A very attractive asshole is still an asshole.*

When I glanced in his direction, he was scrolling on his phone, looking bored (his default expression) as he leaned back in his chair, and I reminded myself that I only needed him for his brain.

Ignore his . . . Damion-ness.

Easier said than done, I thought a few minutes later, because when I held out his drink, he gave me a dickish half smile and said, "Thanks, *Jules*."

"Of course, *Dame*," I replied through gritted teeth as I sat down.

"A pet name already? Sunshine, you flatter me," he said.

I just sighed, because I wasn't equipped to handle him.

"But listen, my student," he said, his eyes nearly twinkling as he made my life hell.

"Please don't call me that."

"How do we feel about 'pupil'?"

"Makes me throw up a little in my mouth," I said, to which he responded with a shrug.

Thankfully, once I pulled out the testing study packet Headmaster Green had given me, Damion straightened up from his I'm-a-bored-duke chair lean. He scooted his chair closer to the table, adjusted his glasses, read over the first page, then cleared his throat.

"Okay, so how do you feel about this unit?" he asked, gesturing toward the paper. "What is your comfort level with these particular problems? On a pain scale of one to ten . . . ?"

I didn't want to, but I admitted, "These are a solid seven for me."

"Okay," he said, nodding. His eyes were serious, entirely absent of his cool mockery, when he said, "We can fix that. What's your first step on this problem?"

He pointed a finger at the equation.

"Um . . ."

"Just show me how you'll attack it, Nebraska, and once I know that, we can start reshaping."

"Okay," I said, gnawing on my lip, nervous to show him more of my lackluster mathematical skills.

Also a little taken aback by the sincerity.

I started working the problem, and just like during our first session, he kind of became a different person when he was teaching. It was like his brain locked in on the information and he forgot who he was. The privileged smart-ass disappeared and was replaced by someone intelligent, intentional, and patient.

He wasn't necessarily warm or nice, but it didn't feel like he was coming *at* me for once.

Which was nice.

"Hold up," he said quietly. "Look at the second half of the problem. Are you sure you want to do that?"

"Oh," I said, trying to remember what he'd showed me on the last problem. "So I should first go here?"

I pointed to the equation in parentheses.

"Bingo," he said, leaning a little closer. "And don't forget about *that*."

His big finger tapped the other side of the problem, but I got a little tripped up by how good he smelled.

It made me look away from the paper and at his muscular neck, just above the collar of that wool sweater, which was probably where the smell was coming from.

Of course, that made my gaze move up to his face, *God*, where hazel eyes were watching me from behind expensive frames.

"I, um, I won't," I said, my voice coming out a little weird.

Stop sounding breathless, you idiot!

"Good girl," he said, but I kept my eyes on the paper as my ears got warm, definitely unable to look at him after those two words left his lips.

I still felt frustrated as I worked through the lesson, because I hated how hard it was for me to *get* it, but he explained things so well that after forty-five more minutes I was starting to feel like connections were being made.

With me and the math, that is.

"It's just like the last one," he explained as he looked at my equation, leaning closer over the paper and pointing at the problem. "You have to find the root of the number first, remember?"

"Duh," I said as I realized my mistake, as I erased my work so I could start over. "Why do I forget that every time?"

"You'll get it," he said, brushing eraser dust off the paper.

"Will I?" I muttered under my breath as I clicked more lead out of the mechanical pencil and rewrote the problem.

"Of course you will," he said, which made my eyes go to his face.

"You will. You have to believe that, Nebraska," he said in a tone that was almost friendly. "This isn't something impossible, right? It's math, it's data, it's unyielding facts. We just have to keep coming at it from different angles until we find *your* path to understanding."

"My path to understanding," I repeated, blown away by his un-Damionness.

I had no idea what else to say.

Because he kind of made me believe.

He made it sound so simple, like there was no question I was going to eventually get it.

Was it actually possible?

"Finish the problem," he said with his eyebrows raised behind those glasses. "Don't get distracted when you're starting to catch it."

"I'm not."

"Sure you aren't," he said, and his little smirk was . . . holy shit, it was *nice*.

I stared into his face and was terrified by how attractive I found him at that moment because he looked like he was being nice, what the hell.

Noooooo!

"Ah, I'll be right back," I blurted as I cranked back my chair and stood, needing to run to the restroom—anywhere—to get my mind right.

But cold liquid splashed over me as I took a step back from the table and bumped (slammed) into a woman who was walking by. I turned around as both of the coffees she'd been carrying crumpled and splurted against me, lids popping off, coffee splashing everywhere.

"Oh my God!" I managed as my shirt was instantly *saturated* with forty ounces of iced coffee. "I'm so sorry!"

I stammered the apology and bent down, trying to pick up the cups and grab a napkin while wiping the dripping liquid off of my hair and body, dear *God*.

"Here, Julia," Damion said calmly.

Without even pausing, he stood and reached a hand over his shoulder, removed his thick wool sweater, and held it out to me, leaving him standing there in a white T-shirt. "Go put this on and I'll clean up."

"What?" I said dumbly as I stood there in a soaked shirt.

As Damion held out *his sweater* to me.

"Here," he said, giving it a shake while also giving the woman whose coffee I was wearing a smile.

"Um, okay . . . ?" I said, taking the sweater from his hand as a fat drop of liquid dripped out of my hair.

The wool was warm in my fingers, and something about that felt wildly intimate. I pushed back my hair with my free hand and asked, "Are you sure?"

"Go already," he said, looking unfazed and also somehow really good in just a T-shirt and khakis.

Although, *of course he did*.

I took his sweater into the bathroom and changed, mortified by my klutziness.

It was totally on-brand for me to do something like this, but did it have to happen in front of *him*, of all people?

But as I slid into the pre-warmed sweater, which smelled like the essence of Ralph Lauren or Calvin Klein, someone rich and well-groomed, my stomach knotted up again.

Because the fit felt too familiar. Oversized and masculine, comfortable, comfort*ing*—the sweater felt like when I used to wear Will's sweatshirts.

Gah! I instantly hated it.

Not that I was in jeopardy of anything happening with Damion, but the sight of me in that extra-large sweater felt like some sort of warning.

I dabbed the coffee out of my hair, and when I came back out to the table with my wet flannel shirt rolled up in my hands, the mess was gone.

No drips, no cups, no napkins.

Damion was sitting there, back in his bored-duke pose like nothing had happened.

"Thank you," I said, making him look up from his phone. "Um, for the shirt and for cleaning up my mess."

His eyes went down to the sweater, and his jaw did a little flex-unflex thing, like he hated the sight of me in his clothing, before he said, "No problem."

"Yeah, uh, I'll bring it to school tomorrow," I said, feeling awkward as hell. "After I wash it."

"Whenever," he said, nodding. "Are we finished here, by the way?"

"Yeah." I cleared my throat, wondering how things with Damion just kept leveling up to even higher levels of awkwardness.

"Great," he said, and two minutes later he was gone.

The boy very nearly *ran* out of the coffee shop.

I left the coffee shop a little unsettled, feeling like my head was spinning as I hitched my bag over my shoulder and walked home.

Because I didn't like Damion. He was a jerk, and I strongly suspected his reputation for rebellion and flirtation was hard-earned.

He definitely seemed to fit the bill.

But I also kind of trusted that Damion could help me, as a tutor.

As in, he was good at teaching.

Really good.

Unfortunately, his tutorhood was actually making things worse for me, socially speaking, at school.

The rumors that we were *something* kept multiplying. And, according to Jasmine the next morning, word had spread that Damion and I were spotted together last night at the coffee shop. Me wearing *his* sweater.

Shit.

Dread settled in the pit of my stomach as I went to English lit, worsening as I walked past the two whispering mean girls in the front of the room.

I wanted to disappear as I took my seat and got out my notebook, as the bell rang and they continued to whisper, even after the teacher came in and took off on his lecture.

He started discussing *Titus Andronicus*, but I couldn't stop watching them gossip because I just *knew* it was about me.

Being invisible sounded like a dream come true.

"Miss Lowell," Mr. Longhaven said from his podium. "What are *your* thoughts on this?"

I felt the blood drain from my face when I heard my name, when I looked up from my thoughts to see that he was calling on me—*ohGod-ohGodohGod*—with every eye in the room turned in my direction.

Mr. Longhaven reminded me of the guy who took over for Keating at the end of *Dead Poets Society*. White-haired and strict, he was the kind of teacher who liked catching people not paying attention, who assigned heaps of homework just because he could. I hated him for calling on me.

"My, um, my thoughts?" I said, hating how breathless I sounded and *loathing* the snicker I heard from the back of the room.

"I think her thoughts are scrambled by too much Rutledge exposure," I heard the girl behind me whisper.

My throat felt tight and my skin was hot as they talked about me like I was a ridiculous punch line. I felt seen in the very worst way, and I wished I could run and hide.

"Yeah, is that actually true?" someone whispered back, and I felt queasy.

"I mean, it can't be, right? Has to be a rumor because ew."

Ew.

I swallowed and blinked fast as my vision went all water-blurred. *Don't cry, don't cry, don't cry.*

But God, I was an *ew*?

I knew I should be above their derision, confident in my own self-worth, but I was so embarrassed I wanted to evaporate into thin air. I was something they found *ew*.

Shit, I thought, biting the inside of my cheek because I was terrified I wasn't going to be able to hold back the tears. I knew if I cried everything would be ten times worse.

"If it *is* true," I heard, "I think the Corn Queen must've cast a spell on him or something, because that's the only explanation."

Why do they hate me so much?

"Maybe the Medusa hair turned his brain to stone."

"Your thoughts on Tamora, Miss Lowell," Mr. Longhaven said loudly, over the mocking and peering at me from behind his wire-rimmed glasses. "Do *you* think she's just as evil as the men in *Titus Andronicus*?"

"Um, no, I don't," I said, swallowing hard, trying to keep my breathing steady and compose my thoughts on the Shakespearian play while everyone stared at me like they wanted me to fail. My skin burned and my hands shook. "I—I think she's also a sort of victim, though obviously not as innocent as Lavinia."

"How can you say that?"

I turned in my seat to see that the red-haired guy from the Toms—Corbin—was leaning back in his chair, looking at me like I was an idiot. His tone was mocking and aggressive as he said, "She's a murderer who cheers on her sons when they attack Titus's daughter. How can you call her a victim?"

He was smirking, like my thoughts were the funniest thing he'd ever heard, and I wanted to punch him right in his tattoo.

God, how does he have a tattoo already?

His white button-down was buttoned down to mid-chest, just enough to expose the Gothic cross tattoo that was inked on the center of his breastbone. His tie was loosened but tied just beneath the cross, and something about the intentionality of his style felt . . . grossly overthought.

Like he'd spent way too much grooming time in front of the mirror.

I hated him and I hated everything.

So much.

"Wait your turn, Mr. Archington," Longhaven said, but he looked happy that *Archington* wanted to argue with me.

Wonderful.

"Explain, Miss Lowell," Mr. Longhaven prodded.

Please leave me alone!

"She's, um, a victim of the patriarchy, I guess you could say," I answered, ignoring the *tsk* sound someone made on the other side of the classroom. "She sees that the only role for her to play, after her husband is murdered and she's taken captive, is that of a victim. So when given the opportunity, she copes—she *survives*—by behaving as violently as the men. I think she makes them forget her gender, temporarily, and forces them to see her as an equal *because* she's as disgustingly fierce and powerful as them."

"Interesting," Longhaven said, tilting his head and narrowing his eyes.

I wasn't sure how he meant that, but in spite of everything I was a little bit proud of my answer. I'd actually made my point, which was a miracle in and of itself with the way everyone was staring at me like they wished one of the overpriced light fixtures would fall from the sky and crush my freak body.

"And as soon as she *stops* behaving that way," I added, "they go right back to seeing her as a woman, and they kill her."

"After they feed her a pie made from her sons," the snotty girl behind me said. "Don't forget that part, *New Money*."

Rage suddenly took over for the sadness when she said that, because who the hell were these awful people? And what kind of place was this, where the students felt completely comfortable being dicks *in front of* the teacher, and in front of the entire class?

I looked over my shoulder and hated the smug expression on her face because I could tell she thought she'd owned me.

Hated it so much that I replied, "I could never, *Headband*."

Gahhhhhh, idiot! I wanted to roll my eyes at my stupid big mouth, but it'd been impossible to keep it closed when the mean girl was wearing what appeared to be a diamond-encrusted headband.

I heard a couple of people laugh at that—*thanks, guys*—but things did *not* get better for me after that.

Oh no.

Because everyone started calling me "New Money."

To my face.

It was no longer a whisper.

When I accidentally bumped into a guy on my way to lunch:

"My bad, *New Money*."

When I held the library door open for the girl behind me: "Thanks, *New Money*."

When I passed out papers in chem class: "I still need one, *New Money*."

The name followed me around all day long. Accompanied by cocky smiles, sneering looks, and piercing giggles.

Why is everyone here so awful??

I somehow made it through the day without melting into a puddle of tears, but my face must've showed exactly how close I was to that when Donovan and Jasmine met me at the exit saying, "You're coming with us."

Ten minutes later, I followed as they strolled through Zabar's, where we'd gone directly after school because Donovan *needed* chocolate babka.

I had no idea what babka actually was. Cake, maybe . . . ?

"It's totally a jealousy thing," Jasmine said as she looked at the cheese behind the glass. "You have the audacity to interest the guy who's never been interested in them and they can't handle that."

"No one is jealous," I said, picking up a package of crackers. "Trust me."

My mood was improving by the minute, mostly because it felt amazing to be with people who didn't hate me after being at the academy all day. And also because Zabar's was the "Happy Thanksgiving back" market from the movie *You've Got Mail*. My brain was geeking out the entire time as I pictured Kathleen Kelly trying to use her card in the cash-only line.

And as someone who'd spent her entire life helping out in a market, I was in *awe* of their inventory and couldn't imagine what their ordering days must look like.

I mean, the cheese alone in this place.

"Yeah, but aside from his heavy flirting, Damion doesn't really *do* the Gardenwood social scene," Jasmine said as we headed for the checkouts. "He goes to the occasional party with Beckett, and he's dated a girl or two over the years, but he's kind of a mystery because, for the most part, he avoids everyone after hours."

"Yeah, it's more of a 'what does she have that we don't' thing that's pissing everyone off," Donovan said, putting her groceries on the belt.

"Agreed," Jasmine said, nodding. "How dare *you*, someone who isn't good enough to fit in at the academy, nab one of their finest?"

Jasmine was blunt and I knew she meant no harm, but her description of me stung.

Not good enough to fit in.

Because I felt that label crushing me like a fist every moment I spent traversing the halls of the academy. Every look, every whisper I couldn't quite make out, every snarky giggle of *New Money*, seemed to repeat that sentiment.

Not good enough to fit in.

"I haven't *nabbed* Damion, for the record," I said as we left the store and started walking down the block. "We're just friends."

Ha! It was almost hard to say that with a straight face.

Friends.

As if.

"Speaking of that," Jasmine said, sounding excited, "my mom said that his mom is *definitely* hosting the ball this year and will *definitely* be forcing him to do the season."

"Shut *up*!" Donovan's mouth dropped open and her eyes got huge. "Seriously? He's for sure going balling?"

"Gross, let's not make *that* a thing," Jasmine said with an eye roll as the light changed and we started crossing. "And yes. The Rutledges are hosting the *Age of Innocence* ball, which means—"

"Which means that Damion and his date are going to be the first dance of the night, where everyone stands around and watches them in awe," Donovan said on a gasp. "Holy shit—that could be you!"

Sounds like a nightmare to me, I thought, but just said, "Trust me, it will not be me."

While we walked, we tore into the babka, which was so good I could've eaten the entire loaf myself. I wolfed down the bread and listened as they described the theme of this year's ball.

As someone with a book obsession, I liked the idea of the book theme.

I might be ass at math, but I *loved* literature.

Thrillers, romance, true crime, horror, classics—I was a *gimme all* kind of reader.

Because there was just something about getting lost in another experience, in forgetting all about your life while riding along on someone else's journey, that was the sweetest escape. I mean, after the day I'd had, I couldn't *wait* to run up to the library when I got home and lose myself.

Yet the fact that someone was using *The Age of Innocence*—a book that explored the falseness of high society—as the theme of an extravagant ball seemed wild to me.

But as Jasmine and Donovan talked enthusiastically about the gowns they were having made, squealing as they used words like "bustles" and "corsets," I figured maybe I was guilty of overthinking.

I was likely the one missing the point, since I knew nothing of the season whatsoever.

Thank God.

CHAPTER FIFTEEN

"Most of the people I'm related to are insufferable."

—Remington

Damion

"For Christ's sake, you can't *make* me go to a dance."

"Damion Rutledge," my mother said in outrage, her eyes huge in her face as a waiter filled her wineglass. She'd gone from squealing like an overexcited tween over the news that she'd been awarded the ball—we were apparently this year's host family—to very nearly spitting my name in righteous anger. "You're going, and stop calling it a 'dance,' for God's sake."

"Isn't that what a ball is, Mother?" My teeth were clenched so tightly that my jaw was starting to ache. "A big, ridiculously expensive dance?"

I glanced over her shoulder and could see that Coco and her parents were being seated beside the fireplace. Members of the Gardenwood Athletic Club didn't technically have reserved spots in the restaurant, but that was definitely their *unofficial* table.

I suspected Coco and her mother—*Chantel*—preferred the way the flames illuminated their perfect skin.

Natural lighting at its finest . . . for people from *hell.*

"Stop it. Stop being obtuse," she snapped, lowering her voice but not even dimming her rage. "How is it going to look if you aren't there?"

"Like a ball full of people minus one Damion," I said.

I wasn't going.

I *wasn't.*

"Listen to me now," she said, leaning in a little. "The season is a fundraiser for *your* school, and all your father's business partners will be there. You *will* be there."

I sighed and dragged a hand through my hair, realizing I needed to calm down.

Making her defensive was a terrible plan.

"I get it, Mom, and I want you to have this, but I'm sure we can find a way—"

"Dammit, Damion," my dad said, slamming his phone down on the table.

Apparently our disagreement had *ruined* the joy of whatever he'd been doing on his phone. His jaw was tight and his eyes told me that he'd *had* it.

"Quit being a child about this—you're going. Period. We're your parents, you live under our roof, and we make the rules," he said, grabbing his Scotch. "If we say you're going, you're going."

"Aww, this is so wholesome," I said, slowly shaking my head because his words sounded so . . . domestic, so familial. "Your house, your rules? Are we on a Disney show now?"

Spoiler: We were not.

We came and went, lived under the same roof, and shared meals as a threesome every evening at a table that actually seated twenty comfortably. That was it. And it'd always been okay because I'd been able to escape to Remi's. But now that escape was gone.

The *Lowells* were living in my oasis.

And I truly had no idea what was going to happen now.

It kept me up at night, wondering how his decision to give away his house and money would affect me, but I trusted him enough to be confident there was still a way. I knew he'd take care of me.

Because Uncle Rem and I had had a plan, dammit.

Once you turn eighteen and graduate, kid, it becomes YOUR life.

Mine to do with as *I* wanted. And what I'd wanted, more than anything in the world, was to move in with Remi.

The plan had been for me to live with him for the summer before going away to college in the fall. He was going to come back from Nebraska in time to "hang with me all summer" before I took off for Colorado.

But here's where it got tricky.

Remi was supposed to help me break the bad news to my parents. He was supposed to be there, by my side, while I told them what I was doing, and then he was going to help me make *my* dream happen.

Because I didn't want that Ivy League life.

"Knock it off," my father said, his eyes telling me he was in no mood for my attitude. His gaze wandered over to the Chattinghams, and he raised a hand in greeting before he said, "It's wasting everybody's time if you rebel on this, because you don't have a choice."

"Come on, Dad," I said, keeping the cool mockery in my tone because I hated letting him think he got to me. "Do you really give a damn about a ball?"

"Of course not," he said with a scowl. "But this is about a lot more than a ball and you know it."

Oh yes, I thought. It was about me imprinting myself upon his colleagues, reminding them with my ass-kissing presence at every social function that I would be coming aboard shortly and I was another one of them.

Rutledge, God of Finance.

"Spare me," I muttered.

"It is exhausting, Damion, the way you're constantly going out of your way to be difficult. Just do the damn season with Coco and get on with it."

With Coco??

I stared at my father and knew, God help me, that he wasn't asking.

Was this why Coco had started acting . . . friendly when I saw her? Were our parents in on this together?

"And it doesn't have to be a big thing," my mother said. "You and Coco have always been friends—"

"We have *never* been friends," I said in disgust, my stomach sinking because I did NOT. Want. To. Take. Coco.

"So you can just take her to the ball—skip the pre-parties if you want, have an easy night with someone you've known your entire life, then put the season behind you. It's not the big thing you're making it out to be."

An easy night.

With Coco Chattingham.

It was like my mother couldn't hear herself or something.

"Easy" and "Chattingham" did not mix. They were old money, owned half of Manhattan, and succeeded at literally *everything* they did.

Everyone knew you didn't mess with Chantel Chattingham. She had a reputation for zero tolerance for anything—or anyone—she didn't like. You still couldn't say the name *Fiona Harper* without wondering what had *actually* happened to the woman who'd challenged her spot on the guild board.

And Charles had the same reputation in his world. He ruined businessmen instead of wives, entrepreneurs instead of PTA members.

"Oh, you have, too," my dad said, looking *this* close to rolling his eyes, if he were the type of person to roll his eyes.

But he wasn't.

He was above that pedestrian bullshit.

"You used to play together at the park, for God's sake," he said. "You've known her your whole life."

"And . . . ?"

"And the fact that Charles is on our board and you'll be running the company someday should make it obvious to you what a great ally she would be."

I am seventeen!

I seemed to be the only one aware that I was a teenager and didn't give a shit about business "allies" and advisory boards. I rubbed the back of my neck and didn't know how to respond, because I also didn't want to fight.

"Can you even imagine the photos?" my mother said with a buzzed smile. "Her pale hair next to your dark curls—"

"The fear in my eyes next to her spinning head—"

"Your height, her petiteness," she continued as if I hadn't spoken.

"My dying soul, her *Exorcist*-style vomiting—"

"Can you stop?" my dad snapped, his nostrils flaring in anger. "Can you stop being the sardonic little shit all the time and just do the right thing for once? There doesn't always have to be a sarcastic monologue to accompany our life, you know."

He literally saw taking Coco to a fucking ball as me "doing the right thing."

I swallowed and wondered what it felt like to have choices. "Will you excuse me?" I said, not waiting for permission as I stood and looked for an escape. "I need air. I'll be right back."

My chest burned because I knew I'd lost.

I liked to think I was smart, but the truth was that I was spineless when it came to my dad. I became the eight-year-old version of myself when he raised his voice and listed demands.

Which meant I was taking Coco Chattingham to the motherfucking ball.

I took a deep breath and exited the dining room. Hopefully a walk to the men's room would reroute the conversation and by the time I got back, we'd have moved on to something less threatening to my well-being.

Talks of proposed lobotomies, perhaps.

Speaking of lobotomies, I'd made it three steps out of the restaurant when I heard, "Well, if it isn't Rutledge."

I looked to my right and there, bellied up to the bar, was Corbin Archington.

"Hey, Arch," I said, taking his offered hand and doing the stupid bro handshake because it was easier than pissing him off. I looked at the empty stools beside him. "Drinking alone tonight?"

The Toms spent a fair amount of time socializing in the club's lounge, mostly because the bartenders got tipped a hell of a lot to spike their sodas with brown liquor.

Everybody knew it; nobody cared.

"Nah, the boys are on their way," he said, and I wondered what would compel a guy like him to think four necklaces and a half-buttoned shirt looked good. He spent half his life trying to showcase the tattoo he'd gotten in middle school, I swear to God.

Corbin had always reminded me of James Spader's character in that old movie *Pretty in Pink*. He moved too fast, talked too slick, behaved too shitty.

"Love that for you," I said. "Life is good when 'the boys' are on the way."

"Right?" he said with a commiserating smile.

Corbin *never* caught on to my sarcasm, which felt disappointing in a way because I really enjoyed ruining his smarmy version of happiness, but it was probably for the best. It was less of a hassle to just ignore the idiocy that was "the boys."

"So let me ask you something," he said, tilting his head. "Are you really having a thing with the new chick from Oklahoma?"

I saw "the new chick" as an enemy of sorts, yet I still wanted to punch this assbag for even mentioning her. That was how much of a douche he was. He made me want to defend the person who'd probably stolen my future.

"It's Nebraska, and nah," I said. "Just talking to her."

"Taking inventory of the new stock, yeah?" he said with a laugh, and I wondered why he'd even asked if he was writing his own version of my reality. "Checking out the new product?"

God, he made my blood boil. "You're hysterical—have you always been this funny, Corbin?" I asked.

"I mean," he said, shrugging and grinning.

"Right? *So* damned witty," I said, wondering how *this* guy was going to Yale next year. Surely there were thousands of rejected applicants more intelligent than he, right? "Listen, I've got to run, but it was great catching up. Buy the boys a shot for me, okay?"

"Sure thing, Damion," he said.

"Asshole," I muttered under my breath as I headed for the restroom, shaking my head.

How the hell was this my life?

CHAPTER SIXTEEN

"I love a woman with a plan."

—Remington

Julia

What is happening?

I was trying to focus on the equation, but Clank had just jumped up onto Damion's lap.

And Damion wasn't pushing her off. He was *petting* her.

"No, you missed a step," Damion said, rubbing a hand over Clank's back as he watched my calculations from behind those glasses.

"What?" I stopped writing and looked down at the paper.

"Here," he said, reaching over the cat's head to point his pencil at my work. "Right there."

Clank had clearly lost her mind. Her ability to read a room and be an asshole *to* an asshole must have taken a vacation, because she was arching into his touch like they were best friends.

She was purring.

So loudly.

"Oh yeah," I said, unwilling to acknowledge the cat in the room because I didn't want to interrupt whatever this moment was. "Forgot."

"Does that make sense?" he asked, and *what the hell?* If I didn't know him, I'd think he was a cat guy. The nonchalant way he was petting Clank was super cat-lady-core.

But that wasn't possible.

This was Damion Rutledge, for God's sake.

"It does," I said, starting over, reworking the problem, amazed that it was making sense.

He was a very good teacher.

Honestly, I was shocked by how smoothly the tutoring thing was going. Aside from the one session at the coffee shop, we worked on math at my house. He seemed to prefer that. Damion stopped by after school, and we settled right into studying and were fully locked-in for an hour.

I mean, he usually had one or two sarcastic observations to make upon his arrival, *of course*, but once we started working, he became my teacher.

The whole thing was surprisingly professional.

As soon as I finished the problem, the alarm on my phone started chirping.

"What's that for?" he asked, still running his big hand up and down Clank's back.

I set down my pencil and turned off the alarm. "I've got a hard stop time today."

Don't ask me why.

"Why?" He watched as I stood and reached for my backpack.

"I . . . have, um, plans," I said, not really wanting to share what I was doing.

"No, you don't," he said definitively, his eyebrows furrowing like I'd said something ridiculous.

"Yes, I do."

"Seriously," he said, his eyes on my face like he was waiting for the *real* answer. "Why?"

"Oh my God—I can't have plans?" I asked, annoyed.

Damion gave me a deadpan stare, a look that told me he definitely didn't think I could have plans. *Rude.*

"Fine," I said, rolling my eyes. "If you must know, I'm going to Times Square."

"Dear God, why?" he asked in disgust, calmly placing Clank on the floor before standing. "I'd rather be drawn and quartered."

"Really relevant reference there, Rutledge, and because I've never been," I said, pulling my backpack over my shoulders. "I know it's touristy and cliché and you're far too sophisticated to ever make an appearance up there, but I've never seen it and I want to."

"Down," he said.

"What?"

"*Down* there," he corrected. "You are *up*town, and Times Square is—"

"Whatever, same difference, you know what I mean," I said.

That made his eyebrows screw together and his eyes narrow. "Are you going with your brother?" he asked, looking down at his watch.

It wasn't the Rolex today, though—it was an Apple Watch. He'd probably decided to go casual with the jewelry since he was wearing the sweater version of his uniform instead of the blazer and tie.

He has a very broad chest, I thought to myself. Not that I cared, but I figured he must work out a lot because it was incredibly . . . solid underneath that V-neck sweater.

My brain remembered from the basketball courts.

The boy was positively pectoral.

He probably swims laps at the athletic club or plays some rich-guy sport I know nothing about, like cricket.

Polo, maybe.

Of course, that made me picture him on a horse, and wow, Damion Rutledge—in my head—looked really natural sitting on top of a horse.

"No—he's grabbing dinner with friends," I said, annoyed over that, because how was it possible that Liam had already found people who liked him enough to want his company on a Friday night, but I'd barely found anyone who didn't want to snarkily scoff at me when I merely passed them in the hallway at school? I had Jasmine and Donovan, thank

God, but Liam already seemed to have an entire army of friends.

I inhaled through my nose, feeling like a loser as I admitted, "So it's just me."

He didn't say anything. Just the typical Damion analytical stare.

"What? I like doing things by myself. Don't judge."

"I'm not," he said. "I *prefer* being by myself, so I get it."

"Yeah, I can see that about you," I agreed as he pulled his leather cross-body bag over his shoulder.

I needed to get going, because I'd selected today, and this specific time of day, for my first subway ride to Times Square, for multiple reasons. I wanted to head there when it was still light out, see all the bright lights just when it was getting dark, and then get home before it was too late.

And before my parents got home.

They were having dinner at the athletic club tonight, and I knew they'd have reservations about me taking the subway and traversing the city by myself when we hadn't really left our neighborhood since we'd arrived.

Damion and I walked out of the house together and said goodbye, and I started walking toward the subway station. My eyes were on my phone's map app as I headed down the street.

I'd made it a block when I heard him.

"Julia!"

I stopped and turned around, only to see Damion walking toward me with an annoyed expression on his face, like a parent who was irritated that their child forgot their scarf and gloves at school.

"What?" I said when he reached me.

His eyes moved over my face, like he was gathering thoughts as his dark gaze roamed, and then they met mine. "Where are you going?"

"To the subway station," I said. "I told you that."

He sighed. "Do you want me to take you?"

My mouth dropped open and I didn't know what to say. Did he mean—

"Don't overthink this, Nebraska, because we both know I'm not a nice guy," he said, sounding like he was unhappy with himself. "But the thought of you wandering through the crowds with your wide eyes and Nebraska face is just too alarming for words."

"My *Nebraska face*?"

"You know what I mean," he said.

"I do *not*, actually."

"Let's just say you don't hide your thoughts well," he clarified. "Every person with bad intentions in that nightmarish square is going to take one look at you and know you're a tourist."

"I'm not a tourist," I replied, offended by his description. "I live here."

"You know what I mean," he said again, this time with a big sigh. "And how well do you know the subway lines?"

I shrugged and tried being cool. "Well enough."

"Really?"

I shrugged again. "It doesn't look hard to navigate. Little kids do it all the time."

"New Yorkers," he clarified. "They're a different breed of toddlers, take it from me. I was one. Listen, I'm not going to force myself on you here, but if you want an escort, just to guide you there and show you a few things, I've got a couple free hours."

"I thought you said you aren't a nice guy."

"Oh, I'm definitely not," he said, taking his turn looking offended. "I just don't want to live with the survivor guilt after you get mowed down by a double-decker bus because you're smiling up at the dancing lights, oblivious to your surroundings."

"For the record," I said, "the first time we met I kicked your ass, so I think I can handle myself."

"For the record," he replied with a smirk, "the first time we met you lost your wallet *and* almost got hit by a car."

"Leave it to you to make it sound negative."

"Leave it to me to make it honest." He put his hands in his pockets and said, "Listen, I can call for a car so we don't have to take—"

"I'm taking the subway," I interrupted, because I'd been dying to try it since the second we pulled into town. My parents seemed to be afraid of it, always insisting we walk or have Bernard get a car, but I wanted to become *that* New Yorker.

I wanted to know where to grab a train, how to take a train, and which train went where—*take the "one train" to Midtown.*

If we were going to live here, I needed to experience all of it.

"Fine," he said. "But you're going the wrong way."

"No, I'm not. There's a station over there," I said, pointing. "And—"

"And it's faster to go this way and catch the express train." He took the phone out of my hand, clicked the button that turned off the screen, then slid it into the pocket of my blazer. "Put the phone away and I will teach you."

I swallowed as I felt his fingers graze the inside of my pocket.

"Wait. Damion the Tutor is taking me downtown?" I said, although as soon as I said it, I got a weird feeling in my stomach.

Because Damion the Tutor.

Oh God.

That guy might be more dangerous than Damion the Evil.

CHAPTER SEVENTEEN

"Poetry hits harder in New York."

—Remington

Damion

What the hell is she smiling at?

We stood there on the platform, waiting for the express, and she was looking down at the tracks with a little half smile on her face.

"What are we staring at here?" The stench was a little stenchier than usual at the moment, the platform was packed, and a baby in a stroller to our left was screaming his head off.

Basically a typical day in the subway, but she was grinning.

"I'm looking for a rat," she said quietly, leaning closer, so no one else would hear what she was saying.

"Why would you be doing that . . . ?" I followed her gaze down to the tracks, where she was peering at a spot where someone had thrown wrappers and empty bottles.

"Because I want to see a New York City rat in person," she said. "I know they're gross dirty little things, the scourge of the city, but after seeing footage so many times of rats carrying off food they find on the subway tracks, I would freak out if I saw it happen in person."

"You'd fangirl over a subway rat."

"Kind of," she said with a giggle.

I wanted to mock the absurdity of the things she was saying, but it was just so disarmingly childlike in the moment that I couldn't.

The sound of the incoming train brought her gaze to mine and she grinned again.

"I think the train is almost here," she said excitedly.

Like a little kid, I thought, but only said, "No shit, Nebraska."

A few seconds later, it came to a stop in front of us. The doors slid open and we stepped inside.

The train was packed, so sitting wasn't an option. I grabbed the first pole inside the doors, and she stood beside me.

But she didn't grab on to anything, so when the train started moving, she lurched, stumbling into me, her hands grabbing the front of my shirt.

"Sorry," she murmured, fast-blinking in surprise but not letting go.

Something about the feel of her fingertips and the press of her soft body as it leaned into mine sent a zap through me, a buzz of tingling awareness as brown eyes looked up, as my brain calculated the distance between her mouth and mine.

Shit.

Her perfume was suddenly all I could smell as *she* took over my senses—sight, smell, touch, dear *Lord*.

As if reading my mind, Julia widened her stance and let go of me, her cheeks going bright pink.

And it was the flush of her cheeks that made me lower my mouth to her ear and say, "Falling for me already, huh?"

Cheesy, yeah, but I swear to God she shivered.

I lifted my head and looked down at her. *Had she?*

She rolled her eyes, *of course*, but then I felt them take a slow stroll over my face, like she was thinking or looking for something.

No, dammit.

I reached down, grabbed her hand, and wrapped it around the pole beside mine. My hand resting softly on hers. Warm, soft, smooth . . .

Fuck.

"Always hold on to something, Nebraska," I snapped, pulling myself out of those brown eyes.

But then her fingers moved underneath my grip to shake my hand off, and I couldn't help myself. I winked at her.

She rolled her eyes again, but her teeth were nibbling on that lower lip like she was thinking hard.

What are you thinking, honey?

I didn't care—I *didn't*—but I'd be lying if I said I wasn't curious about the thoughts that always looked like they were pinging around in that head of hers. Especially as the train traveled downtown, because there was something about the way her eyes darted to the open doors at every stop. The second the doors opened, her brown eyes were moving out to the platform as if she was checking to see where we were or how much farther we had to go.

"We're getting off at Forty-Second," she said to me, trying to prove to me she knew where she was going.

Adorable.

"Works for me," I said with a shrug, glaring at the annoyingly sweet smug look on her face.

"That is so wild," she said quietly, her eyes on a couple with two toddlers. "Both those little kids knew exactly how to step on the train, and they went right over to the seats without even checking with their parents first."

"It's not rocket science," I said, noticing that the freckles on her nose were all kind of the same size. A constellation of tiny dots.

"I know that, but they're so young. How old were you when you did this by yourself for the first time?" she asked, gesturing as if "this" magical subway ride were a beautiful rite of passage, part of some New York coming-of-age story.

"No idea," I said. "Feels like I was born doing it."

That was a lie.

I *didn't* remember how old I'd been, but I'd taken the subway with Remi a thousand times when I was a kid. He'd called it the "quintessential New York ride" and said it was his duty to make sure I was intimately acquainted with the city's "gritty underground." He gave me subway maps to study, and then we'd explore the city with me leading the way. But whenever I took off in the entirely wrong direction, he'd laugh and say we'd get to explore new stations.

Remi had loved New York like it was an actual person, and he'd been determined to show me her every feature, good and bad.

Fuck, even the subway makes me miss him.

I glanced over at Julia and—

"Did you just take a picture of that guy?" I asked, lowering my head to her ear so she could hear me.

That's the only reason. The quick hit of her flowery scent is just a bonus.

"No," she said, turning her head to give me a funny look. "I was taking a picture of the poem."

"What?" *Her hair smells like Bath and Body Works lotion,* I thought, *like flowers and flirting at the mall.*

I squinted and saw the poster hanging right above a guy in red pants. With a poem printed on it, part of a subway art installment.

But—*No way*, I thought as I read the words. The poem was "Thread" by Essex Hemphill.

It was one of the few poems I actually had memorized, one of those poems that seemed like it was for everyone because you didn't need to "get" poetry to "get" that one.

Trying not to think of you
yet your face colors
every contour

of my mind.
And every way I turn
inside of a minute
I collide
with your laughter.
I am wind,
and you
are chimes.

"You like that poem?" I asked, for some reason interested in her response.

She looked embarrassed, like she didn't want to admit it, but she nodded and said, "It's actually my favorite poem in the world."

She has a favorite poem.

I leaned in slightly closer. "Tell me your second favorite."

I don't think I expected her to have an answer, but her eyebrows furrowed for a second while she thought about it and then she said, "It's probably either 'On the Amtrak from Boston to New York City' or 'Stopping by Woods on a Snowy Evening.'"

Sherman Alexie and Robert Frost.

Well, shit, I thought, uncomfortable with this knowledge.

"No comment?" she asked, watching me like she was trying to figure me out.

But what comment could I possibly have?

Do you feel the words like I do?

I straightened, needing space. "Nope."

I cleared my throat and turned my attention to my phone.

We got off at Forty-Second, and just as we were stepping off the train, Lori—the marketing guru at the shelter—was coming on.

"Well, if it isn't my favorite volunteer," she said with a smile. "Long time no see."

"Right?" I saw Julia's eyes dip to the logo on Lori's polo—a dog and a cat wrapped around the letters *ACC*—as I said, "How's it going?"

"Good," she said. "We miss you."

"Same," I said, because it was true.

I'd *loved* volunteering at the shelter. Remi got me the gig when I was in middle school, and it'd been a dream job for a kid whose parents felt like animals and pets were a waste of money, time, and resources. *Bleeding hearts, those two.*

"Then come see us—you know we always need help," she said just as the overhead voice said, "Stand clear of the closing doors."

"Ooh, saved by the bell," I said.

Lori was great, like the mom to everyone at the shelter, and she laughed. "Looks like."

I could feel Julia's eyes on me when the doors closed.

"What?" I said, looking down at her as she glared at me with narrowed eyes and a tilted head.

"Who was that?" she asked.

"None of your business," I said.

"Do you . . . *volunteer* at an animal shelter?" Her tone made it clear that she didn't believe I was capable of doing anything nice, let alone volunteering.

"Again, none of your business," I said, giving her arm a little push to get her moving. "Let's go."

I tried keeping my eyes off her legs when she climbed the steps in front of me, but they were . . . *distracting*, to say the least.

"Holy *shit*," she said when we exited.

We weren't even in the heart of Times Square, but the fact that it was starting to get dark and the lights were so insanely bright set her off.

"Just look," she said, grinning. She stopped still on the busy sidewalk, as I grabbed her sleeve and started her moving again.

"See, this is why I'm here," I said. "You're going to get trampled if you stop and look around."

"Oh, calm down, I can handle myself," she said, and I could tell she believed it.

I felt the bump of people around us, watched a mangy Minnie Mouse walk toward kids who were beaming with too much energy, while eager visitors wearing *I ❤ NY* T-shirts climbed aboard red tourist buses sporting massive Broadway show ads.

What the fuck am I doing HERE?

New Yorkers would rather be caught dead than in Times Square, and everything around me was the reason why. Not only were the tourists wandering around way too slowly, but Times Square was where chaos met insanity at the corner of madness. A place where the absolute pulsing, out-of-control energy of New York decided to meet up and have an obnoxious party. There were hustlers hustling, dudes peddling fake Prada, influencers trying to get photos, cabs and cyclists ignoring the laws of traffic (though traffic laws didn't apply in New York City), and tourists congregating in packs.

It was claustrophobic madness.

And I was standing in the middle of it.

With a girl who was acting like she was enjoying every maddening second of it.

Because Julia was beaming.

"Dear God, look at your face," I said, smiling in spite of myself. "Do you actually love this?"

"No," she said, her grin so big it made her eyes all squinty. "This is madness and I can't imagine anyone liking it, but I'm also amazed that I'm here."

"Isn't this where you wanted to go?" I asked.

"That's not what I mean. I mean I can't believe I'm actually standing *here*, in this place," she explained breathlessly. "It's dirty and disgusting and absolutely magical, because for my entire life, as far back as I can remember, I've seen some version of this on-screen and on New Year's Eve. It's like the center of the world, the place everyone who isn't from here has witnessed from their living rooms. So even though it's madness, it's surreal that I am actually standing here. It's like the intersection of my imagination and reality or something."

I looked at her animated face, at eyes that were practically dancing with excitement as they took in the lights, and I almost felt . . . *moved*, as bizarre as that sounded.

But I'd never *gotten* it before.

My entire life, this hellscape had been a great big question mark to me. I'd always wondered how anyone could like this or why in God's name people would want to sit on those Times Square steps and watch the madness transpiring around them.

But she kind of made it make sense.

I was familiar with the awe of traveling to a place you'd only imagined, the thrill of actually standing in *that spot*. I'd just never considered that Times Square might be *that spot* to some people.

"I've never thought of it that way before," I said, looking around, trying to see it through different eyes.

"Probably because you've always lived here," she said, then added cheekily, "Maybe you need to get out and expand your horizons a little."

"Oh, this from Nebraska," I said to the little wiseass with the know-it-all smirk. "Tell me everywhere *you've* been, world traveler."

She bit down on her lip and raised her eyes before saying, "Florida, Nebraska, and New York."

"Wow," I said. "Quite the explorer."

And quite the shitty liar.

People with millions traveled, so her admission was a dead giveaway. She was New Money if she'd never been anywhere.

I trailed her closely, watching as she took flyers from everyone who offered them and said, "No, thank you," to three separate tour bus operators instead of just ignoring them like I'd suggested.

Which made them follow her and try to convince her she needed to ride.

Which made her utter, "No, thank you," three more times.

"Back the fuck off," I finally had to growl at the especially obnoxious one when Julia wasn't looking, because he wasn't giving up.

"Relax, man," the guy said.

"I will if you do," I said, pushing him out of the way as I walked by.

The crowd was growing tighter as we tried making our way forward.

"Do you have an actual location in mind, or are we just perusing here?" I said, trying to squeeze through the people I was suddenly shoulder to shoulder with.

And that's when I saw it . . .

We were nearing the theater district. Just as people were heading for the Friday night shows. Rookie mistake.

Shit.

The great mass influx of Broadway showgoers was beginning.

Which meant there was a crush of people heading toward us.

But Julia kept forging ahead, going against the grain and slowly creating distance between us, distance that was immediately filled with pedestrian cross-traffic.

I wasn't sure why, but it made me nervous, the way she was disappearing from my line of sight while being swallowed by the crowd. I grabbed the back of her shirt, barely able to reach it, and I jerked her toward me, snaking my hand around her waist to stop her forward motion.

But the movement made her body crash into mine.

Anchoring her against me, her back to my front.

Oh God.

Suddenly my face was in her mass of sweet-smelling curls, my palm on her stomach, my every brain cell exploding from the close proximity of her.

Her.

She looked at me over her shoulder with wide eyes, and I needed to release her. But the way she was looking up at me, so close with the longest lashes, rendered me unable to fucking move.

What is happening?

"It's a little nuts right now," I said into her ear, my voice stupid raspy, *what the hell.* "Stay close."

She nodded, looking slightly shaken.

Yeah, same.

All I'd been trying to do was keep her close so she didn't get trampled, yet suddenly I had a handful of Julia Nebraska that I wasn't hating. Her clean-sweet scent wrapped itself around my head and made me drunk, I swear to God.

Under the influence.

It was the only explanation, because this was *her*, for fuck's sake.

Her.

A guy in a NASCAR jacket and cowboy hat bumped into us—*idiot*—and suddenly I was no longer holding her steady.

Which, like, *thank God* and also *dammit.*

But it left me no choice.

I *had* to.

I grabbed her hand and linked all five of my fingers through hers, squeezing hard. Which wasn't holding her hand, for the record—it was me holding *on* to her hand to keep her out of harm's way.

Her eyes shot to mine again, her gaze no less questioning than when she'd been in my arms.

"That way," I said, my voice still doing that gravelly thing as I pointed toward the cross street. "Let's go."

CHAPTER EIGHTEEN

"I want La Masseria's meatballs in my mouth
every minute of my life."

—Remington

Julia

Damion is holding my hand.

Holy, holy shit, Damion Rutledge is holding my hand.

Sure, I knew it was because I was about to be swallowed up by the massive crowd, but still . . . Damion Rutledge was holding my hand.

What the . . . ?

He'd pulled me against him and spoken like *that*, his lips almost touching my ear, his voice deep and low. Warm breath on my skin as he guided me out of the throngs of people, and when we finally got to a stopping point, he asked, "Where to now, Nebraska?"

I don't know, I'm having trouble thinking right now!

"Umm. Uh . . . Rockefeller Center," I said, avoiding eye contact. My cheeks were hot, my voice caught in my throat. I wasn't ready to meet his gaze just yet.

Maybe ever.

To say I was slightly flustered was an understatement.

He nodded. "Lead the way."

I appreciated what he was doing. That he wasn't trying to change my plans or get in my way. But . . . why?

What is he playing at? I wondered.

I'm sure the lifted eyebrow on my face gave me away when Damion nodded forward. "Shall we? Or would you prefer standing still like this a little longer?"

He lifted his hand, where mine was still securely *intertwined* in his. Dear Lord.

Have I really not let go yet??

As if reading my mind, he let loose with a devilish grin. I felt his thumb slide over mine—slow, soft—as he stepped closer and said with *all* the cocky attitude, "I mean, if you're in the mood to blow off some steam and linger around a little longer, Jules, I know a place—"

"Let's go," I said, ripping my hand out of his, annoyed by his smug laughter.

Welcome back, Damion the Evil.

And, okay—fine. It was nice that he was helping me navigate the chaos of New York City, but did he have to look like THAT while doing it?

Those stupid glasses.

That stupid smile.

That stupid deep . . . deep . . . absurdly deep voice. Low and gravelly—

Snap out of it, Jules!

"So do you never come down here?" I asked while we walked. "One of those things that you do as a tourist but as a local you avoid at all costs?"

"I mean, yes and no," he said. "I try to avoid it because for the most part it's shit, but sometimes you have to head to the shit. The only way to see shows is to come down here."

"You like Broadway plays?" I asked.

"I do," he said, which surprised me. He seemed far too . . . *no-nonsense* for plays. "I mean, don't you want to hit some shows, now that you're here?"

"Uhh . . ."

"Not at all?" He sounded shocked.

"I'm just not a fan of musicals—too much singing."

His scoff was louder than the city traffic. "Come on—*Hamilton* . . . ?"

"I saw it on Disney Plus, and I just couldn't get over the fact that they sang the whole entire time."

"You uncultured swine." He scowled. "Who doesn't love *Hamilton*?"

"I didn't say I didn't love it, I said it was too much singing."

"Maybe you just need to see the right musical," he said.

"Really?" The idea of Damion loving theater was a little bit shocking. But then again, so was the idea of him working at an animal shelter. I still wasn't sure if I believed it.

"Sure," he said. "The thing about a musical is that it makes you feel things deeply, because the music heightens the emotions, so it's worth searching out the ones that might move you. I cried my eyes out the first time I saw *Dear Evan Hansen*."

"You did?" I said on a gasp, more surprised he was sharing this piece of vulnerable info than I was by the image of him crying, which was honestly impossible to picture. "And here I thought you were an unemotional robot."

"I mean, I am, but even robots need their joints oiled every once in a while, right?"

"Wow, so profound . . . and gross."

"Seriously, though," he said, stopping at a red light. "When it comes to film and books and the arts in general, you're rewarded when they make you feel, even when they make you feel bad, right? Some of the best books are the ones that destroy you because they ultimately change the fabric of who you are."

What??

The way he said that, so matter-of-factly, was mind-blowing. Absolutely the most surprising thing he'd done since I'd met him. Because I wholeheartedly agreed with what he said and believed it to my core, though I doubt I could've communicated it in such an eloquent way.

Who is this guy?

"Yeah," I said, trying to recover from this new side of Damion. "I totally agree."

Will hadn't been a reader. His taste in movies tended to skew toward "sporty," and I didn't think he'd ever gone to a play in his life.

He was all about football, football, and more football, which was what made even just *discussing* the arts with Damion feel monumental.

And not just because he was Damion the Evil, but because he was sincerely interested.

"My mom hates anything sad," he said, gesturing for me to walk when the light changed. "Which I get, but I also feel like life is about *feeling*, right? Like really feeling things deeply to your core, good or bad. You can go along for the easy ride, or you can put yourself in the path of the moving train and let yourself feel every bump, every turn, every horrific crash."

I wanted to make fun of him, to mock him for being so deep, to give back at him all the Nebraska jabs he'd shoved my way, but I couldn't.

Was he aware how much he was oversharing with *me*?

Or did he just not care?

"'Poetry, beauty, romance, love—these are what we stay alive for,'" I said, half to myself, remembering the quote from *Dead Poets Society*.

"Are you seriously quoting Mr. Keating to me?" he asked, looking at me out of the corner of his eyes.

"Are you *seriously* saying you recognize that quote?" I asked, beaming in his direction. I didn't *mean* to do it, but this meant that he'd watched my favorite movie more than once.

Which meant I understood something about him somehow.

Is it possible that there's more to this Damion than I thought?

Maybe . . .

We walked around Rockefeller Center, Damion making fun of me for saying "excuse me" too many times, walking too slowly, and making a wish in one of the fountains.

"Locals don't make wishes in wells, Nebraska."

"Maybe that explains why they all seem so unhappy, then, *New York*."

When we finished at Rockefeller Center, I mentioned wanting to stop somewhere to eat.

"Do you have a particular place in mind?" he asked.

"No, not really. Too many choices."

Damion shoved his hands in his pockets, rocking on his heels and acting as if I'd spoken in Klingon. "How can there be too many options for food, Nebraska? An indecisive princess, are we?"

Ugh. That smirk.

"Fine," I said with a sigh. "Suggest something, then."

"You said it, not me," he replied, and then he *winked*. "Don't regret it later."

A wink. *Another* wink.

Seriously, did Damion know any other language but flirting?

"Let me call an Italian place real quick. You like Italian?" he asked.

"Love."

"Perfect." He took out his phone and raised it to his ear. We took a couple of steps toward a building and out of the way of foot traffic. But I swear to God it sounded like he asked for someone by name, and then it sounded like he was speaking in *Italian*.

I watched him, watched his lips moving over words I didn't know, and I was pretty sure I was going to faint. Because what was this? What was my life? Damion Rutledge in all his Damion Rutledge glory was speaking Italian.

And *wow*, it was a powerful thing.

Weak knees powerful.

Smelling salts, please.

"Ciao, a presto," Damion said; then he hung up as I regained my balance.

"I'm sorry, were you just speaking in *Italian*?" I asked.

"Yeah," he said nonchalantly, as if it were normal. "An old family friend can always get me a table at his restaurant, but he speaks way better Italian than English."

"So you speak Italian," I said in awe. "Is that it, just the two languages?"

"French, Italian, Spanish, and Portuguese," he said so shockingly nonchalantly. "Although, my French is not very good."

I don't know what I expected him to say, but it wasn't four freaking languages, holy *crap*. For some reason, this made me feel even worse about my math difficulties, because it was intimidating how smart he was.

Or God, maybe it wasn't just him.

Did everyone with money speak a billion languages? Was I the only student at Gardenwood who wasn't multilingual? That would just be *fan*-freaking-tastic if there was yet another way for me to prove to the world I didn't belong.

"I'm sure it's better than mine," I said dumbly, remembering next to nothing of the language.

"Say something, Jules."

I cleared my throat, then said, *"Où sont les toilettes?"*

Instead of judging my pronunciation or my lame choice of phrase, he said with a dirty smirk, *"J'aime bien le son du français parlé par Nebraska."*

Smelling salts, please. ALL the smelling salts.

I opened my mouth to reply, but the combination of his French, mixed with the half smile, rendered me a tiny bit speechless.

Good God, I've swallowed my tongue.

And he knew, God help me, because something changed in his face. It was like he turned up the volume, the intensity of his flirt.

Damion leaned in a little closer, lowered his voice, and said, *"Tu as perdu ta langue, Jules?"*

A shiver ran down my spine, and I was once again reminded of just how dangerous he was. How glad I was that he didn't like me and I didn't like him, because he was a million miles out of my league of knowledge.

I mean, I couldn't even remember how to *speak* when he turned on the charm.

I cleared my throat. "Are we going to eat or what?" I asked, wanting to sound unfazed, disappointed when my voice came out all breathless.

Totally *fazed*.

Which made his half smile slide into a full-scale grin of satisfaction. "This way."

I followed him over to La Masseria, and when he pulled open the door, I was instantly charmed.

Cozy lighting made the place feel like coming home to a cottage on a rainy day. There was a stone arch behind the bar, making it look like a hearth, and wine bottles were everywhere. White linen, candles, and sparkling glasses were on each table, but somehow this fancy little restaurant didn't feel pretentious.

It felt *perfect*.

And smelled incredible.

As soon as we walked in, an older gentleman came over and gave Damion a hug, and the two of them spoke briefly.

In *Italian*.

And dear God, Damion became the most attractive human on earth as he said words I couldn't understand while smiling and laughing with this man who was clearly overjoyed to see him.

What the hell is wrong with me?

It didn't matter that to the naked eye he appeared—at the moment—to be a *nice* person who was also hot and speaking Italian. It didn't matter because I knew who he was, *what* he was, so why was the sight of him messing with my head?

He. Is. Damion. The. Evil. Rutledge.

Yet . . . I couldn't stop watching him.

Okay, maybe "analyzing" was the right word. This guy looked authentic and happy, sincere in a way I'd never seen him before. No holding back smiles or making internal judgments, no conversation fueled by biting sarcasm. Watching him this way allowed a dangerous thought to enter my mind.

What would it feel like to have him genuinely *like* you?

His friend—Massimo, apparently—led us to a table by a window in the back of the restaurant, and as soon as we ordered and he walked away, I had to know. "What were you saying to him?" I asked.

"We were just catching up," Damion said, brushing it off as if it were nothing to communicate in another language.

"In *Italian*," I muttered, because it was too much.

"I had an uncle who loved Italy," he explained. "So I spent a fair amount of time there."

"You don't say," I said, still in awe of this multilingual Damion.

"I'm surprised someone like you hasn't traveled much," he said.

I could tell that "someone like you" meant "someone with money," and it also felt like he was prying.

Or testing me.

His gaze was watchful behind his glasses as he waited for my response, which made me nervous.

What is he looking for?

I thought back to Bernard's cover stories.

"I think it's a Midwestern thing, sticking close to home. I don't even understand your jet-setting life, to be honest. Like—you said you went surfing in Rio. How on earth does something like that happen?"

"No, I said I *almost* went surfing in Rio," he corrected, and something about the look on his face made me interested.

"Forget your trunks?"

He wasn't exactly smiling, but there was a kind of fond amusement on his face when he said, "Remembered the trunks, forgot my steadfast devotion to staying alive."

"Explain."

Damion seemed almost boyish and self-deprecating—the antithesis of who he usually was—when he finally *did* smile and said, "I couldn't even convince my body to get *near* the water. I was so scared when I saw how ridiculously huge the waves were."

Damion reached for a piece of bread from the table. "But my uncle, who was determined to suck the marrow out of life, and the woman he was obsessed with—her name was Fernanda, and I'll never forget her—she took his hand and they frolicked in the ocean like happy dolphins while I sat on the beach like a pouting baby loser."

"Your uncle sounds fun," I said, trying to imagine what it'd be like to live a life like Damion's, traveling to South America just to surf.

"Yeah, he was," he said, giving me a strange look, like he was trying to measure what I meant by the comment.

"Is he the same one who liked Italy?" I asked.

"Uh, yes." Damion's Adam's apple moved around a swallow, and his eyes were narrowed as he stared at me like I'd just asked too personal of a question.

Like I was doing something *wrong* by asking about his family.

I wasn't sure exactly what I needed to apologize for, but I said, "I—I didn't mean to—"

"So I have a question for you, Nebraska," Damion suddenly interrupted, giving me whiplash with the change of subject. "Are you still carrying around your ex-boyfriend's wallet?"

"What?" I definitely hadn't expected *that* to be his question. "That's none of your business."

"Yeah, but you have to admit it's a really weird thing to do," he said. "Especially when your ex's mustache looks fake."

"No, it doesn't," I said defensively as I cut into the meatball appetizer.

"Oh, but it does, sweetie," he said. "William's got a feathery little mustache."

"First of all, that's not true. Second, I can't believe you remember his name."

"I can't believe you dated his face," Damion quipped, looking smugly amused.

"He has a nice face," I said, because even though his face was no longer mine, it wasn't . . . whatever Damion was painting it to be.

"Is that why you haul around the wallet, to sneak lovesick glimpses of his *nice* face?"

"Oh my God," I said, rolling my eyes and rolling my meatball in the marinara. *"No."*

"Then I don't understand," he said. "I've never known anyone who carries around their significant other's full wallet and uses it as their own. Like, what is Mr. Mullet doing without his identification?"

I sighed. "Not that it's any of your business or that I need to explain this to you, but he lost his wallet and had to get all new ID, okay? *After* he did, we found the old one and thought it'd be funny for me to use it. That's all, no big deal, and I just haven't had a chance to switch it out."

"But I think you have, Jules," he said, pointing his fork at me and shooting me a knowing look. "How long does it take to get a new wallet? You've had time since you dropped it on Broadway, and you've had time since we sat down at this restaurant. I think someone just can't let go of her little farmer boyfriend."

"Stop," I said with a snort because he was ridiculous, and I could feel myself getting angrier. "Yes, I can."

"So you admit he's a farmer," Damion said with a know-it-all little eyebrow raise.

"His *father* is a farmer, yes," I said.

"The ex plays football?"

"Yes." *Ugh.*

"Drives a pickup?"

Damion was starting to piss me off. "Yes," I answered, my teeth grinding.

"Likes to wear flannel?"

"Yes."

"Likes to drink beer from a can?" His voice was annoyingly smug and amused. "Likes to go four-wheeling? You're still in love with him?"

Make it STOP!

"Yes, yes, and yes!" I snapped, slamming down my silverware. "Would you please—"

I held in my gasp. Damion's hazel eyes—more brown than green today—were attentive as he waited for me to realize what he'd asked. What I'd just admitted.

You're still in love with him?

"*No*, not at all," I said quickly, but suddenly I was thrust out of the back-and-forth unseriousness of the conversation, because his pause made me picture Will.

Which made everything come rushing back.

The homesickness for the comfort of *us*, the rejection, the utter disillusionment.

Dammit.

"I'm not," I said pointedly. Slowly, so Damion could believe it. So I could believe it. "Besides," I began, my voice shaking. I could feel Damion shift in his seat, slightly uncomfortable at the topic he'd just unearthed.

Good, you should feel bad.

"Will is in love with someone else. Hannah."

"Oh." Damion's gaze didn't waver.

He watched me like he was absorbing a piece of information, like I'd said something he needed to comprehend. I wanted to say something light and breezy, but my voice seemed to be stuck somewhere inside the tightness of my throat.

I waited for the sarcastic comment. The cocky jab. But—

Instead Damion set his silverware on his plate. He wiped his hands with his white linen napkin.

"Listen." He reached out a hand and carefully grabbed my chin between his thumb and forefinger. And for some reason, I didn't back away. With the lightest of touches, his thumb stroked my skin. It was playful, teasing, and his voice was flirtatious when he said, "If you ask me, someone *should* steal that wallet so you can move on."

Why did I feel like crying all of a sudden? He wasn't being nice, he was being his usual flirtatious and mocking self, but for some reason, his tone made me feel . . . comforted. Understood, even.

We stayed like that for a moment, his fingers caressing my chin, our eyes locked on to each other.

"Sometimes things are hard to let go of, I guess," I heard myself say.

"Yeah," he agreed, and I watched his throat move when he swallowed, like he knew it too. Like we were both admitting to harboring a secret melancholy. Like we were each confessing with just a glance.

Maybe it's just me, I thought. *Does he feel it too?*

Because it was nice and wildly concerning, all at once.

"Damion."

I gasped at the interruption, glancing up to see Massimo tableside with our dinner. His appearance ripped me out of whatever that moment had been, and I was glad.

I needed to shake whatever had been going on in my head. And I did, until we reached the subway platform and were waiting for the train.

When Damion crossed his arms over his wide chest and said, "Are we becoming friends, Jules?"

He was watching me like he'd been giving our . . . *friendship* a lot of thought. Too much thought.

I looked at his suggestive eyebrow quirk and the way his mouth was settled into a teasing little smirk, and my stomach got . . . *flittery*.

Because whenever he said my name in that deep, rumbling near drawl, like his mouth was taking its time slow-slipping over the word, I felt the same way I felt when I consumed one too many energy drinks.

Trembly. Unsteady.

"Oh, I don't think so," I said in a rush, the words falling on top of each other.

"You don't," he said, his tone thick with doubt.

"We're not the type of people who will ever really be friends," I said, tucking my hair behind my ears and trying to put up a shield capable of deflecting his wicked charm. "We don't even like each other. You're just my tutor and I'm your student."

"Yes, but." He stepped slightly closer, just enough to where I had to tilt my head back and look up at him. His ever-changing eyes were heavy-lidded and direct, hot, when he said, "My tutorial areas of expertise are not just limited to mathematics, Nebraska."

I wanted to roll my eyes at his outrageous flirt, maybe push his chest to clear out some personal space, but I was incapable. *Paralyzed.* Immobilized by the power of his ridiculous game. Instead of spouting something smart, I heard myself say on a breath, "Is that right?"

"That's right," he said, the eyes behind the glasses moving over me like a physical touch. "So anytime you want more, all you have to do is ask."

CHAPTER NINETEEN

"A Gardenwood party is the most exclusive, least sensical event you will ever attend. A potpourri of glamour, luxury, and absolute idiocy."

—Remington

Julia

"Your car is here," Bernard said as he walked into the room.

"Finally," my mom said, looking nervous as she stood and ran a hand over the front of her black dress. "Thank you, Bernard."

"Relax, Ma," Liam said, climbing to his feet in that effortless way of his, like he was as comfortable in the tuxedo he was wearing as he was in his pajamas. "These people don't care about tardiness; they're all about fashionable lateness. We're better off running a little behind."

"Really?" she asked, desperate to believe him. "Do you think so?"

"Oh yeah," I agreed, trying to ease her obvious stress even though I had no idea what anyone cared about and was probably more nervous than *she* was.

Because we were going to a cocktail party.

As a *family*.

Quel nightmare.

The "launch soiree" was apparently the first of five parties—*the season*—that led up to the *Age of Innocence* ball. My mother explained when she got the invitation that this was an intimate gathering for all the people planning the balls—and their families—so we had to go.

Thank *God* it was the only one I'd be forced to attend.

Also: "Soiree" attire? We didn't have any.

Knowledge of what a cocktail party even looked like? None.

Awareness of how to behave at a "soiree"? Not a clue.

The thought of a party like this gave me hives, but my mother had said, "We cannot refuse this invitation, Jules."

I'd started to argue, but when Bernard calmly interjected that it was a great opportunity for my family to be officially introduced into Gardenwood society, I knew I'd lost any shot of winning.

Also—*society?*

Seriously, *was* this *Bridgerton*?

I was starting to think that yes—this was.

And also that Bernard was always right.

I shoved my feet into the very uncomfortable pumps that'd been delivered for me, pumps that matched the uncomfortable black cocktail dress that had *also* been delivered for me, and I wished our car would break down. The dress looked fine—it was silky and had cute shoulder straps—but it felt like I was wearing somebody else's outfit that I had no business wearing.

I was grateful Bernard had had someone to call to get us suited up for the event, but I somehow just knew I didn't look . . . *right*.

There was a questionable ruffle on the dress's bodice that I wasn't sure about.

"You look nice, Mom." I tried to sound relaxed and optimistic, calling upon my inner Liam to just be cool about this and not overthink everything. "And we're only staying for like an hour, right?"

"Right," she said, nodding as she started leading us toward the door. My dad hadn't been thrilled by this party either, but my mom told him we just had to make an appearance. "We show up, say hello to a few people while eating hors d'oeuvres, and then we're out of there."

"And you said it's going to be small . . . ?" I asked, following her out onto the stoop.

"Hopefully not too small," Liam said as he pushed past me.

A chilly breeze left goose bumps up and down my exposed arms, or maybe it was the sight of that fancy black car in the darkness—with the waiting chauffeur—that filled me with prickly unease.

"Very small," my mom said, nodding, her heels clicking as she and my dad went straight for the car, somehow looking like lifelong New Yorkers as they slid into the back seat. "I got the impression it's just going to be a handful of the ladies from the committee and a few of their family members."

Thank God.

No one from school would be there.

At least there was that.

As it turned out, "small" meant something different in the big city.

There were people *everywhere*.

Not only was the stunning brownstone filled with people, but the elegance was astounding. Too much for the eye to take in.

There was a man at the grand piano playing classical music in a tuxedo, while three matching tuxedoed men played their string instruments. Servers in black suits milled about with silver trays on their palms—some covered in wineglasses, while others were covered in canapés—and the guests all spoke at a respectably low volume.

Yes. This was *Bridgerton*.

I was living *Bridgerton* right now, minus the attractive suitor chasing me. *How is this my life?*

"Shawna!"

A blonde—probably in her forties—walked toward my mom, her filler-enhanced lips turning up into a photo-ready smile. She was all dewy skin and diamonds, and it was a little jarring to realize that *my* mother knew her.

Mrs. Lowell, Springfield English teacher and former two-time barrel-racing champion, was exchanging air-kisses with a woman who looked like that.

Bizarre.

"This is lovely, Claire," my mom said, gesturing to the *everything* around us.

"Oh, thank you," Claire said, her gaze wandering over to the rest of us. She gave me a smile that didn't quite reach her eyes. "I'm assuming these gorgeous twins are Julia and Liam?"

"They *are*," my mom said, and as she looked at me, I wondered if she was embarrassed.

It was the first time in my life I'd ever wondered if she wished I were more like Liam, prettier and more comfortable in my skin. I knew she loved me, but as she tried fitting in with these people, did I reflect badly on her?

Would my inability to fit in make *her* an outcast?

The idea of that hurt my stomach, though I wasn't sure if it was because I didn't want to hold her back or I didn't want her to regret my . . . *Julia*-ness.

"I'm Liam," my brother said, giving Claire a confident smile. "In case you couldn't tell us apart."

"I assumed," she said, tilting her head a little, obviously charmed by Liam's effortless charisma. "Most of the kids are upstairs, by the way, if you want to escape the boring adults."

Wait. What?

"Yeah?" my brother said, glancing at my parents like he was looking for permission.

Noooooooo! The "kids" were what I needed an escape *from*, for God's sake. My heart started racing as I wondered who was here, and then my stomach clenched as I realized it didn't matter.

No one from school liked me, aside from Donovan and Jasmine.

"Get away. Go hang out with your friends," my dad insisted joyfully.

My *friends*? Ha.

Jasmine and Donovan were on a college visit to Yale, so this "upstairs" she was referring to was likely a hostile environment for me.

"But—"

"Come on, Jules," Liam said, gesturing with his head toward the grand staircase just inside the entry. "Let's go while we can. So nice to meet you, Claire."

"You too," she said, her smile *finally* reaching her eyes as she beamed at my brother.

"Oh my God," I said through my teeth as we made our way through the crowded room. "What is your problem? I don't want to go hang out with a bunch of kids from school who hate me."

"No one hates you," he lied, reaching out a hand to grab something off a passing tray and pop it into his mouth. "Besides, this is a formal cocktail party where everyone's parents are right downstairs. Everyone's going to be on their best behavior."

"*Their* best behavior is still ass," I grumbled, my stomach queasy as we started walking up the stairs.

"Quit being so afraid," he said, giving me a reassuring smile. It was one of those looks that told me he could read my mind and feel every one of my emotions, and for some reason, those looks always made me feel slightly better.

"This is a good chance for you to meet some people outside school and show them who you *actually* are. Tonight could really help your situation."

"My 'situation'? Would that situation be the fact that I'm a walking joke at Gardenwood Academy?" I asked.

"That's the one," he agreed, making me smile in spite of myself as he teased. "Just get outside your own head and talk to people, okay? You'll be fine."

"Well, don't you dare leave me," I said, butterflies flapping all over inside my body as we hit the top of the stairs and surveyed the sight in front of us. "Promise?"

"Sure," he said, but he wasn't looking at me.

He was looking at whatever this "kids" version of the party was.

CHAPTER TWENTY

"A curly-haired woman weakens my knees every damn time."

—Remington

Damion

"Good God, I cannot believe they're here."

Already, Mom?

Barely in the door and they were gossiping.

Wonderful.

My parents had forced me to come with them to the ridiculous cocktail party because apparently, as hosts of a ball, their attendance was mandatory. I'd always been able to get out of shit like this, but my dad had become just as nuts as my mom about the season.

So there I was, at Claire's stupid soiree, counting down the minutes until I could leave. Thank God Beckett was here, upstairs somewhere; at least I could hang out with him until I was sprung.

I reached for a passing scallop, not hungry but needing the culinary distraction, and I'd just popped it into my mouth when I saw her.

Julia.

She was walking toward the stairs with her brother, and I almost swallowed the damn appetizer whole when I sucked in a breath too quickly.

Fuck, I thought as I coughed.

"You okay, Dame?" my dad asked.

"Yeah," I said, clearing my throat.

She looked . . . hell, she looked very Julia.

She was gnawing nervously on that lower lip, walking too fast in high heels as she basically followed at Liam's, and her hair was cascading out from under her headband like a waterfall of long curls.

She looked hurried and purposeful.

Chaotic and fresh.

Unrefined and alive, just like she'd been in Times Square.

She carried herself like a commoner, but dear God, who didn't like watching a commoner running wild in the kingdom?

She was wearing a black cocktail dress that did amazing things for her shoulders and legs, but it had ruffles that probably wouldn't last two minutes without someone commenting on them.

"Did Claire invite them?" my dad asked.

Julia and Liam disappeared up the stairs.

"I mean, of course she did," my mom said in disgust. "Shawna's on the committee."

I turned away, following my parents' watchful gaze until I saw them.

A couple I didn't know, a couple who didn't look like they belonged there.

Holy shit, they have to be the Lowells.

I wasn't sure how I'd expected them to look, but it wasn't like this.

Julia's mom had the same color hair as her, a deep brown that wanted to be red, but hers was straight and ended at her shoulders. She was wearing a black dress—understated and quiet—and sensible high heels, and her smile was warm as she listened to Claire Roth.

She looked smart, like a mom from a sitcom about a working-class family with good values.

Julia's dad was nodding, listening intently to the conversation from behind functional wire-rimmed glasses, his hands in the pockets of his tuxedo pants. His hair was short, like he'd walked into a mall salon and just asked for "a little bit off the top." His goatee looked more functional than fashionable, like he grew it to keep his face warm.

They looked parental; they looked *nice*; they looked responsible.

Definitely not like the grifters that they were.

My jaw clenched as I watched them, because their niceness pissed me off. Was that how they'd latched on to Remi, with Midwestern pleasantries?

"It's insulting, having to work with Shawna on the committee, knowing what she—what *they*—did to Uncle Remi," my mother complained.

"Just keep playing it cool, Whit," my dad said in his best *I need to placate my wife* tone.

His eyes had that Quinn Rutledge burn going on as he glared at Julia's parents, the look of a villain whose mind was running through a million diabolical plans.

"Let her relax into thinking she's gotten away with it, that no one here knows who she really is," he said, his predatory gaze never leaving his prey. "That'll make it more satisfying when we get to rip it all away."

CHAPTER TWENTY-ONE

"It's important to remember, whilst being insulted, that terrible people *will* eventually get theirs. Karma shows the hell up, thank God."

—Remington

Julia

"This is *not* what I was expecting," Liam said, looking around.

"Yeah, same," I agreed, a little relieved.

There was a "living" room in front of us, so big you could probably land a plane in it. A string quartet was in the corner, playing classical music just like the party downstairs, and servers were walking around with the same refreshments.

There were luxe couches and artsy end tables, and a few kids our age were standing around in formalwear, talking.

It looked very elegant, calm, but a total snoozefest.

Thank God.

I didn't see anyone I recognized from school, either, none of the Skins or Toms or the other labels that terrified me, so I breathed a huge sigh and relaxed. The kids who were there looked quiet and composed, not at all like the classmates who always appeared to be judging me.

"Schwab's down the hall," Liam said.

"What?" I glanced over at my brother, who was looking at his phone. "Who's Schwab?"

"Beckett Schwab," he said, as if that explained it.

I waited for another second, then said, "Okay, who is Beckett Schwab again?"

"He goes to our school," he said as if I should know that. "Showed me around the first day. He's cool. Come on."

Right. Beckett. As rich-boy a name as Damion.

"But," I said, trying to grab on to him as he Liamed his way down the hallway.

"Wait!" I scrambled in my heels to keep up with him as we walked past strange antiques, plate collections hanging on the walls (*is that Revolution-era?*), and oil paintings in gilded frames, illuminated by lighting better than I'd ever had in any bathroom. Liam didn't even pause before turning the knob and pushing open the door at the end of the hall. "LIAM!"

What are you doing????

I followed him into a room with only a few lamps illuminating what appeared to be an enormous office *filled* with people. And not just any people.

Oh God.

The room was packed full of people my age, standing around with drinks, talking and laughing as music—"Blame It on You"—boomed from *somewhere* in the dimly lit room.

Oh God, I see the Toms, I thought as those guys appeared to be playing some sort of drinking game on top of the massive office desk.

"Lowell!"

I turned away from the scene in front of me to see a smiling blond guy approaching us.

"Schwab," my brother said with a grin. "Thank God you texted. I was getting a little scared when I came upstairs."

"There's always something happening in one of the back rooms at a Garden party," the guy said with a laugh. "You just have to know how to find the room where it happens."

"Nice reference," I muttered without thinking as the *Hamilton* song settled into my brain.

"'Click boom, then it happened,'" Beckett sang with a smile, "'but no one else was in the room where it happened.'"

"This is my sister, Julia," Liam said. "Julia, this is Beckett."

"Can I just say you're my hero for rocking a headband tonight?" the guy said, crossing his arms over his *purple tuxedo* and giving me a big grin, like he was proud of me. "I heard that you called Cassandra 'Headband,' and I honestly think that might've made my life. Well, until now . . . seeing *you* wearing one."

My cheeks went hot. I was embarrassed and felt caught.

I gave my head a shake and said, "Let's just say I, um, I . . . had a moment."

"You should have more," he said, his eyes squinting around his smile. "Makes things around here more interesting."

"Not my goal," I said with an eye roll, and then I immediately wanted to slap my hand over my mouth.

Shit.

"Maybe it should be," he teased, and I was relieved he didn't seem offended by my remark. "If you can't—"

Whatever he was about to say was interrupted by someone yelling his name.

He turned around, and the Toms were demanding his return.

"Get your ass over here!" the red-haired guy—*Corbin the jerk from lit*—yelled from where he was perched upon the probably priceless desktop. He was literally on his knees on top of the huge piece of furniture as he shouted, "You're up, Schwab!"

"Come on, Liam," he said, and before I could register what was happening, my brother turned his back on me and went over to the game with Beckett.

Leaving me alone.

Noooooooooooooooooo!

I took one step to follow him, because even though the idea of getting closer to the Toms felt akin to moving closer to a starving family of grizzly baby mamas, I wasn't the type of person emotionally equipped to traverse a party alone.

Hell, no.

But someone touched my arm, and when I turned around, it was one of the Skins.

The tall one with the red hair. *Naomi.*

"What are *you* doing here, New Money?" she said with a tight grin. "You don't strike me as someone who'd be *involved* in the season."

The way she said it, like there was no way I would ever land a date, was intended to insult and . . . well, it did. I didn't *want* to do the season, but the implication that I wouldn't be able to if I *had* wanted to stung.

Because it was a hundred percent accurate.

Bella, the Skin with the superlong hair, suddenly appeared by Naomi's side and said to me, "Ooh, I like your dress. Salvatore Sutfan, right?"

That was, in fact, the name I'd seen on my dress's label, so I said, "Right."

"Yeah, I think my grandmother has that exact dress," she said, smiling.

The Skins knew how to make smiles feel like slaps. They grinned, their perfect teeth and glossed lips doing all the right choreography, yet the final pose was somehow a jump-scare.

"Oh, right, she wore it to the Press Club dinner last year," Naomi said, nodding and smiling like this was the funniest thing she'd ever heard. "I remember the ruffle."

"Yeah, it's quite a ruffle," Bella agreed, also nodding. "*Lovely* ruffle."

I stood there, the butt of their joke, and I was overwhelmed with homesickness. I missed being in a place where I knew how everything worked, who everyone was, and where every social situation didn't feel like a toxic trap that would likely end in my demise.

"I'm surprised to see *you* up here at all, to be honest," Bella said, tilting her head. "It doesn't seem like your kind of place."

"That's what I said," Naomi said with a laugh. They looked at me like they were a pair of velociraptors out hunting together.

I searched the vicinity for escape as I stammered, "Um, my, uh, my mom is on the—"

"Oh my God, your mom is on the committee?" Bella asked, narrowing her eyes.

"Yeah, she is," I responded, trying to see my brother.

God, save me, Liam.

"But why?" she scoffed. "Why would she—"

"Because of New Money's brother," Naomi said definitively, nodding as if it made sense. "Liam."

"Well, at least one of the New Money twins has potential."

And that. THAT hurt worse than a slap to the face.

God, please let me disappear right now.

My cheeks were on fire as they laughed at me, as they stood in front of me and mocked me *to my face*.

Dammit, I couldn't let them win.

Couldn't let them see the tears that were suddenly blurring my vision.

Screw that.

I turned to defiantly join my brother and the Toms at the drinking-game desk, but joining Liam and watching him effortlessly blend in was also the last thing I wanted to do. And as I scanned the room, I wondered where the hell I was and what I was doing here.

There was a couple lying on the couch, a girl in a stunning red gown on top of a guy in a charcoal tux, and they were *hardcore* going at it. So hardcore it wouldn't have surprised me if their clothes started coming off at any moment. A group of girls in their finest eveningwear, looking like they belonged in *Vogue* with their necklaces dangling and ties askew, crowded around a table, leaning down and doing something that looked illegal.

Are they snorting something?

I couldn't tell for sure, but it didn't matter because I seriously had no idea what things were even available to snort.

Maybe there's something snortable that isn't an illegal substance, right?

I'd never felt more like I knew nothing about anything.

Suddenly the Toms, shouting about something related to their drinking game, were all I could hear as this montage of sophisticated things I knew nothing about played out before me.

Oh God, oh God, oh God.

I couldn't catch my breath. It was like my heart was beating too fast and my lungs were too shallow and—*what the hell*—the tingly numbness in my hands made me wonder if my circulation was in jeopardy.

My hands were freezing but my body was on fire.

I shook out my hands and tried breathing through my nose, but I needed to get away.

As infantile as it sounded, I wanted my parents.

I turned and very nearly ran from the room, not stopping until I was at the top of the staircase.

"'It *is* the *east*, and *Ju*liet *is* the *sun*. It *is* the *east*, and *Ju*liet *is* the *sun*. It *is* the *east*, and *Ju*liet *is* the *sun*,'" I said under my breath, praying the old trick would work. There was something about reciting the iambic pentameter out loud (thank you, Dr. Allison) that got my breathing back on track whenever this happened.

I took a deep breath through my nose, ran a hand over the front of my dress, and descended the stairs.

"It *is* the *east*, and *Ju*liet *is* the *sun*. It *is* the *east*, and *Ju*liet *is* the *sun*.

It *is* the *east*, and *Ju*liet *is* the *sun*," I whispered to myself because—thank God—it was starting to work.

Be cool, Jules, I thought as I carefully went down the steps. *Act like you've been here before.*

Downstairs, I found my mom right away, but as I approached and looked at the woman she was talking to, I instantly knew who she must be.

"Julia," my mom said with a smile. "This is Chantel Chattingham; her daughter, Coco, is a senior. Do you know her?"

"Um, I think maybe . . . ?" I said, feeling scared for some reason as the woman's pale blue eyes, so similar to her daughter's, bore so deeply into me that I almost *felt* them digging into my skin.

"Oh hey, Whitney!" my mom said to someone who was apparently behind me.

Which made Chantel Chattingham's eyes narrow as if my mother had just insulted her.

I turned to see who *Whitney* was (my mom suddenly had all these new friends) and I gasped audibly, because not only was "Whitney" standing there—yet another flawless woman who scared the shit out of me on sight—but a man was beside her as well.

And Damion.

Damion.

He was watching me, his expression unreadable but intense, and I could do nothing but stare back.

Because I hadn't seen or talked to him since our subway trip.

And I had no idea how to act.

That singular outing with Damion had brought up so many questions in my head.

For starters, who *was* he, really?

Was he Damion the Tutor, Damion the tour guide who spoke Italian and hugged lovely waiters, Damion who had once volunteered at an animal shelter, or Damion the Evil, Gardenwood rebel, who'd once kicked one of my books down the hallway?

I'd slipped that night, at dinner, and I got sucked into the idea that he might be one of those other versions.

Which was so foolish because he was most likely just *that* guy.

The Evil.

How could I ever forget it.

"Hello, Shawna dear," Whitney said to my mother, leaning in for an air-kiss. "This is my husband, Quinn, and my son Damion."

Damion's jawbone flexed before he turned his eyes away from me and smiled at my mom. "It's so nice to meet you."

If Damion looked intimidating in his school uniform, he was downright dangerous in these clothes. The black suit, the thick black tie resting on his crisp white shirt, the messy white pocket square, the messier curls, the black glasses—dear *God*, he was attractive.

And he looked like he belonged upstairs in that office, doing all the scandalous things.

"Did you say Damion?" My mom pursed her lips and said, "Are you the Damion that Julia's been hanging out with?"

Oh God, oh God, oh God.

"I am," he said with a charming smile, his eyes never wavering from my mom's face. "Unless you hate him. Then I am absolutely *not* that guy."

My mom—and my dad—laughed like he was hilarious, and I was mesmerized by his charisma. So smooth. So natural. SO well practiced.

"Well, we very much appreciate it," my mom said, giving him meaningful eye contact that made me uncomfortable. I knew she was trying to convey *we appreciate your math tutorial skills* with her eyes, but it made me nervous because she sucked at subtlety. "Jules is learning a lot—*about the city*—and we're grateful for your help."

Shut up, Ma!

Chantel Chattingham got a wrinkle in her forehead—probably not something that happened to her very often—and she looked unhappy with the conversation. She swallowed as she watched my mom and Damion chat, and then she turned her scary eyes to me.

"So tell me about yourself, Julia."

What? I looked into the eyes of this terrifying woman and didn't know what to say, because who asked questions like that to a stranger? Was I at a job interview?

I didn't have an answer to such a big, general question.

"Well, I, um . . . I'm a senior," I said awkwardly as my face got hot yet again. "I guess I—"

"What are your plans for next year?" she interrupted, looking impatient yet amused by my rambling. Her eyes went to Damion and his parents for a half second as if to say *Are you hearing this?* before coming back to me.

"Oh," I said, clearing my throat. "Do you mean, uh, what—"

"College, dear," she said, her mouth curling up into a smile, like she'd just scored a point by making me stammer like a moron. "Coco and Damion will be going to Dartmouth, and our Chuck is going to Harvard. Where do you plan on attending?"

Yale for sure, maybe Brown.

Not.

I was pretty sure my face was the color of a tomato as she waited for my answer, as Damion and his parents waited for my answer, as the *world* waited for me to piece together enough syllables to form a complete sentence.

But the truth was that I had no idea.

Will and I had planned on attending NU together—that had always been our plan.

So now that he'd dumped me and now that I was living in a surreal world where home was New York, I had no freaking clue.

What is college again?

How could I look at these Ivy League socialites and admit that I had no idea what I wanted to do? Writing, maybe. Teaching, possibly. Running the store in Springfield and dipping on college entirely?

I kind of loved that idea.

But maybe that was lazy, me just wanting to go along with the status quo because it was what I knew. Maybe wanting that meant I was someone with zero drive and no goals, right?

Was I an absolute loser if I didn't go to college?

Shouldn't I *want* a new experience?

I shrugged. "Well, I *was* going to go to the University of Nebraska—"

"A state school?" Damion's mom asked my mom.

"Was?" Chantel said, her tone so thick with mockery that she didn't need to say anything else. She obviously found me to be the most ridiculous human on the planet for not having this already figured out.

"Well, I mean I probably still will, but—"

"Probably, huh?" Damion's dad said with a smile, and my parents laughed like he was just a fellow parent, joking about their silly kids' whims.

But I glanced over at him and could instantly tell he didn't like me. We didn't know each other, but the way he was watching me, the unkind smirk on his *I'm a finance CEO* face, told me all I needed to know.

"I—I'm sure I will, actually," I said, stammering as all eyes stayed fixed on me.

"It's incredibly *charming*," he said, all smug amusement, "this attitude of spontaneity regarding your future. The way you don't seem to have it mapped out at all. No plan. Is that how they do things in Nebraska, or is this a Julia Lowell special?"

Chantel giggled and tilted her head, waiting for me to respond.

Oh my God. *This grown man is publicly mocking me in front of his friends.*

I felt shaken, shaky, as I looked into soulless eyes that held zero adult compassion or any parental responsibility whatsoever.

The man was a grown-ass Tom.

I glanced at Damion and wondered what *he* was thinking. Was he embarrassed by me? Embarrassed *for* me?

Probably, I thought, which bothered me more than it should.

His eyes were all over me as I interacted with his father, like he was taking in the conversation and having major thoughts about it, but I couldn't translate the expression.

Which was good. I didn't want his pity or his judgment. Or whatever the look on his face was. Because in my heart I knew Damion was just like the jerk who'd raised him, thinking I was pathetic for not being like them, for not having Ivy League goals for next year.

Especially when he knew just how far away from that I actually was.

I was lightheaded, feeling like I was going to pass out from the mortification of the moment and my ever-present social anxiety—*It* is *the* east, *and* Juliet is *the* sun—when Damion looked away from me and said to his father, "Actually, Dad, the Julia Lowell special is pretty incredible."

What??

Chantel's narrowed eyes passed over me, bumping around, like she was trying to find something and was coming up short.

"Jules is too humble to admit it, but the reason why she's so indecisive about next year is because she has too many options," he lied, smiling at his parents and Chantel as if he were *actually* my friend.

Whaaaaaat??

"Is that right," Chantel said dryly, as if she didn't believe it for a second.

"Really," Damion's dad said in the exact same tone.

I looked at his face, trying to figure out this game he was playing.

"Beckett's in her lit class," he said, glancing over at me and winking—*dear Lord*—"and apparently Mr. Longhaven was basically letting *her* teach the class the other day because she knew more about a certain Shakespearian tragedy than he did."

Wait, what?

Totally inaccurate, but also what did Damion know about my *Titus Andronicus* moment in lit, because Longhaven definitely *hadn't* enjoyed my response. He'd cautioned the entire class that it was unwise to add "political ideologies" to literature analysis, which made me rage all day, the idea that feminism and the patriarchy could be considered "political ideologies."

Also, isn't that what classic literature is all about?

"She's always loved books," my mom said with a smile, looking absolutely unaware of what'd just gone on in front of her face, "so this doesn't surprise me at all."

"Yeah, well, I was surprised," Damion said, his smile slowly dropping away, his mask of coolness returning in its place. "Never expected this little *Midwesterner* to be such an overachiever. Now, if you'll excuse me, I've got friends to party with upstairs."

The adults immediately started talking again as Damion stepped away, their conversation returning to where it'd been before I'd become the butt of the joke, but I couldn't let him go.

"Damion, wait."

CHAPTER TWENTY-TWO

"The woman was autumn. I swear to God she was autumn personified."

—Remington

Damion

I slowed but didn't stop, because I didn't want to talk to her.

To explain what I didn't understand myself.

Why in the hell did I just defend her?

Jumping upside down into a conversation, simply because she'd looked sad and awkward and embarrassed . . . ?

That wasn't for me.

She—and her family—*deserved* to be awkwardly embarrassed.

God, I needed to check myself.

I was becoming too decent.

"What's up, Nebraska?" I said as she caught up to me, as she dodged Scotch-guzzling bodies while we headed in the direction of the staircase.

"Why did you do that?" she asked, muttering, "Excuse me," to the waiter she nearly mowed over.

"Do what?"

Yes, my plan is just to play dumb and admit nothing.

"Stick up for me, I guess," she said. "You lied to help me save face."

"Did I?" I said, still not looking at her, still walking.

"You know you did. *Damion*," she said, and then she grabbed my arm, stopping me.

"What?"

I sighed and looked down at her, at those big brown eyes that were watching me with a thousand questions in them, like she needed to know if I'd been being kind to her.

Like she *wanted* to discover I wasn't the dick she'd always thought I was.

Sorry, sunshine.

"So, like, why . . . ?" she pressed.

"You know I love having you in my debt, right? We can add this to your tab of my still-to-be-chosen favors," I said, thinking—objectively speaking, of course—that she looked good in red lipstick and bare shoulders.

She was autumn.

"That's all that was?" she asked, long-lashed eyes sweeping over my face in search of the answer she wanted.

Good luck, I thought, *because I have no fucking clue what that was.*

I'd been in my own head during that entire conversation, honestly, because her awkward answer to Chantel had shocked the hell out of me.

She was a senior and still didn't know what she was doing next year?

Like, how was that possible?

The jealousy I'd felt over that had almost knocked me over.

Because I was so jealous, as fucking nuts as that sounded, that she appeared to have no idea what she was doing after graduation. What would that feel like, not having your entire life planned out for you?

No lifelong assumption of a Dartmouth education, no expectation that you'd be joining the family business, no steely presumption that you'd ultimately be at the helm of that mind-numbingly boring financial conglomerate until a heart attack finally took mercy upon your money-worshipping existence and let you off the hook.

God, I couldn't imagine that kind of freedom.

I mean, I *had* imagined it, with Remi, and I was determined to make it happen, but I was jealous that for Julia it required no subterfuge.

The future was hers to decide.

"I'm in it for your favors," I said, snagging a flute of champagne from a passing tray, "and to mess with my asshole father. That's it, honey."

"Don't call me that," she said, looking at the glass in my hand. "And I wanted to thank you, you know, in case you were actually being a nice human."

"Nice?" I reached out my free hand and tugged on one of those long curls, then let my finger hold on for another moment. "Now why would I want to be something like that?"

"Because sometimes people do that," she said, smacking my hand. "I should've known *you* wouldn't."

"Oh, don't be disappointed in me, Nebraska," I said, leaning just a little closer because it was noisy and I needed to hear her and not at all because I wanted to smell the perfume on her neck to figure out the scent. "I just couldn't bear that."

"Sure you couldn't."

"Listen, I'd love to chat about human kindness," I replied, not wanting to talk about being nice when her smell was going straight to my head, "but I'm ready for a good time. Have you seen Beckett anywhere?"

Her eyebrows furrowed and she watched me for a long second before answering, "Yeah, um, he's upstairs in the office at the end of the hall, somewhere between the booze-guzzling Toms on the desk and the couple getting down on the couch."

It was clear from her tone that she wasn't a fan of the "kids' table," and there was a challenge in her eyes, like she was hoping I'd be surprised by the side party going on upstairs.

What? Kids from Gardenwood are misbehaving upstairs?

Impossible.

But the truth was that the kids' table had been a thing since middle school; feigning shock wasn't possible. Or helpful in this instance.

It was better that she thought I was a reprobate.

"Then that is where I shall be as well," I said with a lascivious grin. "Later, Lowell."

And I walked away before her perfume had the chance to pull me back in and make me forget who she was.

CHAPTER TWENTY-THREE

"There's something about being invited to a party in the city that makes you feel like you've landed."

—Remington

Julia

If there was a bright side to my unpopularity at Gardenwood, it was Donovan and Jasmine.

Somehow, in spite of my poor reception by everyone else, they actually seemed to *like* me.

The group chat they'd started with me on my first day, to use just in case I had any questions, had become our constant conversation. We liked a lot of the same books and watched a lot of the same reality TV (hello, *Below Deck*), so what'd started as a resource had become an actual—dare I say it—friendship.

It was a lot like me and my friends back home.

Thank *God* for Don and Jaz.

"Julia!"

I turned, surprised to hear my name when I was walking down the hall with the only two people who ever talked to me at school (aside from my brother when I happened to see him and Damion's "Lowell" whenever he passed my desk in transition). Everyone else usually just whispered and murmured *about* me; they didn't shout my name.

"Julia, have you been holding out on us? Are you friends with Beckett Schwab?" Jasmine asked, tugging on my sleeve as Beckett stood in front of his locker, grinning and gesturing for us to come over.

His tie was completely untied, just hanging around his collar like a border separating his dark blazer from his white button-down.

"I exchanged like two sentences with him at the preseason soiree," I said out of the corner of my mouth, "before he ran off to do keg stands with the Toms. That's it."

"I still can't believe you were at the kids' table," Donovan said, sounding in awe. "I've never been invited and I've been here my whole life."

"I *wasn't* invited," I said, irritated that this place had a cute nickname for whatever that upstairs party had been. "Liam was. And it sucked, trust me."

"Come on," Jasmine said, pulling me with her toward Beckett's locker. "Let's see what he wants."

"What do you want with our Julia?" Donovan said, skipping right over to him.

"Well, Donnie, if you must know," he said, his amused gaze moving back and forth between her and me, "I feel like I blew an opportunity to get to know the new girl the other night. One second she was there; the next she was gone. So I thought I'd see if you guys want to come to my birthday party tomorrow night so I can rectify that situation."

"Absolutely not," Jasmine said. "The last time I attended one of your birthday parties I got puked on."

"Come on, that was in the third grade," he said with a laugh. "Give me another chance, Jaz; I promise I can hold my soda now."

Donovan looked at me with her eyebrows raised and said, "His parties are legendary."

I pictured the Toms and had zero interest. "I don't know, I think maybe—"

"And they're always super chill. The Skins *never* go to them because they don't like Beckett," she said, sounding like she was trying to convince me.

"You're not supposed to call them that," he chided with a smile. "And I suspect they *secretly* like me."

"Coco *hates* you," Jasmine insisted.

"Beckett is one of those wildly honest people," Donovan explained to me, "who you either love or despise."

"Choose love, Julia Nebraska," Beckett said to me. "And Liam's coming. You guys should totally come with your brother."

"No offense, but our fellow classmates haven't exactly been welcoming to her," Jasmine said, looking over at me sympathetically.

"You mean New Money here?" he said, acknowledging the insult with a warm smile, somehow making me feel . . . *not* attacked.

"Yeah, there's that," I said, rolling my eyes but giving in to a smile.

"What if I told you that none of the assholes will be at my house, and I will personally ensure that you have a great time? It's casual, jeans and sneakers, it's on the roof of my building, so we can use our outdoor voices, and we're talking twenty people max. Very low-key vibes."

"I'd say thanks—seriously," I said, meaning it. He really seemed like he was trying to be nice, which felt shockingly great, like stepping into warm sunshine after being stuck in the bone-chilling cold. "But I think I'll—"

"Julia," he said, and suddenly Beckett was lowering his head, his eyes looking straight into mine. "I promise you'll have fun."

And as he smiled at me, as the *three* of them smiled at me, I wondered if maybe they *did* want to hang out with me.

I was fun and I could be brave, right?

I looked at Donovan and Jasmine and decided, for the first time since being in New York, to take a chance. "You said jeans and sneakers . . . ?"

"Attagirl," Beckett said. "Get ready for a good time."

I was in a surprisingly good mood the rest of the day because I finally had something to look forward to. Something to do with friends. And apparently I wasn't great at hiding my happiness.

"Are you *humming*?" Damion asked while he tutored me after school.

"Hmm?" I looked up from my worksheet and Damion was scowling at me. "What?"

"You're humming while you work," he said, his eyes narrowed. "In a good mood, are we?"

Since the soiree, things had snapped right back into the "before" with us—before Times Square. He didn't talk to me at school, and if our eyes happened to accidentally meet, he either threw me one of those ridiculously overdone flirtatious gazes or stared at me like he hated me.

Fortunately, when he came over to work with me on math, he slid right into his Tutor Damion identity.

Helpful, patient, absurdly smart.

"I kind of am," I admitted, reaching for my Dr Pepper.

"Is there a reason?" he asked as he ran a hand over Clank's back.

It was confirmed—my cat was officially obsessed with him and jumped on his lap every time he sat down in our kitchen.

Traitor.

For a second I thought about telling Damion the unbelievable fact that I had extracurricular plans coming up that didn't involve math, but then I thought better of it. He'd probably just mock me somehow, and I didn't want him to say anything to ruin my hopes.

"Nah," I said, shrugging. "Today just sucked a little less than other days."

"Don't forget the final step," he said, pointing down at the paper.

I hate your slutty little glasses, I thought, because I didn't hate them at all.

"I'm *not*," I said, giving him an overexaggerated eye roll. "I was about to do it."

His eyes told me he didn't believe me. "Sure you were."

I was about to argue, but I could see Bernard was headed our way, walking in that way that meant he had important business to discuss. Very *serious* business, by the intense look on his face.

Which made me wonder why his stern gaze slipped right past me and landed squarely on Damion.

CHAPTER TWENTY-FOUR

"Liars lie, and that's the truth."

—Remington

Damion

We were in the middle of our tutoring session when I came face-to-face with Bernard Elizando.

"Miss Julia," he said as he walked into the kitchen, looking down at a piece of paper in his hand. "I was thinking perhaps this evening—"

His words stopped when we made eye contact, and I felt like I was going to fucking pass out as no less than a thousand emotions and panicked thoughts shot through me.

For starters, *holy shit*.

I hadn't known Bernard had come back and was working with the Lowells. *How did I not know that?* His last known location was Nebraska, and I'd just assumed he was still there.

Hell, I'd almost sent letters to him at that address.

But it hit me like a ton of bricks what his appearance was capable of.

Holy shit, he could ruin everything with Julia.

The second she saw we knew each other, it'd be all over. She'd realize my connection to Remi and I'd be done.

But as these thoughts sprinted through my panicked brain, I also wanted to bawl like a baby at the sight of Remi's best friend.

Bernard had always been right there alongside Remi, working with him.

Being beside him.

In São Paulo, Paris, Madrid, Nebraska—if Remi was there, so was Bernard. If they'd been in an old mob movie, Bernard would've been Rem's consigliere.

"Oh hey, Bernard," Julia said, her eyes moving between me and him. "This is Damion—he's my tutor."

I jumped to my feet and held out my extended hand, meeting Bernard's gaze, hoping he'd go along with my deception while knowing he probably wouldn't. "Nice to meet you, Bernard."

He took my hand and shook it, but he didn't say anything. Those sharp eyes stayed on me, like he was assessing my presence and drilling into what I was actually doing there.

"You are Miss Julia's . . . *tutor*," he said, doing that whole it's-kind-of-a-question-but-not-in-the-form-of-a-question thing that he did.

"Yes, sir," I confirmed.

"That is admirable work," he said, "Helping other people. The last time I checked, it's an unpaid officership at the academy. Is that still the case?"

I swallowed and gave a nod, knowing exactly what he was doing. "That is correct."

"It's nice that there are still honorable organizations," he said, "where young gentlemen like yourself put the greater good above their own time. Altruism over selfish machinations."

"Chill, Bernie," Julia said, glancing at him out of the side of her eyes. "He gets extra credit for it or something."

"Yes, you're probably correct," Bernard said, and it was clear by the way he looked at her that Bernard *liked* her. That he saw *her* the way he used to see me, like she was a priority in his life. "Miss Julia, your mother is looking for you upstairs."

"Oh, she is?" Julia asked, crinkling her nose.

"It's why I'm here."

"Oh, okay," she said. Then she looked at me and said, "I'll be right back."

She got out of the chair and left the room.

Immediately, Bernard stepped closer to me and lowered his voice. "What exactly do I need to know here?"

"What do you mean?"

His shrewd eyes narrowed and I felt like he could see into my very soul. "Do not pretend you're unaware of what I'm saying, and please know that I refuse to lie for you."

"Listen, Bernard, I—"

"Do not mistake my silence regarding our previous acquaintanceship as a willingness to deceive. I am simply trying to assess this situation."

"So you're going to tell Julia that I'm Remi's—"

"Stop," he interrupted, holding up a hand. "*You* are going to tell Julia, of this I am certain. It's simply a matter of when your good conscience decides to kick in."

He didn't get it. I said, "I don't know—"

"Yes, you do," he interrupted, again giving me a knowing stare. "I believe we've both been fortunate enough to know some very honorable people in our time, people who left behind a lot of invaluable lessons for us to learn."

Shit, shit, shit. "Yes."

"People who exited the world with more lessons still to teach. It's not up to me to understand or translate those lessons for you, but merely to guide the steps of—"

"What does that mean, Bernard?" I snapped, wanting to hug him and punch him because he reminded me so much of Remi. "Stop talking in Bernard Elizondo and give it to me straight."

"It means that I have faith in you. In your ability to do the right thing."

I don't know why, but all of a sudden the sight of him in the kitchen, *their* kitchen, hurt me. "So are you on their side now, is that it?"

"There are no sides, Damion."

"Bullshit there aren't—"

"I can't find her," Julia said as she walked into the kitchen. "Where's my mom?"

Did she hear us?

Bernard adjusted his cuffs, his eyes on his sleeves. "She just left for a committee meeting."

"I thought you said she was upstairs and was looking for me," Julia said, looking confused.

"She was but she left," Bernard said in that Bernard way that left no question whether or not his words made sense. Because if *he* said them, they made sense.

"This whole season thing is nuts," she said, looking over at me. "Your mom and my mom, planning the insanity together. So weird."

"*Your* mother is also on the committee?" Bernard asked me.

"She actually is," I said, positive he already knew that because the man knew everything.

"Perhaps they'll become friends," he replied.

I looked at him, my mind racing. I wasn't sure if he was threatening me or dropping one of his proverbial pearls of wisdom, but I didn't like the way it felt, regardless.

I snuck a glance at Julia, her eyes all bright and shiny in that very Julia way. My chest squeezed.

No. I didn't like how *anything* was feeling lately.

CHAPTER TWENTY-FIVE

"Always carry an umbrella. You're covered if it rains and covered if you need to kick someone's ass."

—Remington

Julia

"You look amazing, Jules," Donovan said as the elevator took us up to the rooftop of the Henry. Because, yes, Beckett lived in the *penthouse* of a luxurious building, and his party was on the rooftop.

Did that mean he was the richest of all the rich people who lived there?

"You really do," Jasmine agreed, reaching out a hand and adjusting the right side of my hair.

"Thanks to you guys," I said, feeling a tiny bit amazing.

I'd gone to Donovan's to get ready for the party, opting to go with my friends instead of my brother, and she and Jasmine had insisted I borrow something from her closet. And I was glad for the offer, because for the first time since our arrival in New York, it seemed like I looked pretty okay.

I was wearing Donovan's white off-the-shoulder cashmere sweater, a trio of chunky necklaces that managed to look effortlessly cool and twinkly, and a pair of weathered jeans with loafers the color of my hair.

And my friends had somehow managed to make my hair look *good*.

It was down, with zero pins trying to force it into place, but the product they'd used had somehow transformed it. The wild curls were as wild as ever, but they looked soft and intentional, like I wanted my hair to look that way.

I was in love with it.

So much so that I'd begged them to let me keep the five bottles of *whatever* they'd used on my head.

The elevator doors opened, and you'd think, as someone who actually lived in a spectacular house, that I would stop being so starstruck by the grandioseness of Gardenwood.

But that was impossible.

Because it was hard not to stare with a gaping mouth as we walked onto a stunning—and huge—rooftop patio. A patio larger than the main level of our old house. There were couches and tables, perfectly placed, roaring fireplaces illuminating the dusk, and music coming from the DJ . . . *stand* (was that what it was called?) that was set up near luscious botanical plants.

"Have Your Lovin'" by Johnny Orlando. *Nice choice.*

Immediately I saw kids I recognized from school, but unlike at the soiree, I didn't want to run away screaming.

Because people were laughing. Talking with actual volume.

I could breathe out here.

The smells of the city came at me on the autumn breeze, and I wondered if I'd taken a wrong turn and was on the set of some really cool streaming series instead of at a high school party.

Instead of red Solo cups, I saw wineglasses, pint glasses, lowball glasses. Instead of beer pong, there were guys *my age* playing cards around a table. While smoking *cigars.*

It was like these people were grown-ups in teenagers' bodies or something.

So, so douchey.

"Julia!"

I squinted and saw that one of the cigar smokers was the birthday boy himself, so we approached their game.

"Happy birthday, Beckett," I said, my cheeks getting hot from the attention, but this time no mean girls were eyeballing me like they wanted me to disappear, no Toms were scoffing like my existence was screwing with their world aesthetic.

"Where's the food, Beckett?" Donovan asked, fluffing her hair as her eyes scanned the rooftop.

"No 'happy birthday'—just 'where's the food?'" he said, looking at his cards.

"Happy birthday, where's the food?" she corrected.

"Inside." Beckett rearranged his hand. "The chef's got a helluva spread in there whenever you're hungry."

I realized as I stood there that Liam was sitting next to him. My *brother* was one of the douchey bros.

"You smoke cigars now?" I said without thinking.

He didn't look up from his cards. "Do I really have to answer that?"

"Let me rephrase. Have you always smoked cigars and I never knew, or is this your stogie debut?"

"Yeah," Beckett said with a smirk. "Is this your stogie debut, Lowell?"

My brother laughed as he puffed. "You don't know everything, Jules."

"Can I get you something to drink?" A waiter popped up at our side, apparently ready to take our drink orders.

This definitely doesn't happen at parties back home.

"Oh. A drink. Um . . ." I said, wondering what in the world to order. I didn't want to seem gauche, like a kid ordering a Shirley Temple at her first big Gardenwood party, but I also didn't want to seem try-hard by going with something like a vodka cranberry.

"Um, I—"

"She'll take a Dr Pepper," I heard from behind me.

I turned around and there was Damion.

He was wearing jeans, a charcoal sweater with a white T-shirt underneath, and a backward baseball cap that teased his dark curls through the opening. A different pair of black glasses were on his face, these with thin frames, and the overall look was a tiny bit overwhelming.

I was used to the prep-school version of Damion, but the casual iterations of him kind of took my breath away.

"You're ordering for me?" I said, managing to sound unaffected even though I was definitely affected.

"Just offering a suggestion," he replied, his eyes dipping down to my exposed shoulder, making me want to tug nervously at the sweater.

"Well, I *will* take a Dr Pepper," I said to the server, "but not because he's suggesting it."

"Okay, miss," the waiter said, before turning to my friends and taking their orders.

"You are the last person I expected to see here," Damion said quietly.

"Why is that?" I asked with an eyebrow raise, even though we both knew why.

Nobody likes me here, so why would I be at a party?

"Because you didn't mention it yesterday, and Beckett is one of my best friends and he didn't mention inviting you either," he explained.

"Beckett's one of your best friends?" I glanced over at the guys playing cards, and for some reason I couldn't imagine him hanging out with them. "I can't see it."

The guys at the table seemed way too . . . *not* Damion.

"I get that," he said. "He's a club-joining, extroverted little frat boy, but for some reason I still love him."

"I heard that," Beckett said, pointing his cigar in our direction. "And being involved in school activities doesn't make me a 'frat boy,' for the record."

"You're puffing a cigar whilst wearing a shirt that says 'Birthday Daddy,'" Damion said, but he looked amused as he mocked his friend.

"Okay, so a teeny bit fratty," Beckett corrected, not looking remotely apologetic as the breeze played with his spiky hair. "If you remember correctly, I bought this shirt for *you* on *your* birthday, but you refused to wear it."

"That's called taste."

"That's called a missed fucking opportunity, Rutledge."

"Come on," Donovan said, grabbing my arm. "Let's go drool over the hot DJ."

"What?" I allowed her to pull me alongside her as she and Jasmine crossed the rooftop patio, relieved to be taken away from Damion while also feeling a little disappointed. Relieved because I didn't need any more gossip about the two of us, and disappointed because . . . well, I wasn't sure *why* I felt disappointed.

Probably because he was one of the few people I sort of knew from school.

"Did I hear that you're wearing a Jessi McSullivan design to the ball, Don?" A girl with bright red hair, wearing a crewneck that said *BATSHIrT* and the cutest jeans I'd ever seen, approached us.

"It's true," Donovan said, looking like she'd won something. "I nearly died when my mom told me."

"I'm so jealous," the redhead said, holding her wineglass and shaking her head in disbelief. "The best we could do was Dempsey."

"He's incredible, are you kidding?" Donovan replied. "He's going to make you look stunning."

"I mean, I'm happy with him; Dempsey's really talented," she agreed. "But he's no Jessi."

"You two need to shut up," Jasmine said, "Because I still don't have a dress."

"Only because you know your mom can get *anything you want* from *anyone,* be serious," the redhead said, and then she said to me, "I'm Addison, by the way."

"Julia," I said, pointing to myself. "Nice to meet you."

"You're the one who called Cassandra 'Headband,' right?"

I would've died of embarrassment, but all three of them started laughing like it was hilarious, so I just shrugged. "That would be me, yes."

Her friends, Jo and Grace, joined the conversation, and all three of them seemed . . . pretty okay with me.

As in they weren't gushing warmth and begging me to be their friend, but they weren't calling me New Money and looking at me like I offended their eyeballs by existing, either.

So that was a definite upgrade.

Everybody started talking about the season again, because that was all anyone could talk about, it seemed. There had been another party since my ill-fated soiree, so they were all sharing stories of everything that'd transpired at the event.

"By the way," Addison said, lowering her voice and looking over her shoulder to make sure no one was listening. "My mom thinks, um, *you-know-who*, the Dead Poet king with the glasses, is going to go to the ball with Coco."

"I don't believe for a second he's going," Grace said in a whisper, like she was scared of being overheard, even though we were outside and it was noisy. "I can't picture any scenario that ends with him dressed in a tux and dancing at a ball."

"Who is the Dead Poet king?" I asked, also whispering.

"Rutledge," Donovan said, giving me a look like she thought I might have more information. "Do you know, Jules? Is he going with Coco, or does he have *someone* else he might be interested in taking?"

"What?" I wasn't sure why, but the thought of him and Coco together made me feel . . . not good.

Not good at all.

It seemed right somehow, but also somehow gross and disappointing.

Oh, don't be disappointed in me, Nebraska. I just couldn't bear that.

"He hasn't said anything to me about her, but he probably wouldn't tell me anyway," I said, throwing a lot of *who cares* in my tone when everything about the idea of them as a couple made me feel panicked. "Why do you call him that, by the way?"

"Because he was, like, the original member of the Dead Poets before he became too cool for—gahhhh!"

It was like the sky opened. One minute there was no rain aside from one suspicious sprinkle, and the next it was pouring.

"Oh my God!" Jasmine screamed, laughing as she raised her hands to cover her head. "What the hell?"

It was a cold autumn rain, the kind with big fat drops that slapped.

"My makeup says no to this bullshit, come on!" Donovan yelled.

Everyone took off running toward the side of the rooftop where the elevators were located, and I was about to follow—because my hair didn't need this kind of help—when suddenly an umbrella appeared over my head.

I glanced to my right, half expecting to see Bernard because that was the sort of magic he always managed to perform, but it was Damion instead.

Towering over me, seeming even taller than usual, the umbrella *high* above my head.

"Am I the only one who checks the weather before I go out?" he said calmly, his voice low in the quiet of the underbrella we were sharing.

For a second I forgot how to breathe, because all my existence knew in that moment was him, standing over me, eyes dark and lazy. And the tiniest bit of water droplets hanging onto the curls of black hair.

Oh no.

"I think you must be," I said, finding my words. I smiled in surprise, the twinkle in his eyes making it impossible not to.

“Care to accompany me down the stairs that no one else seems to know about?” He gestured with his head toward the bar.

“Yes, please,” I said, still a tiny bit breathless from whatever this rescue was.

I walked with him over to the bar, our steps in time as he held the umbrella over me. And behind the curtain that ran parallel to the wall of bottles—*voilà*—was a staircase.

“After you, Nebraska,” he said.

When we reached the bottom, he calmly closed the umbrella, leaned it against the wall, and pushed open the nearly invisible door that blended into the wall. *Magic.*

Just like that, we were in the back hallway of a stunning home. The wood floor was gleaming, a long white rug stretching to places unknown like the carpet had been rolled out to lead us home. The walls were beige, trimmed in white, and covered with paintings that were both quiet and bold and luxurious, all at once. Like monochrome finger paintings.

“Come on,” he said, lightly grabbing my sleeve as he led me down the hall toward the noise.

I followed, passing door after door, and when we turned the corner, I gasped when I saw them.

The Skins.

No, no, no.

They're not supposed to be here.

They were standing in a group, blocking the hallway from whatever living space was on the other side of them. Wineglasses were in all their hands, and they saw us at the same time.

“Look who's here,” Naomi said, her eyelids heavy like she was totally out of it. “It's Damion and New Money.”

“You look like you're having a good time,” Damion said, and I felt his fingers tug me and my sleeve a little closer. “How long have you been here?”

"Oh, we've been pregaming all day," she said. "Coco's dad is still overseas, so I've been staying with her all week."

"While the king is away, the princesses play," he muttered, so quietly that only I could hear it.

"Oh my God, you are everywhere, Corn Queen," Coco said, walking over with a mocking smile on her perfect face. "I cannot seem to avoid you."

"Yeah," I said, my heart pounding in my chest as the mean girls grinned like they were happy to see me.

Jackals.

"I mean, that's what they have in Nebraska, right?" She glanced at Damion; then her pale eyes came back to me. "Corn?"

"There *is* corn in the state of Nebraska, yes," I said, ridiculously, horribly, *terribly* embarrassed for Damion to witness this. It shouldn't matter to me, because he was one of them, but for some reason, it did.

"What are you doing?" Damion calmly asked Coco. "Do you have to be snarky all the time?"

Oh.

"You've known me since kindergarten," she said in a bored tone, her pale eyes all over him. "I think you know the answer to that."

"So yes, you *do* have to be snarky all the time," he quipped, looking irritated.

"I just like to be honest and say what everyone else is thinking," she said, glancing over at her sidekicks.

"Everyone is *not* thinking asinine words like 'Corn Queen,'" he said dismissively. "And why are you even here? You hate Beckett."

"Actually, everyone is *absolutely* thinking 'Corn Queen' when they see your adorable little country buddy here," she said with a sneer. "And I came to this pathetic excuse for a party because I need to talk to *you*, Damion."

I felt like passing out as she made fun of me, but I also wasn't going to stand there and let her crap all over me either. But before I could open my mouth to utter something brilliant like *headband*, I saw Damion's face change. His *I don't give a shit* mask slipped for a second, and he looked . . . *hunted* . . . ? He visibly swallowed and seemed nervous.

No. Damion Rutledge didn't *get* nervous.

But he looked uncomfortable as he cleared his throat and said, "Listen, Coke, I don't have time for—"

"It'll only take a minute, *Dame*," she interrupted, her lips curling into a flirty smile as her long eyelashes fluttered. She stepped closer to him, put her hand on his arm, and said, "We can use this bedroom right here, have a nice . . . *conversation*, and you can go find your Midwestern buddy when we're finished."

Her tone was thick with suggestiveness, as if the word "conversation" were a synonym for "sexual encounter."

Which made something animalistic rise up in me.

"Actually, *Coke*," I said through gritted teeth, grabbing his sleeve with all ten of my fingers. Between the way she'd insulted me, her *I am queen* demeanor, and the terrified look she'd put on Damion's face, I was suddenly infused with a purpose so strong it was almost overwhelming.

That purpose—making sure she didn't get what she wanted.

I tilted my head. "We were literally looking for a bedroom when we ran into you, because we're dying to have our own private conversation, so I think you'll have to *chat* with Dame some other time."

"Jules," Damion said, and when I looked at him, he was watching me through narrowed eyes, like he wasn't exactly sure what I was doing.

Like he wasn't sure *I* understood the undercurrents that were buzzing in that hallway.

"Hmm?" I said, raising my eyebrows, hoping he wasn't mad that I was attempting to save him.

Something about my expression must've answered his question, because his mouth slid into a filthy smirk, a half smile that set loose a thousand butterflies in my stomach. His eyes were downright wicked when he said, "If you and I have our conversation, there's no way in hell I'm chatting with anyone else tonight."

I smiled, and with every ounce of courage I had left, I turned back to Coco and said, "Some other time that isn't tonight, apparently."

The words were barely out of my mouth before Damion pushed open the bedroom door beside him and shoved me inside.

CHAPTER TWENTY-SIX

"I'm great at flirting. I might've invented it."

—Remington

Julia

Oh God, I thought as we went into what appeared to be a *very dark* bedroom with a huge king-sized bed in its center.

And I thought *oh God* yet again when Damion closed the door behind us.

"Oh my God," I whispered as darkness engulfed us. "I am *so* sorry about this—what was I thinking?"

He sounded like he thought it was funny when he quietly murmured, "You were trying to stick it to Coco, I think."

"I *was*," I said, hating her so much. "She was just so . . . *rude* with the Corn Queen stuff that I wanted to piss her off and make her jealous."

"And you probably succeeded," he said, sounding absolutely unfazed. "She's probably losing it right now."

"I'm such an idiot, though," I said, my eyes adjusting enough for me to see the outline of him as he stood beside me in the dark. "How long do you think we need to stay in here?"

"That depends on what you want them to think we're doing," he said, and I knew if I could see his face, he'd be smirking.

And if he could see my face, I'd be dying of mortification.

"Can we turn on the light?" I asked, suddenly nervous.

"Same answer," he said.

"Is fifteen minutes a respectable amount of time to spend in here?" I asked, feeling absolutely unsettled as I whispered to him in the darkness.

"You'll *ruin* my reputation," he teased with a laugh. "You gotta give me at *least* forty-five minutes."

My stomach went all light as I forced myself not to think about what that meant.

"Can I call in a bomb threat?" I said, sighing as I stepped away from the door, as I tried adjusting the slouchy sweater that kept sliding off my right shoulder.

"I'd advise against it," he said, laughing. I could feel him stepping closer toward me. "You don't want the cops here."

"Well, what are we going to do in the dark for forty-five minutes?" I whisper-yelled, panicking at the thought of it. My steps led me backward, away from his presence, but he was right there with me.

Back, back, back . . . until I hit the wall behind me.

And he was still there, towering over me.

Damion's voice tickled my skin when he said, "Oh, Nebraska, you're killing me here."

I laughed in spite of the tension. Nervous laughter because what else was there when I was alone in a bedroom with Damion Rutledge?

"I suggest we move to the bed," he said when I finally caught my breath. "We can get comfortable until the bomb squad arrives."

"Well . . . ," I said, trailing off because the idea of being on a bed with him, in the dark, was too much for me to handle. Just like this current situation, this very minute. His face inches from mine. The smell of whatever cologne he was wearing, suffocating my senses as I tried to guess if his eyes were more blue or green today.

"I'll be a good boy, I promise," he said, pushing himself away from me as if he weren't all up in my personal space. Then again, maybe he'd made that move dozens of times. Maybe even with Coco. "We can play a game."

You mean besides the one you just played with me?!

“Or maybe we can just talk?” I asked, trying to regain my composure and avoid something nightmarish like truth or dare.

“Come on,” he said, and I felt his hand grab mine. *Oh my God.* I let him pull me through the dark room, and then my heart stopped when we reached the bed and he gave me a tiny push.

He immediately followed, jumping boyishly onto the surface beside me, flipping onto his back so he was lying flat and staring up at the ceiling.

Blue or green eyes right now?

“I’m not playing *this* game,” I said nervously.

That made him laugh. “I won’t bite, Nebraska. If we’re going to be in here for a while, I want to be comfortable. That’s it, I promise.”

“Oh.”

There was a safety in the removal of eye contact, like the darkness was making it okay to take a risk. So I lay down (a safe distance) next to him, and we both stared up at the ceiling. It was oddly comfortable, the silence between us. And I was glad for it, to be honest, because how could I ever explain to him why I’d inserted myself into this situation?

You looked like Coco made you nervous.

It made zero sense. If there was anyone in the world who *didn’t* need saving, it was Damion Rutledge.

But eventually he asked, “Are you okay with this, or are you going to die of embarrassment when we exit the bedroom?”

He probably didn’t know just how many rumors were already flying about us and the fact that we’d been “hanging out” since I moved in. I didn’t love what this would look like to a lot of people, but I was used to the judgment.

Okay—not *used* to it, I would NEVER be used to it, but I didn’t think this would make it any worse.

“I’m good,” I said. “The embarrassment will be debilitating but not fatal.”

"Worth it?"

"I mean," I said, shrugging. "Sure. It felt good to ruin her happiness."

He made a noise in the back of his throat. "Believe me, I get that."

"Yeah, what's the deal there?" I asked nonchalantly, positive he wouldn't give me a straight answer. "Maybe I misread it, but you definitely looked like you *didn't* want to talk to her. You looked . . . hesitant."

"Hesitant," he repeated, reaching behind his head to fluff the pillow he was lying on. "Yeah, that's a good way to put it. I'm always hesitant to go anywhere near her because she's not exactly nice."

"Like any of you are," I said without thinking.

"*Any* of you?" he said, sounding amused *and* outraged. "Who specifically are you referencing here?"

It wasn't wise, but I admitted, "The entire student body of Gardenwood Academy . . . ?"

He made a noise in the back of his throat, some sort of an agitated sigh. "It's a little insulting, Jules, for you to lump me in with Coco and the Skins or the Toms. Talk about a gross generalization."

"But . . ." Even more unwise, I heard myself ask, "How exactly are you different?"

"Are you kidding me right now?" he asked, his voice quiet but thick with outrage, like I'd *actually* insulted him. He turned over on his side to face me, a challenge, so I did the same. I rolled over, and even though it was dark, my stomach flipped because I could see how intently he was watching me.

I couldn't have actually insulted him, right?

Impossible.

"I mean . . ." I didn't have any explanation, any words of clarification, but I wanted to know. I wanted him to tell me how he was different from everyone else at the academy. "You just said Coco isn't nice, and you've specifically told me that *you* aren't nice, either, so how exactly are you different?"

"For starters, Coco tears people down for fun. It's like a sport to her."

I bit down on my lip, but then I thought *screw it* and said, "Again, you're different how?"

He made that offended noise again. "I only do it when I have good reason."

What in God's name could he mean by that? "Good reason? When have I ever given you a good reason to tear me down?"

At that his stare lingered on me for a bit too long. It may have been dark in that room, but I knew when Damion Rutledge's hazel eyes peered into mine. It was a unique feeling all its own. It made a shiver trip down my spine, especially with what he said next.

"Maybe it isn't 'tearing down' at all." His voice was as dark as the room when he said, "Maybe it's flirting."

"Oh, okay," I scoffed, because *of course* he would say that.

"Speaking of flirting," he said, his subject change silky smooth. "Since we've got time to kill in this cozy bedroom, I'd be more than happy, as your tutor, to volunteer to give you a flirting lesson."

He was so close, it was so dark.

"Oh my God, I don't need a flirting lesson from *you*, Mr. Ego," I said, sounding as flustered as I felt, "but thank you so much for the offer."

"No, think about it," he said, scooting slightly closer, a smirk in his deep voice. "I'm an expert in Gardenwood flirting. You are not. Let me tutor you in something fun, free of charge."

"Wow, a flirting lesson *free of charge*? From Damion the Expert?" I mocked, but my brain was kind of crashing out because this was too intimate of a topic to be discussing in this dark of a room.

On this big of a bed.

I said, "Oh my God, you're so selfless."

"Right?" he replied, and I could *hear* he was grinning his dirty grin, the one that always made my stomach dip.

My stomach was dipping just from picturing it, actually.

He said, "I mean, eventually you're going to meet someone you're interested in, and won't it be nice if you're equipped with the skills to land them?"

How can he be so arrogant? I wondered.

"How do you know I haven't already met them?" I said, annoyed by the way he was acting like I was a clueless child when it came to flirting.

He said, "I'm flattered—"

"Not *you*," I scoffed, even though there was, of course, *no one* I was flirting with in this hellscape where people hated me.

"Really." His tone changed. "Then who, Miss Lowell?"

Miss Lowell.

I don't know why, but I just couldn't let him win. His cocky know-it-all attitude on full display in this very intense moment was too much. It was the only explanation for why I said, "Not that it's any of your business, but your friend Beckett is interesting."

"Beckett?" He sounded shocked.

Good.

"You're interested in *Beckett*?" he repeated, his voice a little louder. Less smooth. More agitated.

"I mean, I don't know if I'd say I'm *interested*," I said, suddenly feeling good about my lie. I liked that I'd caught him off guard. Made him lose the cockiness in his voice.

It inspired me. And suddenly I wanted to shock the hell out of Damion the Rebel. I smiled at him in the darkness and said, "But Beckett is definitely interesting."

"Interesting." He was quiet for a second, then he said under his breath, "Huh."

"Interesting and not an asshole," I added, feeling a little light, a little playful.

"Is that what you look for?" he asked, his tone unreadable from the small space between us. "Not an asshole? Seems like the bare minimum."

"It's a good start."

"So somewhere between 'dickhead with a mullet' and 'non-asshole' is your starting spot," he said. "That's a low bar, Nebraska."

Was it just me or did he sound . . . mad? Annoyed. *Big bad Damion can't handle someone else messing with him for change?*

"Don't you worry about my bar, *New York*."

"Oh, I'm not," he said, a distinctness to his tone. "But I'm going to need you to move a little closer."

"What? Why?"

"Because our lesson is about to begin." Gravelly and low, his voice came out with an extra something that I felt in every cell in my body. It sounded like his usual arrogant flirtatiousness, but there was an edge to it.

An urgency, maybe . . . ?

No.

Impossible.

"I told you I know how to flirt," I said, and I was impressed by the confidence in my tone when I *so* didn't feel it.

"Sure you do." The mattress dipped and suddenly his face was right beside mine, his head closer on the pillow next to the pillow my head was resting on.

I was looking into his hazel eyes, and *God*, they were watching me as the smell of his wicked cologne slithered around my consciousness and made me hyperaware of every detail about him.

Glasses, eyebrows, sweater, cheekbones, eyes that seem to see everything . . .

"Has it ever occurred to you that you *aren't* the best at everything?" I asked, trying not to focus on the fact that we were *lying on pillows on a king-sized bed, dear Lord.* "That your self-professed expertise might simply be that, your own opinion?"

"Nope," he said quietly, reaching out a hand to touch my hair on the pillow.

I held my breath, unsure of what was going on as his eyes—and his long fingers—offhandedly trailed along a curl.

I was pretty sure I was going to spontaneously combust.

Get it together, Jules!

"Maybe I don't need tutoring," I said, ignoring the way my pulse was running wildly erratic. "Maybe *you're* the one who needs tutoring."

And then.

His hand stilled and his eyes shot to my face.

His Adam's apple moved when he swallowed, and I watched his jaw flex.

Shit!

"Well, well, Nebraska," he said, lifting his hand to set that exploring fingertip on my bare shoulder instead. The warmth of it sent a shiver down my spine. "Here you are, in this sweater, blowing my mind and giving me ideas."

"That's not what I meant," I said in a rush, but my voice came out so, so quiet, far too breathy. "I didn't—"

"Teach me, teacher," he said, the warmth of his hand still sliding along the skin of my shoulder as his gaze slid over my face.

My eyes wanted to close and my voice didn't seem to want to work. "You misunder—"

"Apprendez-moi, maîtresse," he said, his eyes playful and so, so, close, *oh my God, what is happening?*

I couldn't seem to speak, to move, to do anything as his voice toyed with me in another language, as his fingers toyed with my sweater, tugging it into place on my shoulder.

"Mi insegni, Maestra, in italiano," he said on a breath, his lips so close to mine, his hazel eyes dipping to my mouth.

My heart was pounding in my ears as Damion leaned—

"Time's up, we need this room!" I heard as someone banged loudly on the door, snapping me back into reality.

I gasped as the door flew open and the lights came on, and two people I didn't know stumbled into the room.

I scrambled to sit up, squinting into the jarringly bright light as I very nearly leapt off that bed.

"Fine, it's yours," Damion said, and when I glanced over at him, he was smirking and climbing leisurely off the bed like this was no big deal.

Like he'd just been woken from a long nap or something.

He looked rumpled and beautiful, a fallen angel or boyish devil, as he adjusted the backward hat on his head.

What what what just happened with him??

I was totally freaking out.

He wasn't looking at me, so I couldn't read his expression, though I wasn't sure if I wanted to or not.

Because I had no idea what was going on.

What in God's name had just almost happened in the dark??

I followed his watchful gaze to the doorway, where Coco was standing, glaring back at him like they were having an angry, wordless conversation.

Fabulous.

"You ready, Jules?" Damion asked, and when I looked at him, he winked and grabbed my hand.

I forced my lips into a smile and nodded.

And then he lowered his head and said, loud enough for everyone to hear, "That was one hell of a conversation, honey."

CHAPTER TWENTY-SEVEN

"Sometimes doing the right thing sucks, but other times, it can be fun as hell."

—Remington

Damion

"I'm just saying it's hella ballsy," Beckett said as we walked into the cafeteria. He went straight for the sushi bar, just like he did every day. "*I* invited her to my birthday party, yet *you* celebrated with her in my bedroom, you dick."

"Whatever," I said, irritated by the way everyone was making such a big deal about what went down—or didn't, actually—at Beck's party.

People needed to mind their own fucking business.

"She looked good the other night, though," he said, grabbing a platter of California rolls. "And I don't care what anyone says, she seems pretty cool."

"Okay," I said.

"I mean, I'll come out and say it—I like her."

"Fantastic," I said, wanting him, the most interesting man in the room, to shut the hell up.

Interesting. Julia thought he was "interesting," whatever the hell that meant.

Not an asshole.

Which, okay, fair.

I *was* an asshole, and I tried my damnedest to be the biggest asshole I could be around her, but it was still annoying, the way she barely knew Beck yet she assumed he *wasn't* an asshole.

I mean, he *wasn't*, but still.

I took some tuna rolls and followed him over to a table.

But *dammit*, he went straight for the Toms and I wasn't in the mood.

"What the hell, Rutledge?" Corbin said when I sat down, giving me one of his skeevy smiles, like we were in cahoots together or something. "I thought you said you were just 'talking' to New Money, but it sounds like that was a lie."

Shut up, jackass.

I said, "Yeah, uh—"

"So she's . . . fun?" he asked, raising his eyebrows and grinning. "I trust you had a good time, yes?"

"Christ, Archington, don't be such a douchebag," I said, wondering why anyone liked him.

At all.

He was an asshole.

"Relax," he said with a cackle, and as I looked at him, I thought of Julia's comment.

How exactly are you different?

Julia Nebraska thought I was no different from Corbin Archington, and that was depressing as hell. I took pride in the fact that I was nothing like the rest of the sheep at Gardenwood, so having someone make that assumption made me feel like trash.

How exactly are you different?

I kept hearing her question, but I refused to entertain it.

She didn't know shit about me.

"So are you and New Money official, then," Corbin asked, "or is she still—"

"Is she still what—*available*?" Beckett finished, scowling. "Are you seriously asking that two fucking days later, Arch?"

"Hey, I'm not one to let the dust settle; I jump when it's hot," he said, rubbing his hands together.

"You're fucking gross," I said, feeling even worse about Julia's assumption. "Shut the hell up."

The idea of her thinking I was no different from these people was kind of disgusting.

And hearing her name come out of Corbin's mouth made me want to beat his face in.

Underneath it all, too, was the uncomfortable truth that I knew Remi would be disappointed I hadn't done enough good to distance myself from my classmates.

"So it *is* more than just talking," Corbin said smugly. "Why can't you just be honest about that? Just admit that you're feeling the fuck out of Miss New Mon—"

"Will you shut your goddamn mouth?" I said, grabbing the front of his shirt and jerking him closer, seeing red as I looked at his smarmy little face. "Or I'll shut it for you, I swear to God."

"What's your *problem*?" Corbin said in a high-pitched voice.

"Cool it, Dame," Beckett said, leaning forward to remove my fist from Arch's shirt. "Your dad will kill you if you get another suspension."

"Shit," I muttered as I let him go. *Shit.* "You're right."

"Yeah, maybe chill the fuck out," Corbin said, running a hand over the front of his shirt, scowling down at it as if my fist had marred the fabric. "I just got this, for Christ's sake."

Things didn't get any better after that, because all anyone could talk about was me and Nebraska and Beck's bedroom. Even though my stern declarations of NOTHING HAPPENED fell on deaf ears.

If I was getting shit for it, that meant she was getting it ten times worse. And that thought pissed me off.

Me worrying about her pissed me off more.

Not my problem.

Her unhappiness had nothing to do with me. I hadn't been the one who suggested we go into the bedroom, but still . . .

Fuck.

It also pissed me off that I couldn't stop thinking about her on that bed, in that dark bedroom. It'd been insane and stupid—insanely stupid—the way she smelled like flowers and made me come this fucking close to kissing her, but I was also smart enough to realize that it'd been nothing more than chemistry.

A biological reaction to being in a bedroom with an attractive person.

That was all.

I gritted my teeth and made it through most of the afternoon, but my annoyance hit a new peak when I saw the photocopied pictures of Julia, hanging in random spots all over the senior hallway.

What the hell?

They were taped up like flyers, printed in black and white. I pulled one off a locker and holy God, it was a photo that had been taken at the party.

Specifically, it was from when we were interrupted.

Holy shit, who would do this?

Julia was standing next to the bed, her white sweater hanging off her right shoulder, looking like she'd pulled it on in a hurry. Her hair was wild, curls everywhere, and she looked surprised and sleepy.

She looked *bedded*, holy shit.

The photo was nothing, in a way, just a not-so-great picture of someone.

But in a place where appearances were everything, it was like the ultimate insult.

An act of war.

I looked at her startled expression on the paper, and suddenly *not an asshole* didn't seem like such a low bar at all.

I crumpled the photo and tossed it into the trash, but when I turned the corner and saw Julia standing in front of Coco's locker, talking to Bella and Coco, I slowed.

Because her face.

Shit, shit, shit.

Her face was red, splotchy, almost as if she'd been *crying*, which wasn't possible, right? Sure, she was awkward as shit and pretty introverted, but Julia was also skilled at trading quiet barbs with me.

I mean, she'd literally run me down when she thought I'd stolen that stupid fucking wallet, so the girl could hold her own, right?

But the sight of her, looking . . . Jesus, so damn broken, made something in my chest feel uncomfortably tight.

And I fucking lost it.

"Listen, Miss Bedhead," Bella was saying, her smile garishly huge as she looked at Julia like she was being ridiculous. "Someone snapped a funny picture and I just printed it off. I think you need to lighten up."

"For sure," Coco agreed, tilting her head and crossing her arms, looking like a fucking evil queen.

"And it's *Corn Queen*, not *Bedhead*," Coco added, her tone dripping with condescension. "I like that better."

Bella said, "And here I thought she was New Money. Gosh, it's hard to keep track of *which* adorable nickname suits her best."

"I'd go with 'Damion's date,' I said, stepping forward, wanting to crush those assholes.

I shoved my hands into my pockets, trying to be chill when I really wanted to unload on them for being such dicks.

But it wouldn't do any good.

I'd learned a long time ago that they were entirely incapable of seeing themselves as anything other than the main characters in their world, the girls who were always in the right.

"What?" Coco said, looking confused, and her look fueled me.

I *loved* when she was confused, when everything *wasn't* going as she'd planned.

Which was why I enjoyed every second of what I did next.

I said, "Since Julia is my date for the season, maybe *Damion's Date* is the best nickname for her."

Suddenly I was moving to stand beside her, looking down at Julia's fast-blinking gaze as I said, "I mean, it's a hell of a lot better than the lazy shit I just heard. You're still using *Corn Queen*? Absolutely lacking in creativity, Coke."

"I'm sorry," Coco said, her perfect face contorting into something ugly as her brows crammed together and her eyes narrowed into little slits. "Did you just say you're taking *her* to the ball?"

"That's right," I said.

But when I looked down at Julia, at the way she was watching me with wide eyes, I realized I was going to have to do it.

Aw, shit.

I'd said it to make waves, to shut them up, but as Julia looked up at me, it was obvious that she thought I was messing with her, too. Her expression told me that she didn't think for a minute that I was serious, that she thought I was just another asshole playing with her.

And I mean, I *was*.

But I couldn't shake that damn Remi epiphany I'd had earlier, either, the one that reminded me of everything he hated about Gardenwood. Of everything he'd raised me not to be.

And I really REALLY couldn't shake the tears still staining her freckle-sprinkled cheeks.

Shit, shit, shit.

I swallowed, clenched my jaw as the everything of what I'd just done punched me in the chest, and I announced, "I'm doing the season with Julia."

And then I turned and headed straight for the exit, just as Liam appeared and rescued his sister from the girls staring at her in shock.

Dear God.

What did I just do?

But when my nerves settled and I stopped focusing on what my dad would do when he found out I'd asked Julia Lowell to the season, I took a deep breath of fresh autumn air and thought of Remi.

Of Julia's face as she was being mocked.

Hunted.

Remi would want me to take her, to rescue her from the assholes, regardless of what her family might've done.

I knew that without a doubt, and I hated it.

Because now I had no choice.

CHAPTER TWENTY-EIGHT

"You might hate life in New York from time to time, but it's impossible to hate the city itself."

—Remington

Julia

"Why are you in bed?" my mom asked. "Do you feel okay?'

She looked concerned as she stood there in the doorway, and I was torn between wanting to lie and say I was fine and wanting to sob out the truth in hopes that she could somehow make everything all better.

Like she'd always been able to do when I was little.

But I was afraid if I started crying again I wouldn't be able to stop.

It'd been almost impossible earlier.

"I'm fine," I said, sitting up. "I'm just tired."

"Oh. Well, Damion's at the door," she said with a smile. "So maybe run a comb through your hair."

Shit. I'd forgotten all about our tutoring session.

NO.

I didn't want to see him, and also her comb comment made me think of *Miss Bedhead* and my throat got all tight again.

I hate it here so much.

"Can you tell him . . . ," I started, but then I trailed off because if I told her I was canceling a lesson, she'd get all in my business wanting to know why, and I just couldn't.

Explaining, out loud, what everything was like in my life was too embarrassing for words.

Everyone hates me and I'm a laughingstock, Ma.

I also supposed I should thank him, or at least be polite, for rescuing me from the Skins. I wasn't sure why he'd said what he said, because everyone was ultimately going to know the truth when we didn't go to the ball together, but I'd been grateful for the moment.

"Okay, I'll be down in a sec," I said.

I pulled my hair up in a ponytail, not even looking in a mirror because what was the point, and I ran down the stairs. I wanted to get this over with so I could climb back under the covers and go back to hiding.

He was standing in the living room, staring out the window, his back to me.

How is he so tall?

"Hey, um," I said, but my words got a little tripped up when he turned around.

His eyes were sharp, his face serious as he looked at me.

His thick hair was tousled, like he'd been out in the wind, and the collar on his blazer was turned up. The top button on his white Oxford was undone, his tie was loosened, and his hands were in his pockets.

It was a disheveled version of Mr. Perfect, although as soon as I thought that, I realized he looked really *good* disheveled, so perhaps it was more of a testament to how perfect he actually was.

Ugh.

I cleared my throat and started over. "I think we cancel tutoring today."

His jaw flexed and unflexed, his gaze tough to read. "But your practice test is coming up—"

"What the hell *was* that, Damion?" I interrupted, suddenly drained of the ability to engage in cat-and-mouse Gardenwood games.

"Whatever do you mean?" he asked, his mouth going to the sardonic half smile that was his signature expression.

"Seriously?" I said with a sigh. "I'm really not in the mood, come on."

He echoed my sigh, but his was in mockery of mine. "It was a promposal, sweetheart."

"Don't call me that," I snapped. "And don't be ridiculous."

"Who is being ridiculous here, Nebraska?"

"I'm pretty sure it's you," I said.

"Come on, honey, don't be testy," he purred. "You owe me a favor, remember, and I've decided that favor is going to be you going with me to the ball."

"No," I said, shaking my head. There was no way he was being serious, but even if he was, I *didn't* want to go. I mean, I wanted to stick it to Coco, but I definitely didn't want to attend yet another fancy social event where I didn't fit in. "Absolutely not. I don't want to go."

"Too bad. You agreed to the favor," he said dismissively, shrugging.

I looked at his face, so cocky and sure, and wondered what his endgame was. Had he done this—as a nice guy—to save me from bullying, was he using my favor to snag an easy date to the ball he didn't want to attend, or was there something else in play that I was missing?

My head was constantly spinning as I tried figuring out the manipulative motivations of the characters who lived in this world.

"The good news," he said, crossing the room to stand directly in front of me, "is that now we can spend time together openly, in a different way, without all these tricky mathematical equations getting in our way."

"What do you mean?" I asked, putting my hands on my hips as I tried to figure him out.

Impossible, that.

"I mean that if we're going to the ball together, we need to plan our outfits," he said, his eyebrows furrowing in that mocking way, like I was the ridiculous one. "Seriously, Nebraska, you act as if this is your first time attending the season."

"You know, you're really kind of a jerk," I said, half wanting to laugh but too emotionally drained to pull that off.

"A jerk who is your date," he said, that smirk turning into an actual smile.

I gave my head a little shake and bit my lip to keep from smiling back at him. "How can this be true?"

"You're a lucky girl, it seems," he said, his voice dipping into its low, flirtatious octave, reminding me of whatever had gone down in that dark bedroom.

My throat was dry, but I cleared it and said, "Then why do I feel so incredibly *un*lucky today?"

CHAPTER TWENTY-NINE

"When the fall breeze whips itself into a bluster, pull down your hat, because a fuckin' storm is coming."

—Remington

Damion

I nearly ran over her brother when I walked out the front door.

"Hey, man," he said, leaning against the building with his arms crossed, like he'd been waiting for me.

"Hey," I replied, hunching my shoulders against the brisk wind as crunchy leaves blew across the sidewalk between us.

I did my best to avoid Julia's brother, because I didn't like the way he'd looked at me.

Like he thought I was up to something.

So when he said, "You and Julia. Going to the season? Together?"

Yeah, I could hear the accusations in his voice.

Dammit.

"Is this a rhetorical question?" I said, not wanting to admit to anything more than that.

"Yeah, I guess I don't get it," he said, his eyes a little narrowed like he didn't trust me or was suspicious of my motives. "As far as I can tell, you don't really seem to be into my sister, and aside from the tutoring, you two don't hang out. So why do you suddenly want to take her?"

Good question, bro.

I opened my mouth to speak, but then he said, "Or does this have to do with the bullshit rumors about Beckett's party? Is that your game, you want to start some shit about the thing that didn't happen but everyone seems to think *did* happen?"

Well, hell.

Liam wasn't holding anything back, was he?

"Listen, Liam—"

"No, you listen, Rutledge," he snapped, straightening and stepping slightly closer. "To be honest, I think you're a prick for not shutting down the gossip, but that's just me. I'm a decent guy."

A decent guy who I want to hit, I thought, a little in shock that he was coming at me like that.

No one came at me like that.

"But what I want to know—and I'm asking you straight, so don't give me that rebel-without-a-cause attitude—is what your endgame is. Everyone at Gardenwood is an asshole to my sister, so if you're doing this as some sort of grand asshole gesture, you're not gonna like what happens afterward."

What the hell?

"Are you *threatening* me?" I asked in disbelief.

"I'm not usually that douchey, but I'm also not going to let somebody treat her like shit for entertainment."

"I know we don't know each other, but do I seem like that big of a dick to—"

"Yeah, kind of," he interrupted. "The fact that Beckett likes you is the only reason I'm even considering giving you the benefit of the doubt."

"Well, then, praise God for Beckett Schwab's friendship," I muttered under my breath.

"What was that, Damion?" Liam stepped even closer, in my fucking face, raising his voice like he had the right.

Oh, hell no.

Not. Happening.

"Listen, why don't you calm down, *Lowell*," I said, pushing him out of my space with both hands because who the *hell* did he think he was? I was doing my best to stay calm, but I wasn't about to let his protective-brother energy suffocate me either. "I'm leaving, all right?"

Jesus. I'd never wanted to kick someone's ass and also proudly pat his back at the same time. The way he was looking out for his sister was admirable. Impressive, even.

Because, yes, she needed looking out for.

Especially from me.

But, like, was this sort of sibling dynamic normal? The way the Lowells treated each other, like they *liked* each other and worried about each other's happiness—was that how other families behaved?

I knew my parents *loved* me, but my emotional well-being wasn't a high priority for either of them.

Uncle Remi had given me a taste of that when he was around, but it was tough to imagine it on a daily basis.

Fuck, was I *jealous* of the Lowells?

Yes. The answer, I realized as I got home later that day, was yes, I absolutely was.

"Tell me it isn't true, Damion," my mother said as I walked into the den. "Tell me you didn't ask that girl to the season."

That girl.

She was sitting on the couch with a glass of wine in her hand and a washcloth folded on her forehead, which meant she had a tension headache. My dad was seated beside her with a generous pour of brandy in his snifter and a red face, which was how *he* dealt with her tension headaches.

"It's not true, it can't be," he said definitively, dismissing the notion. "Our son isn't a fool."

"It actually *is* true," I said, my stomach suddenly dropping to the floor, because the flare of his nostrils and the hawklike stare he was pinning on me meant this was going to be a much bigger deal than the big deal I'd been worried it was going to be. "You wanted me to do the season, so I found a date."

"Oh, come on, Damion!" my dad snapped, his eyes flashing. "Don't give us that shit. Of all the people you could take, you chose *her*? This is bullshit rebellion and I'm not having it!"

"The Lowells are the ones who stole your house, who bilked Uncle Rem out of his estate," my mom said, her voice rising in pitch and volume. "How could you do this to us? To him?"

Ouch, I thought, my gut clenching.

"You're not taking her," my father said. "Period. That's it and that's final. I don't care who you have to replace her with, this is not—"

"I can't dump her now," I interrupted, knowing how bad that would be for Julia. "Are you serious? Do you know what everyone would say—"

"I don't care!" my dad yelled. "I don't care *what* everyone would say about her getting dumped. We are hosting the ball this year, so the optics, for our family, are a very big deal. You will not use this once-in-a-lifetime opportunity to parade around the daughter of our enemy! Honestly, with how close you were to Rem, I can't believe you'd even consider this."

He looked at me like I was a traitor, and even though I knew he was working an angle, it made me *feel* like a traitor for every time I'd been with Julia.

"He's probably rolling over in his grave at this slap in the face, at your disloyalty after the way he always took care of you. Here I am, working my ass off to find a way to get rid of those vultures—"

"So am I!" I said, hating him for making me feel shittier than I already did about Remi. "Do you honestly think I'm not *also* actively trying to get the house back?"

"What?" My dad held up a hand, cutting me off as his shrewd blue eyes narrowed and searched my face. He tilted his head. "Hold up. What does that mean?"

Shit.

It meant nothing.

I might've been trying to find something at the beginning, some piece of evidence that'd prove the Lowells were grifters, but I didn't have jack.

I rubbed the back of my neck, agitated as hell, trying to think of words that would defuse this situation.

"Just that, uh . . ."

"So *that's* why you've been spending time with that girl," my mother said, her pinched expression morphing into an understanding smile. "You're trying to get information."

"Is that it?" my dad asked, eyebrows raised.

"Would it matter?" I said with a sigh.

I'd let them think that if it calmed their asses about the ball.

"It would." He sat back and swirled the liquid in his glass, staring at the amber liquor as if it held answers. His voice was low when he asked, in an approving tone, "Having any luck?"

I hated this feeling.

I hated *myself* for feeling this feeling. The feeling I got when my dad gave me an ounce of attention, of credit, of a smile or a goddamn "attaboy." It was so rare, his approval, that the dopamine spiked hard every time. The pathetic little boy trying to impress his dad never disappeared, no matter how much of an asshole his dad was.

"Maybe. Time will tell," I said vaguely, shrugging. I felt sick.

"Well, then I'm going to trust you on this," he said quietly, watching me like he wanted me to squirm. Like he wanted to make sure I understood everything he *wasn't* saying.

"You and I might be different, Damion, but I have faith in your loyalty to this family. And I trust that this disturbing plot twist is going to result in the same net positive for the Rutledges."

My gut clenched as he spoke of our "family" like we really were some sort of crime syndicate.

I wondered if Clint Lowell had ever used the term "net positive" in regard to *his* children.

CHAPTER THIRTY

"Sometimes October bashes you in the face
with gold-tipped joy."

—Remington

Damion

"Damion!"

I closed my locker, glad the day was over, and turned just in time to see Julia running toward me.

Literally.

She was grinning, her smile enormous as she waved a piece of paper in the air and jogged in my direction, all long legs in motion.

And I felt . . . lost.

What the hell?

For starters, she was wearing tall socks today, tall socks with tiny bows on top that made it impossible not to notice the soft skin between the hem of her skirt and those flirty little bows.

Dear *God*.

But also I was lost because, like . . . was she yelling to some *other* Damion?

Because she never looked at me like that, like raw happiness was coursing through her veins.

No, she usually looked at me like she expected me to pick her fucking pocket or slip her a roofie.

"What's up?" I asked, very interested to know what the hell was going on.

I could see over her shoulder that other people were noticing her running toward me as well.

"My practice test scores—look." She was beaming, holding out the paper, and I swear to God she made a little squealing sound.

I snagged the results and as my eyes scanned the numbers, I whistled.

"Holy shit, Nebraska, you nailed these."

"Right?" she said, and that squeal was still there. "Five points over the cutoff."

"I told you," I said, and I couldn't *not* smile back at her as she beamed up at me like an overexcited puppy. I looked down at those glossed-over grinning lips and said, "I knew you'd kill it."

"Thank you!" she said, and then she threw her arms around my shoulders.

Around *me*.

My chest pinched a little as she squeezed the shit out of me, because she'd worked her ass off for this. She'd studied hard and it hadn't come easy, yet she'd pulled it off. It felt great.

Wait. Hell, was I *proud* of her??

Before I could let my thoughts settle, I felt her.

All of her.

Dear Jesus.

Because when she hugged me, I'd reflexively hugged her back. My arms went around her body naturally. Easily. *Perfectly.*

But suddenly all I could focus on was the feel of her arms pulling me closer, the press of her soft body against mine. I wrapped my arms around her waist—because what else would I do when she was gluing herself to me—and crushed her more tightly against me.

Julia. Julia. Julia.

She was warm and short and smelled like something I wanted to taste as she gripped me like this was completely normal for us.

But it wasn't.

This was Julia, for the love of God, so why wasn't I pulling back?

"I hate to admit it," she said, looking up at me with a teasing grin. Her arms lowered but slowly, where I felt the relaxing drag of her fingertips as they left my shoulders. "But it's kind of all because of my tutor."

"Careful, Jules," I said, staring into a face so full of unchecked joy that I kind of didn't want to ever look away. "You sound a little grateful. To *me*."

"I know," she said with a giggle, her nose crinkling. "It's nuts to let Damion Rutledge feel my gratitude, right?"

How is a nose crinkle so cute? It was just a movement on her face, but something about the way it paired with the squint of her eyes when she laughed made it seem like the physical embodiment of her joy. This version of Julia had forgotten about everything in the world except happiness, and it was . . . really something.

It was *her*.

Get a grip, Rutledge.

I needed to look away from that face, so I lifted my hands and adjusted her crooked tie instead.

Said with just the right amount of innuendo, "I mean, I'd be all in on feeling your grat—"

"Stop," she interrupted with a laugh as she looked down at where my hands were fixing her Windsor knot. "Don't ruin my gratitude by being a pig."

I tilted my head to see if the tie was straight now, needing another minute of looking at something other than her face. I nodded. "Much better."

"What are you doing now, Rutledge?" she asked, running her hands down the silky tie.

"Besides fixing your abominable knotting work?" I said, dropping my hands. "I was going to go to the park," I admitted, though I *wouldn't* admit to what I'd been planning on doing there.

"Well, I'm going with you," she said, "because we need to celebrate."

"Celebrate as in . . . 'cel-e-brate good times—come on . . .'?" I asked, still feeling out of sorts and confused by this happy-little-elf version of Julia who was being all fucking . . . nymphish. With *me*. "Is the park really the best place for a cel-e-bration?"

"Just shut up and come on," she said, grabbing my sleeve.

What was *with* her today? I'd be lying if I said I didn't like it, but that was just because the juxtaposition was entertaining and I loved to be entertained.

I liked the unpredictability of whatever this was.

She said, "Save that sarcastic wit for later. Right now I'm going to shower you with a few of my favorite things on the way."

"Sounds messy," I complained as she started walking, as she jerked my arm and pulled me behind her.

"You're going to love it."

"I cannot believe you walk your cat."

"I know. Clank is a weirdo," Julia said, holding the leash as the cat paraded around the Upper West Side like a little boss.

"A weirdo who knows what she likes," I said, because I fucking loved it.

I wasn't sure I'd ever seen anything as adorable as her fluffy white cat walking around like a dog.

"Yeah, she *loves* it. Just like *you* are going to love this place." Julia grinned as we entered the bodega around the corner. She went straight back to the deli counter, and before she even opened her mouth, the old guy behind the glass said, "Where's your coat, Jules? It's cold out there today."

"This blazer's warmer than it looks," she said with a grin, gesturing to her school uniform. "Where's Chippy?"

"She got sick of my jokes and went home, but she left your book on the table," he said, his shrewd gaze moving over to me. "Who's this guy?"

Julia looked at me with an overexaggerated sneer as she stepped over to a tiny table and pocketed a book that I was actually very familiar with.

She said, "Just a prep-school kid who followed me here. His name's Damion or Dave, I can't remember which."

"Dave?" I said quietly, a little . . . mystified by this carefree version of her.

Who was this fucking girl?

Was this who she was in Nebraska?

Or was this just the version of her that existed when she wasn't being bullied at the academy?

She grinned at me before saying to the guy, "He seems hungry, Saul, so can I get two red dogs with onions and mustard?"

"I'm afraid to ask," I said. "But what's a red dog?"

"Do *not* waste one on this guy, Jules," Saul said, shaking his head. "I can tell by looking at him that he won't appreciate it."

"Ouch," I said, not sure what the hell that meant, but I was certain it was an insult.

"He keeps surprising me, though," she said. "Every time I think he's the biggest jackass in the world, he does something . . . slightly less jack-assy. And he helped me with my math, so I figure I owe him one."

I owe him one.

Was that all this was? Just paying back a debt?

And why did the thought physically hurt me?

"Then two red dogs with onions and mustard, coming up."

As it turned out, "red dogs" were Fairbury brand red hot dogs that apparently came from somewhere in Nebraska and couldn't be bought outside the Midwest. When Julia told Saul (who she called the sweetest old grump) about them, he managed to get his hands on a few boxes and kept them in the back, just for her.

And him.

It sounded like she and Saul—along with Chippy, his wife—shared hot dog lunches on a regular basis.

Again—who the hell *was* Julia Lowell?

Because I didn't know this carefree girl who was apparently friends with boomer grocers, who leash-trained her cat, who exchanged books of poetry with people named Chippy.

"This is so fucking good," I said, chewing as we walked toward Riverside Park, doing my best not to get onions and mustard all over the front of my shirt. "I'm sure the dye in this hot dog is going to kill me, but I think it's worth it."

"Right?" she said, nodding through a mouthful. "But hurry up and finish, because it's almost time for your dessert."

She made me wait outside with Clank when she ran into a bakery with a sign so faded it looked out of business, but when she emerged from the place with a box in her hand, she was grinning. "Now take me to the best place in the park to sit and eat cake."

I didn't plan on taking her *there*, but as I listened to her ramble while we strolled leisurely, my legs just went in the direction of my bench.

"So Liam thought it'd be funny to take her for a walk, but he basically just dragged her down the hallway because the old girl refused to stand once the harness was on." She laughed and said, "She looked like a corpse."

"So then you trained her?" I asked as the cat strutted along the path beside us.

"I did, and now she's insane about her walks."

"Insane like her owner."

"Haha, you're hilarious," she said.

"Yes, I am," I said, giving her a push because something felt right about being physical with her.

Julia drew out the part of me that was compelled to tug on her hair, pinch her chin, pull her by her sleeve, and deliver teasing little pushes.

Christ, I thought.

She drew out the eight-year-old in me.

I wasn't sure what it was, but I always wanted to be closer.

I always wanted *hands-on*.

"You *think* you are," she replied, rolling her eyes and giving me a one-handed nudge.

Yes, please.

"So what was with the *Milk and Honey*?" I asked, dying to know. "Is Chippy a poet?"

She looked surprised, though I wasn't sure if it was in response to the question or the fact that I'd seen the book. She blinked, thinking hard, then finally shrugged and said, "Chippy is an avid consumer of literature who *thinks* she detests poetry."

"So the book . . . ?" I prodded, fascinated by this unexplored side of her.

Christ, had she always been there and I'd never stopped to look?

"My attempt to change her mind," she said with a self-deprecating smile.

"Give me a line, Nebraska," I said. "And choose carefully, because I judge harshly."

"I am aware." She coughed out a little laugh, and I wondered if she'd balk, if she'd brush me off.

I *was* an asshole, after all.

But instead her gaze went forward, looking at the path in front of her, turning her profile into art, a form framed in pin-oak curls. Her voice was soft and butter-smooth when she said, "'When I am angry / I don't yell, I burn.'"

I wanted to laugh but I was too stunned.

It was like witnessing a transformation, only the transformation didn't exist.

I strongly suspected this had been her the whole time, only my blinders were just now being removed.

I knew she wouldn't ask, but I wanted her to.

I wanted to give her a line, God help me.

I didn't need anyone's approval, but like a child, I wanted to impress her.

If I said, *the two of us combined / could set it on fire,* would she be impressed that I *also* devoured Rupi Kaur?

I shoved that ridiculous thought out of my head—*what the fuck is wrong with me*—and asked, "What's your favorite book, Nebraska?"

Suddenly I needed to fill in all the blanks.

"Impossible question," she said with a dismissive head shake. "If we're talking classics, I love *The Awakening* and *Pride and Prejudice*. *The Hunger Games* series is my jam if we're talking dystopian, *The Wife Upstairs* is *such* a great domestic thriller, and I have read *The Duke and I* at least fifty times if you're counting romance as a genre, which you absolutely should."

"She contains multitudes," I said quietly.

"Don't sound so surprised," she said, a smile in her voice. "Now give me yours."

"Babbitt," I said without thinking.

"Wait—did you just say *Babbitt*?" Her eyebrows went together and she looked shocked. "I've never heard anyone else talk about that book. Like, ever."

"Yeah?"

"Yeah," she said, looking . . . *weird* about it.

Like it'd shaken free a buried memory.

Oh, and how I want to dig for it.

"Which way?" she said, still looking distracted by my answer.

Wow.

I'd been so lost in our conversation that I hadn't realized how close we were.

"That bench over there," I said, pointing to *the* bench.

My bench.

The bench I'd been going to my entire life.

My happy place.

I'd spent so many hours there, just watching the barges go up and down the Hudson while thinking about every little thing in my life, but the only other person who'd known it was my favorite spot was Remi.

So it was wild the way Julia looked at the bench with her eyebrows all scrunched together, like she was surprised to see it or had thoughts about it.

"That one?" she asked, her eyes narrowed as she pointed. "That bench right there?"

"Is that okay?" I asked, puzzled. "Or does Nebraska need something else?"

"No. It's actually perfect." She shook her head, then plopped unceremoniously on the bench, her smile returning. "*Perfect.* Now let us eat cake."

Something about the sight of her there, smirking while holding that bakery box, felt *right,* God help me.

Like this was a sight I'd seen before, or wanted to see again, or . . . hell.

It didn't make a damn bit of sense, but I felt like she belonged there.

I liked her on my bench.

I cleared my throat.

"Well, sit down," she said, patting the spot beside her. "You are about to enjoy the most delicious cake of your life."

When I sat down, the view I knew so well felt different with her there.

It looked the same, but now it smelled like rose-infused curls, sounded like her laughter, and was dusted with bow-tipped socks as she opened the box on her lap and handed me a plastic fork.

We sat there, side by side on my bench, devouring chocolate chip cake at an unhealthy pace while talking about everything and nothing. Crisp leaves blew past us on the ground while the trees overhead waved in the autumn breeze, slowly releasing more gold and red into the world like someone was perched above us, gently shaking down falling leaves to set the scene.

"Jesus, slow down or you're going to choke," I teased as she wolfed down the cake.

"I can't," she said with a giggle. "It's too good."

"I'm not Heimliching you," I warned.

"Because you'd have to stop eating the cake and you can't bring yourself to do that, right?" she said, pointing her fork at me. "Admit it."

"Hasn't anyone ever told you it's rude to point your plastic fork at a person?"

"You with those fancy Manhattan manners," she teased.

And then a bird flew into the tree beside us.

The yellow on its chest caught my eye and I said, "Holy shit, that's a dickcissel."

"Your *mom's* a dick weasel," she muttered with a snort.

Cuteness overload.

"Not a dick *weasel*," I said, pointing up at the branch where he'd landed. "*Dickcissel.* That bird right there."

"Hasn't anyone told you it's rude to point your plastic fork at a bird?" Julia squinted in the direction of my finger. "You mean the one with the yellow?"

"Yep," I said. "They migrate to Colombia and Venezuela for the winter, so this guy's a little behind. And lost."

"How do you know it's not a female?" she asked. "Maybe she's an independent lady bird who just didn't feel like following her loser boyfriend to South America yet again."

"Because, wiseass, males have that black V on their throat—see it?"

She nodded, staring up at it.

I swallowed down the sadness I felt every time I saw a bird Remi would've appreciated. I mean, dickcissels weren't *rare* and we'd seen them before, but they mostly stayed in the Midwest, so he'd always called it "a treat" when we happened to come across one.

"So you're *actually* a birder," she said, and her tone made me think she wasn't wholly surprised. "Does the wild and dangerous Damion Rutledge come to the park to bird-watch?"

I looked at her crinkled nose and teasing smile and I did it.

I confessed, "He does, actually."

Her smile changed, settled into something less teasing and more sincere.

Her eyes roamed over my face, and it felt like everything around us dimmed, faded into the background of her light.

"He contains multitudes," she said quietly.

No, more like she *breathed* it. Soft, sultry breath that did things to my head.

I looked down at that pretty face, at the soft warmth radiating from her, and I felt like I *knew* her, all of her.

And that she somehow knew exactly who I was.

The good and the bad.

The *real* me, not the Rutledge.

And I realized that whenever I was with her, there was zero expectation for me to be anything other than myself.

This was just a passing minute in the middle of a city park, a nothing moment surrounded by chocolate chip cake and dickcissels, but for the briefest of seconds I felt warm and home and like I wanted to pull her closer and beg her not to go anywhere.

Please stay.

"Jules," I said, reaching out with both hands to push back those long curls, to allow my fingers to feel their wavy softness.

God, that hair.

How had I ever thought it was anything less than spectacular?

My heart was beating hard as I focused on the sight of those strands surrounding my fingers, those electric eyes on mine.

"Hmm?" she said, and as I looked at her face, I realized I could describe her eyes in great detail.

Holy shit, I *could*.

Yes, they were brown, but they were more of a glowing amber than something so basic as brown. "Brown" could fucking never. They were alive, twinkling more often than not, and the long lashes that framed them were like a middle finger to all the girls who hated her. Mother Nature's extra-credit points.

Suddenly I was leaning closer, my breath frozen in my lungs as I looked down at her mouth, at her pretty lips that probably tasted like chocolate chips and strawberry gloss. I wanted to kiss her more than I wanted anything in the world, but even more than that, I wanted her to *want* me to kiss her.

Those lashes fluttered as she blinked, blinked fast like she was considering her options as she met my gaze.

Trust me. Please.

It was impossible to breathe as the distance between us slowly disappeared, as my lips hovered just above hers.

God, yes.

"Damion," she said, her voice nonexistent, her eyelids heavy as her gaze went to my mouth.

"Yes," I said, unsure if I was asking or answering.

"Ah," she blurted out, her eyes growing wide. "I have to go."

What?

She scrambled away from me and jumped up off the bench, still blinking fast as she grabbed her backpack and hurriedly threaded her arms through the straps, looking like she'd just woken up from some deep sleep, surprised to find herself in the park with me.

"What?"

"I, um, I have to go," she said, waving a hand to act like this wasn't a big deal even though it obviously was. "I forgot I have a thing so . . ."

So . . . ?

So . . . *what*?

My gut clenched as I tried figuring out what'd happened to make her face look like . . . *this*.

This look—whatever it was—gutted me from top to bottom.

"It's nothing," she said, shrugging and giving a breathy little fake laugh, even though her voice came out as sad and panicked.

Nothing? It's EVERYTHING.

"I just forgot that I have to get home and I can't be late. You keep the cake because I bought it as a thank-you, and I'll talk to you later."

"Julia—"

"I gotta go," she said. "Thanks again!"

And she turned and literally started jogging up the path.

Running away.

From me.

CHAPTER THIRTY-ONE

"Nebraska takes its time . . . all the time."

—Remington

Julia

"I can't believe you're here," Lauren said as she pulled away from the Omaha airport. "It seems like you've been gone forever."

"Trust me, I know," I said as I buckled my seat belt, so happy to be in her old yellow rust bucket.

I'd made plans for this little trip—Teanna's birthday weekend—before we'd even pulled up stakes and moved east. Your best friend only turned eighteen once, and my parents were cool about me missing one day of school to return for the tiny celebration.

Plus, the timing of this trip was so perfect.

Because I couldn't shake what'd almost happened at the park with Damion yesterday, and I needed this escape. It was messing with me so badly, that thing on replay that wouldn't go away, no matter how hard I tried blocking it out.

What. The. Hell.

I'd run all the way home from the park after . . . *that*, so freaked out and more homesick than ever, ready to forget everything and celebrate at the house in Springfield, with our dogs and our ratty sofa that was the perfect napping couch.

It sounded so good that it made me cry.

Because nothing in Gardenwood made sense anymore, not that it *ever* had. I wanted to go home and be with people who liked me, to be in a place where I knew everyone and felt comfortable in my own skin.

Where pretty boys with pretty glasses and pretty words weren't following me around.

And I just wanted to blend, for God's sake, and not be a constant topic of conversation. Damion and I were now the *only* gossip that was gossiping at school. If I'd foolishly thought things would slow down once Damion's grand display of chivalry happened in the hallway, well, I was wrong.

It amped them up to an eleven.

Thus the escape. From school and from Damion.

Damion.

God, the moment he leaned down close, his face not flushed with teasing and snarky flirtations but with what felt a lot like something more, something . . . *real*, I lost it.

Panic flooded my insides because it *wasn't* real.

If I gave him an inch, he would take everything from me.

Just like Will had.

No. *Nope.* I knew better.

I wasn't going to be seduced by the New York City lights, by talks of literature and poetry and shared delicious cake under the cover of fall foliage.

And especially not by ever-changing hazel eyes that made my stomach drop.

Those things had tricked my brain into forgetting that as good as things might *feel* with a boy, it wasn't worth the crushing blow of the *after*.

Time had moved on, but I hadn't.

I'd never be over the shock of how wrong I'd been about everything.

How kisses behind school bleachers at thirteen, declarations of love, and promises of forever had ultimately ended in tears and emptiness.

And if Will Malone, the world's biggest green flag, was capable of making everything hurt that much, what the hell was I doing, playing with someone like Damion Rutledge, rich playboy and renowned rebel?

But dear God, when he leaned in, his hands playing with my hair, the only thing that'd been on my mind was what it'd feel like to kiss him.

And I'd *wanted* to know.

So badly.

I am such an idiot.

How can I be so foolish again?

This weekend was going to be a perfect recovery, a forty-eight-hour return to reality.

"By the way," Lauren said, grinning as she merged onto I-80. "What the hell happened to your hair?"

"What kind of question is that?" I asked, raising a hand to touch it. I'd done my best, with the help of Donovan and Jasmine's bag of hair products, to make it look like it'd looked at Beckett's party. "I tamed it a little."

"I mean, you did," she said, "But I always thought your wild hair was kind of your signature, like your trademark asset. Now you just look like every other girl."

"Oh wow, such a nice thing to say," I said.

"You know what I mean—you look fine, but you don't look like my fun cousin," she clarified. "The Jules who flipped the golf cart with me had Heat Miser hair."

"Is that how you think of me? Your fun cousin?"

She was my cousin, yes, but she was also my *other* best friend.

Teanna, Lauren, and I had always been inseparable, regardless of familial connections.

"My fun cousin with Heat Miser hair, yes, that is correct," she said. "The one who used to get me into way too much trouble because she liked doing stupid things but never actually knew how to pull them off."

"Yeah, thank God for Liam," I said, nodding. "He usually made our idiotic ideas less idiotic."

"The smart twin," Lauren said with a smirk.

Relaxation washed over me as I looked out the window because I *knew* this landscape. I recognized the buildings and the billboards and it felt *calming*. Warm and wonderful as we got closer to Springfield, and when we finally turned onto Main Street, I was pretty sure I looked like a happy dog, head out the window with my tongue lolling out the side of my mouth. We passed the market—where the heaping display of fall pumpkins looked amazing—and the tiny little two-block stretch of downtown, and I wondered if it was the prettiest town I'd ever seen or if it was just my nostalgic heart drawing it that way.

I smiled as I saw our neighbors' houses pass by, and I smiled at the way the town already had the Christmas lights hung in preparation for the season even though it was only October.

The things that'd always been mundane suddenly seemed magically charming.

And when we pulled up in front of the house, I had to blink fast to hold back the tears.

I knew I'd missed it, but as I stared at the old farmhouse with the black shutters and wide porch and white picket fence that desperately needed to be painted, my heart felt hurt and healed, all at the same time.

"Your face," Lauren said as she turned off the car, "is ridiculous right now."

I cleared my throat. "I guess I hadn't realized how much I missed it."

"It's a great house," she said as she opened her door. "I mean, not a Manhattan mansion, but it has its charms."

It was the only house I'd ever lived in before Riverside Manor, and I wasn't sure I'd ever really given it a single thought.

It was just home.

My house.

No big deal.

"Oh my God, I can hear the dogs already," Lauren said with a laugh. "They've missed you." I could see the golden retrievers barking, their noses glued to the window. My heart filled with warmth as I took a good look at the place.

It was old and outdated and the air-conditioning never really kept up on hot days, but suddenly it looked like the most beautiful place in the world.

Later that day, while the sun shone brightly through the big windows over the kitchen table, Lauren and I sat on the kitchen counter and chatted away, me doing my best to fill her in on all my New York City drama. Papers from last summer were still stuck on the front of the refrigerator with magnets, Liam's old baseball hoodie was still dangling from the hook on the back of the door, and the photo of our family from the Fourth of July was still smiling out from its frame on the top shelf of my grandmother's china cabinet.

Everything felt the same. And *smelled* the same. Somehow, the house still smelled like Downy dryer sheets and fresh air, making me long for the "before," when life seemed so much easier.

"I don't get it," Lauren continued. "Everyone at your school is a prick to you, but you're going to their ball . . . ?"

"I owe Damion a favor for the tutoring," I explained, even though I'd already told her that.

"That seems flimsy. I wouldn't do it."

"Yeah, but he volunteered his time, and because of that, I'm actually going to pass," I said. "I owe him *hugely*."

It was that massive feeling of gratitude that'd messed up everything.

Because I'd been *so* relieved by my scores, so overjoyed, that I'd *wanted* to be nice to him. Instead of looking at his arrogant smart-ass face and feeling the usual way I felt about him—suspicious and cautious—I'd felt . . . *fondness* for what he'd done for me, an unexpected warmth that challenged me to try and tease him out of his Damion-ness.

To see if he could play.

And God, it'd worked so incredibly well.

Too well.

I fear I'll never recover.

"You should get a dress at the Satin Hanger while you're here," she said, referencing Springfield's bridal shop.

"I don't need a wedding dress," I said, my stomach getting a knot just thinking about wearing a fancy gown in front of *those* people. "And I'm pretty sure it's supposed to be costumey."

I told her about the ball's theme, which made her roll her eyes. "That sounds stupid, and also, it's a 'theme.' If it's truly like the Met Gala, you wear your *interpretation* of the theme."

"You don't get it—I just need to blend," I said with a sigh.

"No, seriously," she said, looking offended. "Why not get a sick dress that *makes* you stand out? Let those jackals wear bustles and corsets and stupid hats while you show up looking like a fucking queen."

I loved the idea of that, but who was she kidding? There was no way I was brave enough to pull something like that off. I could just hear the new nicknames the Skins would come up with for me. *As if I need more.* The though made me sick to my stomach.

"Can we talk about something else?" I said. "What time are we meeting Teanna?"

Lauren looked down at her watch. "One hour."

"Okay, I'm going to take a shower and change."

"We probably have time to pop into the Hanger before dinner," she said as I hopped off the counter. "Just to look."

"We can look, but I guarantee we won't find anything."

"Bet."

CHAPTER THIRTY-TWO

"Love is spring, lust is summer, yearning is autumn, and heartbreak is deadass winter. Those are my four seasons."

—Remington

Damion

I looked out at the river and texted: Can we talk?

Because what was up with her?

She hadn't been at school, and she hadn't responded to any of my texts.

I wasn't one to beg, but God help me, I was begging. Something had happened with us yesterday, something that felt important enough to *make* me beg.

I waited another thirty minutes, then sent: JULES. Please??

Oh shit, I am literally begging.

It was even colder today, blustery and raining, as I sat on the bench among wet leaves and wondered where the hell she was and what was going through her mind. I could go to her house and force her to talk to me, but that wasn't the point.

The point was for her to *want* to talk to me.

I was dying to talk to her.

Because I realized after lunch, when Beckett said *where is your little Nebraska today,* that there was something about his verbiage I liked.

Something I craved.

The possessive part of it.

Mine.

Because on paper, I had everything, right? Money, clothes, a good family—Damion Rutledge had it all.

But none of it felt like *mine*, like mine alone.

It all belonged to my family.

And not that Julia "belonged" to me—or to anyone, for that matter—but her presence in my life had nothing to do with anyone, or anything, but the two of us.

And that felt like something I wanted to protect.

I sighed and shoved the binoculars back into my bag, because I hadn't touched them since I'd sat down. Instead of doing the thing that usually relaxed me, I'd stared at the barges through the autumn rain and thought about her.

I texted: Are you there? JULES.

I sat there for another twenty minutes, but my phone didn't make a single buzz.

Me: JULES!

Now I was panicking. Where was she? *Does she regret it? Is she pushing me away?*

Me: Jules. Can we talk?

Worried thoughts picked away at me one by one. I squeezed the phone in my hand, wondering what else I could do, what else I could say.

Another ten minutes went by. Nothing. Then another.

I started typing again, but nope.

Fuck it.

Twenty minutes later I pressed the doorbell and waited.

Waited with my hands in my pockets, wondering what the hell I was going to do, what I was going to say once I saw those amber eyes.

But it wasn't her that answered.

Shit.

Liam swung the door open, looking shocked to see me. "Rutledge? What're you doing here?"

"I need to talk to your sister," I said, trying to see around him. My eyes searching for wild hair, long lashes, and perfect freckles.

"Too bad, she isn't here," he said, looking happy to deliver the news.

"Where is she?" I asked.

"Not telling you," he replied, arms folded across his chest. "Because it's none of your business."

And so I lied. "Fair, but it actually is. We had a tutoring session and she was supposed to meet me, so consider this me doing the responsible thing and making sure she's okay."

Even *I* was impressed at how easily the lie had slid out. Especially when I added, "Isn't that what you wanted from me, to be responsible for her?"

I couldn't deny myself the extra bit of snark when he was looking so smug.

Liam scoffed at me, his eyes sizing me up.

Jesus, this guy.

"She's in Nebraska," he said, narrowing his stare at me. "She went home."

She went home?

"She . . . went home?" I asked, feeling even more panicked now as cold rain tapped the back of my neck like busy fingers.

"Yeah. Nebraska. Heard of it, right?"

Seriously. This fucking *guy.*

"Relax, Rutledge," Liam added, the smugness growing. "And like I said. It's none of your business."

And with that, he slammed the door. *Remi's* door.

Right in my fucking face.

CHAPTER THIRTY-THREE

"Wanting to stay forever while at the same time wanting to run away as fast as you can? That means you've gone home again."

—Remington

Julia

"This is SO good," I said, shoveling beef fried rice into my mouth.

"Right?" Teanna agreed as she twirled drunken noodles around her fork. "The best."

As if it weren't enough to come home for Teanna's birthday, she was having her dinner at Sweet Rice, my absolute favorite Thai restaurant, which sat right on Main Street.

Talk about a win-win.

"I might have missed the food here more than I missed you two."

"Ha. Ha. Ha," Lauren teased. "Liar."

I was so happy to be back with my friends, but as I watched them together, I felt lonely.

Alone.

I missed being part of our little threesome, having friends who cared about making me happy. Donovan and Jasmine were nice, but I didn't feel comfortable with them the way I did with friends I'd known my entire life.

These were the two I'd chased fireflies with during countless Fourth of July block parties, the two who'd been there for me every time I'd ever been sad, the two who'd sat with me huddled in blankets and given me tissues when Will decided it was over between us.

Will, the other "friend" I'd known my entire life.

Ugh.

And as we continued eating and they were catching me up on all the gossip of Springfield—apparently Mr. Fabian, who owned the hardware store, had gotten a pet iguana that he let run around the shop, quite the scandal—my world suddenly came to a screeching halt.

Will and Hannah were at the restaurant.

Together.

Walking through the door, hand in hand.

Springfield was a town of under two thousand people, so it wasn't unusual to see someone you knew at a restaurant.

No, not unusual. Heartbreaking.

Oh God.

Everything went quiet as I watched him set his hand on her lower back as they walked to a table. As he looked lovingly at her, and as he smiled at her like he was completely obsessed with everything about her.

Has he ever smiled at me like that?

God, why did it still hurt so much to see them together?

He looked the same, right down to the NU hoodie that I knew smelled like Downy. Blue eyes, baseball cap, a kind face that was warm and handsome.

Will.

He was easy, he was happy. He was a golden retriever. The kind of guy who'd pull his car over during a raging thunderstorm to help a stranger change a flat tire or carefully give you directions if you were lost.

The kind of guy who took care of everything.

My stomach hurt as I watched him giving *her* all that happy energy.

I went silent. Head down, pretending I was enjoying my food too much to join in on Lauren and Teanna's gossiping. I was afraid to look up and spot Will treating Hannah like he used to treat me.

But the nausea I felt as I avoided watching them wasn't exactly about him anymore.

Not really, not specifically.

It was more about me missing the past, missing *this* life that I knew.

And it was about the pathetic fact that since the breakup, I'd *done* nothing. All these wild things had happened to me, but I hadn't *done* anything.

I still had no idea what I was doing with my future, where I was going to college.

This past version of me, with Will, had at least known she was doing something *with him*, because steadfast Will was going to make sure that she did. He was there for her, at her side, so *of course* she was going to figure everything out.

But I didn't even know who I was without him.

And that thought completely and utterly crushed me.

Who am I?

"Do either of you have any ibuprofen?" I asked Lauren and Teanna as we drove away from the restaurant. "I've got a screaming headache."

Somehow, neither of them had noticed that my ex and his new girlfriend were cuddling at a table nearby. They'd been facing the other way, thank *God*, but my friends were clueless over the emotional trauma I'd just endured.

"Yeah, in my purse," Lauren said, gesturing to the bag that was sitting beside me in the back seat.

I rummaged through her purse until I found a bottle, and I popped two tablets. "Thanks."

She glanced at me in the rearview mirror. "Did you just take a PM?"

"What?" I looked at the bottle in my hand. It was dark and I had to squint to see the label, but then I saw it. The little "PM" and the picture of the moon. "Oh my God, I *did*. Why do you have sleeping pills, Lo, and what's going to happen to me now?"

She rolled her eyes and smiled. "They aren't sleeping pills; they just make you a little drowsy. And I only have them because I was sick last week and my mom thought they'd help me sleep."

"Oh my God," I said, picturing my slightly irresponsible aunt. "That's not reassuring at all."

"It's just pain reliever with diphenhydramine," she said calmly, looking at me in the rearview mirror and reminding me that she wanted to be a pharmacist, that she was going to school in order to eventually *become* a pharmacist. "No big deal, Jules, I promise."

"But I'm always super sensitive to, like, cold medicine," I said, trying not to worry. "I have ZERO tolerance. And I took two!!"

The look Lauren and Teanna shared did not ease my concern.

"Guys??!!"

"It's nothing illegal, calm down," Teanna said.

"I promise, you'll be okay," Lauren reassured me. "You'll be drowsy and *preeeetty* sleepy, but you will be fine."

My cousin was a liar.

Because *fine* I was not.

They dropped me off at the house so I could start "calming my pants and settling in" while Lauren took Teanna home, so I went straight upstairs.

Or . . . crawled into bed, more accurately.

But even with the accidental sleeping aid, sleep was elusive. I couldn't find anything to watch that'd take my mind off Will, off Damion, off my uncertainty about the future. I lay there, staring up at the ceiling, where a few random glow-in-the-dark stickers (with no more glow) still hung from middle school, as it all raced through my head.

I kept picturing Will and Hannah, how happy they looked, and it kept bringing the tears back to my eyes. I didn't want him anymore, but it felt so . . . sad, *I* felt so sad, that he looked so unbelievably happy in his new life, where I didn't exist.

And what was my new life? Every time I started shifting my thoughts to New York, Damion's face sprang to mind.

His beautiful, bespectacled, gorgeous face that was *not* to be trusted.

Like, at *all*.

Yes, he'd shown me a new side of himself while we'd hung out at the park, but that didn't make him any less of a rebellious, arrogant, wildly flirtatious trust-fund baby. It was possible for him to have a fun side and still be the poster child for affluent bad boys.

Honestly, it added to his dangerous charisma.

When I forced myself not to think about *him*, all I was left with was my confusion about college and the painful way it felt to have everyone at the academy hate me.

That picture of me, printed out and hung all over the school, still haunted my thoughts.

I felt helpless.

"Gahhhh," I moaned into my pillow, wishing for sleep. Wanting to do anything except the one thing I was about to do.

Cry.

I rolled onto my side and grabbed my phone. Drowsiness was starting to set in, but I wanted to text Liam before my phone, which was just about dead, shut off.

My brother always made everything a little better, made me feel a little less alone.

I noticed a few missed messages. *Of course* Liam would be checking in on me. He said he would the moment my plane landed and I completely forgot.

I texted: Hey.

Sadness and drowsiness and all the things weighing on my head were pressing down on me.

I texted: I hate everything right now.

Which I did. The fear crawling up my spine. The worry, the sadness. The smile on Will's face. His hand on another girl's back.

That used to be my back.

Nebraska was supposed to be an escape, but it felt more like a crushing reality check that I wasn't prepared for.

I waited a few moments but Liam still hadn't responded. *That ass.* No joke, no "keep your chin up."

Nothing.

I felt myself dozing off.

Me: Why aren't you here with me??

I flipped over onto my other side and pulled up the covers.

I was suddenly *very* sleepy.

Which was good, I thought. If I fell asleep, all the worries would be gone. I sent Liam one last text.

Me: HELP me.

CHAPTER THIRTY-FOUR

"I've said, 'What the hell?' at least twenty times today. What the hell is that about?"

—Remington

Damion

What the hell?

CHAPTER THIRTY-FIVE

"There's nothing quite as painfully
blinding—and beautiful—as a Midwestern sunrise."

—Remington

Julia

The doorbell woke me up.

That and the ridiculously bright morning sun that was shining directly into my bedroom when I opened my eyes.

Wow.

I got up and went over to the window, but there wasn't a car in the driveway.

Awesome, I thought, and hoped that Lauren would beat me to the door because I wasn't in the mood for visitors.

I shuffled out of my room and down the stairs, feeling like I'd been sleeping for a hundred years. *Must be the medicine.* I was relieved the pills hadn't killed me, and I *did* feel pretty well rested. Fourteen hours of sleep would do that, I supposed.

Whoever was at the door kept ringing the bell over and over again, which meant it was maybe Teanna, because who else would be that obnoxious?

"Will you relax on the doorbell, you idiot?" I said as I grabbed the doorknob, but when I pulled the door open, it wasn't Teanna on the porch.

"Oh my God," I said, because *oh my God,* it was Damion.

Damion Rutledge was standing on my porch.

In Springfield.

Damion. Rutledge. Was. In. Springfield.

"So you *are* alive," he said, looking pissed.

What????

He was wearing jeans, a Mets hoodie, and wire-rimmed glasses, and his curly hair was all tousled, but his general appearance paled in comparison to the expression on his face. Those dark eyebrows were down, his jaw was tense, and his hazel eyes were all over me like they were searching for something.

"What are you doing here, Damion?" I asked, sounding a little like I was seeing Santa Claus on the front porch.

How could Damion Rutledge be in Springfield, Nebraska?

"I had to make sure you weren't *dead*," he said grumpily, "because you wouldn't respond to my texts or calls last night."

"What?" I looked at the big angry boy on my porch and I was totally confused.

"You texted me, and then when I responded," he said through gritted teeth, "you went radio silent."

"I didn't text you," I said, even more confused.

I'd ignored his "can we talk" text from the day before because I'd had no idea how to respond, but we *definitely* hadn't communicated last *night*.

I'd been groggy as hell, but I wouldn't have—

"Yes, you did." He angrily pulled the phone out of his pocket and held it in front of my face. "Look."

I squinted, trying to read while my eyeballs were being assaulted by the sun.

Julia: Hey.

Julia: I hate everything right now.

Julia: Why aren't you here with me??

Julia: HELP me.

"Oh my God, I meant to send those to Liam," I said, half to myself, as I realized what had happened, as total mortification set in. "I sent those to *you*?"

His gaze swept over my face, eyebrows down, before he swallowed and said, "You did."

"Oh geez," I said, feeling like *such* a moron. "I'm sorry, I mean, I accidentally took a wrong pill last night and got too groggy to charge my phone so it was dead before I—"

"Everything's okay?" he interrupted, looking less mad but still serious. "You're fine?"

I nodded, but I wasn't sure how I felt. Because—

"Why are you in Springfield?" I asked. "How did you get here?"

"I *flew*," he snapped, and then a wrinkle formed between his eyebrows, like he realized how weird the situation was. He blinked and watched me for too many long seconds.

"Because." He cleared his throat and it was as if a switch had been flipped; he shrugged and his face turned casually arrogant. Indolent and lazy, like he didn't give a damn about anything. He put his hands in his pockets and said, "Because there was no way I was going to let you bail on me for the season. I have a reputation to protect, remember, and you *owe* me."

"So that's why you're here. For your . . . reputation?" Sensible, sure, but the look of . . . *concern* on his face said something completely different.

Something I was scared to even think about because of what it meant.

Is he here because he is worried about me?

Not possible.

Right?

"You came here because you thought—"

"Liam said you were in Nebraska, I assumed you were being a coward and running away, so I put my frequent flyer miles to work and grabbed a first-class seat to Omaha." His rich-boy smirk was back when he added, "I couldn't let that happen."

"Ah," I said, even though something about that didn't seem exactly right. "Just a Rutledge using his money to close a deal?"

A chill slid over my skin, leaving goose bumps in its wake as I watched and waited for him to tell me I was wrong. To give me some other explanation as to why he was inexplicably on my porch.

In Nebraska.

On the other side of the country from where he lived.

How had he even known how to find my house? So many unanswered questions, but then his eyes—more green than brown today—dipped to my mouth for the *briefest* of seconds, and that chill turned to a crackle, dear *God.*

It's still there.

Whatever had existed between us at the park was still there.

Damion swallowed. Cleared his throat. "Exactly," he said, nodding. "That is exactly what this is."

"Okay." I *also* nodded, struggling to keep up with anything and everything because Damion was on my porch, *what the hell.*

"So." His voice suddenly got louder and he pointed at the screen door. "This is the house . . . ? This is where the Lowells lived before they became Upper West Siders?"

"This . . . is it," I said, taken aback by the small talk.

"Who's this?" I heard from behind me.

"Shit," I muttered, because Lauren scared the crap out of me as she popped up over my shoulder.

"Wait—is this Beckett?" she said with a warm smile, squeezing around me in the doorway.

"Beckett?" Damion's eyes darkened as his eyebrows shot up. He looked

at me like an accusation. "You've talked about *Beckett* to your friends?"

I hadn't—Liam had mentioned him a few times to Lauren—but the assumption seemed to annoy Damion and amuse Lo.

"I'm her cousin," Lauren clarified. "Lauren."

"Oh, well, I'm Damion," he said, giving me a look that I couldn't quite decipher. He looked irritated and almost like he was about launch into a lecture. Jaw clenched, nostrils flaring. "You talk about Beckett to your cousins?"

"I'm the only cousin she talks to on a regular basis, so that'd be cousin *singular*," she said.

I nodded dumbly. "Singular."

"For Christ's sake," he muttered under his breath, raising his hand and rubbing the back of his neck. "That's not the issue here."

"Then what is the issue here?" My tone matching his.

AND WHAT ARE YOU REALLY DOING HERE, DAMION??

It was all coming at me so fast.

Damion was here.

In Springfield.

How is this happening?

"So . . . ," Lauren began, trying to break the tension and the strange staring contest Damion and I seemed to be in the middle of. "I have to head to campus in a few to work on a group project." Lauren put her hand on his arm and gave it a pat, which for some reason made his face change. He looked slightly less intense when she said, "Damion, can you keep an eye on Jules? Maybe have her give you a tour of our booming little town?"

"Oh, ah," I said in a panic, because I wasn't mentally prepared to spend time alone with him at the moment.

Not in Nebraska, not in New York.

Not *anywhere*.

"That sounds perfect," he said, the cocky smile I was so familiar with returning to his face. Hazel eyes squinted behind those wire-rimmed glasses as he tossed me that grin.

"No but, I, um, I still have to take a shower," I explained, running a hand over my hair and looking down at my wrinkled outfit as my brain scrambled to keep up. "I fell asleep in my clothes last night—"

"Loser," Lauren teased.

"And I literally just woke up, so maybe—"

"I can wait," he said, his gaze dipping down to my clothes, then coming back up again.

Stop it, everyone!

Everything was still moving too fast and I couldn't get a grip. Only ten minutes ago I was in the deepest sleep of my life, trying to recover from seeing my ex being wildly flirtatious with his new and pretty girlfriend, and now this?

"I'm going to need at least, like, a half hour," I said.

"Take your time," Damion replied, looking like he wanted to laugh, that *ass*. "I can get to know your friend while we wait."

"Cousin," I corrected, feeling like this was a terrible idea but not really knowing why.

"Go shower," Lauren said. "And we'll play with the dogs."

"Yeah, Nebraska, we'll play with the dogs," Damion said in a quiet voice, "while you go take a nice, loooong shower."

CHAPTER THIRTY-SIX

"Nebraska feels good on the skin, like the slow lick of warm afternoon sun when it crawls all over the planes of your face."

—Remington

Damion

"So why are you here?"

I looked at Julia's cousin and respected the way she wasn't wasting any time. It kind of reminded me of Liam and his assholery when he found out I was taking his sister to the season.

"On earth?" I quipped as I followed her around to the backyard.

I still couldn't believe I was here. In *Nebraska*.

Holy shit, what am I even doing?

I'd been so shaken up by her texts and the momentary panic of thinking she was gone forever that I'd knee-jerked and bought a plane ticket. I'd told my parents I was going with Beckett to Aspen for the weekend and they didn't even blink; they just reminded me to have Donna overnight my skis to the condo so I wouldn't have to bother with them at the airport.

Such concerned parents.

But I wasn't going to overthink my Julia issues anymore because I was getting sick of trying to figure out what the hell was going on with me when it came to her. I'd hopped on a plane out of concern for a fellow human, and now I was going to check out this insanely small town before heading back to the hotel for a day of relaxation.

That was it.

Nothing to figure out.

"No, seriously, why are you in Springfield? I'm just curious," Lauren asked as she unlatched the fence gate and pushed it open. "Jules looked shocked to see you."

"Julia texted me last night," I admitted. "And I . . . *misunderstood*."

That earned me a raised eyebrow from Lauren as I followed her into the backyard, and into—*wow*—a yard just as small-town charming as the house itself. A big grassy rectangle with bushes on its border and party lights draped across a few trees. Looking around, I had the fleeting thought that it'd probably been nice to grow up here.

And just as I thought that, two golden retrievers came running at us.

"Meet Bo and Bobo," Lauren said.

"Julia named them, didn't she?" I said as the dogs started happy barking.

"Duh," Lauren said, smiling at the dogs. "And yeah—Jules texted me last night, too, panicking that my meds were going to kill her. She's got no chill about pills, I swear to God."

"So she accidentally took *your* medicine?" I asked. "Is that what happened?"

"Pretty much, but in her defense, she's allergic to like *everything*, so she's smart to be paranoid." Lauren knelt down to scratch the bigger of the two dogs, the fluffier of the two. "One time they gave her Benadryl for a mosquito bite and she ended up with a head-to-toe rash. Resulted in the unfortunate nickname of Pink Julia."

"When was that?" I asked, dropping to a sit on the grass as the smaller dog approached me.

"She was in third grade," she replied, then added, "I remember because Will got a time-out for pushing CJ McCallum because CJ made her cry. Little Will took him down good."

Will. Will. Will.

She laughed at the memory, but it was like his name was being hammered into my brain on repeat.

With a really painful nail.

"Is that the same Will . . . ?" I said, acting as if I knew something about that guy.

I knew nothing, of course, other than the fact that he had an ugly wallet that Julia was still using.

And that he was her *ex.*

And that he didn't look *close* to being in her league with that stupid hair and even stupider 'stache.

"The one and only Will Malone," she said, nodding.

One and only. *You have got to be kidding.*

The one and only *douchebag*, maybe. The one and only *asshole who broke her heart*.

Fucking one and only my *ass.*

Sticking to the whole *what am I even doing* theme of the day, I asked, "So things with Will are over but also . . . ?"

"Complicated," Lauren said with a smile, nodding like we agreed on something. "I'm pretty sure she's over him but would still like to punch him in the face if she ever saw him again."

"Ah," I said. "So what happened?"

Lauren said, "He and Jules were together since like seventh grade."

Seventh grade! That was like five fucking years.

Christ. I'd barely dated anyone for five *months*.

"But then last year he started texting the new girl, like all the time, but he told Jules it was no big deal. That they were just friends."

Classic asshole.

"He made Julia feel like she was being paranoid, like *she* was the one out of line whenever she brought up how much it was bothering her. But then two days after they had a little argument and 'took a break,' he started seeing the new girl. Literally two *days* later. And then we started hearing all sorts of rumors that he'd been cheating on her for weeks. We still have no idea if it's true or not."

"So she was gaslit and blindsided," I said, bothered way more than I should be over the thought of Julia brokenhearted. "What a dick."

"Who's a dick?" I heard, and when I looked up, there she was.

Julia stepped off the deck and started walking toward us, and dear God, she looked incredible. She was wearing faded jeans with holes all over the place and an oversized NU football jersey, her long curls were wet and wild, and a pair of black Converse high-tops covered her feet.

Somehow she looked fucking *perfect*.

Jesus, Nebraska looks good on her.

"Will," Lauren replied.

Who were we talking about? Because only Julia existed right now. The clean smell of her—shampoo or soap or lotion—floated around me on the breeze as she stopped in front of us.

"Will?" Julia said, her eyes darting to me briefly before she said, "Why are you talking about *him*?"

"He asked," Lauren said with a shrug.

"I was curious about Wallet Boy," I said, feeling busted. "Your little mullet man sounded *interesting*."

The Beckett thing still annoyed the shit out of me. Maybe that was why I was messing with her now.

"Oh my God, that's right—the tutor was your pickpocket!" Lauren said with a grin.

"I'm *not* a pickpocket," I said, wondering what *else* Julia had told her about me.

But also . . . she talked about me?

"And I heard she kicked your ass, too," her cousin added in a singsong voice.

"Is that what she said?" I tilted my head and wanted to laugh as that little shit gave me the most unapologetic grin I'd ever seen.

A grin that was one hundred percent the version of Julia I'd had at Riverside Park.

Cake Julia.

Bodega Julia.

Julia with a wealth of smiles, all for me.

I wanted to step closer just to make her look up at me.

"Okay, I'm taking off," Lauren said, pulling a set of keys out of her pocket. "You two have fun," she shouted, walking toward the car. Leaving me and Julia—*my little Nebraska*—alone. *Finally.*

"So about that tour . . . ?" I began, and I could tell Julia was nervous as she rocked on her feet. God, she was cute nervous.

"Uh, right. The tour." She ran her hand through her hair, the movement giving me a strong hint of whatever the hell that shampoo was. *Easy, honey.* "Maybe we should take the golf cart."

"Why would we take a golf cart to town?" I asked.

"Because it's more fun to drive than a car, I guess."

Oh, Nebraska.

"Is it legal to do that?"

She shrugged. Nibbled on that lower lip. "Everybody does it."

"You're telling me that everybody drives golf carts on city streets?" Somehow the image of her drifting in a golf cart, hair flying, just fit. But I leaned a little closer and said, "How about we walk instead?"

Julia toyed with that lip a little more, distracting me with the sight.

"I mean, I guess," she said, looking so pouty I wanted to laugh. "Let's go."

We started down the sidewalk, the morning sun bright and warm, and I was a little surprised by how picturesque everything was.

Actually, I was shocked that *I* found it to be picturesque. Autumn yard decorations, the old houses lining the road, pumpkins everywhere.

And what was with the smell? I took a deep breath through my nose and smelled . . . *nothing*.

No food, no garbage, no exhaust fumes. It just smelled like . . . morning.

Grass, sunshine . . . *air*, maybe.

And it wasn't like I'd never been outside the city; I'd communed with nature before. But this somehow felt . . . more pure.

Like I could take more oxygen into my lungs in this place. Breathe a little easier.

God, it makes perfect sense that Uncle Remi loved it here.

And there was something about knowing this was the town where he'd lived that made me feel . . . *connected* to it somehow, like this random town was something to *me*.

"Do you really want a tour?" Julia asked, pulling me out of my thoughts, and God—it was almost hard to look at her.

She was too gorgeous.

The freckles on her nose, the fire in her hair, the sheen of those glossy lips—too much. The football jersey, the worn jeans, the cheap sunglasses—MUCH too much.

I wanted to stare, to just look at Julia without stopping, because suddenly I couldn't get enough.

"Hell yes, I do," I said.

She nodded at me skeptically, her eyes glancing over me.

"So"—I cleared my throat—"tell me who lives there."

I pointed to a big blue house with a white porch as we walked past. "The mayor?"

"Don't be ridiculous," she said, shaking her head. "The mayor lives over in the Pines. Dr. Butters, the principal of the high school, lives here."

"His name is seriously Dr. Butters." I snorted. "You're kidding."

"It's too outlandish to be a joke, right?" she said with a smile.

"And who lives *there*?"

"I don't actually know every single person who lives in Springfield," she said, her eyebrows pressing together. "You know that, right?"

"I doubt it, but okay, fine," I said, wondering what it must've been like to grow up here, in all this quiet. "So tell me, Jules. What's your favorite thing about this place?"

Her face turned warm, and for the first time since I'd come here, I noticed her guard drop. Just a little. "I don't know. It's hard to say because it's just, you know . . . *home*."

I was envious of the expression she wore, of the relaxed softness on her face as she reminisced about *home*. I loved the city, but I wasn't sure I'd ever spoken about it with so much contentedness in my voice.

Although, *shit*—something about this place just coaxed out contentment.

Maybe it was the leisurely way the town was waking, like all its inhabitants were still lounging under their sun-warmed blankets. It felt like sleep as we strolled under the autumn sun, like languorous waking with zero alarms.

My father would hate it here.

When we passed Woodland Animal Hospital, I wondered if Rem had taken Mr. Dipshit there for shots, and I also wondered what life was like for the DVM who ran that clinic.

Did he make house calls and spend half his days looking in on sickly horses? All the times I'd imagined it, a career in animal medicine, I'd never considered *that* a part of the job.

What would that look like?

"Wait—is that the store?" I pointed at Lowell's Market on the other side of the street. It was next door to a dentist's office, and the exterior was everything I would've imagined after seeing their house. Brick facade, painted front window, piles of pumpkins.

"Yeah," Julia said, shooting me a weird look. She almost looked nervous.

"Well, tour guide, let's take a tour."

"Wait—" she began, but my hand was on her arm and I was tugging her forward. "Please."

"Fine," she relented, nudging me with her elbow.

Yes, honey.

Julia waved at the man at the counter as we walked in. Carl Sr. or Kevin Jr. or something.

"So this is the store," she said, holding out her arms.

"Aisle by aisle," I demanded. "Don't rush it."

"You're a real pain in the ass about this," she said, a laugh in her voice.

There was something about the place that felt more personal than most of the markets in the city. Instead of a thousand products jammed onto the shelves, there were fewer selections, but set up in small displays that made it feel like it was curated *for* the townspeople.

Like *specific* townspeople, I realized when I noticed a big, handwritten sign taped to a display that read *LOU'S SECTION*.

The shelves of Lou's section were covered with an array of products, none of them seemingly tied into the others. Cans of Campbell's Chunky soup, spaghetti, Oreo cookies, Fancy Feast cat food—

"Who is Lou?" I asked.

"Our favorite customer," Julia quickly said with a bright smile. "He was this old guy who lived in a fishing cabin outside of town. He had very specific tastes and always ordered the same exact things: soup, spaghetti, Oreos, and Fancy Feast."

"Refined," I teased, but I'd spent plenty of weekends devouring Oreos at my uncle's. They were a fucking delicacy, if you asked me.

"Right?" she said. "After we found out he passed away, everyone at the store agreed that we had to put his favorite things in one section and make it a permanent display. Our town's quirky little way of honoring him, I guess."

My eyes slid over her face as she said this. Because even though she was smiling, her eyes shimmered with tears. Tears.

And that was when it hit me. When everything got messed up in my head as I looked at the display again.

Soup, spaghetti, Oreos, and Fancy Feast.

Suddenly it felt like I couldn't get enough air into my lungs.

Soup, spaghetti, Oreos, and Fancy Feast.

Shit, shit, shit.

I was staring at a display of Remi's favorite things.

Oreos, Barilla, Chunky, and Mr. Dipshit's favorite, *Fancy Feast*.

And as my eyes dropped down to the bottom shelf, I saw the photo next to a can of clam chowder.

Before I could think better of it, the picture was in my hand. I felt almost dizzy as I looked down at his face.

It was Remi, sitting at a desk with a pen in his hand, smiling as Julia's parents stood behind him.

Beaming, like they'd just accomplished something monumental.

"Lou had a great smile, right?" Julia said, stepping closer and looking down at the photo.

I nodded and wasn't sure I could speak, but then I managed to say, "Tell me more about this Lou."

That was when Julia stepped back, a beam of realization flooding her face, and said, "Actually, I have a better idea."

CHAPTER THIRTY-SEVEN

"Someone who wants to explore with you
is someone to explore."

—Remington

Damion

"This is it," Julia said, pulling up in front of the tiny cabin.

It'd been a shock to my system when Julia suggested we visit "Lou's place." She said I had to "see it to believe it," and then she explained that since she hadn't had a chance to visit since his death because of their move to New York, she "wouldn't mind the closure."

And, honestly, I didn't know how to feel about that.

Before I could figure out how to navigate this emotional roller coaster I suddenly found myself on, Julia and I were using the grocery store delivery truck to head out to Remi's fucking cabin.

On the way there, she told me how she and her family got to know "Lou" when they started delivering groceries to him. How that led to inviting him over for Thanksgiving and Christmas, then barbecues on weekends when they realized he was living alone.

She told me about how Lou told wild stories about his travels and waxed poetic about even the most mundane things.

And as she kept on going about how amazing Lou was, how important he was, every word was like a painful, emotional punch.

She rolled down both windows as she put the truck in park. "It's hard to believe he's not inside."

What a perfect place for Remi, I thought, completely able to picture him sitting out on that porch.

It looked small and simple, like it probably only had three rooms, but it reminded me of all the places he'd flocked to when I traveled with him. He'd had all the money in the world, and used it to do everything he could to *live* life, but he never cared about the finer things. The flashy things. He was simplistic in a way very few people were.

He'd take a cabin with a funky backstory over a five-star hotel every time.

"Is this the way it always looked?" I asked.

I could tell that there was a lake behind the cabin. Well, more like a fishing pond. It was small, but surrounded by cottonwood trees, with a wooden dock that screamed of something Remi would've loved. In front of the house, tall shrubs lined the property, shrubs that were overgrown but beautiful. Wild.

"It's exactly the way it always looked," she said. "The first time I delivered here, I remember thinking it looked run-down, but then I was blown away when I went inside."

"What's it like?" I asked, wanting her to slow down and describe every tiny detail. Hearing about him from someone else, details I'd never heard about things he'd done that I knew nothing about, made me feel closer to him somehow.

Which was probably why I'd taken that picture of Remi and slipped it into my pocket.

The second I did it, I convinced myself I'd nabbed it because it could be evidence of . . . *something.*

But that was bullshit.

The truth was that I hadn't been able to let go of the image because, *fuck*, Uncle Remi was smiling at me.

The thing no one ever told you about death was the way the door to a person just slammed shut in an instant. Suddenly, without notice, your contact with them was gone forever. And I was only realizing now that I'd been unprepared for the sudden blackout. Since no one in my family really ever wanted to talk about him, sometimes it felt like Remi had never existed at all except in my mind. We'd had a memorial service right after we got the news, but the very next day, everyone immediately behaved as if it'd never happened. As if Remi wasn't here a minute ago, and then gone for good in the next.

"When you walk inside, there's just one room. It's small, but all the walls are covered in wood. There's a surprisingly well-equipped kitchen, but it's just a tiny galley-style off in one corner. The place is all about the view. You sit in that cabin and you could just stare out at the pond for hours."

I wondered if my face was giving away what an absolute heart twist this visit was turning out to be, holy *shit*.

"Yeah?" I said, trying to keep it together.

"And Lou was a crazy reader. Shelves and shelves of books in the cabin, books in closets, books in the bedrooms; I swear to God all the man did was fish and read."

"Sounds like a pretty great life," I said, feeling way too fucking emotional because that was the way every place I'd ever visited with Remi had been.

Full of books and stories.

That made her look over at me. "I cannot imagine you, Mr. New York, being happy fishing and reading all day every day."

"You don't know," I said, throwing her words back at her. "That sounds pretty fucking great right now."

"It does, doesn't it?" she agreed. "I think you might be in danger of liking Nebraska, Damion."

"If I didn't have to deal with Nebraskans, it isn't half bad," I replied, needing to lighten the tone because I was in serious danger of bawling soon.

“Do you want to go around to the back?” she asked. “I mean, from what Lauren told me, no one has bought the house yet, so all things considered, it’s still Lou’s. Someone might kick us out, but there’s nothing illegal about going in someone’s backyard and peeking through their windows, right?”

Hell yeah, I wanted to. “Come on,” I said, opening my door.

We walked around to the back of the cabin, and my throat got ridiculously tight when I saw the fishing boat tied to the dock.

Because he’d sent me a picture of that boat. It was Remi’s boat, his pride and joy.

He’d built the red cedar dinghy by hand—multiple letters had described the process—and it was gorgeous. That shiny ten-footer was a gleaming throwback that screamed Remi’s name.

“Lou loved that little boat,” she said as we walked through the grass. “One day when he was sanding it, he turned on the *Dracula* audiobook and we listened to the whole thing in its entirety. I sat in a chair and got a terrible sunburn while he worked his ass off. He wouldn’t let me help.”

I was torn between jealousy and absolute fucking joy as I pictured it.

“Let’s go,” she said. “I want to peek in the window.”

She pulled me with her as she climbed up the stairs to the deck, and I didn’t give a shit about anything except the way it was making me feel, hearing her talk about my favorite person in the world.

I was starving and she was nourishment.

I grabbed her hand and instead of removing it from my sleeve, I wrapped my fingers around her cold ones, needing the contact.

Her eyes narrowed as she glanced over at me. “What are you doing?”

“Trying to warm my cold hands,” I lied, shrugging.

“You’re a little clingy for a city boy,” she teased, those amber eyes playful as they moved over my face like she was trying to figure me out.

"And you sure are mouthy for a country girl."

When we got onto the deck, she put her hands up to the window and peered inside like a little kid. It warmed the sadness in my chest, making me laugh.

"Nothing's changed," she said on a gasp. "It looks exactly the same as it did when he lived here."

I mimicked her actions, putting my hands on the glass and peeking inside.

And it looked exactly like she'd described, more Remi-coded than I even would've imagined.

"I'm sure it's locked," she said, but when she tugged on the sliding door, it opened.

"Jules," I warned. "You know you can't go inside, right?"

She ignored me and pulled the door open a little farther. "I just want to say goodbye."

Goodbye?

I swallowed and gave her a nod, feeling more fondness for her than I had since we'd met because no matter what was real or fake with us or real or fake with her and her family, the emotions she had for Lou—*Remi*—were authentic.

And that made me feel close to her in a way that I'd maybe never felt with another person.

She'd known, and loved, the person I'd known best in the world.

The person who'd *shown* me the world.

I followed her as she walked around the rooms, taking pictures with her phone. It was hard to breathe, though, because I saw things I recognized as his. The book-page paperweight that I'd given him as a birthday present, the framed picture of him in Nepal when he'd climbed Everest, the compass; it was almost too much.

I felt overwhelmed by emotion as I soaked in every last bit of Remi.

The place somehow even smelled like his place, like a cross between mothballs and Gain laundry detergent.

But we both nearly jumped out of our skin when we heard the cat.

"Mr. Dipshit!" Julia squealed, her voice coming out a little strained.

I glanced over and she had tears in her eyes—again—as she grinned at that stupid cat.

"So whoever is taking care of the house is taking care of you, too, huh?" she said in awe. "Hell, it wouldn't surprise me if this cat figured out how to live here alone. He's a total independent asshole."

I know, I wanted to say.

"All cats are," I managed, kind of wanting to cry right along with her as we both dropped down to pet the stupid cat.

The cat, who leaned into my touch like we were old friends.

Because we were.

Yeah, I remember you too, buddy, I thought, really fucking struggling to keep it together as Mr. D. started to purr.

I didn't believe in bullshit like reincarnation or spirits, but as the cat butted his soft head against my hand, I felt like Remi was close, somehow.

"Are you okay?" I asked as we both stood, as I watched her unshed tears finally spill over. My thumbs seemed to find her cheeks, and I watched as they brushed away her tears, feeling like I couldn't breathe again.

"Yeah," she croaked. "I just miss him, even though it's ridiculous, because he was as much of a stranger as he was a friend."

"I get it, though," I said, my voice cracking.

She went a little blurry then, and I was pretty sure I looked like a psycho, because why would I be blinking back tears over her old friend "Lou"?

"Most of the time I think you're a huge New York jerk," she said, "but sometimes you surprise me by how decent you are."

"Why are you saying this?" I asked, clearing my throat and looking away from her.

"Because I literally just saw a tear in your eye, so unless you have allergies, you are being a good human, empathizing with my emotional ridiculousness."

And just like that, I fully trusted her.

I mean, if I was being honest with myself, I'd been trusting her for a while.

But as I looked at her, I realized that she was a thousand percent who she said she was. She was a girl from Springfield-fucking-Nebraska who'd been kind enough to my uncle to make him want to make sure her family was okay when he was gone.

Family.

A family of warmth, hugs, and kindness. Tough love and inside jokes.

Would I ever know that again, now that Remi was gone?

"Are *you* okay?" Julia asked, and I realized as she blinked up at me that my thoughts must have been painted all over my face. I was losing it.

Whatever dam I'd built to try to keep the emotions of Remi from surging was about to break.

What the hell am I doing here?

"I'm not sure," I admitted, unsure how to explain my reaction, relieved that she didn't appear to be looking for an explanation.

"Is there anything I can do?" she asked.

"Actually—" I cut myself off because it was stupid.

"Actually, what?" she said, her mouth turning up in a little grin. "What were you going to say?"

My eyes dipped down to that gorgeous smile and I said it. "Do you want to take the boat out?"

CHAPTER THIRTY-EIGHT

"Sometimes you have to stop thinking
and make shit happen."

—Remington

Julia

"Don't say *The Notebook*," he said, shaking his head.

"I can't help it," I said with a laugh. "It's the oars. You rowing while I sit here and watch just *screams* of that movie."

"It's nothing like that. It's sunny out, not raining," he said. "We're in Nebraska, not wherever the hell they were, and there are no ducks to be found."

"I think they were swans," I said under my breath.

"Regardless of the species of waterfowl, know-it-all," he said, giving me his patented mocking stare, "this is nothing like that. We aren't about to fight, you're not engaged to a rich dude, and I'm working up a sweat over here. For the record, this isn't as easy as Gosling made it look. My shoulders are screaming."

"Do you want me to help?" I asked. "I can do one oar while you do the other— "

"And make me feel like less of a man? I don't think so."

"Is that fragile masculinity talking?"

"Knock off the shit or I'm dumping you in the drink, wiseass."

I laughed as I leaned my head back, letting the warm autumn sun heat my face.

"This is nice. I'm glad we're doing this."

"As long as we don't get arrested for trespassing," he added.

"Don't worry. My Uncle Dave is friends with the sheriff. It'll be fine."

That made him scoff in disbelief. "So are you related to everyone in town? Is that how this works?" he asked.

"No," I said. "My parents are kind of transplants. When they got married, they were both desperate for this small-town sort of life, I think because they both had suburban childhoods with divorced parents and a lot of unhappiness. They *wanted* a life where they were connected to a lot of people. So they bought our house when they were completely broke but wanting the American dream. They fixed it up themselves because they couldn't afford to pay someone else, and they *made* this whole vision of theirs happen."

The second it came out of my mouth I realized what I'd said, and I wasn't sure how to recover. But I also trusted him.

Oh my God. I trusted him. As much as my brain told me better, my heart told me he was safe. Worth the risk, maybe.

He wasn't looking at me like he'd caught on to the fact that we hadn't always been rich. No, he was looking at me like he wanted to know everything about the real *me*.

And I wanted him to know.

So I continued. "Then the previous owner of the store put it up for sale and they did it again—they bought the market and worked like crazy. Now we have all those small-town connections, and my parents love it. I think they love all the connections and relationships they made through the store more than actually having it be a source of income. And my Uncle Dave technically isn't my uncle, by the way. He is my dad's best friend's cousin."

"This place is so backward," he teased.

"I know."

"And it feels a million miles away from New York." He let go of the oars and we just sat there, soaking up the sun. His eyes were on the pond, like he was trying to memorize the spot, and there was a soft vulnerability to his face that I wouldn't have imagined before today.

Although, today's version of Damion was impossible to comprehend.

I'd never be over the fact that he'd had tears in his eyes when I was talking about Lou. That he empathized me with that much. That he cared. And that it was real. All of it felt real. Him showing up here. In Nebraska. On my front porch because, let's face it, he was worried.

About me.

I felt special, as lame as that was. I felt important to him, like my happiness mattered, and as I watched him stare out over Lou's pond, I was scared.

I'd been deluding myself since the day we'd met.

I was very, *very* into Damion Rutledge.

And the thought was terrifying.

"It's a different genre of beauty," he said, his eyes still on the horizon. "Because, God help me, there *is* something about this. It's like a pared-down, shaved-off version that's raw and simple. Uncomplicated."

My heart squeezed as I watched him take in the surroundings. "You love Nebraska, don't you?"

His gaze slowly left the sky and inched its way toward mine. Blue eyes today as he looked at me. "I kind of do."

Oh God. I'm in trouble.

After we finally tied the boat to the dock and walked back over to the truck, he grabbed the front of my jacket and pulled me a little closer to him. My stomach went weightless as he gave me a look that I couldn't read, as his eyes slid over my face in a way that made the oxygen get sucked out of my lungs.

"Thanks for showing me this," he said, swallowing.

"Thanks for letting me," I managed, my voice coming out all breathy and soft. His face was so close, above mine but so so close, and I wondered again what it'd be like to kiss him.

God, what am I thinking??

I cleared my throat and stepped back, tucking my hair behind my ears. "We should go?" I managed to say. "There's a party tonight. I promised Lauren and my friend Teanna I'd be there."

He looked at me, still impossible to read, and then he gave me a nod. "Right. You have to go."

And because there was something in the tone of his voice that reminded me of a sad puppy, I heard myself say, "Do you want to come?"

"This is a first for me."

I looked at Damion in the darkness, and the funny grin he was giving me made my heart pinch in my chest. We were sitting on the tailgate of my dad's truck and he was smiling like a little kid.

"Which part?" I asked, taking a gulp from my red Solo cup.

"All of it." He could've meant the vehicles (mostly trucks) parked out in the middle of the mowed-down cornfield, the groups of people standing around, someone's radio playing "Love You Tonight" while the only light was the bright harvest moon above, or the key bucket.

He'd seemed downright shocked when I had to dump the truck keys in the bin and he learned I couldn't get them back until I—or someone with me—blew a good number into the traveling breathalyzer.

Party rule number one was *If you wanna go, you gotta blow.*

Memorial crosses next to dirt roads resulted in unwritten traffic rules.

He said, "Saturday night hits different here."

"Yeah, it's light-years away from Gardenwood, isn't it?" I agreed, inhaling a deep breath of air that smelled like dried leaves and bonfire smoke.

He gave a nod and looked into his cup before taking a drink.

I glanced in the direction of the makeshift bonfire, feeling relaxed and terrifyingly happy, but then I saw Will and Hannah approaching.

No, no, no.

My eyes met Will's and my stomach got the feeling it always did when I thought of him, a mix between butterflies and the world's biggest stomach pain.

"Hey, Jules," he said when he reached the tailgate, a can of Busch Light in his hand and a carefree expression on his face.

God, his smile was the smile I knew as well as my own, and I wanted to hug him and scratch his eyes out, all at the same time. I missed him, the boy who'd always been there in my life. But I also wanted to push him to the ground for destroying a lifetime of memories.

I *hated* him for destroying that.

Hannah gave me a polite smile that didn't reach her eyes.

"I didn't know you were back," he said, his gaze shifting over to Damion.

So they didn't see me at the Thai restaurant.

"Yeah, I just came back for the weekend, for Teanna's birthday," I said, hating the way he smelled the way he always did, the way his smile looked the same as it had when he used to smile at me in his basement while we watched movies together.

"Ah," he said, nodding with another smile.

God, don't smile at me.

I didn't want him back, and I didn't care about him—not really—but it still hurt to talk to him.

His smile was something that still had the power to crush my heart.

"Who's this?" I heard, and then I felt Damion's arm settle over my shoulders as he pulled me closer to him.

Holy shit, I thought, glancing at him out of the corner of my eye. He had me in one of those adorable-couple headlocks, where the crook of his elbow cradled my neck, and he gave me a look that I couldn't quite interpret. There was something teasing about it, but there was also heat there, like he was intense or jealous or . . . *something*.

He couldn't be jealous, could he?

No way.

"This is Hannah and Will," I managed, suddenly breathless, and I wasn't sure if it was because of his hands on me and his cologne in my nose or the presence of Will after all this time. "I went to school with them here."

"Nice to meet you. I'm Damion," he said. "Jules told me about most of her friends, but I don't think she mentioned you."

"She didn't?" Will said, his eyes lingering on my face.

"Why would I?" I said, feeling absolutely like I'd won something as he looked even more surprised by those three words.

I wasn't sure what Damion was doing or why, but I didn't hate it.

"So you're from New York, then?" Hannah asked Damion.

Duh, I thought.

"I am," he said.

"You came back for the birthday party too?" Will asked.

"Not exactly," Damion said. "*Jules* came back, but then I missed her too much, so I flew in this morning."

Damion the Rebel, maybe he isn't too bad, I thought as he messed with Will.

"Yeah?" Will said, his eyes darting between Damion and me like he was trying to figure something out.

I just raised an eyebrow and smiled, because it felt good. Will knew me well, so I knew he could see on my face what I was thinking, the smugness of it all, but I didn't care. I wanted him to know that I was smug about this, about the fact that he didn't matter to me anymore.

"Well, we're going to go grab another beer," he said. "Nice meeting you."

"Yeah, you too," Damion said.

"I'm sorry," he said quietly as soon as they walked away, his voice low and kind of rumbling in my ear. His voice did wild things to my stomach, and I couldn't bring myself to look at him, not when his arm was still around me and I was still resting so close to him.

When his mouth was that close to my ear.

"Don't apologize," I managed, wondering why he wasn't letting go. "That was perfect."

"I don't like him," he said.

"You don't like him?" I said with a laugh. "You don't even know him."

"I know what he did to you and that's enough," he said, and the accusation in his tone made me weak. He sounded like he wanted to slug Will even though he really knew nothing about him, and something about that was unbelievably swoony.

"That little shit keeps looking at you," he murmured in my ear. "He knows what he lost."

"You're wrong," I said, wondering how I was supposed to keep my thoughts in order when the warmth of his breath was on my cheek as he said ridiculously incredible things, oh *God*.

"Would it matter to you?" he asked, and God help me, something in his voice made me think he cared about the answer.

"No and yes," I admitted, surprised that I wanted to talk about Will at all, much less with Damion.

I finally looked at him, at that ridiculously handsome face, and said, "It'd matter because I want him to miss me, but it wouldn't change anything. I'd never get back with him."

"So it feels a little good, yes?" he teased, giving me one of his wicked smiles. "You like the way it feels to mess with them, don't you?"

Oh, hello, Damion the Rebel.

I looked at his mouth and thought again, *Maybe he really isn't TOO bad.*

"Yeah," I admitted, my stomach dipping because I had no idea what was happening. Damion and I were together in the back of a truck in a cornfield, talking about Will.

Like, *what*?

"I love it," I admitted. "I don't care that it probably makes me petty and small—I love it. Feels good."

"See," he whispered. This time there wasn't space between us. His lips brushed my ear, and his tone shifted to something . . . dangerous. "Being a rebel can be a lot of fun."

Oh God.

"Follow my lead," he said, and then he leaned closer. His eyes were . . . *something* as they went down to my lips.

Oh my God, he's going to kiss me.

He raised one eyebrow, a wordless request for consent, and I couldn't help myself.

I smiled. *Permission granted.*

His mouth came down on mine. Hard and soft at the same time. Damion Rutledge held me in place and kissed me, his hands finding my cheeks, gently angling my head as his lips slid over mine.

There had never been a question that he'd be a good kisser. You met Damion Rutledge and you just *knew* that the boy could kiss.

But he only gave me a sample. *Always a tease.* I felt his breath lingering between us. Could feel his deep sigh as he pulled back.

He looked down at me, his eyes asking a million questions, and it felt like my heart stopped beating as I met his gaze.

Because the question no longer had to do with making anyone jealous.

The question had to do with me and Damion.

The moment paused, frozen, as we looked at each other.

What are we doing? I thought as he watched me.

What do I want? I wondered, and then the Ella Langley on the speaker hit, the moonlit country lyrics crashing over me.

When the stars are out, boy, I want you to hold me . . .

And then I lost my mind.

My fingers found the hard line of his jaw, and pulled him right back to me.

CHAPTER THIRTY-NINE

"Kissing is worth it. Every time."

—Remington

Damion

Yes, yes, fucking yes.

I didn't give a shit where we were, how many people were around, or that we were sitting on the tailgate of a pickup truck in the middle of a cornfield.

All that mattered was kissing Julia.

Because for that brief second, when she looked at me with a thousand questions in her eyes, I realized the absolute truth.

I was gone.

I was head over heels, lost to Julia Nebraska with the *Pretty Woman* hair. I'd somehow managed to fall for my enemy, even though she actually was *not* my enemy, and all that mattered was her.

My fingers might've been a little too rough, pressing a little too hard on her perfect skin as I angled her head, but I needed more. I needed all. I opened her mouth with mine and went all in, kissing deep, wanting to consume every bit of her.

And then she made the tiniest sound in the back of her throat.

Oh God.

That sound, a hum or a moan or whatever the hell it was, made me rear up in need because that sound was exactly how I felt.

Urgent.

Desperate.

Desperately hungry.

For her.

I'd waited too long for this, even though I hadn't even known I'd been waiting. Suddenly it was like I couldn't get enough, like I'd been Julia-starved my entire life and had just been given my very first taste.

And it wasn't enough.

Not nearly enough.

More.

Fucking more.

I need so much more.

She nipped at my bottom lip and I heard myself growl, helpless to behave because how could she kiss like this? How could she respond this way, lick into me this way, destroy me this way with her sweet strawberry-glossed mouth?

The blood pounded in my ears as I felt the drag of her tongue against mine, as she let me go wild in her mouth like she wanted me there, like she'd been waiting for me to kiss her like this.

Like nothing else mattered.

She kissed me back with a ferocity that sent sparks of heat burning through every one of my nerve endings, torching me with the need for more, setting my skin on fire as I sought every bit of her I'd yet to try.

Holy shit, Julia Nebraska.

She kissed the way she drove a pickup, the way she loved a poem, the way she leaned her head all the way back and worshipped the sun out on Remi's boat. She was reckless and wild, sincere and intentional, and quite possibly the most devastating thing I'd ever experienced.

I felt everything, every single fucking emotion, as she met me where I was. Her kiss was liquid sunshine against my tongue, the highest of highs, yet my heart was already breaking at the low-low realization that it would eventually have to end.

And her fingers, my God.

Her fingertips were like branding irons on my skin, ten searing touches that made me weak as she flexed on me and kissed me back like it was her idea.

God, I loved her ideas.

"MAY I HAVE YOUR ATTENTION, PLEASE, YOU LITTLE SHITS?"

I pulled back at the sound of the bullhorn and looked at Julia's face. "What the hell is that?"

"Oh no," Julia said, her eyes fluttering open. She looked sleepy and sexy as hell as she smiled at me and said, "The farmer."

"The farmer?" I repeated as movement exploded around us.

I didn't know what was happening, but I needed everything to pause.

Freeze.

Hold on a damn minute!

I needed to stay in that moment a little longer, because her glossy lips were grinning at me and her mouth was still so close to mine and my nose was still drunk on the smell of her—

"We've got to go," she said, dropping her hands from my face, breaking the spell.

And everything was suddenly on fast-forward.

The fire was extinguished with someone's drink and people started running around, grabbing shit and tossing it into truck beds.

A small crowd formed around the key bucket almost instantaneously.

"I WOULD SUGGEST YOU GET YOUR VEHICLES OUT OF MY FIELD, BECAUSE I'VE CALLED THE SHERIFF AND HE'S ON HIS WAY."

"Where is he?" I asked, looking around in the darkness.

"Probably up on his porch," she said, jumping off the tailgate and gesturing for me to do the same. "You can't see it from here, but his bullhorn's got great range."

"I WOULD APPRECIATE, MOVING FORWARD, IF YOU WOULD HAVE YOUR LITTLE GATHERINGS ON SOMEONE ELSE'S PROPERTY. I AM AWARE THAT MY NEPHEW, COLT, IS AMONG YOU, BUT THIS HAS NOT BEEN AN APPROVED EVENT. TAKE YOUR TRASH WITH YOU AND GO HOME BEFORE YOU GET AN MIP."

"What's an MIP?" I asked as engines started.

"Are you serious right now?" Lauren asked, she and Teanna suddenly emerging from the darkness, pushing me toward the cab of the truck while Julia ran over to get her keys. "Minor in possession?"

"You don't want an MIP, New York, because you have to come back for your court date," Teanna said. "Get in the truck."

What the hell what the hell? I had no idea if this was serious or not. But the next second we were all piled inside the truck, Julia climbing behind the wheel, starting the old pickup.

"Your boyfriend doesn't know what an MIP is," Teanna said as Jules slammed her door.

"That's because there are no rules where he comes from," Julia replied, buckling her seat belt. "The kids do everything the adults d—"

"AND DON'T BE STUPID. IF ANYONE'S NOT OKAY TO DRIVE, I'LL GIVE YOU A RIDE HOME BEFORE THE SHERIFF ARRIVES. JUST, LIKE, HONK YOUR DAMN HORN OR SOMETHING."

Julia didn't wait around for a horn. She jammed the truck into first gear and hightailed it out of the field, following the line of vehicles in front of her, a convoy of headlights exiting a dark field of corn.

"What the hell is this?" I asked, looking out the back window for cops or farmers with pitchforks.

"It's fine," Teanna said calmly. "People don't love it when you throw impromptu parties on their property, so sometimes they call the cops."

"This is *normal*?" I asked.

"Not *normal*," Julia said. "But it happens."

"Have *you* ever gotten an MIP?" I asked her.

"No," she said. "And I'm not about to get one tonight."

I watched in disbelief as Julia jerked the wheel and took off in an entirely different direction from every other car on that field.

And with a wicked smile on her lips that made me want to kiss her all over again, she hit the gas and said, "Hang on."

CHAPTER FORTY

"Grand gestures are cheesy as hell.
Never fucking skip them, son."

—Remington

Julia

I went into my room, shut the door, then let out a silent scream as I leaned against it because *OH MY GODDDDDD!*

The adrenaline was still pounding through me, and I was pretty sure I'd never really be able to sleep again.

Because, yeah—running from the cops. That was pulse-jarring. *Sure.*

But the kiss??

"Holy *shit*," I whispered into the empty of my room. I could die. "Holy *shit*!"

Damion's Uber had pulled up in front of my house the second we got home, so I was disappointed we hadn't really had a chance to say goodbye. Or kiss again. Or talk about whatever this meant, *oh God*.

I leaned down to turn on the lamp when I heard the tap.

I froze, then heard it again.

The quietest tap.

On my window.

My heart was in my throat as I crept closer in the darkness I knew by heart, my pulse pounding.

Because Will used to climb the trellis and tap on my window.

All the time on warm nights.

I swallowed and felt unsteady as I approached the window and looked out, searching for ghosts of summers past.

But I saw *Damion* instead.

Damion was dangling from the trellis.

I yanked up the window, leaned out the opening, and asked, "What are you *doing*?"

He shrugged and gave me a rebellious smile, his confident hands resting on the white lattice. It should've looked wrong for the city boy to be dangling off the side of my house, but he looked somehow just right.

Like he'd been born to climb my walls in expensive glasses and a backward ball cap.

"I didn't like getting interrupted," he said with a shrug.

"You didn't like getting *interrupted*?" I coughed out a laugh in disbelief, ignoring the way *my* hands were shaking just the tiniest bit. "So you climbed my house?"

Will might've done it before, but Damion doing it felt like a much bigger deal.

"I just . . . ," he said, his smirk falling away, sliding into something more . . . honest. He glanced below, toward the ground, and when his gaze returned to mine, something about the way he looked at me made me feel weightless. "I wasn't ready yet, Jules. Were you?"

Even though I was inside and he was outside, our faces were close.

A breath apart, only the space of a sigh between us as I leaned out the window and he leaned closer.

And I wasn't exactly sure what he was asking.

All I knew was that I hadn't been ready either.

He reached out a hand, taking my chin between his fingers like he had at our Italian dinner. His warm thumb traced over my skin, back and forth, as his eyes were all I could see.

Can I trust you? I wondered.

Could I really trust this rich boy from New York?

Could I really fall again?

The pad of his thumb moved slowly, sliding back and forth over my skin as hazel eyes watched me, and, God help me, I wanted to fall.

I felt hypnotized, *electrified*, as he slowly leaned closer.

Said my name in the softest whisper.

"Jules . . ."

"Hey, Julia, can I borrow your shampoo—" Lauren asked, barging into my room, her eyes going wide as she saw Damion's head in the window. "What the—"

I gasped—I think Damion did too—at the sound of Lauren's voice, which made Damion falter on the trellis.

"Shit!" he said as he grappled on the half-dead climbing branches and lost his footing.

"Oh shit!" I repeated, watching in horror as he lost his grip and fell. "Oh my God!"

Being the Mr. Perfect that he was, though, Damion somehow did the whole six-foot-drop thing, yet managed to land on his feet.

"Are you okay?" I shouted, too loudly.

"Did I interrupt something?" Lauren asked, but I ignored her.

Damion smirked and gave me a thumbs-up, but not before I heard the ominous—and oh, so familiar—creak of the Whittles' front door.

Nooooooooooo.

The last thing I needed was Edna, the next-door neighbor, calling my mom about a handsome young intruder who happened to climb up her daughter's window while she was back in town. Mrs. Whittle had ratted on Will and me one too many times.

Her eavesdropping was legendary.

And always resulted in a grounding.

"You better go." I straightened up from where I'd been leaning out the window, suddenly feeling awkward and unsure how to act. "The neighbors will be gossiping."

"Or I could come inside, and we could . . ."

"Could what?" Lauren asked, pushing her face out the window.

Could what? *We could what, Damion??*

"Uh. Yeah," he said, swallowing. "Never mind. I'll get going."

He started to walk away, toward the Uber waiting for him at the curb.

But then he stopped.

We could what??

He looked almost . . . timid, his eyes down like he was nervous.

Or . . . *something.*

God, does he regret it?

"I'll see you back in New York, right?" Damion said, looking up at me.

Looking curious. Looking . . . worried.

Oh, that face.

But his words—New York—reminded me of things I'd temporarily forgotten.

New York, where reality was waiting for us.

I nodded. "I'll see you back in New York," I replied, my heart doing cartwheels at I watched him walk to the Uber and get inside, unable to figure out what the New York version of me and Damion would look like now.

"Jules." Lauren's stern voice pulled me from my wondering. I turned around to see her standing in my bedroom, holding an empty bottle of shampoo in her hand.

"Are you sure this is a good idea? I don't want you to go through another destructive heartbreak like you did with Will."

She didn't even have to ask how I felt about Damion. She could see it written on my face. Hear it in my voice. She knew me that well.

"He's not Will, though," I said, feeling the need to defend him because he *wasn't* Will.

He was everything I didn't understand, everything I wasn't sure how to handle, but he definitely wasn't Will.

And maybe I *liked* that about him.

She shifted on her feet, hand on her hip. She wanted more.

"Plus, I don't know . . . he makes me feel *alive*," I said.

"Alive?" she repeated.

"And brave," I added, realizing it was true. "He makes me feel brave."

Something about that made her stern motherly look of concern melt. "Well, being alive is good. Being brave is better."

"Feels great, too." I agreed, then coughed a ridiculously lovesick giggle as I thought of the kiss and added, "*Unbelievably* great."

"I can see it's too late for warnings. You're too far gone."

"Am I?" I said, because even though I'd been with Will for so long, this feeling for Damion was something entirely new to me.

Does he feel the same way, though?

I couldn't help but notice the way his shoulders slumped and his voice got heavy when he asked if he'd see me in New York. *What did it mean?*

But I shook the thought out of my mind.

"You are so far gone you are no longer on the map. And besides," she added with a sly smirk all her own, "a rebel might be good for you."

I let Lauren's words sit for a while.

"I think . . . ," I began, smiling as I remembered Damion's voice in the back of the truck. "I think I want to be rebellious for a change."

CHAPTER FORTY-ONE

"Loneliness hits harder in New York."

—Remington

Damion

Why haven't I heard from her yet?

All I could think about since the minute I'd landed was when I was going to see her.

Hell, all I'd thought about since her lips met mine was when I could kiss her again.

The three-hour flight from Nebraska to New York had been the longest of my life. I couldn't text her, couldn't call her, couldn't make sure she was coming back to the city, where we could reenact what happened in the back of her pickup truck.

God, I am addicted to her.

Addicted and terrified.

Terrified that she'd woken up the next morning and thought it was all a mistake.

Terrified she'd want to pretend that kiss had never happened.

The thought made me want to run to her.

What the hell is wrong with me?

"I cannot believe you're wearing that," Beckett said as we both stood in front of the mirrors.

Neither of us wanted our mothers involved in our fittings—they had way too many opinions—so we met up at the Claude Karrgens boutique instead, cutting out the overbearing middlemen.

"I look great, are you kidding me," I said, hating the idea of wearing a tux and parading around in front of everybody.

"You're totally missing the theme, though," he said.

He was dressed in a top hat and wearing a ridiculous ruffled shirt under his jacket—on theme—whereas I was wearing a modern-cut suit that happened to be white.

With a white pocket square, white tie, white shoes.

Julia and I had only spent five minutes discussing our dress for the ball after her cousin brought it up, but I loved her idea. Instead of being literal about the novel itself, she was inspired by Wharton's real life. According to her, Edith Wharton spent her entire life in love with a man named Walter Berry, even though they never ended up together.

Wharton referred to him as her "blank canvas."

So I was literally the canvas, and Julia was going to find something . . . berry-related.

"It just seems like since this is your family's ball and you get the first dance," Beckett said, adjusting his ruffles as he looked at himself in the mirror. "You might've gone a little more on-topic."

"Like you?" I said with a snort. "A top hat and walking stick? You look like Mr. Peanut."

"Mr. Peanut has a monocle, you cretin," he said. "I look nothing like him."

"You kinda do," I heard, and when I turned around, Liam Lowell was walking in.

Fucking awesome.

"What the hell does your shirt say?" Beckett asked, looking at Liam in the full-length mirror.

THINGS RICK ASTLEY IS NEVER GONNA DO was printed on Liam's hot-pink T-shirt, along with the lyrics to *that* song.

Yeah, he was fucking Rickrolling anyone who read it.

"It's hilarious," Liam said, looking down at himself. "Better than your boring-ass style."

"Fuck off," Beckett said, laughing.

"So what did you think of Springfield, Rutledge?" Liam asked as one of the employees brought out a suit for him.

So he knew. Did Julia tell him? Lauren?

"What?" Beckett asked, giving me a surprised look in the mirror. "You went to *Nebraska*?"

Dammit.

I really didn't feel like discussing it with Beckett *or* Liam, but definitely not with them together. I wanted to guard it, to protect the sanctity of this new chapter with Julia, and opening it up for discussion with those two felt wildly unsecure.

Especially when I hadn't had a chance to talk to *her* yet.

"Yeah," I said, meeting Liam's eyes in the wall of mirrors. He was watching me suspiciously, like he didn't trust me—shocker—and something about it pissed me off more than usual.

Like, I got the whole protective-brother thing, but he also needed to chill the hell out.

I told Beck, "Julia went home for a birthday party, so—"

"So you went with her, huh?" Beckett said. "I think you've been lying to me. I think you're into her."

"Have you?" Liam asked as he took the hanger. "Have you been lying, Rutledge?"

None of your damn business was what I wanted to say, because it wasn't. It was no one's business.

Was I into her? Had I been lying—to Beck, to everyone, to *myself*—when I said I wasn't?

Yeah, maybe definitely.

Did I feel like admitting it at this moment?

Not fucking really.

And I was dying to know what Liam knew . . . about anything and everything.

"Maybe," I said with a noncommittal shrug, untying the tie, ready to get this fitting over with.

"What the hell does that even mean?" Liam asked with a scowl, like he was pissed I wasn't opening up to him and sharing my innermost thoughts and secrets. "Always fucking hedging, I swear to God."

Liam's posture instantly changed. He was staring at me, frozen, and I wasn't sure if he *wanted* me to have feelings for his sister, or if he wanted me gone.

He just looked . . . on edge as he glared at me.

Why am I giving a shit about Liam's approval?

I didn't need *anyone's* approval.

"I'm saying I *want* there to be more," I confessed, watching Liam's glare soften slightly to more of a disapproving stare.

I'll take it, I guess.

"Holy shit, Rutledge likes a Gardenwood girl?" Beckett said with a laugh. "Surely this cannot be true."

"It's probably because she's *not* a Gardenwood girl," I said.

"You don't think so?" Liam asked, his tone still full of interrogation as he slid into the jacket. "You don't see Jules as a Gardenwood girl?"

"You know she isn't—now who's hedging?" I said, unwilling to kiss his ass anymore. "Julia might go to our school, but she's a Springfield girl."

His eyes narrowed. "I'm not sure if you mean that as an insult or a compliment."

"Oh, it's a compliment," I said. "Trust me."

"You actually liked it there?" Beckett asked in disbelief.

"I'm as shocked as you are."

"I heard your presence caused a fight between Julia's ex and his new girlfriend," Liam said, tugging at his cuffs as he looked at his reflection in the mirror. "So I appreciate *that*."

What else did you hear?

Had he heard about the kiss? Again, not that I gave a shit, but still.

"Why is that?" I asked, wondering if he wished his sister were back together with that douchebag.

He shrugged. "I just like to see assholes suffer."

"Same," I said, although as we eyed each other in the mirror, we both knew who he was really talking about.

Again. This fucking *guy.*

"I also heard Will got an MIP, along with ten other people who all turned out onto Platteview Road just as the sheriff arrived."

"No shit?" I looked at him in disbelief. "Are you serious?"

"Yeah," Liam said, and his glare dimmed just a little. He wasn't smiling—*fuck, no*—but he looked mildly amused as he said, "You're lucky my sister's an impulsive idiot when it comes to driving. Apparently everyone who went out the other way got clocked."

I started laughing because, damn—what a night.

Every time I thought I had her figured out, Julia Lowell surprised me.

By the time I got home, I couldn't handle another minute of not hearing from her.

So I sent a simple text.

Me: Meet me at my locker as soon as you get to school.

CHAPTER FORTY-TWO

"Falling in love in New York? In the fall? It's absurd that someone could be so lucky."

—Remington

Julia

I was nervous as I walked in the direction of Damion's locker.

He'd texted me, but what did it mean?

Damion: Meet me at my locker as soon as you get to school.

Did he want to shut me down, to talk to me before the news of us went wide, or did he just want to see me? The Damion I knew at school was not the Damion I'd hung out with in Nebraska, so I had no idea what to expect. I was terrified I was going to reach his locker and find out he'd returned to his former self and had no interest in being close to me whatsoever.

That he'd be pissed about the whole almost-MIP thing. I kept thinking about that night, the kiss. His breath on my neck, the whispers in my ear. Him being all Romeo-like and climbing up my window.

But I also remembered the nervousness in his voice when he hit the ground in front of my house, the way he'd looked . . . *conflicted* when he asked about New York.

What the hell did that look mean??

I just couldn't bear the thought of the guy who'd shed a tear for Lou, who'd embraced my town like it was his own, who'd kissed me like his life depended on it, disappearing.

I was kind of obsessed with that guy.

I could see the back of his head as I got closer. And I mean, how was it that even the *back of his head* was attractive?? He was talking to somebody—it looked like Beckett—but the second I got next to his locker and he saw me, Damion stopped talking mid-sentence.

"Hey you," he said, those eyes all over me, making me a little breathless as they reminded me of the way he kissed. The way his hands had flexed on my face like he was losing control, the way his teeth had nipped my bottom lip like I made him a tiny bit feral.

"Hey, you," I said back, my voice ridiculously breathy.

Be cool, Jules.

"Come here for a sec," he said, and then he grabbed my hand, linking his fingers through mine. He turned and started walking, pulling me behind him.

"What the hell?" Beckett yelled. "We were in the middle of a conversation!"

"I don't care," Damion yelled back. "I need a minute with my girl."

My girl? I thought.

He said "my," right??

Then Damion opened the door to a classroom and pushed me inside.

"What are you doing?" I managed, but he was looking at me with an intensity I hadn't seen before. Teasing and sexy, *absolutely* naughty.

"I didn't get enough time with you Saturday, and I didn't talk to you at all yesterday," he said, letting go of my hand to close the door. "I need to make up for lost time."

"You do?"

"I do," he said, his fingers grazing my waist. "It's been far too many hours since I had a taste."

He stepped closer and didn't stop coming until my back was pressed against the classroom door, the front of his body leaning into me.

I set my hands on his hard chest as his lips met mine, as he kissed me like he'd been planning it since the last second we were together. It was hot and big and wide and perfect, proving to me he had absolutely mastered the art of kissing. Actually—"mastered" was ridiculous.

"Mastered" didn't begin to explain it.

I was fairly certain he had pioneered the art of kissing. Probably no one had kissed before him, and no one would ever kiss like this after him. Because the way he kissed felt like Damion the tutor, patient and thorough and brilliant, immersed in all the knowledge needed to pass any test that might be given.

The way his mouth was overconfident but all finesse, the way his teeth toyed with my bottom lip like we had all the time in the world, the way his—

"I'm sorry," he said, barely lifting his lips off mine, the heat in his eyes enough to make my toes curl. "I'm an animal and I didn't even ask."

"Ask what?" I managed, drowsy and breathless.

His mouth curled up into a sleepy half smile, which matched his heady-lidded gaze. "For permission to kiss you."

"You have it," I said quickly, on a breath. "You've got it. Permission granted please and thank—"

He growled and kissed me again before I could finish speaking, so intent—dizzyingly intense—that all ten of my fingers could do nothing but clench against the front of his sweater, digging into pectorals that were . . . *hell's bells,* so unbelievably solid.

The way his mouth was absolutely *devouring* mine, feverish and hot like he couldn't get enough, was overwhelming and too much and yet not enough, all at the same time. He was wicked with his lips, filthy with his teeth, and downright dirty with his tongue, *oh God.*

I was very nearly panting, breathing like I'd run a mile, as the space between the door behind me and the body before me disappeared.

But my heart nearly exploded when I felt his hands on my waist.

Those long fingers brushed over the tiny strip of bare skin that'd become exposed, the barely there distance between the bottom of my shirt and the top of my skirt, but I felt it.

The tremble.

While he kissed me like *that*, boldly audacious and cocky as hell, his fingers were shaking.

Damion Rutledge's hands were shaking.

And I loved that more than everything else.

Someone pushed on the door, jiggling the handle behind my back, so I jumped out of the way. Students poured into the room, glancing at Damion and me, but Damion just grinned down at me and grabbed my hand.

"Not that I don't mind an audience," he said, leaning down and saying it into my ear, "but we'll be late. Let's go. We have transition to get to."

We started walking down the hall, and I felt the eyes of everyone on us. I felt flustered and lightheaded, giggly and unsettled, kind of like everything was happening *to* me and I was just along for the ride.

How has this happened?

I was scared, to be honest, scared of the way I felt about him. It was too big, too much, too soon, especially when he gave me that blinding smile.

But he was holding my hand, so I didn't care.

It was impossible not to smile as all eyes took notice that we were together.

Suck it, jerks.

"I hope you wanted to hard launch this," he said quietly, his fingers squeezing mine as heads turned our way, "because I don't think there's any going back now."

"If you're good, I'm good," I said, hoping it was what he wanted.

I was scared to trust him, to trust this, but it felt so good that I had to force myself to give it a try, right?

Just let go and fall.

"Oh, I'm so good," he said, giving me yet another look that made butterflies go wild inside my body.

When we got to transition, he leaned down into my space, *oh, so close*, his mouth traversing my hair to find my ear and whisper—in the most intimate way possible, "See you at lunch."

And then he straightened and walked to his desk in the back of the room.

Yeah, the entire class murmured in shock (while I suppressed a shiver, dear *Lord*).

Subtlety and Damion did *not* go together.

True to his word, Damion sat with me at lunch. There I was, across from Donovan and Jasmine, when he plopped down beside me as if that spot belonged to him and him alone.

"What are you doing here, Damion?" Donovan asked, but she was smiling as she looked between the two of us. Word was traveling fast, and I felt like the entire school knew that we were official.

Dear God, are we actually official?

"You know exactly what," he said. "I have an affinity for your little friend here with the auburn curls and amber eyes."

"You did not just call her eyes amber," Jasmine said with an eye roll. "Please don't make me nauseous."

"What do you want from me here, Jaz?" Damion said, his forehead falling to the table in defeat, which made all of us laugh. "Should I do away with talking completely and just lock in on the PDA?"

"Please, God, no," Donovan said with a laugh.

I had trouble swallowing as he raised his head and looked at me like *that*, my cheeks on fire because Damion's romantic attention was an intensity level I wasn't used to.

Holy *God*.

"Maybe we can do that later," I joked, clearing my throat.

"Speaking of later," he said, leaning a little closer.

Oh God, what now?

"What are you doing after school?" he asked, hazel eyes sucking me in and making me want to do whatever *he* was doing. I felt like I had whiplash from how quickly we'd gotten here.

Zero to one hundred in a hot minute.

It scared me, the way I already felt about him, but it also felt so . . . so *right* that it was hard to pump the brakes. Slowing down was the safe thing to do, but his speed was making me an adrenaline junkie.

"My mom told me to come right home after school because she has a thousand things to do before the season kicks off and she needs help."

"How about you tell her you have more important things to do?" he said in that arrogant way of his. "Like hanging out with your new boyfriend."

New boyfriend??

I looked at his insanely handsome face and couldn't quite reconcile the fact that he was that.

My *boyfriend*.

"I definitely don't think she'll approve that," I said, catching a whiff of his cologne. How did he *always* smell like a Ralph Lauren advertisement? I had to be careful not to hyperventilate on his scent.

"Oh, sorry, what I really meant was *tutoring*," he said, oh so quietly so no one else could hear, inching his way closer to me, closing the space between us.

Damion was a very physical guy, where Will hadn't been. He was always grabbing my hand, pulling my sleeve, nudging me with his big body, tugging on my hair; I *loved* it. It almost felt like he needed to touch me, and I was obsessed with the idea of Damion needing *anything* from me.

"Fine, I'll tell my mom I have to stay home and study."

"Wait," he said, a tiny crease forming between his eyebrows. "How about you come to my house to study, instead?"

"*Your* house?" I repeated, hating that idea. I pictured his father's face and NO—no way. "No offense, but I don't think your parents are going to be happy to see *me* crossing their threshold."

"They're never home until well after eight, so it isn't going to matter," he said, his voice quiet and deep.

Sending a shower of sparks through every nerve in my body as those eyes, behind ridiculously hot glasses, watched me like they were looking for my reaction.

"Oh," I said, torn between wanting desperately to go and being wildly intimidated at the thought.

And it must've shown on my face, because he leaned even closer and said, "I'll take care of you, I promise."

My heart was in my throat as I looked at him, at his up-close-and-personal jawline and smirking lips, and I wondered what exactly that reassurance meant.

"So give me your address, then," I said quietly, my insides buzzing with nerves, worry, excitement, fear, anticipation . . .

"Attagirl." Damion winked as he tugged on one of my curls and said, "I can't wait to spend a few hours alone in my house . . . *studying*."

Dear Lord. Help me.

CHAPTER FORTY-THREE

"There's nothing quite like being led through the streets of New York by the girl of your dreams. Grab on to those fingers, and just let her show you the way."

—Remington

Damion

"You are impossible, Nebraska."

"But I was right," she said with a giggle, dropping her pencil onto the table. "So tell me how to say it."

I rolled my eyes because she was ridiculous.

Ridiculous in *my* kitchen, praise Jesus.

"Avevo ragione," I said, leaning closer, my arm resting on the back of her chair while I made sure my lips touched the shell of her ear, because I fucking loved the way that always made her shiver.

"Avevo ragione," she repeated with a huge grin, and I felt like I'd won something when I felt the shiver. "I. Was. Right."

"You're really becoming an obnoxious student."

"I learned from the very best tutor," she teased, and then she dropped a smart-ass kiss on my cheek. "Am I done now?"

"One more problem," I said, pointing my finger at the math worksheet.

"Fine," she said with a pout, then started in on the equation.

I watched her, the way her arched eyebrows scrunched together and her teeth clamped down on her bottom lip while she made her calculations, and I wondered if I had time to sneak her up to my room before my parents got home.

I knew I didn't, and I also knew she wouldn't blow off the math.

My dedicated pupil.

I took a long drink of water and wondered how it'd only been two weeks.

Two weeks of this. Two blissful fucking weeks.

Meeting at her locker every morning so I could get my Julia fix before the day began. Lunches in the courtyard, away from everyone else. Long strolls in the park, walking her cat while the trees shed their leaves, while her gloved hand warmed mine and she attempted to recognize birdcalls.

Texting and FaceTiming, kissing in bodegas, showering her with the Zabar's chocolate babka she was a hundred percent obsessed with; I was obsessed with all of it.

I was obsessed with her.

Because being with her was different from being with anyone else. She gave me all of her, every little bit, with zero expectations.

She didn't care what I was going to do with my life, she didn't care what my last name was, and she didn't give a *shit* about what my reputation was at the academy.

She wanted nothing from me, and it was perfection.

Julia just smiled and I was happy, happier than I'd maybe been in my entire fucking life.

That sounded asinine, pathetically lovesick, but it was the honest-to-God truth.

Honestly, *life* would be perfect if it weren't for the tiny fact that I was avoiding her house.

Avoiding my lies.

It somehow hadn't occurred to me until the first day we were "official" that I was screwed.

So, so screwed.

How would I ever explain to her that my uncle was her benefactor and that I'd been in her house *hundreds* of times—but never mentioned it?

She'd never understand, and with each passing day I didn't say anything, it got worse.

Suddenly the house I'd always loved was the one place I was avoiding.

"Oh no—look at the time," Julia said, jumping out of her chair and grabbing her coat. "I have to go before they get home."

I glanced at my watch and she was right. My parents would be home soon.

She had to go.

I helped her shove her books into her backpack and we were out of there, and the second we stepped outside, I felt better.

Because this was my favorite part of the day.

Walking her home in the dark, listening to her ramble about anything and everything while we traversed the blocks between our houses; I loved it.

"I can't believe the ball is this weekend," she said, lowering her chin more deeply into her scarf as the breeze blew in our faces.

God, I love what the wind does to her curls and her cheeks.

"I can't wait to see you in your dress," I said, chomping at the bit for that.

I still didn't want to do the damn thing, but knowing she'd found some long red gown when she was back home, a gown that left her shoulders bare, had me in a frenzy.

It was obscene how into her I was.

"I'm so nervous, though," she said, and I hated the look that crossed her face, the way that tiny crinkle of concern settled between her eyebrows whenever she worried about being judged.

It made me want to fight every single person who'd ever been an ass to her.

My past self included.

"Don't be nervous," I said, pulling her closer as we walked into Amsterdam Marketplace, where we had to stop and get her a side of fries every day on the way home. It was out of the way, but they were her favorite, so we made it a priority, mostly because neither of us minded extending our time together with a longer walk. "You'll be with me, Nebraska, and I'll take care of you."

She grinned up at me as we approached the counter. "Remember that time you told me you weren't a nice guy?"

"Yeah?" I said, grabbing a bag of cassava chips.

"Well, you lied," she said, grabbing a pack of bubble gum.

"No, I was telling the absolute truth," I said, pulling out my phone to pay for the snacks. "I'm still not a nice guy, but being nice *to you* is my new favorite hobby."

CHAPTER FORTY-FOUR

"I fucking love to dance."

—Remington

Julia

"Are you quite all right, Miss Julia?"

I glanced over at Bernard. "Huh?"

"You appear distracted," he said, gesturing to the way I was sitting on the couch, gnawing on a pen cap and staring into space.

I was definitely distracted, obsessively distracted by the upcoming ball. I couldn't stop dreading it. I'd started *dreaming* about it, for God's sake, nightmares that wouldn't go away; that was how stressed I was.

Because I couldn't help but feel like this was everyone's chance to mock me while I was *in* the spotlight. If they'd enjoyed messing with me during mundane weekday classes before Damion and I became inseparable, imagine how much *more* they'd enjoy it while at an elegant ball, all dressed up in formalwear?

And the idea of something happening in front of Damion was too much to bear. I was so into him—too into him, really—that the idea of him seeing me ridiculed, even though he'd seen it before, was beyond embarrassing.

I didn't think my heart could take it.

I was still getting the chilly reception from the Skins at school, the mocking laughter every time I walked by, but he was never around to see it, thank God.

"I'm just thinking about the ball," I said, "and how it has the potential to be quite the spectacle."

"In a wonderful way," he said assuredly.

"In a wonderfully awful way," I corrected, shaking my head. "I mean, I don't even know how to dance, not formally, so I'm probably going to look like a fool when the spotlight is on me and Damion."

He looked at me for a long minute, then pulled the phone out of the breast pocket of his suit jacket. A minute later, after a few clicks, he set it down on the coffee table, and classical music began playing from its speaker.

"May I have this dance, Miss Julia?" he asked.

I wanted to say no, but as he gave me that knowing look, it occurred to me that I needed him.

Desperately.

"Of course," I said, climbing to my feet. "Please help me, Bernie."

"At your service," he said with a warm smile, lifting his arms and straightening his posture, gesturing me to step forward. Then he calmly ran through the basics of a waltz, showing me the steps. *Box step, step-step turn, change of places.* Once it started to become less . . . *foreign* to me, Bernard stopped talking through it and just danced with me.

"So how are you adjusting to life here?" he asked, leading me around our huge living room. "You seem more . . . *content* since returning from Nebraska."

More *content*.

Yeah, that was definitely one way to put it, I thought as I followed his steps. *Box step, step-step turn, change of places.*

The truth was that I was head over heels for Damion, content because we'd been spending so much time together.

Blissfully, magically content, but also terrified.

Because it felt too perfect in its wild imperfection.

He was cocky and sarcastic like no one I'd ever known, yet he randomly texted me poems—at all hours of the day—that he thought I would like.

He was waiting at my locker *every day* after school so he could walk me home.

He trash-talked at the courts like he'd been hired to roast his friends, yet he brought Clank catnip every time we went to the park so she wouldn't freak out when we stopped to bird-watch.

I mean, he looked like *that* and he freaking *bird-watched*, for God's sake.

He was a walking contradiction that I had fallen *so hard* for.

"Yeah," I said, nodding. I wasn't sure what to say about that to Bernard. I knew he knew everything that went on in Gardenwood, but I wasn't sure I could talk to him about Damion.

It felt like I liked him more than I'd ever liked Will, which was terrifying. I was so "in like" with him it was mind-blowing.

"Things are good with the young Mr. Rutledge?" he asked, *of course* reading my mind.

"They are," I said, failing to hold in the smile.

Box step, step-step turn, change of places.

"Excellent," he replied, his grin warm and fatherly.

"Do you like him?" I asked. "I mean, do you approve, Bernie?"

"Your opinion of him is the only one that matters," he said stoically, ever the diplomat. "But I strongly suspect there are many layers under Damion's rebellious exterior."

"You *do*?" I was in shock. "How well do you know him?"

"Everyone knows everyone in these circles," he said enigmatically. "And I just think he seems like someone who might be more complicated than he appears."

Yeah, that was probably true.

Sometimes I worried about his "rebel" reputation. Like, was there more to it than I knew? What things *had* he done to make all of Gardenwood think of him that way?

Because he wasn't that way when he was with me.

But he *did* have his complicated layers.

The other day when we were studying, Damion's dad was text-yelling at him about something to do with Dartmouth, and he shocked the hell out of me with the confession that he didn't actually want to go to an Ivy League school at all.

And he had no interest in studying business. He hadn't wanted to talk about it and immediately changed the subject, but I'd been surprised by the resolution in his voice. From the look on his face, I wondered exactly how much pressure his father put on him about his future.

I wasn't a fan of my own cluelessness regarding college, but I'd definitely hate a forced plan even more.

Which was why I'd been *forced* to distract him in a delightful way.

"How do you read people so well?" I asked Bernard, and I also wondered how my family was lucky enough to know him at all. He'd become a part of our family somehow, and we were all better because of it.

"A lifetime of experience," he said. "Now tell me, young lady, have you ever heard of the cosmic dip?"

"The *what*?"

"Watch and learn, Miss Julia."

CHAPTER FORTY-FIVE

"Is there anything as painful as
waiting for the love of your life?"

—Remington

Damion

"You have to respect the location," Beckett said, pointing at the stone walls and high ceilings. "Gothic glamour on Halloween night? Your mom fucking killed it with this."

I looked around and yeah, he wasn't wrong.

The ball was at the Cloisters, the medieval museum that was part of the Met, and the setting was money. Candlelight, sconces, Gothic artwork, stone floors, dark corners—it *worked*.

Hosting the ball was a coup and the only reason my mother had volunteered on the committee for half my life, and the fact that she'd been able to book space *there* gave her ball GOAT status.

She was winning at everything, it seemed, although she was still pissed at me for wearing an all-white modern suit (instead of a ridiculous costume) and for taking "that" girl.

But my parents had been surprisingly nice since the minute we got into the waiting car.

My mom was in her long black gown, my dad in his black tux, and they seemed almost *smug* when we left the house, like they were A-OK with the situation. Which probably should've worried me, but I was too excited to care.

Not excited about the ball, but about having this night with Julia. I was excited to see her in her gown, to dance with her, to have permission to keep her out until all hours of the morning.

I just hated that I had to wait to see her. It was a Gardenwood tradition that couples didn't show up to the ball together. The guys waited in the huge ballroom, and the girls were presented at the top of the stairs. It allowed for big drama (and wasted a lot of time in my opinion), but if I started picking apart all the details of the season now, I'd never stop.

"I like this buzz," Beckett said, gesturing to the crowded ballroom. "If I have to stand in the middle of a massive man sandwich, it's fun that we're all standing around, waiting for the women to light up our world."

"I cannot believe you just referred to this as a 'massive man sandwich,'" I said with a laugh. "And I cannot believe that you like this."

"Anticipation is an underrated drug," he said with a grin.

"Yeah, that it is," I agreed, my eyes going to the top of those stairs, desperate for a glimpse of her.

"I think this is the first time I've seen you without Julia in weeks," Beckett said out of the side of his mouth. "You doin' okay, kid?"

"Not really," I joked. "I haven't seen her all day."

She'd spent the day getting ready with Donovan and Jasmine.

"Well, it won't be long now," he said.

I was ready with a smart-ass jab, but when I looked at him, Beck was giving me a genuine smile as he said, "You seem different now."

"Different how?" I scoffed.

Beckett's eyebrow rose as he shrugged. "I don't know, dare I say . . . happy?"

"Happy" didn't do what I was feeling justice. No.

Was it bliss? Contentment? Fucking pure and indescribable joy?

Yeah, maybe all those things, God help me.

"Don't jinx it," I responded as Beckett jumped when three men with trumpets started playing the fanfare.

"Dear Jesus," he said with a laugh as the horns signaled that the announcements were to begin. "Scared the shit out of me. Is that really necessary?"

The announcements were basically just an excuse to have all eyes on the girl in the gown. To give every girl an opportunity to shock and awe with her appearance. And our jobs, as the dates, were to meet them halfway up the staircase, lend our arm, and walk them down to the bottom, where the ball awaited. As the "host couple," Julia and I would be announced last. Julia would probably hate it, all that attention on her, but I kind of thought she deserved the spotlight.

The announcements began, and for some reason, I was stupid nervous. I just wanted everything to be perfect for her, but I knew she was worried about the Skins or the Toms doing something to ruin the night for her.

And I wasn't about to let that happen.

I watched as they announced one couple after another, impatient for the sight of her. I watched as all the girls I knew descended the stairs in immaculate costumes, pale pink and white dresses with matching hats and parasols. Corsets and high heels. Diamonds fucking everywhere, twinkling in the shadowy medieval lighting.

Everyone was well-dressed and glamorous, and I was dying to see mine.

So when they finally said her name, my heart was pounding in my chest.

"Miss Julia Lowell, daughter of Clint and Shawna Lowell, partner of Mr. Damion Rutledge."

Julia stepped forward, and I literally felt my heart pinch in my chest.

Dear God, she is so beautiful.

I heard a collective gasp go up around me.

I mean, no one would be so gauche as to *actually* gasp, but there was an undercurrent of surprise, of awe, as everyone looked up at the most stunning girl in the room.

She was Cinderella, if Cinderella had fire in her veins and was fucking hot.

Instead of a period piece, Julia was wearing a long gown. It was made of red silk and tulle, with a corset top that had two straps of silk bows, bows with long, dangling ribbons just begging to be pulled. The skirt was frothy and lush, looking like hundreds of handmade roses were folded into the transparent fabric, making the entire thing a hazy tease.

Fucking Springfield, Nebraska, I bow to your fashion, holy shit.

Her hair was down, all pulled over to one side and falling in the softest curls, like a waterfall of waves. It looked brighter against the shocking color of her gown, almost like an accessory.

The dress and her hair were an homage to the trees outside, I swear to God, the brightest hues of autumn's palette.

Diamonds twinkled in her ears, and a thin diamond necklace sat at the base of her throat.

But her smile as she looked down at me was what made me feel like dropping to my knees and saying a prayer of thanks. I didn't wait for the cue but started walking up the stairs, needing to get to her.

Unable to wait another second.

I heard Beckett laugh as I ran up the stairs too fast, as I reached her side before she'd even come down three steps.

"Slow down, Mr. Rutledge," the announcer said with a smile in his voice. "The lady is worth the wait."

"I've never loved Edith Wharton more than I do right now," I said as I grabbed Julia's hand.

"Why?" she asked, and I could feel her hands trembling. I didn't want her to be nervous. I wanted her to feel as alive as I felt, looking down at her perfect face.

"Because somehow her life led to this moment at this ball, with you as my date, wearing this dress that I want to bow down and worship. I can't think of an adjective strong enough to describe how you look right now, Lowell."

"Oh my God," she said, her smile growing wide, her eyes crinkling at the corners. "I've stumped the smartest tutor at Gardenwood."

I think I love her already.

It was impossible, too soon, and what the hell did I know about love anyway?

But I was enamored with everything about her.

The poetry of my Julia.

I am wind, and you are chimes.

The way she thought, the way she grinned, the way she moved.

"'The two of us combined could set it on fire,'" I said to myself, delivering the line under my breath.

"What?" she asked, those perfectly lined amber eyes meeting mine.

"Nothing," I said, swallowing down the unexpected swell of emotion. "Shall we do this ball thing, Miss Lowell?"

"Yep." She nodded, but then stopped herself and lifted her chin with a regal air. "I mean, yes, please, Mr. Rutledge."

CHAPTER FORTY-SIX

"The brightness of the city lights can make you completely forget that it's dark at all."

—Remington

Julia

I was shaking as we walked into the ballroom, but there was something about Damion's hand holding mine that made everything less scary.

It was a little jarring, realizing how wrong I'd been about him.

It was a little unfair.

I'd judged him by the way his parents behaved, by how much money he had, by how he looked, and I had a lot of guilt for that because, clearly, underneath it all, he was an amazing guy.

Worthy of the trust that I had taken so long to give him.

"By the way, you look surprisingly nice in all white."

"Did you doubt me?" He looked at me out of the corner of his eye and made a face. "I look hot, right?"

"A little bit, yeah," I admitted with a laugh. "Actually, kind of a lot."

"You stop that right now, Julia Nebraska," he said, his fingers tightening around mine, his voice low. "Flirting with me in front of all these people is a terrible idea."

"Why is that?" I couldn't stop myself from teasing a little more because, God help me, I loved his tone when he acted like I made him weak. "You can't handle it, Rutledge?"

"No, it's just a terrible idea because I don't give a damn what they think," he explained, looking like the rebel he was. "I'm on my best behavior right now, for you, but I have zero qualms about kissing the shit out of you right here in front of God and everybody."

"Oh," I managed, feeling a little lightheaded, wishing we were alone.

"So if you want that, keep it up," he said, his eyes holding mine like he was waiting for my next move.

And I'd clearly lost the ability to make good choices, in my rebellious era, because I leaned a little closer and said, "You talk a big game for someone in a white tux—"

His mouth cut off my words.

In an instant, his big hands were on my face, holding my cheeks, angling so our lips were perfectly aligned. He kissed me with everything, deep and thorough, but it was a tiny bite, like a nipping sample of the real big thing, and I was disappointed that he pulled back so quickly.

"I need more," he said, his mouth a breath from mine, "but I don't want to mess up your pretty lipstick."

I could barely speak as he looked at me like *that*, like he wanted to push me into a closet and show me everything he knew but was too thoughtful to be selfish.

"I appreciate that," I whispered, wondering how I was so lucky, wondering how it was that Damion Rutledge was looking at *me* that way. "Perhaps later?"

"Oh, there's no perhaps about it," he said, and then, as if it hadn't happened, his fingers were back between mine and we were walking again. "So did Bernard or your mom tell you how this first-dance thing goes down?"

"They told me we have to do a first dance," I said. "That's really all they said."

"Well, apparently my parents are going to welcome everyone to the ball and say a bunch of things to the donors about the school. After that, the band leader will call for the host couple to dance, which is us."

"Have I mentioned this is insane?" I said, feeling faint at the idea of dancing in front of everyone.

"You have and I agree, but seeing you in that dress and knowing I'm allowed to put my hands all over you makes me somehow appreciate it."

I took a deep breath and nodded.

At least we were doing it together.

No big deal, right?

My eyes traveled over the room, seeing the Toms, who were all wearing top hats and ridiculous shirts; the Skins, who looked like they belonged *in* the movie the ball was inspired by; and all the parents, who were dressed in elegant black formalwear.

And I felt like I wanted to pass out when the man said, "Let's welcome our host couple for the first dance of the night."

Everyone applauded as the lights dimmed, and Damion snatched the glass from my hand and put it on the table beside his. "Are you ready, Cinderella?"

His words, and the expression on his face, warmed my goose-bumped arms. "I am."

"Then let's do this. Let's give Edith and Mr. Berry the dance they never got to have."

We walked onto the dance floor, where a literal spotlight awaited us. When we reached its center he leaned close, lowering his head and saying into my ear, "Just keep your eyes on me. You won't be nervous if you're only looking at me, right?"

"Right," I lied, nodding like I was capable of non-nervousness at that moment.

He straightened to his full height and lifted his arms, and I stepped into them, positioning myself the way Bernard had taught me. The music started, and the combination of Damion's one hand on my body and the other one in my hand felt like it was more than him dancing with me; it was holding me up.

It was partnering.

It was all the support I needed.

Box step, step-step turn, change of places.

"Attagirl," he said quietly, smiling down at me like he was proud. "You're killing this."

"Bernard taught me," I admitted.

"Well, you're a natural," he said. "Although, it could just be your incredible partner."

"Yeah, how did *you* learn?" I asked. "Did you take manners and dancing classes when you were little?"

"No," he said. "But I had an uncle who thought it was important to learn to waltz. He grew up in another time, I guess."

"Well, you're pretty okay at it," I said, wanting to memorize the way his face looked at that moment, relaxed and teasing and so ridiculously handsome it was almost hard on my eyes.

"He also taught me the cosmic dip, but that's a little advanced for you," he said.

"Oh my God, are you serious?" I said with a laugh, unable to believe the words he'd just said. "Bernard literally taught me the same thing and he *called* it the cosmic dip. Was that a thing?"

Damion got the tiniest wrinkle between his brows, and his smile slipped for a second as his eyes moved all over my face.

"Hello?" I said. "Cosmic dipper . . . ?"

"Do you want to do it?" he asked, cutting me off, his eyes getting that devilish twinkle as he waited for my answer.

"You want to cosmic dip me in front of everybody? What if you drop me?"

"Oh, I won't drop you," he said, every word dripping with overconfidence. "The biggest risk is that you'll fall so madly in love with me you'll never see another man the same way again."

"Wow," I said, grinning up at him. "I am not risk-averse, it seems, because I think we should try it."

"Wait," he said, his jaw flexing before he swallowed hard. "You're willing to risk it? The idea of falling in love with me doesn't send you running?"

I knew I shouldn't admit to it or fall into these feelings again, but I meant it with my whole chest when I said, "Not even a little bit."

His smile grew as he looked down at me, the power of his full-scale grin warming every goose bump on my skin as we both realized what I meant.

"Here we go, then, Jules," and then he dipped me so far back that I could feel the tips of my hair brush the ballroom floor. All I could see was his face, leaning down over me as he said, "Let's fall together."

CHAPTER FORTY-SEVEN

"Sleeping in the bed you made can feel pretty disgusting."

—Remington

Damion

"Look at that jackass," I said as we watched Liam standing in the center of a circle of six girls. He was just one of those guys who everyone liked, who people gravitated toward.

Hell, even *I* liked him. Even though I suspected he still didn't like *me*.

"And not one of them is even his date," Julia said, laughing. "I don't know where Lana is."

"She's over there next to Beckett and Donovan," I said.

"I still can't believe *they* came together." Julia was smiling as she looked at them, and I wondered how I hadn't fallen for her the second we met, when she'd been jumping for that ridiculous wallet.

"Listen, I should probably make up some elaborate scheme to get you into a darkened hallway, but the way you look makes it impossible for me to formulate plans."

"Oh really," she said, smiling and blinking fast like she was embarrassed by the compliment.

Which was too damn bad, because I couldn't keep my mouth shut when it came to how she looked that night.

"I do have to say, though, as good as you look tonight," I said, "I still think about the way you looked in Springfield. In your backyard. When you came out the patio door with your wet hair and you were wearing that stupid Big Ten football jersey. I swear to God you were walking perfection."

Her eyebrows went together. "You think I looked better in my old jeans and no makeup?"

I lowered my head and pressed a kiss to the side of her throat because I was drunk on her. "You looked so incredibly *Julia* that it took my breath away."

"Are you kissing my neck in public?" she said, but her breathy voice suggested she wasn't complaining.

"My apologies," I said, breathing in her perfume. "I should stop?"

"Definitely not, but maybe we should find that dark hallway you mentioned," she said, stepping closer to me and grabbing my hand.

"We definitely should," I said, but as we started walking toward the unknown areas of the venue, I heard a commotion.

More specifically, I heard my dad's voice.

My dad's *raised* voice.

I wanted to run away from that tone I knew all too well, but Julia was already turning to look in that direction. "What the hell?"

And not just Julia, but nearly everyone in the venue was craning their necks to see what the disturbance was. One by one, people started inching toward the tense scene. Whispering to each other, eyebrows raised as they held their glasses of champagne.

My gut was twisting as my eyes searched for my dad, who was with my mom and—

Oh no.

Shit. Shit SHIT!

Who was with my mom and Julia's parents. And they were arguing.

Loudly.

Fuck. No.

Julia charged over there and I followed, panicking because there was no way this could be good.

"What does this even mean?" Julia's dad said to my father. He was holding a packet of documents that looked legal, and he shoved it in my dad's face. "You can't seriously be suing us."

Fuck fuck fuck.

"We can, and we are," my mother said, lifting her chin. "You might want to lower your voice, *Clint*, before everyone here knows what you really are."

Too late for that, Mom, thanks to you and your loud voice.

I was going to be sick.

"Again, what the hell does that even mean?" Julia's dad said, louder this time.

"It means that we know what you did. You met a rich old man with dementia—my uncle—and you bilked him out of everything and moved into his house. But what you didn't count on was the fact that we weren't going to let you get away with it."

"Wait—Remington was your uncle?" Julia's mom said, her face draped in shock.

I swear to God I heard a roaring in my ears as I looked at Julia and watched a million thoughts going through her head. She stood there in silence as my parents laid out all their facts, as *her* parents refuted them.

"What?" Julia's voice trembled as she spoke.

God help me.

She walked closer to my parents. "You are related to Remi. To Lou?" she asked them.

It was like her brain couldn't handle the information slapping her in the face. I could see her slowly putting the pieces together, my gut clenching as she lined everything up.

And then she looked at me. With those eyes. Those amber eyes.

"Damion, did you know?"

I'd been punched before, but this was worse. I didn't want to lie to her, but I also didn't want to lose her. I stood there, frozen, incapable of formulating any words or thoughts to defuse or contribute to this situation. "Did I know what?"

You're a coward, Damion.

"You did," she said, her eyes moving all over my face. "So you knew the whole time who I was, that my family—"

"What is going on here?" Chantel Chattingham said, stepping into the middle of the group like she belonged there. She had her responsible adult face on, but her eyes were glowing like she was excited to jump into the center of this scandal. "This is taking away from the children at the ball, so let's get it together. What happened?"

My mother used every ounce of dramatic training she'd had as a girl when she said, "As it turns out, the Lowells are not what they seem."

I grabbed Julia's elbow, wanting to pull her away from all this, because I knew in that moment that she was about to be pulled away from me.

Forever.

Don't leave me.

"So you're Lou's nephew," Julia said quietly, her eyebrows furrowed.

"Great-nephew," I admitted softly, reaching for her. But she was backing away. Away from *me*.

Please don't let me lose her.

"And you knew the whole time," she said, blinking fast. "Like since the day we met."

"Yes," I said, my entire body frozen with panic as she looked at me like she didn't know me. Like she didn't *like* me.

The suspicion was back in her gaze and she was watching me the way she used to, like she didn't trust a word I said.

Still, I said, "But I didn't—"

"Oh my God, when we went out to Lou's cabin and I was telling you all about him and crying, you didn't think to mention you knew the guy I was crying over?"

God, why hadn't I? "I was going to, but then—"

"The tutoring?" Her eyes grew large, worry filling them with fear.

I shook my head. "The tutoring? What do you—"

"Was that part of your plan? You parents' plan?" she asked, her pitch rising. "To get you in our house?"

"No," I said. *Don't lump me in with them.* "It wasn't like that. You need to let me explain."

"I don't need to do anything," she said, biting her lower lip like she was trying to hold back emotion. "When did y—"

And then she gasped when those amber eyes, starting to glaze with tears, landed on the folder in her father's hands. I followed her gaze to see that stapled onto a document was the photograph I'd stolen from the store.

Along with the photo of the information I'd found on their legal pad my first day tutoring her.

Fuck, fuck, fuck.

"Oh my God, you gave that to your parents?" she said, looking at me with wide eyes, like I was a stranger. "You stole that picture and gave it to your parents? Why, Damion?"

"He found a photo that shows *your* family taking advantage of ours," my dad said, looking *proud* of himself.

"It's a photo of him *smiling* with us," her mom snapped. "What are you even talking about?"

"No, I swear to God I didn't!" I said, panicking as I realized just how shitty this looked.

"You used her, you *dick*," Liam said. "You were planning to from the very start."

My breath got stuck in my chest when I saw Julia blinking back tears.

"That's a picture of information from our house. A house that you had access to because you were Julia's tutor," Liam continued as my eyes begged him to stop. "And then you fucking flew to Nebraska and took advantage of the fact that she liked you in order to steal from us."

I had no idea how my dad got that photo—he must've taken it out of my room—or the picture I'd taken in the kitchen—holy shit, he'd gone through my phone.

Of course he had.

I looked at my dad's victorious smirk and I wanted to hit him. I wanted to hit him and I wanted to rage, because what kind of a father fucking did that?

"No, it wasn't like that—I didn't give it to them!"

"You were the only person who could've grabbed that picture," Julia said, her cheeks pink, her eyes glassy.

"I was going to give it back," I said, and as I desperately looked for any rescue, my eyes settled on Bernard's face.

"Tell her, Bernard," I said. "You know me! Tell her that I wouldn't—"

"Oh my God, you too?" Julia said, and it broke my heart how hurt she looked as she stared into the face of the most honest man I'd ever met. "Bernie, you knew?"

Bernard looked down at the floor.

"Oh honey," Chantel said, smiling and looking around at the rather large crowd that had surrounded the public argument. "There are no secrets in Gardenwood; you should know that by now."

"Julia, listen to me," I said.

But those eyes were full of tears, and she just shook her head before turning and running off, the crowd parting as she sprinted out of the ballroom.

No!

"Wait! Jules!" I moved to go after her, but Liam grabbed my arm and jerked me back.

"Let go, I have to stop her!" I said, seconds from hitting him.

He looked murderous as he scowled and said, "You don't get to stop her, you—"

"The fuck I don't," I said, ripping my arm free and taking off in the direction she'd run.

I needed to get to her, to find her and make her understand. Everything around me—the stone walls, the candles, the medieval artwork—felt dark and foreboding as I ran as fast as I could.

Through the cavernous hallways, down the echoing stairs.

Away from the crowd and into the darkness.

And then . . . then I saw red.

A dark hallway to the right, a blip of red in the corner.

Oh, oh God.

She was facing the wall, her arms wrapped around her body, her forehead resting against the cold stone. My heart felt like it was being ripped out of my chest when I heard her hiccup out a sob—*she's crying, she should never be crying*—but it got worse when I heard what she was chanting under her breath.

"It *is* the *east*, and *Ju*liet *is* the *sun*. It *is* the *east*, and *Ju*liet *is* the *sun*. It *is* the *east*, and *Ju*liet *is* the *sun*," she whispered.

Her poem of self-preservation.

"Julia." I said it quietly, afraid of scaring her off.

Terrified of her running off and disappearing forever.

She lifted her head and turned toward me, and her tear-streaked face broke my heart.

"Please," I said, slowly walking closer. "Please let me explain."

"No," she said, shaking her head.

"Please," I begged, trying to swallow around the lump in my throat. "I know we can work this out if you'll—"

"Seriously?" Her eyes narrowed as she looked at me like I was out of my mind.

I was panicked, desperate to get her to stop looking at me like *that*. I took a couple of steps, needing to be closer, and said, "The past few weeks, since Nebraska, it has been . . . like, fucking perfection, right? I don't know how, but it's been—"

"A lie, Damion," she said, shaking her head.

She blinked fast, amber eyes full of thoughts that I couldn't decipher, thoughts I *needed* to tap into.

I swallowed down the fear as she continued watching me like I was a stranger. "I know this looks so bad, Jules, but you have to know how I feel."

She shook her head, lips pressing together. I could fix this, right? Make her understand.

I had to.

"My parents were wrong about your family, but I figured that out a long time ago. The only reason I haven't told you everything is because I didn't know how, but you have to believe me that everything between us is one hundred percent real."

"It's not." She said it matter-of-factly, shaking her head.

"No, but it is," I argued, stepping closer.

She took a step back, then two, like she needed distance. "Stop it."

"I can't because I can't let you go, Julia," I confessed, my chest burning as I looked into her eyes. "I know I sound nuts, but it's the truth. I don't want to be without you."

Her eyes narrowed. "Damion—"

"God, that was ineloquent, right?" I said with a laugh, even though nothing was funny. I felt *this* close to tears because *please God, help me*, I couldn't get her to stop looking at me like *that*.

Like she felt nothing. And the idea of my Julia being numb, of not feeling, was devastating. Because I felt every fucking thing when I was with her.

"But I'm so damn *deeply* into all of you," I confessed, my heart pounding in my chest. "Like, head-over-heels *entranced* by the person you are."

Her eyebrows scrunched together and she bit down on her lower lip, which fueled me. Made me believe she *was* feeling something.

I stepped closer, gently setting my hands on her shoulders, and she didn't move away from me, *praise Jesus*.

"I love that you can drive a stick shift through a goddamn cornfield, and I love that you came gunning for me when you thought I'd stolen your wallet," I said in a rush, my brain giving me a montage of so many Julia moments.

"I'm obsessed with how funny you are and the way you tried to find accessible poetry for your boomer bodega friend. You leash-trained your cat and you eat french fries every day. You are the most interesting person I know, the breath of fresh air that I *need* to breathe when all my life I've felt suffocated. I might've fucked up by being too much of a coward to tell you about Uncle Remi, but you can't give up on us because I was an idiot."

She made a noise in her throat that I couldn't translate, and she crossed her arms protectively over her chest. Those eyes stayed trained on me as she stood there, but she said nothing.

I needed her to say something.

She stared up at me, her expression unreadable.

Tell me what you're thinking, Julia.

"Say something," I begged. "Tell me—"

"It is unbelievable that you think I care how you feel about me right now," she said, narrowing her eyes as she brushed my hands away from her shoulders. "That 'us' matters at all. God, Damion, your parents are suing my parents, accusing them of fraud and theft, and you think I give a damn about your feelings?"

Shit.

Shit, shit, shit.

"They don't have anything, though," I said, wanting to reassure her, needing to reassure her so we could move on to getting everything back on track with us. I'd just confessed, to her *and* to myself, that I was fucking in love with her. "There isn't any proof. The suit won't stick."

"Oh, well, if you say so," she said bitterly, rolling her eyes. "My parents were just served legal documents in the middle of a ball, in front of everyone, but as long as *you* think—"

"Jules—"

"You know that you're no different from the rest of them, right?" she said in disgust. Her voice was raspy when she glared up at me and said, "You like to think you're this rebel who does whatever he wants, but Damion, you're just better at pretending."

Ouch. I swallowed and wanted to throw up as she glared like I was the world's biggest disappointment.

"Underneath it all, you are nothing but a Skin. A Tom," she said, giving her head a shake. I felt gut-punched by the hate in her eyes, but that was nothing compared to the pain when she ripped my heart out.

She looked me in the eye and said, "I bet your father is so proud."

CHAPTER FORTY-EIGHT

"Don't let the October rain trick you with its softness. It's got bone-chilling teeth."

—Remington

Damion

I walked in the front door—*stumbled*, actually—and couldn't believe my eyes.

Somehow, I'd imagined my parents not being there, but they were both at the dining room table, waiting for me.

At two a.m.

I'd been walking around the city for hours, feeling numb. Broken. And, *oh yeah*, like the biggest asshole on the planet. Her betrayed face and tearful voice were all I could think about, all I could see.

It was on repeat in my head: my punishment.

Did I really lose her already?

But whatever numbness I'd been feeling was instantly replaced with an all-consuming rage at the sound of my dad's voice.

"Damion," my dad said, not looking up from whatever he was doing on his phone as he chewed on a bagel. "If you're going to be out until all hours of the night, you need to let us know. Your mother was worried."

My mother smiled at me and didn't look worried at all.

In fact, she and my father didn't look like they cared that they'd blown up the motherfucking *Age of Innocence* ball. That they'd completely humiliated a nice family.

I dropped my tuxedo jacket on the chair beside me, dumbfounded.

Fucking stupefied by the fact that this was real life.

And as I looked at his blasé face, I *wanted* to argue.

I needed to fight.

"What the fuck *was* that?" I asked.

I didn't speak to my parents like that. I didn't shout.

Especially at my dad.

Both of my parents looked up at me in shock.

My dad gave me a measuring look, eyebrows raised over his glasses and chin down, like he was assessing the situation. "You're going to have to be more specific."

"Okay, well, *specifically*," I ground out through my teeth, "why did you do what you did? Why would you serve the Lowells in the middle of the ball, in front of everyone?"

My dad crossed his arms, and I couldn't tell if he was surprised I was questioning him, or pissed off that I dared.

He just stared me down.

And then he said, "You know why."

"Do I?" I asked, hungry for this fight. "Actually, please enlighten me, because I don't have any idea why you would do that to someone."

"Don't be a child, Damion," he said, his furrowed brow and dismissive tone letting me know I'd disappointed him yet again by not understanding his ways. "There are always strategies when it comes to business."

"But this wasn't business!" I said, so frustrated that I wanted to kick things over. "The Lowells have nothing to *do* with Rutledge business!"

"Riverside Manor is our business," he calmly stated. "They put themselves in our business when they stole our house."

My house, I wanted to correct, because I knew Remi hadn't wanted my parents to have it.

"By serving the papers publicly," he said, "we've taken the upper hand. Everyone now knows that the Lowells are not to be trusted, and the

Lowells now know that the Rutledges are not playing around."

I felt sick as I looked at him, as his air of superiority wafted around him like a scent.

"But you don't have proof of *anything*," I argued, wondering how in the hell to get through to him. "Trust me, I tried to find some, but it doesn't exist because they didn't steal anything."

"Perception is reality," he replied with a cool shrug. "And trust *me*, if these small-town nobodies start worrying they're going to lose everything, then they'll be more than willing to make a deal that leaves us with the house."

I pictured the Lowell family—Liam, Julia, and her parents—and it just felt *wrong* that he was still categorizing them as "small-town nobodies" when we knew them now.

And they *weren't* that.

But it was clear that he wasn't going to back down.

He was going to do whatever it took to win, regardless of anything else.

"You seriously still want to evict them, even if they inherited it fair and square?"

"*You* wanted to evict them not so long ago, Dame," he said with a half laugh, sounding like I was a ridiculous little boy. "Is this about the girl, is that what this is? And now you want to give away a fortune?"

"It's not mine to give away!" I said in disgust, picturing her tear-streaked face.

You're a Tom.

I couldn't stop hearing her say it, the accusation in her tone, the disgust in her eyes.

I said, "This belonged to Remi, and he wanted them to have it. It's not about a girl, it's about right and wrong—"

"Protecting our family isn't wrong," he interjected.

"Protecting from *what*?" I yelled, my voice echoing off the walls. "We're not protecting shit—we're trying to steal something from people who did nothing to deserve this!"

"Damion!" my mom said, her mouth dropping open in shock. "Will you please calm down? Everything is going to be fine."

"How can it be fine?"

I looked at my dad and wanted to rage.

I wanted to cry, actually, because I felt so helpless. I cleared my tight throat and said, "And how could you steal from *me*?"

"I'm sorry—what?" he said, *his* voice loud now. He looked at me like I was out of my mind. "What are you talking about?"

"The photo of Uncle Remi with the Lowells that was in my room . . . ? You *took* it and used it without even telling me. The picture from my phone too. Those were *mine*, but—"

"I'm trying to get *your* house back, Damion," he said, cutting me off. "I know Remi didn't particularly like me and he damn sure didn't want *me* to have Riverside Manor, but I'm trying to get it for *you*!"

"We both know that's bullshit and you're just trying to get a win," I said, suddenly out of fight. I just shook my head, so fucking done. "Don't pretend it's for me."

"Damion." My mother tilted her head and her eyes narrowed. There was disbelief in her tone when she lowered her voice and asked, "Are you okay?"

I shrugged and coughed out a laugh, unsure how to respond to that question when I was suddenly too fucking emo to speak. My chest hurt and my shoulders were sore and I was struggling to keep it together, so I just said, "I. Am. Fine."

"*Are* you?" My father got out of his chair and crossed the room, not stopping until he was standing right in front of me. He looked into my eyes, his hawklike gaze unreadable, and he said, "Because you don't look fine."

CHAPTER FORTY-NINE

Two weeks later

"Melancholy hits harder in autumn. The gloomy skies, the shedding trees, the awareness of the unavoidable frost—those things insulate the sadness."

—Remington

Julia

I said goodbye to Carl Sr. (who was in a hurry because of a "hot date" with Ida the librarian) before locking up the store. I flicked on the timer for the window display lights and got into the pickup truck.

I pulled away and started driving home, making lists in my mind of the things I needed to order the next day. I'd been *obsessed* with updating everything since I'd returned, obsessed with the distraction of throwing every bit of my energy into the store.

Thankfully, my parents thought it was a "good use of my time" and were all in on allowing me to run wild, so now the market had a Great Pumpkin window display, a newly expanded cheese inventory, and a bakery table dedicated to New York's finest babkas.

I still had no idea what I was going to do with my life after high school, but now that I was allowing myself to consider the market as a possible option, I was focusing on exploring the concept.

Unfortunately, all distractions seemed to wear off whenever I drove the short stretch of road between my house and the store.

Because now, thanks to Damion, the sight of it hurt my heart every day when I saw it through the windshield. No matter how hard I worked to block it out, *that* day always popped into my head.

Every. Single. Time.

Damion's smart-ass grin when he joked that the big blue Victorian house *had* to belong to the mayor. The way I'd been distracted by his cologne when we'd walked past the gray ranch on the corner.

"Stop it," I said to myself, but when I pulled up in front of my house, all I could see was Damion dangling off the trellis because he *didn't like getting interrupted*.

Oh God.

I didn't want to miss him, but I did. Every damn day.

After the scandal at the ball, it was decided that some time at home—my Nebraska home—would be best for me.

I'd been an emotional wreck when we got back to the house that night, collapsing on the staircase. We were on the brink of ruin, maybe losing everything, all because *I* had led them into Damion's trap.

The beautiful rebel in glasses had betrayed me.

I bawled like a baby while my mom held me close, as I stressed about what I might've gotten my family into.

"The lawsuit," I said, my voice gravelly as I struggled to make it work. "Do we know—"

"Forget about the lawsuit," my dad interrupted. "We'll figure it out."

Liam and Bernard had stood behind him, nodding in agreement.

I'm so sorry was all I could keep thinking about. That and Damion.

His face wouldn't stop popping into my head, making my chest feel like it was being squeezed when I heard his deep, patient, oh-so-sweet voice on repeat.

I'm so damn deeply into all of you.

LIAR!

Those thoughts had me chanting Shakespeare and trying to catch my elusive breath.

"It *is* the *east*, and *Ju*liet *is* the *sun*. It *is* the *east*, and *Ju*liet *is* the *sun*. It *is* the *east*, and *Ju*liet *is* the *sun*," I whispered.

"You need to calm down, sweetie," my mom said, her hands gently grabbing my shoulders. "It's okay."

"It's not . . . okay. Nothing is okay."

"Honey," my dad said sympathetically. "I promise. Take a deep breath, everything is going to be fine."

"*Nothing* is going to be fine!" I cried, shaking my head as my hands got tingly and my breath got faster. "Nothing is ever going to be fine here. It isn't. I want to go home."

"Home?" Liam had asked, giving me *that* look, the one that told me he could feel exactly what I was feeling.

"Home," I said, my voice cracking on a sob. I pictured our house in Springfield, so far away, and I cried, "I just want to go home."

After a call with Mr. Green, it was decided that I would take online classes for the time being, which ensured we still met our stipulations. He was reassuring and sympathetic to the fact that I was feeling a lot of pressure, agreeing that my time at Gardenwood had indeed been difficult.

News to my parents, which led to an honest conversation about the bullying, which led to my parents apologizing for not seeing what was going on with me.

And the very next day, holy shit, I got a text from Coco Chattingham.

Just heard that your social experiences as a student at GA have been . . . less than satisfying. If you're ever back and want to talk, let me know and we can grab a coffee. —Coco

It was very formal, likely insincere, but something about it felt oddly satisfying.

Especially because, according to Jasmine and Donovan, Headmaster Green met with multiple students—and their parents—after my departure, and he didn't hold back. Apparently he said that "Gardenwood Academy has zero tolerance for bullying."

That was two weeks ago. Since then, I'd settled into the comfort of Springfield. After Gardenwood, the decency and simplicity of life here felt like a refuge.

I felt safe.

But I also couldn't shake the feeling of being *out of sorts.* Like I didn't quite belong here anymore, but I didn't belong in New York, either.

I was lost.

Where do I fit?

My lostness kept leading to moments like this, to me backing out of my driveway so I could just drive around aimlessly while rehashing the everything of my life. I cranked the stereo, singing along to "The Hudson" because it reminded me so much of the city that I loved and hated, all at once.

I missed the house, the neighborhood, my bench, Clank; I was crazy homesick for those things. Online classes from Nebraska were great, truly, but my heart couldn't forget my Upper West Side, as hard as I tried.

This never-ending search for a kind of "happy place" was the only explanation as to why I pulled up in front of Lou's cabin a few minutes later. I almost felt surprised to find myself there, even though I'd been the one driving.

I shifted the pickup into neutral, letting my eyes drink in the sight of that little cabin. It looked exactly the same as it always had, the home of a kind old man, but now it just left me with this aching emptiness I couldn't escape.

It made me miss Lou and that easy pre-Manhattan life, but it also brought back a million moments with Damion. Sneaking around inside, taking out the boat, tear-filled hazel eyes . . .

No.

NOPE.

No more.

I had been crying too much over that guy. Too many nights thinking of him and his kisses, of broken promises and confessions of how much he cared for me.

NO.

No more tears over him, over his lies.

I sighed and flipped on the truck's heater, my hands cold as I wondered how it'd all gone so wrong. That day had been perfection, that night pure magic, so it was almost impossible to believe that everything fell apart *so badly* after that.

But I knew *exactly* when it'd gone off the rails, right down to the minute.

It was when I'd decided to trust him.

My head had known better, but my heart had refused to listen.

Foolish, silly girl.

CHAPTER FIFTY

"Fighting doesn't solve anything, but sometimes
it feels really fucking good."

—Remington

Damion

For two weeks I'd been losing my mind, thinking only about Julia and the last time I saw her.

Not getting to touch her, talk to her, see the warmth of her grin and the lingering stare of those amber eyes; it was torture.

A torture I deserved, a torture I didn't know how much longer I could take.

"Oh. Hello again, Damion," Julia's mom said as she pulled open the door, as she angled her head and looked up at me like I was a lunatic.

"Hi. Um, is Julia here?" I asked, knowing full well that my visit was futile.

"No," she said patiently, looking concerned. "She's not here right now."

"Do you know when she—"

"Why the *hell* are you here again?" I heard, and then the door behind Mrs. Lowell flew open. Liam stood there, arms crossed, glaring at me. "Stop coming here; she doesn't want to see you."

"I understand," I started, trying to be cool because I knew why he was pissed. He *should* be pissed, I thought as I stood there like an obsessed stalker, but that didn't mean I was able to stop myself. "But—"

"I don't care if you understand or not," he snapped, and his mom just watched me, not interjecting because truly, I *was* the asshole. "She doesn't want to see you, so you need to stop showing up on our porch multiple times a day like a psycho. If she wanted to see you, she'd find you."

I nodded, clenching my jaw to keep calm, because this was all my fault. I deserved his scorn, dammit. "That's totally fair, and I know I don't deserve for her to hear me out. But she hasn't been at school, so if I could just have—"

"If you could *just have*?" he mocked, loudly and with so much disdain it was almost palpable. "You *just have* fucking enough. That's probably why you're such a dick, because you *just have* so much. I always knew you were a rich-boy asshole who'd hurt my sister, but you outdid yourself. Not only did you hurt her, but you used her to try and hurt my *family* while also hurting her. You're just a scumbag—"

"I know," I said, my stomach knotted and my whole fucking face on fire as he read the list of my crimes while his mother watched. "And I'm sorry I—"

"Fuck you and your apology," Liam said, his voice so loud it echoed in the area between the buildings on the block.

"Liam!" Mrs. Lowell said, objecting to his language, though I suspected she had no issues with the truth he was speaking.

"No, get the hell out of here," he said, hatred in his glare. "Do *not* come back or speak to us again unless you want my fist in your mouth."

And just like that, the door slammed in my face.

It slammed and then I heard the sound of the dead bolt locking.

Instinctively, my hand went for the knob, my heart pounding because I wanted to fucking go. I wanted to punch him in the face; I wanted to throw down at this asshole who wouldn't let me talk to his sister.

Oh God, unloading on Liam would feel so fucking good.

But then I heard it.

Not gonna work, kid came from somewhere in the back of my brain, and God help me, it was Remi's voice.

"I'm losing it," I muttered under my breath, to myself, as I stood there on the stoop of Riverside Manor, hearing voices.

But saying that didn't change the fact that I actually had heard him.

"Really, Uncle Rem?" I muttered, shaking my head in disbelief as I started walking toward the steps that led down to the park, mocking my own insanity while also fully believing I was hearing the voice of my dead uncle as I passed the statue of General Franz.

I knew I was never going to get Julia back in my life as what I wanted her to be, but suddenly I felt like I had to make things right with her. Even if she never spoke to me again, I needed to explain myself and apologize because God help me, I *was* better than that.

I was better than the version I'd given her ninety percent of the time I'd known her.

I stopped on the stairs, frozen, because I wasn't really sure what to do next.

So when my phone buzzed with a text from Beckett that just said what are you doing right now? I knew what I needed to do.

I needed to get help.

I needed the help of someone decent.

I needed the help of Beck.

I was nervous as I approached the courts the next day, mostly because I knew this was going to be my only shot.

But the second Liam spotted me, I knew I was toast.

He let go of a shot that banked off the rim, and instead of saying anything to me, he just yelled to Beckett, "Did you tell him I was here?"

"Just hear him out," Beckett said, catching the ball and giving it a dribble. "What'll it hurt?"

"Oh my God, did you lure me here for this?" Liam asked, looking disgusted. "Fuck you, Beck, and your rich douchebag friends, too."

"Come on," Beckett said, unfazed. "He just wants—"

"Five minutes," I said, coming around the fence. I held up my hands and approached, letting him know he had the upper hand.

"Get the fuck away from me," he warned, stepping close, crowding me. Liam was my size, which was a little unusual, so he was *in my face* in a way most guys weren't when he growled, "Now."

"Lowell, I need—"

He responded with a punch. One second he was growling at me, the next his fist was fucking slamming into my eye.

Shit, shit shit. I stumbled backward, raising my hand to cover the spot where it felt like every bone in my face was surely fucking shattered. *"Shit!"*

"Whoa, whoa, whoa!" Beckett yelled, running over to step between us.

But I deserved this. If I was ever going to get Liam to let me talk to her, this had to happen. "Stay out of it, Beck," I said, or *groaned*, actually, because my eye felt like his fist was still there, planted in the jagged space between my eye socket and my cheekbone.

And I had no clue where my glasses had gone.

"What?" Beckett said.

I dropped my hand and straightened up. "I'm good."

"Jesus, your eye," he said under his breath.

"I need you to listen to me, Lowell," I said through teeth I was gritting against the searing pain, every fiber of my being wanting to put both my hands over my eye and drop to the ground.

Liam lifted his fist and tried throwing another one, but I ducked and missed it.

And then I couldn't stop myself from clenching *my* fist and ramming it into his face.

He dodged, lucky bastard, so he didn't get the full force of the shot.

"Fuck!" he yelled as my fist grazed his jaw. "Are you serious right now?"

And then it was on.

"You piece of shit," he said, grabbing the front of my shirt with both hands.

"Takes one to know one," I said as I ducked his right cross; then I pushed his hands off me, seeing red even as I knew I didn't deserve to be angry.

"Fucking Rutledge," he said, and then he bull-rushed me, running at me and tackling me to the pavement.

My shoulder blades hit the ground hard, *shit*, but then I shoved him and rolled, managing to throw an elbow that landed somewhere solid as I struggled to sit up.

"Christ," I said, breathing deep and running my fingers over my eye socket. "Why does everyone like you?"

"Because I'm a nice guy, not an asshole," he said, sitting up and raising a hand to where I'd hit him. It looked like my ring might've cut his cheek.

Good, I thought, even though I knew I shouldn't have gone after him.

He looked over at me through glasses that were bent all to hell, and it was clear the physical part of the fight was over.

I sighed, because I was bruised and bloody and hadn't made a damn bit of progress.

After what felt like an eternity of silence, I knew I had to speak first.

"I didn't mean for any of this to happen." I huffed, running my hand through my hair. "Remi was my uncle, my friend. Shit, he was a father to me."

That made Liam sit up, his gaze shifting to something slightly less hostile.

"I won't lie to you. I didn't like you guys when I found out you moved into Riverside Manor. That you guys—strangers—swooped in and settled into the house where I'd spent every day with him. It pissed me off because I'd shared so many fucking memories with him inside those walls. I can still hear his smart-ass remarks when I'm there, I swear to God."

"He *was* a smart-ass, wasn't he?" Liam said, a small laugh escaping his mouth.

"Yeah, he was. In the best way."

Liam nodded in agreement, his eyes searching my face, reminding me of *her* eyes. "Beck told me Lou—*Remi*—meant a lot to you."

I had to choke down the heaviness in my throat, so I just nodded.

"I'm sorry he died."

The emotions started to pound through me, but I swallowed them down. I couldn't, not now.

"I didn't want this, truly. Hurting you, your family . . . Julia," I said, my voice cracking, *dammit*.

Liam's eyebrow lifted, his expression turning serious. I took a deep breath. "I'm sorry, Liam. Really."

Liam just stared at me, silent, before shaking his head and standing up. I watched him walk away, feeling like an absolute failure until . . .

"I'm not telling you where she is and I'm not letting you see her," he said, and there was zero room in his tone for doubt. "But I'll tell her you stopped by."

"Serious?" I shouted, quickly getting up to follow him. It may not have been a lot, but it felt like . . . something. "Thanks," I said, wondering just how bad my face looked.

"Your right hook is shit, by the way," he said, his mouth moving into a dickhead smirk.

"Well, your jab is ass, too," I said, coughing out a laugh in spite of myself.

"You two are idiots, you know that, right?" Beckett said, staring at us like we were nuts.

"Yeah," I said as Liam tossed me the basketball. "First one to eleven wins."

CHAPTER FIFTY-ONE

"Never let your past socialize with your present.
The two don't play well together."

—Remington

Julia

I was pulling a load of laundry out of the dryer when I heard the doorbell.

Wonderful, I thought. In the time I'd been back, I hadn't really connected with anyone, aside from Teanna and Lauren, and I was good with that. I wasn't a big "social scene" kind of girl, and even if I had been, I felt far too closed off right now to want to open up anything new.

I sighed and walked over to the front door, seeing through the bay windows that it was still windy and raining, and the cottonwoods were nearly bare, the grass littered with their dropped yellow leaves.

But when I opened the door, instead of some Springfield resident, it was Bernard.

"Oh my God," I said, shocked. "Bernie, what are you doing here?"

"May I come in, Miss Julia?" he asked, removing his hat.

"Of course, of course," I said, gesturing for him to come inside.

He glanced over at the piles of laundry on the couch and looked like he wanted to laugh. "Someone has been putting this off," he said, calmly removing his loafers and propping his umbrella in the corner of the entryway in that Bernard way of his.

"Yeah, that someone is me," I said, my heart kind of hurting with how much I'd missed him. "I've kind of been living out of my suitcase, and today I realized it's probably time to unpack."

"I see," he said, nodding.

"Why are you here?" I asked, curious. "I mean, did my parents send you to check in on me or something?"

My parents had been pretty okay with the idea of me coming back to Springfield, staying at our house with Lauren, and doing the online school thing. We had a family FaceTime at dinner every night, and it didn't hurt that my Uncle Dave stopped by in his patrol car every day, and our next-door neighbors—Milt and Edna Whittle—were always popping in (whether we wanted them to or not).

"No," he said. "I was actually gathering some things from Remi's cabin, and I wanted to stop by and have a conversation."

"Oh," I said as Bernard sat down. I sat across from him, strangely nervous in front of this kind yet intimidating man.

"I disappointed you," he began.

"Bernard, I—"

"Allow me to finish, Miss Julia." Even in his sternness, the man had a way of making it impossible to stay mad at him.

"I don't expect to be forgiven, but I need you to know that Remi and I had been friends since we were children, if you can picture it." He smiled, a warmth that radiated from his core. "I knew him better than anyone, and what I know for certain is that Remington thought of Damion as his son."

I thought of Lou, with his funny old-man grin, and tried picturing him with Damion.

For some reason it made sense, even though it also didn't.

Because Lou seemed too . . . *sweet* for Damion, yet they seemed remarkably similar when I thought of the "good version," aka the lie, of Damion.

"But Damion has always had a . . . *complicated* relationship with his parents," he continued.

"What do you mean?" I asked, wanting to know the backstory even though I wasn't sure what it would change. Everything still hurt so much. But maybe if I could understand Damion, I might be able to feel less awful about everything that'd gone down.

Maybe I could move on.

"I mean that his parents aren't like yours," he said, leaning forward to grab two socks and fold them into a ball. "They love him, sure, but they don't always put him first."

It wasn't surprising, this information. Even though I'd only seen snippets, the way Damion interacted with his parents wasn't anything close to the warm relationship I had with mine.

But still, that didn't excuse his lies.

"I'm not going to get into all of it," Bernard said, reaching for another pair of socks. "But Mr. and Mrs. Rutledge have always treated Damion more like an accessory to their life than their child. When he makes them look good, they're happy, but they don't have a lot of use for anything that doesn't align with their . . . *goals*."

I pictured his parents and the harsh way his father had spoken to me, a stranger.

The way his mother had spoken to my mom at the ball.

I couldn't imagine what it would be like to have *them* as my parents.

It made me sad.

In spite of everything, I hated that for him.

"Remi was great with him, though, filling in as a stand-in parent while Damion was growing up. And those two—they were like-minded souls. The books they read, the movies they loved, the birds they watched; they were two peas in a pod."

"They were?" I asked, my heart hurting for what Damion didn't have with his family, for what he'd lost when he lost Remi. In my anger and hurt, I hadn't really allowed myself to think of Damion's loss.

Even though Damion had lied to me, it wasn't fair that I hadn't given him that grace.

"They could finish each other's sentences, I swear to God," he said with a smile, his eyes warm with the recollection. "So when I discovered Damion was your tutor and it was clear he didn't want you to know, I wasn't sure how to proceed. I trusted he'd do the right thing, and I didn't want to hurt him, but Miss Julia, I also trusted that he wouldn't hurt *you*."

"Well, he did," I said quietly, but I felt the hurt a little less at that moment than I had, probably because I was imagining *his* hurts.

"I know," Bernard said with a nod. "Sometimes we make the wrong decisions with the right heart."

I looked at him and wasn't sure if he was referring to himself not revealing the truth, or if he was talking about Damion.

After he left, I took a long walk, trying to process everything he'd told me. I walked laps around Buffalo Park, cranking the Favors on repeat, thinking about the kid version of Damion, trying to imagine him with Lou, trying to imagine him with Lou *and* Bernard.

While tiny montages of Riverside Park played along like the music.

Watched the sun descend on the Hudson . . .

If I let myself think about the good version of Damion, or the version where he'd *pretended* to be good, I could sort of see it.

You touched my hair and kissed my neck

And I felt so bad for him, for what he didn't get from his parents.

What he *deserved* from his parents.

Still, it didn't excuse his behavior. I'd trusted him and he'd let me down.

He let me down.

I was lost in my thoughts, so lost and far away that when I got back home, I literally gasped when I saw who was on my porch.

"Holy shit," I said out loud, because sitting on the stoop like he was waiting for me was *Will*.

Oh, great—just what I need.

"Hey," he said, looking up at me.

I swallowed as familiar blue eyes met mine, as his smile made me remember the time he'd chipped a tooth while ice-skating up the road.

"Hey," I said, knowing I was scowling but not caring, because why the heck would *he* be on my porch? "What are you doing here?"

"Sit?" he said, patting the spot on the step next to him.

"Um, I don't think I want to," I said, sounding punchy. "Why, um . . ."

I just shrugged and trailed off because *what the hell?*

"Come on," he said calmly. "Just for a minute."

"Um." I awkwardly sat beside him, plopping down onto the step, too shocked and confused to do anything but obey.

I kept my eyes on my shoes because I couldn't look at him. I didn't know his face anymore and had no idea how to talk to him. I'd had enough of boys hurting me in a year to last a lifetime.

"Remember when we used to sit here and watch the lightning bugs at night?" he said, a hint of a smile in his voice.

"Stop, Will," I snapped, hating how pouty I sounded, but I didn't need whatever this was. "I don't want to remember."

A pause.

"But of course I do," I added, because it was impossible, pretending I didn't remember our childhood. We'd spent *so many* hours on this porch, in this yard, running around this neighborhood.

Hide-and-seek, riding bikes, playing on the playground.

Then . . . older things.

Holding hands and kissing in the moonlight.

God, I realized as I looked at him that I had trusted Will since I was seven years old.

"Right," he said, his hair falling into his eyes.

Is it weird that part of me still feels like I should brush it away?

"I know I was a jerk," he said.

"Yeah, well, you're a guy. It's what you do," I muttered with a shrug, because this wasn't going to help anything.

"Is it too late?" he asked.

That made my head snap in his direction. "For what?"

"To apologize?" he asked, and the smell of Downy from his sweatshirt hit my nose, sending me straight into the past.

"For being a jerk?" I asked.

"Yeah, kind of."

"Apologize?" All the feelings I'd been burying rose to the surface, but I realized I meant it when I said, "It doesn't matter anymore."

"The point is that you didn't deserve it, and *that* matters. I was wrong and you need to know that. I am truly so sorry for hurting you, but, like . . ."

He trailed off, rubbing the back of his neck like he was searching for the perfect words to explain it all away.

But how could there be any?

"But like *what*?" I said, surprised at how calm I sounded. Equally surprised that I didn't feel any anger. Not anymore. I looked at his face, at the face I'd known since before I could ride a bike without training wheels, and suddenly I just genuinely wanted to know how it'd all fallen apart so quickly.

How two people who used to do everything together had let it all go.

"What follows the apology?" I asked. "An explanation of what happened?"

"I don't know if I have that, Jules. I mean . . . what *did* happen?" he said profoundly. "Sometimes I think I just got scared, I don't know."

"Scared of *what*?" I asked, annoyed by that response because we'd been far too *easy* together to ever be scary.

"Maybe . . . I don't know, the way everything felt so decided for us. It was like our whole life had been planned out for us since we were ten years old. You and me, college together, picket fences, dogs, even kids. I feel like it was what we were 'destined' for, regardless of what either of us intentionally thought through or wanted. I think I felt a little backed into a corner, but it was a stupid way to act on it. You didn't deserve that."

"I didn't deserve you cheating on me?" I said with a scoff, because his version was far too sanitized.

"I swear to you on my life, Jules, that she and I were never together like that when you and I were together."

I looked into blue eyes I'd known as well as my own and I believed him, not that it made much of a difference.

"But you were texting her all the time," I snapped as it came back to me. "You talked to her more than you talked to me. And then you made me feel like I was insane for being paranoid."

"I know," he said, nodding. "I may not have been doing anything with her physically, but I leaned on her a lot, and that was wrong. And to be honest, I think it's why I knew we had to break up. At some point, I realized maybe you and I were together because we didn't know anything else, right? Like, we were comfortable with each other, but I don't know if we were in *love* with each other."

Huh? I couldn't believe he'd said that. "Maybe *you* weren't, but I know what I felt."

"Do you?" He looked skeptical, his eyebrows cocked together in that *nuh-uh* expression of his when he said, "Because I know for damn sure you never looked at me the way you looked at the rich New York kid the night of the party."

"What?" I said, shocked and slightly flustered by Will bringing up Damion.

"And not to sound like a creep, but your PDA in the back of your dad's pickup . . . ," he said, his jaw clenched. "I think you know that we never kissed like that."

Oh God. He was right. The universe *had* shifted when Damion and I kissed, and I'd felt wholly changed afterward. No matter how hard I tried to forget it, I had every second of that kiss memorized. From the way his big hands had felt on my cheeks to the sound of his breathing to the smell of his cologne, that kiss had felt . . . *right*. Natural.

"We *didn't* ever kiss like that, did we?" I said in disbelief, looking up at one of the nearly bare cottonwood trees.

"Don't say it like that, like I'm not *good* at kissing," he said with a little smile, breaking the tension between us. "All the time we were together, part of me wondered if we gave up ourselves in the name of 'us,' you know?"

"What do you mean?"

Will sighed, searching for the words. "I just mean that in hindsight, we became each other's shadows. I liked watching football, so you liked watching football even though I knew you hated it. I liked horror movies, so you watched them all with me, even though you had to cover your eyes and peek through your fingers. I wanted to go to the University of Nebraska and suddenly so did you."

"Fair, but . . . ," I said, trailing off.

"But did you ever think about what *you* wanted, Jules?" he asked.

I wanted to respond with something snarky, but his face was too . . . *genuine*. He gave me an authentically kind smile as his words started to sink in.

Was he right? Had we become too much of an us that I didn't know what *I* wanted anymore?

His smile lingered—all kindness and the Will I remembered.

It made me miss my former best friend.

"I truly am so sorry, Jules, for everything."

I nodded, unable to say anything because my eyes were slightly itchy.

As the reality of what he was saying really hit me.

"Do you know what I'm the sorriest about, though?" he asked.

"Your terrible mullet?" I suggested.

"No," he laughed before looking seriously toward me. "I'm sorriest for ruining the friendship," he said. "You were my best friend for so much of my life, and then you weren't, and I regret that part of it more than anything."

"That *was* the worst part of it," I agreed, watching as the wind made the leaves circle wildly in the air, sadness hitting me hard in the chest.

He left not long after that, but I stayed outside, just sitting there on the porch, staring out at the yard as I processed everything he'd said.

Everything Bernard had said earlier.

They were two wildly different people with two entirely different reasons for visiting me, yet the things they'd left me with felt . . . similar.

Related to each other.

Tied together with an invisible string.

A string I wondered if I was brave enough to pull on.

CHAPTER FIFTY-TWO

"Heartbreak feels heavier in Manhattan. The cacophonic sounds and bustling crowds just illuminate aloneness."

—Remington

Damion

My birthday started out as crap.

Because for starters, my father got an unofficial acceptance notification for me from Dartmouth. It was nothing—early decisions didn't go out until next month—but one of his contacts had let him know that I was "in."

He was on cloud nine and I was nauseous, because I realized that I had no plan to change the prophecy. I knew where and what I wanted to study next year, but zero idea on how to make it happen.

I was going to end up at Dartmouth, God help me. And I knew I was privileged. It wasn't some tragically sad story that I was going to have to go to an Ivy League school and take over my family's very lucrative financial empire.

Poor little rich kid, poor little Tom.

So I smiled and pretended to love the birthday crêpes my mom had the chef prepare for breakfast (like she did every year), but I didn't feel like celebrating.

Because in addition to the bad news about Dartmouth, I kept hearing Remi's voice every time I started to accept my fate. Whenever I thought, *Maybe I'll like finance once I start working at Rutledge,* I instantly felt like I could hear him dropping f-bombs and telling me life wasn't supposed to be easy.

For fuck's sake, if you're not out there living in the grit of it all, you're not living at all, *kid.*

But I had no clue how to see it through.

School also sucked that day, which was no surprise. It'd become sort of a numb place for me since Julia left. It was like she'd opened my eyes and now everyone's hypocrisies and behaviors looked more egregious than they ever had before.

Or maybe it was because I missed her. So much.

Nothing was the same without her.

It felt like everything was dimmer. Darker.

Like the light was gone.

But when I got home from school, I was shocked to find Bernard waiting for me in the study. Seeing him felt so familiar that I half expected to look around the corner and see Remi, because those two had always been inseparable.

"Your eye," he said, gesturing to the ugly bruises.

"It's fine," I said dismissively, because I'd been wishing I could apologize to him since the night of the ball. "Listen, uh, I'm really sorry about everything I started—"

"Say nothing," he said, calmly raising a hand. "Sometimes life is messy."

Bernard was so Bernard that I wanted to hug him. I realized at that moment that as much as I missed Remi, I missed Bernard, too. He was essentially another uncle to me, and here I was hiding things from him. *What would Remi think?*

"Thanks, Bernard" was all I could say, trying for a polite smile while feeling overwhelmed with regret. About everything.

"I have a birthday gift for you."

"You do?" I said, shocked. "I can't believe you know it's my birthday."

"You doubt me?" he teased, making me feel slightly better.

"Of course not. No one has ever doubted you, Bernie," I said.

"You know, she calls me that too," he said quietly.

I swallowed and didn't know what to say as I pictured her smile. God, I missed her so much that it *hurt* to picture her face.

I cleared my throat and managed to say, "Yeah?"

"Yeah," he said. Silence lingered between us as he looked at me. I could tell he missed her too.

"Well. Your present," his kind voice said, interrupting the silence. "From Remington."

"What?" My voice came out in a croak. The surprise hitting me hard. I cleared my throat again. "What?"

"I was instructed to give you this on your eighteenth birthday." He bent over and grabbed a wrapped package that I hadn't even noticed on the table beside him. Bernard smiled softly, sadness in his eyes, as he said, "Happy birthday, Damion."

"He seriously left me a present?" I said, my throat tight as Bernard held out the box.

"Of course he did." Bernard pushed it toward me. "Open it."

I took the package and ran a hand over the wrapping, wondering if he'd wrapped it himself or if Bernard had.

"He wrapped it," Bernard said, reading my mind.

"Don't make me open it," I said, finding it hard to swallow as so many emotions filled my entire body. I didn't know how I was going to handle seeing the last thing Remi ever gave me.

"He wanted you to open it," he said, then gestured with his hand for me to keep going. "Let's go."

I ran my finger under the seam, sliding it under the clear tape before pulling back the wrapping. I pictured Remi's weathered hands wrapping the present, and I knew I was going to save the paper like a fucking lunatic.

But my heart stopped when I saw the gift.

Birds of the World, I read, my heart hurting, burning in my chest as I looked at the bird-watching book in my hands.

"He loved sharing that with you," he said. "He was always tickled by the fact that you seemed to enjoy it as much as he did."

I nodded, unable to speak. Uncle Remi had left behind a birthday gift for me. A bird-watching book.

"I, um, I just miss him so much, you know?" I managed, my voice cracking as I swallowed again and clenched my jaw against the pain.

"I understand completely," he said, his voice rougher than usual.

"If you go back to the index," he said, pointing at the book, "there is a letter."

"A letter?" I flipped through the pages, and when I reached the back of the book, there was something stuck in the pages. "From Uncle Rem?"

"You know how he loved correspondence," Bernard said with an affectionate grin.

"Yeah, I do," I said, watching my fingers tremble as I unfolded the letter, as my eyes saw that familiar handwriting.

Oh God.

I wasn't sure my heart could take this, to be honest.

Dearest Damion,

Happy birthday. I hope your day is filled with life and love and laughter. You have been eighteen years of pure joy—for me and for everyone—and I consider your life a gift.

I imagine you've probably been wondering about my will. I bet the shit has really hit the fan since I croaked. It was never my intention to leave your family out, but as I thought about you and your parents, it occurred to me that your family has enough money. Too much, if you ask me. I wanted to free your family from the curse of more, if that makes sense at all. Because if I left your parents the inheritance, I knew your father wouldn't do good with it, Dame.

So I decided to use it to help a nice family. Selfish of me, perhaps, but I think a dying man can be a bit selfish, right? I just want Riverside Manor to go to a family that can fill it with the kind of joy we've always found in it, you and I.

There is a trust set up in your name and Bernard is the executor. It's enough to support you completely while you go to school in Colorado, but after that, you need to make your own way, Damion Rutledge, DVM. It's because I love you and want you to find fulfillment that I'm cutting it off at that. If living in Gardenwood has taught me anything, it's that money does NOT bring happiness.

I hope you know how much I love you, that you are 100% what I would've wanted if I'd ever had a son. In my heart, you are—and always will be—my son.

Love,
Uncle Remi

I stared at the letter in my hands, hands that were shaking *hard* now, and then I couldn't see the words anymore through the tears.

Because, God, I'd just heard from him. It felt like Remi had stopped by and had *spoken* to me, literally, and now the grief of him being gone again felt worse.

Bigger. Harder.

Unbearable.

How can he be gone forever?

I wanted another letter. I needed more sentences. Dear Jesus, I couldn't go back to hearing nothing from him again.

It was like a match had been lit in the darkness, showing me what I'd been desperate to see, but now it'd flared out and everything felt darker than it had before.

"I should've visited more," I said, dropping into the chair because my legs didn't feel like they could hold me up any longer. I tried keeping everything in, but it came out as a sob when I said, "Why didn't I go see him after he moved to Nebraska?"

"You did exactly what you were meant to do," Bernard said, setting a hand on my back. "He loved his quiet life at that cabin."

"Still," I said, swiping at my eyes, which wouldn't stop fucking leaking tears. "I should've made him a priority."

"You wrote him every week," Bernard said with a patient smile in his voice.

It wasn't enough, I thought.

Not nearly fucking enough.

"I just wish—"

"Damion, look at me."

I wiped at my eyes again and raised them to Bernard.

"Listen to what I'm saying. Remington *chose* to live out his final years in that cabin. He *wanted* it to be exactly how it was. He wanted you to find your way without him, and trust me, he wasn't lonely or isolated, and he definitely wasn't being taken advantage of. The Lowells became another family to him. Not a replacement, but an addition. And it was *their* time to make him happy."

I hoped—so badly—that he was right. I searched his face for the lie, but I couldn't find it. I sounded like a little kid when I asked with a hoarse voice, "Do you really think so?"

"I know so," he said. "They needed him, they loved him, and he loved and needed them right back. It was beautiful."

All the grief was hitting me at once. It was too much and I just wanted to curl up into a ball. I just wanted *more* of him, dammit.

But then . . . I turned the letter over, where more of Remi's scribbled handwriting stared back at me. Writing I hadn't noticed until now, next to his tiny doodle of a crimson-red cardinal with a black face and a fluffy crest that looked like tousled hair.

P.S., it said . . .

> There is a girl here in Springfield you should meet.
> I think you'd like her.

And that's when I fucking lost it.

CHAPTER FIFTY-THREE

"There's always time to get off your ass and fix your shit.
So do it already."

—Remington

Damion

I knew what I had to do.

"Hi, Damion," Beverly said when I walked into the offices of Rutledge Investments. "I haven't seen you around in a while."

Beverly had worked for my father and his colleagues as an executive assistant for longer than I'd been alive.

"Your dad's on a call right now," she said.

"Okay," I said, infused with such a sense of purpose that I was ready to break down the damn door. "In his office?"

"Yes, sir. I can let him know—"

"No," I said, a fake smile on my lips. "He knows I'm coming. Thank you."

I cruised past her, grabbing the doorknob and knocking as I entered. My dad looked up, *not on a call*, sitting like a king in his high-backed desk chair.

"Damion," he said, looking shocked to see me. "What are you doing here?"

"I need to talk to you," I said.

"Well, it's not a great time," my dad said, his eyes narrowing in measurement. He'd gotten far on his intuition, his ability to read people, and I saw in his face that he knew he wasn't going to like whatever this was.

"You need to drop the suit against the Lowells," I said.

"Oh, now come on, Damion," my dad said, shaking his head and looking like he was beyond frustrated with my unwillingness to let this go. "Let's not—"

"No, seriously," I said, talking over him. "This isn't—"

"I know exactly what this is. This is you wanting to defend the girl you like," my dad interrupted. "Even if it means rolling over on your family."

"You're wrong. Actually," I said, "you might've been right a day ago, but I got a letter from Remi."

He looked at me confused. "A letter? How?"

"He left me a letter that he wanted me to open on my eighteenth birthday," I explained.

My dad took off his glasses and pinched the bridge of his nose. "Do I want to know this?" he asked quietly.

"I think it's important that you know this," I said.

I handed over the letter and said, "There's stuff in here you won't like, but it's absolute proof that the Lowells didn't do anything. Just read it."

"Fine, fine," my dad said impatiently.

He started reading the letter.

"Damion Rutledge, DVM," my dad muttered under his breath. "God help me."

I watched his face as he read, and I wondered how he felt, if Remi's words about my family and money bothered him at all. The letter *wasn't* complimentary, but was my dad capable of even caring?

He read the entire thing and then calmly folded it up. Set it on the desk.

"This doesn't prove anything," he said, sitting back in his chair and steepling his fingers in front of him. "We don't know that Remi actually wrote this."

"Bernard brought it over and said that he did," I said. "And it's his handwriting."

"Well, Damion, we don't know that this wasn't dictated to him by the Lowells, do we? Not only that, but no one but you and Bernard know that this questionable letter exists. In my opinion, nothing has changed."

I stared at the man who'd taught me to ski, the guy who'd never missed one of my school events and had donated millions to charity, and I wondered how he could lie so easily.

"But what about right and wrong, Dad?" I asked. "Regardless of whether or not we *can* proceed after seeing this letter, what about the morality here? What about the fact that we *shouldn't*?"

My dad looked at me for a long second, like he was considering my words. And as his eyes moved over my face, for the briefest of seconds I almost felt like he felt bad about the chasm between us.

"Listen, Damion," he said. "I know we butt heads a lot, and I *do* care about right and wrong. But that doesn't change the fact that sometimes in business, you have to do the responsible, intelligent thing. You have to weigh the overarching evidence, the overarching facts, and make a smart decision. The unknowns regarding this letter are greater than what's written on the paper."

"Dad, please." I could hear my voice break as his eyes stayed locked on mine. For the first time in a while, it felt like he was really looking at me.

"I know you miss him, Dame," he said. "This must've been hard to read, hearing his voice again."

My dad was being surprisingly soft, and it made me wonder, for the first time.

Shit, did my dad miss him too?

"But I worry you may be acting on your emotions right now."

"That's not true," I said, clenching my fists because it was so fucking wrong that this wasn't going to work.

My dad leaned back in his chair. He looked like he was battling his own thoughts. God, maybe I was getting to him.

"Please, Dad. *Please.* Drop the suit. If I learned anything from Uncle Remi, it's that life is about doing the right thing, even if it isn't what you *want* to do."

It was about family, and even if my family sucked, *her* family didn't.

"And I'll go to Dartmouth," I said. "I'll go to Dartmouth and study business."

"You will," my dad said, watching me like he wasn't sure if I was telling the truth or not.

"I promise," I said. "I'll sign a legal document or whatever you want. Just don't do this to them. I'll go to Dartmouth and be a good boy. Just let them have this. We have enough."

And for the second time that day, I felt like crying.

But I wouldn't.

Not over this.

The disappointment was what made me feel devastated, but there was enough anger to offset that.

I could feel my dad's eyes burning into me. Studying me. "You'd do that? For her?"

"For what's right. And for him." I said, pointing to Remi's letter. He sighed deeply, his eyes running over Remi's swirling handwriting.

God, he does miss him. And for a split second I wondered if everything my dad was doing against the Lowells was because he believed he was doing what was right.

"You know, Damion," my dad said, standing up and walking toward me. "Your mother mentioned that Cornell, in addition to having a good business school, also has some other programs you could study as a minor." He was having trouble making eye contact. As if he was . . . nervous. Uncomfortable.

What is he saying? Remi and I had spent so much time looking at colleges that I knew Cornell had one of the best veterinary schools in the country.

But he couldn't be suggesting that, could he?

"You'd still need to get your degree in the appropriate field to take your place in the family business, but if you work hard, I don't see why you couldn't take classes in animal medicine or whatever it is your stubborn brain has latched onto. It may not be Dartmouth, but it is Ivy."

There it was. A compromise.

My dad was definitely telling me that I wasn't allowed to study what I wanted to study, but he was also giving me the option of taking classes in something I was passionate about.

For him, that was a lot.

My dad trying to compromise felt like the closest thing to something fatherly he'd done in a very long time.

"Deal," I said.

My father extended his hand, and I took it. But it felt like more than a handshake in that moment. It felt like maybe the beginning of something.

An understanding between us, maybe.

Some sort of a start.

A few minutes later, Jeffrey came into the room with a legal document that tied up all the loose ends. My father and I had reached an agreement, and in turn he was dropping any and all suits or interests in Remington's estate.

"I'll send a courier over to Riverside Manor, letting the Lowells know the estate is theirs, free and clear," my father said.

"No," I said. "Can I tell them?"

"This really isn't all about the girl, Damion?" my dad asked, sounding curious.

"Not at all," I said truthfully, my gut burning as I pictured her face. "She moved back to Nebraska, and I'll probably never see her again. This is about me wanting to be the one to let them know that the Rutledges are doing the right thing."

My dad handed me the document and the letter, and though he wasn't smiling, there was something warm in his eyes when he said, "Whatever you say, kid."

CHAPTER FIFTY-FOUR

"There are thousands of beautiful homes all over this amazing city, but she's the only one I want to live and love in. Riverside Manor is my refuge."

—Remington

Julia

My duffel bag was full, but I shoved my lit book inside anyway, holding the two sides together as I tried getting it to zip. It took a lot of work and grunting, but after a few minutes, my overstuffed bag was finally closed.

Whew.

I plopped down on my bed beside it, looking around my room, trying to gauge what else I needed to grab. I was back in the city for a day, just to collect a few more things to take back with me, things I needed to finish out the first semester.

But as I let my gaze move around the bedroom, I found myself missing it, and I hadn't even left yet.

The soft bed, the heavy comforter, the thick rug that felt like a blanket under bare feet. The way there was a perfect mix of insulated quiet, yet with the accompaniment of random city sounds from outside, like garbage trucks and honking horns.

I walked over to one of the windows, looking out at the incredible view of Riverside Park. The trees had shed most of their leaves since I'd left, so it looked like a different place than it had while I'd lived there. It was like the curtains had been pulled back on the space, and now I could clearly see the walking paths below, the stairs throughout, the river beyond that'd always called to me like a voice.

God, I missed it so much.

This place had become so much more than a house, which still surprised me.

Maybe it was because while everyone at Gardenwood had made life here pretty crappy in my short time there, these beautiful walls had held safety for me.

It'd been the refuge home base during all the storms.

I heard the doorbell ring as I moved to the other window to look out onto the street, but I couldn't see anyone or any car dropping someone off.

"I'll get it," I heard my dad say, followed by the creaking of the front door. And then, "Oh. Hello, Damion."

Oh my God, oh my God, oh my God.

My dad sounded more snide than was typical for him, but still. Why was Damion there?

What did he want?

And why was he here??

There's no way he knows I'm back, right?

"Hi, Mr. Lowell," he said, and the sound of his voice sent chills through my entire body, chills that were cold yet also crackling like flames.

It's him, oh God.

My pulse pounded in my chest as the huskiness of his deep voice wrapped itself around my heart.

"I was wondering if I could talk to you and Mrs. Lowell for a second?"

"Sure, um . . . ," my dad said, sounding like he didn't want to say yes. "Come in."

My heart was pounding in my ears as I heard the door close, as I heard him walk into the foyer.

Damion is downstairs! Damion is in the house!

What the hell??

I could hear murmured small talk as my dad yelled for my mom, but I couldn't make out exactly what was being said, so I crept out of my room and moved closer to the stairs.

God, against my better judgment, I missed him so much that his sudden unexpected presence in my world was almost overwhelming. Knowing those stupid glasses and that arrogant smirk were right downstairs, *right down the stairs*, had my hands trembling.

I definitely didn't want to be seen, but I needed to know what was going on. I leaned against the railing and found it hard to listen when I was holding my breath.

"Thank you," he said, his voice rich and deep.

God, hearing his voice was brutal. I wanted to cover my ears and hide from it, but I also wanted to roll around in the sound. I wanted to record it and save it to listen to on repeat, or find a way to shove it into the pages of my lit book in the overstuffed duffel.

"Do you want something to drink?" my mom asked, as if Damion were just a nice boy stopping by for a visit and not the guy who'd tricked us all.

"Listen, I don't want to be rude," my dad said as if reading my thoughts, "but you keep stopping by to apologize. You're sorry and we get it, yet nothing has changed. I'm not sure how much else we have to discuss—"

He what?

He what????????

"No, um, this isn't that," Damion said, sounding flustered. "I don't know how to say this, so I'm just going to be honest. Here."

I leaned forward, trying to see without being seen. What was he giving them? What did "here" mean??

What is going on??

"What is this?" my dad asked.

"My parents are dropping the suit," Damion said. "No one is going to contest Remi's will."

"What?" I heard Liam say. "Are you serious?"

I covered my mouth and leaned even closer to the banister. They were seriously dropping the suit?

"Yeah," Damion said. "This is legit. The Rutledges are done and stepping away. What's yours is yours and all that."

"Wow," my dad said. "This is . . . unexpected."

I felt almost dizzy as I listened, because could this be real? Were we actually going to be able to keep everything?

And hearing the news coming from *his mouth* was really messing with me.

My dad asked, "What triggered the change of heart?"

"Some evidence came to light that proves Uncle Remi was in his right mind when he wrote the will. He definitely wanted you guys to have his estate, so the only right thing to do is ensure that you get it."

"Where did the evidence come from?" my mom asked.

"Um," Damion said, and I could hear the hesitation in his voice. *He doesn't want to say,* I thought, and I knew the exact expression that was on his face that very moment.

I closed my eyes and swallowed as the image of his hazel eyes came at me so strong, it was almost like he was standing in front of me.

I heard him clear his throat before he said, "My uncle left me a letter."

Lou left him a letter?

"Oh," my dad said. "And this letter just surfaced?"

"Yes, sir."

Yes, sir.

I blinked fast as Damion's respectful response made me want to cry.

Because he *was* a good guy, dammit, in spite of every not good thing he'd ever done.

I heard my dad say, "Can I tell you that I'm proud of you? I know that's probably weird, and I know you aren't out here looking for my approval, but I know how difficult this decision must've been. Thank—"

"Don't thank me," Damion said, sounding embarrassed. "We accused you of some terrible things."

"Why do I feel like *you* had something to do with this turnaround, though, Damion?"

"No idea," Damion said, and I could tell by his tone that he was giving my dad a little half smile. "The bottom line is that it's settled now and we can all move on."

Move on. My heart pinched at the sound of those words, because I missed him so much and I'd been trying to move on, but moving on was also the very worst thing.

"Really appreciate you dropping this by," I heard my brother say.

"The very least I could do," Damion said. "Later, man."

It felt like my heart was shattering because he was leaving. It was good he was leaving, because he was an asshole, but it didn't change the fact that I missed him.

Dear Lord, I missed him so much that every bone in my body *ached*.

I missed his face and his sarcastic sense of humor and the way his hazel eyes looked when he called me Nebraska.

God, I needed to hear him say it again.

I couldn't seriously never hear him say it again, could I?

The sound of him pushing on the front door was devastating.

Don't go! I thought. *Wait!*

"Wait," I heard my brother say, which made my breath catch in my chest.

I was almost dizzy as I stood there, listening.

"What's up?" Damion asked, and I leaned forward a little, trying to see him. Desperate for a glimpse of him. For dark curly hair, wide shoulders, dirty smile.

"Between you and me, how did this happen?" Liam asked.

Yes, yes, how DID this happen, Damion?

"What do you mean?" he asked, his deep voice climbing all those stairs to settle into the hairs on the back of my neck.

"I mean that when your dad served us, it was obvious he had no intention of backing down, and I don't suspect he backs down very often. So, what did you do to make this happen?"

"I didn't do anything," Damion said.

"Bullshit," my brother said, and I dropped to a squat to try and see down the stairs. "You obviously did something to convince your dad."

"It was nothing," Damion said with a sigh. "Easy. I go to an Ivy, go to business school, he drops the suit."

"Why would you do that, though?" Liam asked. "Beck said you'd never go to business school."

I remembered the way Damion had looked when he talked about his future, how much he hated the thought of going to Dartmouth and working for his dad.

"It doesn't matter," he said in his bored, blasé tone, the one I'd always suspected was an act.

"If it doesn't matter, then say it. Why the hell would you give up on the dream of a shitty public university, Rutledge?" Liam was challenging him, his voice rising.

And I wanted to scream.

I wanted to yell at Liam to stop interrogating him while at the same time I wanted to demand he give us every single answer because *Damion, what did you do??*

"Jesus. Ease up, Lowell. You guys get to keep the house, so can I please leave it? Like I said, it doesn't matter."

It does, it does, it SO does!

Why??

Liam's voice lowered, but it was still loud when he said, "It does and we both know it, so just fucking admit—"

"For her, okay?" Damion snapped. "And screw you for making me say it when you know damn well she's done with me. Fuck."

I clenched the stair railing tighter as his voice cracked. As he said, "Even so, she still deserves everything."

"She 'deserves everything'?" Liam scoffed, and I could almost see my brother lift his eyes toward the staircase, in my direction.

He knew I was listening.

Liam, don't! Don't do it.

"God, you sound like you're in love with her."

The seconds passed by like hours as I crouched there on shaking legs, until . . .

"I am," he said. "Doesn't matter, though, does it?"

With that, he left. I flinched at the sound of the door closing.

I rose to my feet on wobbly legs, feeling shell-shocked.

Oh my God.

Liam shut the front door and turned around, looking at me standing at the top of the staircase.

Where I was an absolute wreck, my face no doubt blotchy and smeared with tears.

Liam smiled at my awful appearance. "I've got three words to say to say to you regarding Damion Rutledge."

I looked at my twin brother, who knew me better than maybe I knew myself. "Yeah? What are they?"

"Go get him."

CHAPTER FIFTY-FIVE

"Everyone should fall in love in Riverside Park."

—Remington

Damion

"Well, I did it," I said to myself as I sat there on the bench.

I looked out at the Hudson, thinking of how many times I'd sat there with Remi, and I wondered if he'd be proud of me.

I felt like he would be.

Not that I deserved it after I tried to wreck things, but he was always good with forgiveness. He was the kind of guy who thought if someone did the right thing by the end, that kind of made things okay.

So I felt good.

It finally felt like I was doing right.

"Hey."

Oh God.

I was afraid to turn around because there was no fucking way I was going to see what my mind wanted me to see. It was kind of like the day I'd stared at the picture of her in the wallet, so alive and laughing in the photo, and then she just appeared in front of me.

I think that's when it started. When I fell for her.

But lightning didn't strike twice, so there was no way I was going to turn around and see her standing there in a blaze of curly glory.

"Hey," I said to whoever was behind me. I kept my eyes on the river as I wished so hard it was almost painful.

Wishing it *was* her, glad it wasn't.

"I heard you're going to business school."

My heart sank.

Her voice.

It *was* her.

I turned around slowly, afraid to have her see me. Fucking terrified of what she might say to me. *Goodbye forever.* But those thoughts disappeared when I saw her because *dear Lord.*

She was so beautiful that it almost hurt my eyes.

Her hair was down and curly, blowing in the breeze, and she was dressed in jeans, square-toed brown boots, and my stretched-out sweater, the one she'd never given back.

My sweater.

On her.

God, the things that did to me.

I tried to read her expression, the lines of her face. She looked soft, but determined.

Is she happy to see me? Pissed that I went to her house?

She cleared her throat and said, "I just wanted to let you know that if you need a tutor, I might be available."

"You're . . . you're, uh, you're wearing my sweater," I said dumbly. I really couldn't get it out of my mind. *My* sweater. On *her*.

"Oh. Yeah." She blinked fast, obviously thrown off by my inane comment.

But I just fucking *loved* the way she looked right now, her . . . *Julia*-ness all wrapped up in my favorite sweater.

I dared to stand up and walk toward her, drawn to her like a magnet to steel, not stopping until the tips of those Nebraska boots were touching my loafers. Until I was so close I could look down and see the flecks in her eyes.

"Did you hear me?" she asked, soft lips saying pretty things.

I clenched my fists to keep myself from touching her. "You, tutor? You're available?"

"I just might be," she said, reaching out a hand and tugging a little on my tie.

Tugging on my heart, waking every molecule in my body.

"Are you *actually* a tutor, though?" I asked, quoting the response she'd given me the day I showed up on her doorstep, offering my services. "Like, you've tutored other students?"

"I'm actually the best at Gardenwood," she said, those pretty glossed lips sliding up into a big smile. "Ask anyone."

"Is that right," I said, my hands finding her waist and pulling her against me.

"Oh, for sure it is," she said breathlessly. "So how about it? Try me for one session? If you don't like it, you can find somebody else—"

"I don't want anybody else," I said, meaning it in every cell in my body. "You've been the only one I wanted since the minute I looked at that stupid picture of you and the dogs."

"You better be careful with that. I'm a Gardenwood girl, and I heard you don't have any love for them."

"You're not a Gardenwood girl," I said, lowering my face because I needed to kiss her.

"I'm not?" she asked, her eyes heavy-lidded as she rose onto her tiptoes. "You think I'm just a Springfield girl, is that it?"

"I think you're just *my* girl," I said, taking her mouth because I couldn't wait another second.

But I immediately pulled back because I had to say it. I looked down into burnt amber and said, "Words cannot express how sorry I am, Jules. For everything."

She blinked fast, like she was processing, and then she gave me a tiny nod. "Okay."

"Okay?" I asked, pressing my forehead to hers, needing the connection.

"Okay, I'm going to take a risk and trust you one more time," she said, her mouth soft and oh so tempting. "But please don't let me down."

"I won't," I said, then I couldn't stop myself from giving her the line. "Because 'the two of us combined could set it on fire.'"

Her nose crinkled with her sweet smile as she raised her fingers to my cheek and said, "He contains multitudes."

Wild horses couldn't have stopped me from kissing her then, and when she kissed me back—*thank you, God*—Julia kissed me back the same way Julia drove a pickup truck out of a cornfield.

She was bold and impulsive, wild in the very best way, and there was zero doubt in my mind, as her fingers trailed down to grip my shoulders, that she was going to get me exactly where I needed to go.

Home.

EPILOGUE

Spring

"Look for the cardinal and you'll find me, kid."

—Remington

Damion

"Don't say *The Notebook*," I said, shaking my head.

"But it's just the way it is, every time we take out the boat," she said with a laugh, leaning back on her arms as the sun licked over her pretty face. "I swear to God you turn into Ryan Gosling whenever I sit here, watching you row."

It was a stunningly gorgeous afternoon, one of those spring days where everything was finally turning green and the sun was warm in the sky, so *of course* we were out on the water. I'd flown in two days ago to spend spring break in Nebraska, with her, and I was out-of-my-mind happy.

"Shouldn't that be changing, though?" I asked, obsessed with the big black sunglasses that were covering half her face. Julia Nebraska had her own aesthetic, and I was so there for it. "You should just see me, the love of your life, rowing your wiseass around the lake now that this is going to be the norm, right?"

The norm.

It was still impossible to believe.

The day after my birthday, Bernard had delivered one additional piece of legal documentation: a belated final gift from Remi that had rocked my world.

The cabin.

Remi had left me his fishing cabin.

So even though I was still living in Gardenwood and going away to Cornell in the fall, I had a place in Nebraska I could get away to whenever I wanted.

And I wanted to get away to Nebraska as often as possible. Hell, I'd basically been visiting on a monthly basis.

And since Jules had been flying back to New York every couple of weeks to spend time with her family as they figured out the best way for her to finish her remote school year, it felt like we were together more than we weren't.

It was goddamn perfection.

"Wow," she said, shaking her head. "'Love of my life'? That's a little aggressive, don't you think?"

"I'll show you aggressive," I said, letting go of the oars to gesture with both hands for her to come closer. "Get over here, Nebraska."

My stomach dipped as she smiled at me, because even when she wasn't trying, her teasing nature always hit me like a drug.

Her phone buzzed, which made her hold up a *one sec* finger as she pulled it out of her pocket.

Which made me give her a dramatic sigh. "Your phone is more important than my . . . *aggression*?"

She looked at me over the top of those shades, long lashes fluttering. "Absolutely not, Rutledge. But you know I'm waiting on my . . ."

She looked back down at the display and her eyes went wide. "Oh my God, they're in!"

I didn't have to ask what she was talking about. She'd been watching and waiting every day to see her test scores. Even though she was no longer worried about screwing up the inheritance with bad marks, mastering the math section had become important to her.

Which meant it was important to me.

"Oh my God," I said. "So . . . ?"

She bit down on her bottom lip as she looked at her phone, and I was surprisingly nervous as I waited. She'd worked her ass off, my Jules, and I wanted so badly for her to see that reward.

It was so on-brand for her to care.

She'd already been accepted to NYU (she wanted to study literature and writing while deciding if running Lowell's Market was her "destiny"), yet these inconsequential scores meant the world to her because *she* needed to know she'd done it.

Her eyes moved over her phone as she scrolled, and then she let out a squeak.

"Jules?" I asked, dying to know. "Tell me."

Her gaze met mine, her mouth slid into a huge grin, and then she was jumping at me in the middle of the boat. "Six points higher than the practice test!"

I caught her as she threw herself into my arms, as she hugged me and squealed, and I was pretty sure I'd never been happier in my entire fucking life.

"You're going to tip the boat!" I yelled, laughing as I squeezed her harder, trying to keep her still so we didn't end up in the cold water as the boat rocked back and forth. "Calm your ass down, Nebraska."

"I'm sorry," she said with a giggle, her hands sliding to settle on my chest. Those perfect eyes were wild when she looked up at me in the rocking boat and said, "But I'm too excited. We did it, Damion!"

"*You* did it," I corrected, so damn proud of her that it kind of made my chest hurt a little. Julia was so full of everything good that looking down at her face was like freebased happiness, I swear to God.

"But I couldn't have done it without the best tutor in Gardenwood," she teased. "*Mon beau professeur.*"

She'd been studying French in her spare time and it was *sending* me, dear Jesus. Even when she didn't get it exactly right, she got it exactly right for me.

"Mon élève bien-aimée," I said, lowering my head to kiss the side of her sun-warmed neck.

"I can't believe you're the same guy who stole my wallet," she said, a smile in her voice.

"I can't believe you're the same girl who broke my nose," I said, dragging my teeth over her pretty skin.

"Was that our meet-cute?" Julia asked with a laugh, her fingers sliding into my hair.

"More like a meet-ick," I corrected, drunk on her scent, surrounded by the soft blanket of her hair. "Because we hated each other on sight."

"But then we didn't," she said on a sigh.

I heard the two-part whistle of a cardinal, and when I raised my head, I saw a crimson-red male fly over and land on the dock, his crest fluffy like tousled hair.

Holy, holy shit. Remi?

That shrewd little face and pointy beak almost appeared to be watching me.

"Right?" she said quietly, a tease in her voice.

Quit interrupting me, old man, I thought with a smile.

"That's right, then we didn't," I agreed, and as the cardinal sang and I fell back into the pure magic of my Julia Nebraska, a quote from Remi's favorite book came at me like the warm reflection of the sun on the pond, like the whistle of that little bird on the chilly spring breeze.

"There's so much spring in the air—there's so much lazy sweetness in your heart."

—F. Scott Fitzgerald

THE SOUNDTRACK OF DAMION AND JULIA

1. Hate Myself | Ruel
2. New Girl | FINNEAS
3. she got a thing about her | Thomas Day
4. Parasite | MICO, Haiden Henderson
5. Father Figure | Taylor Swift
6. Drive | Audrey Hobert
7. i wish i knew how to quit you | sombr
8. Julia | Mt. Joy
9. Blame It On You | Daniel Seavey
10. obvious | Aidan Bissett
11. Have Your Lovin' | Johnny Orlando
12. Bleed | Malcolm Todd, Omar Apollo
13. Misery | Alex Sampson
14. The Crowd | Johnny Orlando
15. Symptoms | Stephen Dawes
16. blind | ROLE MODEL
17. This Song | Conan Gray
18. Eu Posso Ser Como Você | Jão
19. Small Town Joan of Arc | Del Water Gap
20. Backyard Boy | Claire Rosinkranz
21. yard sale | asiris
22. Nice to Be Known | Late Night Thoughts
23. love you tonight | Ella Langley
24. THINGS YOU DO | Justin Bieber
25. her | JVKE, Annika Wells
26. imperfect for you | Ariana Grande

27. Dumb Sh*t | Jack Gray

28. Deadbeat | Mathias Julin

29. Time | In Color

30. Don't Say That | Ruel

31. what's wrong with me | Olivia Rodrigo, Robert Smith

32. The Hudson | The Favors, FINNEAS, Ashe

https://open.spotify.com/playlist/0VDsDauESxuYzoeZwq7aJz

ACKNOWLEDGMENTS

First and foremost, thank you, God, for giving me this incredible journey that I absolutely can't believe I'm on and definitely don't deserve.

Thank you, thank you, THANK YOU SO MUCH, READER, for making my wildest dreams come true. I get to spend every day with my imaginary friends, doing my favorite thing in the world as a job, and it's because of YOU. I'm eternally grateful for this gift that you've given me.

And an extra special thank-you to all the creative geniuses who make book edits. I'll never understand how I'm lucky enough to witness your vision, but I'm obsessed with it, for real, and am humbled by your time and your talents.

Kim Lionetti, I love you more than people who love Benson Boone love his flips. I appreciate you more than people who appreciate Benson Boone's flips appreciate *him*. You are the one who makes sh*t happen, the wind beneath my wings, and I will never be able to properly thank you for being so much more than an agent. You're, like . . . my COOL friend who is a total badass when she has to be, and I adore you.

Thank you, Nicole Ellul, for being the perfect editor. You make everything I write better, and I'd be lost without you. And thank you for giving me the gift of New York City! You FORCED me to dig deeper into the setting, which led to the BEST trip to the Upper West Side, and now we love the city more than we already did. You are amazing, and I promise that one of these days, I won't make you work so hard.

And the incredible team at S&S—where do I even begin? Anna Elling, Deane Norton, Stephanie Voros, Jess Egan, Maryam Ahmad, Trey and Seven, Kendra Levin, Anne Zafian, Amy Habayeb, Nicole Benevento,

Michelle Leo, Shannon Pender, Erin Toller, Cassandra Fernandez, Nicole Russo, Justin Chanda, Amy Lavigne, James Akinaka, Julia Ashley Romero, Jon Anderson, Amanda Brenner, Sara Berko, Liz Casal, Sarah Creech—you're all so incredibly wonderful, and I'm so lucky to work with you. Also thank you, thank you to the very important people that I'm probably forgetting—please forgive me!!!!!!

Also—a world of thanks to my foreign publishers. You've given me such a gift by translating my stories; I suddenly find myself with friends in places I never imagined I'd visit—Brazil, France, Germany, Poland, Belgium, Turkey, and Spain—and I'm forever grateful.

And, of course, thank you to my incredible family for being incredible.

Cassidy, Terrance, Tyler, Jordyn, Zealous, Breeze, Matt, Joey, and Kate—you guys are my favorite humans, 10/10 would recommend. Who would've thought the kids who created—and were tortured within—"armpit jail" would end up being so cool? You're the Pablo Sanchezes of the world, and "On the Grind" from *Nellyville* is your walk-up song, whether you like it or not.

And finally—finally—KEBBIN. Kevin. Kevvvvvv.

How is it that life keeps getting MORE fun with you?? You would think it'd be boring by now, or far less stupid-silly, but you still make me belly-laugh over dumb things every single day. I think I like you more now than that day I saw you at Uno and lied about being stung by a bee so I could call out of work, and that is saying a LOT.

I mean . . . I think this might be serious, Kirkle. Five kids and a million meatballs later, you're still the one I want to watch old TV shows with. Like, I am SUPER into you, bro, and feel like this could be the endgame for us. I'm thinking we should take it to the next level . . .